The Syndicate

ROSALYN ST PIERRE

For travellers and adventurers who venture far, face dangers, find love and return.

And for the amazing Komodo dragons and communities who live together.

I owe a debt of gratitude to my husband Sam for his endless patience, to my children for their continual encouragement and to my wonderful grandchildren who have brought me so much joy during the days of writing.

I am indebted to Tony Parker for his information on shipping, shipping lanes and avoiding pirates. I am also indebted to the many bloggers who record their sea journeys out of Freemantle Western Australia in their tiny boats to the Pacific and Indian Oceans. I am grateful to those who had more substantial yachts moored in Fremantle who shared their experience of the sea and of course of the unique culture of the city.

Most of all I am grateful for the time I spent with children in care, to learn and understand their brave journey, their determination and their resilience

Many thanks are due to the East Sussex officers who offered advice dealing with plastic waste. However any miscalculation is mine.

I look back to the many stories my students, who came from all over the world recounted while they were studying in the UK and some of which are woven into this story. Thank you.

I am grateful for my eagle-eyed readers, Vera Gajic and Carole Buchan.

Finally, none of this would be possible without the amazing Roddy Phillips and his creative writing workshops, Bourne to Write. His encouragement and the kind criticism of my fellow writers provided the milestones that mark this story.

Rosalyn St Pierre

PROLOGUE

Some people keep skeletons in a cupboard. I could never see the point. I learned at a young age that hiding something in plain sight is a far safer option. So I keep the ashes in transparent plastic boxes on the mantlepiece, just with stick-on labels. No names, just the instruction: 'DO NOT THROW AWAY'.

There are four boxes, two large ones, one marked DOG and a very little one. If asked, I only talk about DOG. I know how to deflect any interest from the others. I keep them to remind me that I have changed, more than just a name. Perhaps my old self still lurks beneath the facade. The boxes looking down at me each evening telling me I can still be in control.

Sometimes the smell of vanilla jolts me to the very centre of my being, so I avoid sponge cakes and white ice cream, which is sad. Have I got used to these vibrations? I cannot work it out, for that dreamy perfume revitalises the memory of my metamorphosis, but to wasp, or to bee, or maybe the elusive dragon?

INTRODUCTION TO THE PLAN

June 2017

It was an auspicious day, when not only did a shower fall from a cloudless sky, but sails of an approaching yacht were observed and from that time life on the island was about to change.

From the air the island resembled an hourglass, two bulbous ends and the centre dominated by a volcano, so high, so hot and so feared that none of the sparse population would think of a name foul enough for the fire breathing, foul belching monster that dominated their lives, for even when it was quiet there was a watch to make sure anyone climbing the lower slopes could be rescued and when it was active to give thanks that no one had been trapped on the sulphurous slopes.

The island was relatively new, soaring out of the Pacific Ocean in one intemperate spasm unnoticed by the world at that time. Life did not develop there it just got washed up or dropped from the skies in an unmanaged migration. Birds dropped seeds, kernels washed up on the shore, turtles struggled in to lay eggs on a possible paradise, until the very same happened to the humans. A few were from shipwrecks and three were put ashore as mutineers. A party of exploring Polynesians also settled in and from time to time they were joined by pirates looking for a place to bury treasure, adventurers from far off Europe looking for gold and once by a lady whose plane crashed a place in the nearby reef.

The early human arrivals set up camp, built settlements at either end of the island, cut off by the dominating volcano.

When the rain fell from cloudless skies on the northern end of the island, it was interpreted as an omen of doom, when the fish would depart the local reefs as monsters of the deep were aroused from their slumbers. At first someone who claimed to have experience in appeasement said that virgins should be sacrificed, initially in accordance to remembered custom, it had to be girls, but then, as the shower continued, perhaps boys until doubt was expressed whether any of the intended victims were actually virgins and no mother would contemplate donating a son. So the custom of singing dirges and a great degree of loud wailing was tried out and yes in due course the unusual showers ceased, the fish returned and there was no sighting of sea monsters.

In the southern regions when showers falling from a cloudless sky covered everyone and everything in a white paste of volcanic ash and water, it immediately dried in the hot sun. Perhaps the dark skinned people remembered the days of attempted invasion by pale skinned intruders, or celebrated their own ancestors arrival on the island, so the day was spent in carnival. There would be good times to be had, drinking and cavorting. Myths were retold, probably expanded and re-enacted in joyous celebration.

The people from the north made the long trip over the mountains to the south and brought incoherent news of a disaster, a catastrophe. Patient questioning eliminated the more usual reasons for panic: not showers from cloudless skies, not more active belching of smoke fumes and ash from the volcano; not plague or illness, but something more sinister, inexplicable, words could not be found.

So much of the day had been spent in wailing and dancing and debate, until a sudden cessation, an approaching vessel was spotted and silence fell as all eyes scanned the horizon. The progress of the vessel was met with some astonishment for it looked as if it was heading on a course to the very beach where all were gathered, staggering around lost, not a sign of damage. And this caused consternation, was this a further omen of disaster? In past times, there was once a raiding party that sought lost gold, twice there were landings or rather abandonment of sickly crew members who had eventually recovered.

The debate started as to how they would defend themselves, to launch the canoes and attack or wait.

As tropical evening ended first with speed then the long blast of the sun's rays turning the skies to all shades of red and orange, the villagers gathered on the beach. Fires were lit and stories told, about other landings while the yacht rested outside the reef.

There was only one passageway through the reef and wind and tide had to be correctly judged to pass through. Many vessels had misjudged the approach, which accounted for some of the humans being dumped on the beaches if they were lucky or the sharp crags of the reef if not, with no hope of return home. The islanders debated for some time about how the yacht had fortuitously anchored in the just the right place, sheltered from the prevailing winds of that night and why a yacht would voyage with intent to their island and unlike others who had in happenstance arrived, blown off their intended courses.

As in all communities, the young women sat apart, oiling their hair, chatting and laughing, never still, rarely quiet and always vigilant, watching the yacht. One by one they confirmed that there were at least two crew and all agreed they looked liked fit young men.

But, as they waited their astonishment grew, for it was a fine yacht and more importantly had anchored just off the treacherous reef, near the gap that could only be crossed at high tide. So throughout the night as the fires on the beach gradually burned down, watch was kept on the yacht and talk of who was onboard, why they had come to the island and what would happen surfed from the south islanders to the north islanders until dawn emerged, when it was agreed to eat and see who was about to land.

Above the tree line in dense undergrowth the wisest and the eldest of the Komodo dragons observed the gathering of the people on the beach, could see the sails of the yacht being lowered and the anchor dropped in the deep pools being the reef and as the night are called slunk slowly purposefully into the burrows to dream of what could be caught and eaten in the days to come.

PART ONE

In which our heroine encounters unexpected events a number of deaths and is given strange advice.

ONE
H

The glutinous tentacles of coincidence stretched some 8000 miles, to an island in the north where a day without rain would have been recorded, and on that very same morning, as a yacht approached a remote island, dawn was greeted by silence, nothing from the railway line, no traffic, even the seagulls were sitting wet and miserable, on the dark roofs of suburban houses. It was minus fifteen hours to the explosion that would alter the life, not just of a community, but a sole woman, me, suddenly waking in the dark.

I had woken up in those unforgiving hours before dawn, wondering if I'd had a premonition, you know like those young people on the telly say, 'I just gave him a special kiss this morning just before he left the house, don't know why, then wham! he's dead ten minutes later.'

I found myself thinking what would happen to me? Perhaps this was going to be my last day after all. And in a most unanticipated way that was what happened.

Looking out the window towards the bleak gardens and watching the lights come on in the houses that backed onto ours, I saw my neighbours stumbling around in some dreadful nightwear, though that was better than the couple whose morning ritual was to stand by their window, starkers, I long suspected they knew I watched them every day from my dark bedroom.

In those hours just before dawn, in our back bedroom, it was the combined snores and occasional, though not unbearable flatulence, of both my husband Harry and my beloved old mongrel Bertie that awakened me and constantly reminded me I had duties, I was their carer after all.

And yet, and yet, I could feel that this day was going be different, that change glimmered in the dawn light with all the intensity of a gypsy's prediction.

I went slowly down the stairs. Photographs of Harry's previous wives lined the wall. He said that he liked to be reminded of them even though they were long departed and he had me beside him in his twilight years. Harry said that all his wives names began with an H, 'Such coincidence,' he said when I moved in and was introduced to them.

'I'm a Londoner and there's one thing I cannot do is say me H's, so let me introduce you 'elen, 'ilda, 'annah and olly.' He gave me a hug. 'But you my pet, I will just called 'aitch' then you know I will never drop you.'

At the bottom of the stairs there was a mirror, and looking at myself that morning I had a shock. It was the realisation that each day I was to getting to look more like his former wives. My hair, once thick and blonde now hung lacklustre, my vibrant colour had become the very epitome of ditch water, my skin was pallid and, yes, my eyes were as dead as those departed women. I knew I was stuck here.

In the kitchen Bertie fell, whined and could not get up. So, it wasn't going to me that 'popped my clogs', or as they say 'fell off the perch today,' it was going to be Bertie. We English do not like to use the death words.

At 8.30am precisely I called the Vet and the very kind receptionist said someone would be with me by lunchtime and would make Bertie 'comfortable'.

We had a chat about 'afterwards,' did I want a burial in my garden, a pets' cemetery or a cremation, did I want the ashes returned, in a plastic box or perhaps a nice casket? Who would have thought there would be so many choices? I sat on the floor and cuddled my old dog, I could see he'd had enough of life, chased his last stick, stolen his last bit of chocolate. Let him go in peace, cheapest option, a plastic box on the mantelpiece, or, in my special place alongside the others.

Sunrise in *Lopeham* is not the dramatic event I see on the television, where a blazing sun leaps from golden seas, bringing warmth, light and good times for the day ahead. No, here the sun jerks up. Its progress measured by light forcing its way through the gaps of the semi-detached houses, creeping around sheds and garden paths, almost apologetic in its struggle to reach the sky. First, a struggle getting above the bungalow roofs over the road before disappearing into the sky, challenging the planes making their unsteady way to Gatwick.

That morning had its usual dismal routine. I got dressed, washed, combed my hair without looking in the mirror, I did not like that mirror as it traced my time in the house, too depressing. Looking back, I remembered as a sixteen-year old girl, being flattered and delighted to have the attention of a gallant older man.

He used to call me his 'little woman' in those early days, his best 'gel'. I had not realised how much older because he lied about his age. To think I thought he was only thirty at the time when he was nearing fifty, God I was naive, but by the time I found out, our wedding day, the very day I could be legally married, when we signed the book, I did not care. But what I did care about was the control he gained over me, the quiet menace. Strange to think I did not notice as my life quickly developed from wife to carer.

Until yesterday.

TWO

H

Tuesday, a knock on the door and there was Chardonnay, always known as Cherri. We had shared a room for two years when I was in Care, and, I could not believe my eyes, here was Lucy Carruthers, the oh-so-very-posh key worker in the Children's Home.

'Is your husband at home?' an odd question, not preceded by any greeting, any question as to my well-being and general state of health.

'Upstairs snoring his head off having his afternoon nap,' I replied.

'Good, Can we come in?'

I admit I had a moment of panic, what had I done wrong now? But then I pulled myself together for it was some years since I left Care, they did not have any hold over me now. My mother had died of an overdose and no one knew who my father was. The care-home-kids did form a loose bond, though easily broken in adult life.

'I know we've lost touch,' Lucy began, 'I was very fond of you, a real fighter, or as we professionals say, you have resilience.' she smiled at me fondly, I was astonished. Not many people have ever expressed fondness for me.

'Oh how true, you little cow, remember our fights?' said Cherri giving me a hug.

The difference was Cherri was my friend and when the fights broke out she was at my side. I was about to show them into the front room, a mess with Harry's huge chair drawn up so he could watch the TV in comfort.

'No, the kitchen,' said Cherri leading the way. We crammed in, and Lucy quietly and firmly shut the door. 'We have news for you,' she began.

'We are concerned for your safety, you understand,' Lucy blurted out.

'Don't be daft,' I said absent-mindedly, searching for uncracked mugs. Harry did not encourage visitors and resented buying new mugs till all the old ones were broken.

'Well, I have heard rumours,' Lucy again, 'actually perhaps more than rumours from colleagues in Adult Social Care.'

Cherri laughed, 'and that's a first, those two departments, geriatrics and children actually talking to each other!' Then, 'You know you've always been a survivor, not a victim of the past of your bloody awful family and that episode in Care.'

I hesitated, where was this going, 'suppose so' I muttered, 'keep your voice down, you'll wake him up.'

Lucy lent back on the work surface and looked out of the window, not meeting my eyes, 'what do you know about Harry, do you know about the other wives?'

I almost exploded, a strange sense of loyalty or perhaps I did not want to admit there was anything I did not know.

'His wives' pictures are lined up on the stairs so I know all about them, can't forget them,' I muttered, 'I met Harry when he was visiting Holly in the old folks place I was working in up the road.'

'Very early onset of dementia, very, very early, I believe,' said Lucy.

'And then she pegged it unexpectedly, according to the Coroner and straight after a visit from Harry,' Cherri leaned towards me conspiratorially, 'and not the first one.'

There was a moment's silence.

'What do you mean not the first one?'

'All the others, all unexpected or disappeared,' said Lucy.

And those were just the wives, there were others you know, girl friends, he used to call them but some were just a one night stand.'

'Serial Killer!' that from my friend the go-to person for background on any TV crime drama, could have won Mastermind on the topic.

'No!' Was my voice lacking conviction?

I thought that all through our marriage, he used to say, 'I can't lose you. You are my woman, stay with me or I will die.'

I had no intention of leaving, I was fond of him plus I had the security of a nice little house. There was some condition I once read where victims became too fond of their captors and did not want release. Something from Sweden? But now?

Cherri interrupted my thoughts,

'Make plans my friend while you're safe,' then seeing me look at my dog sighed, 'I suppose you'll hang around while that poor old dog needs you.' And surprisingly I found myself agreeing.

We could hear Harry stirring up stairs and so they left silently.

15

'Who's there, you got visitors, you know I don't want visitors here.'

The incessant grumbling had started accompanied by belches, loud farts and shuffles as Harry made his way slowly downstairs.

'No one here Harry,' I lied with considerable ease, a skill I thought I had left behind with my destructive mother, 'just the radio.'

And so I left things as they were, but like a seed, the warnings grew until yesterday.

Harry decided from then on to take his afternoon nap in the sitting room. I suspected he did not believe my story about the visit. I could see him peering, trying to keep awake, listening to my every move. But yesterday he crashed out and I quietly, step by step, moved up the stairs to the spare bedroom, more of a cupboard really, where Harry kept his 'boxes'.

'Nothing for you to worry about, H,' he used to say with a giggle thwarting my occasional attempts to get in, 'no need to dust in there, I likes to do it, gives me a feeling I am helping with the housework.'

The door was never locked, but he closed it firmly after being in there, with a look and sometimes, 'not the place for you gel.'

But yesterday, I crept in. As I got to the door I could hear the snores rumbling up to the rafters, so far so good. I turned the handle, a small squeak and another as the door opened. I stopped and listened, a pause in the snores and then they started up again.

There were piles of boxes, all shapes and sizes from large plastic ones that must have been made for office files, cartons that might have held radios, small televisions, Amazon deliveries that I never remember ever arriving at our address, well not during my time, even old cereal packets.

One fell to the floor, and photographs fell out. A very young man, looking closely I thought it was Harry with a young girl his age, around fourteen I would guess. And then on the floor fell a little bracelet and when I looked closely the girl was wearing an identical one.

Another box, more photographs, Harry older, but who was the woman? Not one of the wives I was sure. A scarf fell out. I picked it up, heavy sweet perfume, old fashioned scent I thought.

Then I heard a whimper, it was the dog, my guardian. 'Get out of my way you filthy cur,' Harry was on the move. Shuffling, grunting he was making his way to the foot of the stairs.

He called out, 'H, where are you?'

I could not reply, he would know I was in the room, I threw everything back more or less as I found it.

'Hey my little wifey, where are you?'

I made it out of the room and was trying silently to close the door, when, there he was at the bend of the stairs staring at me with loathing and menace. He started to lick his lips, how reptilian his face had become, how lizards-like his movement as he crawled limb by limb extending an arm, a hand with long yellow nails, clasping the bannisters.

'So what's you been looking at little wifey?' his words spat out, 'you'd better be careful, you'd better look out.'

'What me?' I looked right back on him, 'you'd better get down stairs right now, before you fall down, if you get my meaning.' I felt like a panther ready to spring.

There was a look first of surprise. I had never spoken to him like that before, never challenged his order. Then fear, then perhaps horror as he turned to walk, very carefully, back to the sitting room. He spent the rest of the day, shaking or rather trembling. Maybe he realised two things that afternoon, first I was no longer under his control and secondly and of more significance, he was dependent on me for food, for drink, for life itself and that frightened him. How could he have changed so much? There was no trace of the debonaire man who had seduced me, a hybrid part saviour giving me a chance to escape institutional life part an experienced lover who would offer far more than the groping I had endured.

My secrets so hidden were coming to the surface, I was changing, never a victim and for a time was a survivor I was leaving the past and seeking the future.

THREE
H

But that was yesterday. This morning there was for once a break in the routine. The vet arrived, a lovely young man. He actually gave me a hug and told me I was so brave. It struck me as very modern behaviour not like old Joy Bliss, an oxymoron of a name. When she turned up both animals and clients bellies turned to water.

'It's a hard decision,' he said, 'to put a dog to sleep. This old dog,' he added unnecessarily pointing at Bertie in his basket while looking at Harry in his chair, 'has had a good life I can tell. Why don't you give him a last pat, and I will give him an injection, he won't know anything about it.'

It seemed to me that a tremor began in the ground, a shaking of the world around me as I held my beloved and loving dog. It was no time at all, old Bertie did just what they say, gave a little gasp and then was dead but somehow there was a perceptible shift in the universe.

I was sad and shocked, and unusually I started to cry. Harry, who was as always sitting in his chair started grumbling because I had turned the telly off.

'What's up with you woman? It's only a dog. I hope you cry like that when I'm gone.'

For once I was lost for words. The vet waited a while, holding my hand, then, glancing at a magazine page that was open said, 'look at that lovely island in the sun,' he turned to me as I sobbed even louder,

'No chance of a little break perhaps?' And then sighed seeing it was unnecessary for me to say, what chance?

The vet filled in some forms then wrapped Bertie in plastic to take him out to his car. As he bent down to lift the package up he said, very quietly, 'have you ever heard of *The Syndicate*? It might do you good to find out. A client of mine is thinking of booking up, it would be quite an adventure for you.'

'What are you talking about?'

I replied sotto voce, for there was something conspiratorial in his manner, 'I am not one for buying racehorses if that's what you mean.'

Annoyingly he did not stop but continued down our path to

his car, nodding at our neighbours, Peter and Angela. With a cheery wave, he added, 'ask around, you might find it fun,' and sped off.

My neighbours unusually came out of their house, standing on their front doorstep, drinking coffee from identical mugs.

'Bertie died this morning,' I said dolefully.

'We wondered, so not Harry then?' Peter said but did not add any kind comments as they returned to their house shutting the door with unnecessary firmness. I knew I was right about those two, would one person actually carry Harry out in a rolled up bit of plastic?

The afternoon could, very accurately, be described as deathly quiet. Most afternoons I would saunter down to the little parade of diminishing shops, now looking as bleak as my soul. I suppose I was facing up to the fact that, in recent years I could not see any change, no modern housing estates here, no trendy shops.

However, this day continued to be different, I could feel a tremor again, so strong I even asked the lady on the till in the shop if she had noticed anything peculiar. But she looked at me blankly. It reminded me that I should write to the owners of this branch recommending it be renamed so as to drop the title 'Super'.

I am convinced that any staff with any communicative skills are encouraged to find employment elsewhere. However, I did try.

'Can you feel that?' I asked.

'You what?' the reply.

'That tremor.'

'Where?'

'Everywhere, the ground, the air around.'

'Nope, that'll be five pounds ten. Next.'

I know when I am beaten so I trudged back along dismally named roads, avenues and closes which lack the bizarre flair for highway naming that I saw in Peacehaven. Who were the lovely ladies of that little town near Brighton, Phyllis, Edith, Dorothy that had won such an eternal accolade? Here the imagination stretches to West Close, East Avenue and other points of the compass.

I was sure that I had only been out for half an hour and what did I find when I get back but old Harry lying on the floor still and barely breathing.

'What a coincidence, what a relief,' I thought, then reflected whether I had murdered him by telepathy or by severely rationing his pills, best not to mention that to anyone.

I rang the doctor's surgery but gave up after endless instructions to press this and that and then being told a house visit was out of the question.

I rang the ambulance and said the old man was on the floor but on reflection did not stress that he was very poorly. In fact he died within seconds of my call.

I had a moment's panic. I had heard of stories of paramedics resuscitating victims due to their fanatic belief in prolonging life even an hour or more after the last breath. How ghastly it would be if my newly won freedom were to be snatched away. Predicting such an occasion I had obtained the essential paperwork. We had both got Do-Not-Resuscitate certificates that the doctor told me to keep in the fridge, and so kindly gave me a plastic tube to keep it in so any spilt milk did not spoil the writing just in case I am found on the floor close to death. That's where the paramedics look first, in the fridge, on the shelf with the milk I am told. Now who would have thought of that?

After half an hour the ambulance turned up, the speed of the paramedics noticeably slowed down and relaxed as I met them at the door with the Certificate in my hand. They were very kind, but took their time looking at old Harry's medication. They said they had to call in the doctor for a Death Certificate, more and more paperwork I thought.

The doctor turned up an hour later, all in a rush and confirmed that Harry was very old and had been poorly for a time.

'I expect he hasn't been takings tablets again,' she said, but with a questioning look, but did not wait for an answer.

As she took out her pen, to sign the Death Certificate, she had Harry's notes from the surgery and I saw in pencil the letters MOB. I knew what they meant. When I was once looking at my notes, I think I was only six, I saw MLS and later found out it was for Miserable Little Sod, so, I knew what the MO stood for Miserable Old B... but wondered what the B stood for, Bastard, Bugger, any of those would be an appropriate diagnosis.

She had taken up a magazine to rest her forms on as she sat to write down all the details. Putting it back on the table she noted it was open at the page of the deserted island.

'Gosh,' she began in a weary voice, 'doesn't that look lovely, just to be able to wander along a quiet beach in the beautiful sunshine, sipping some wicked cocktail from a coconut shell?'

She suddenly said that a patient of hers was thinking of signing up for a fun expedition to an island somewhere off Australia, and asked did I know about *The Syndicate*, which truthfully I did not, though I failed to mention I had first heard of it this morning.

She said, 'you must look after yourself now, I think it would do you good.'

But wasn't it odd that in one day two professionals had mentioned that name? She wrote heart failure, which it was, because it had definitely stopped and then added stroke to be on the safe side. I said goodbye to Harry as he was carried out of the door, but with far less sadness than when Bertie had made the same journey only that morning.

The only thing that gave me a little joy on the sad journey from house to undertaker's wagon was that Angela and Peter had made their once-in-a-month trip to the supermarket, so his departure was only noted by that strange woman who as a one-person project is the local equivalent to Neighbourhood Watch, and whose daily task is to endlessly circle our roads on foot or in her little car.

It was evening. I had disposed of all the pills, which had been prescribed for Harry. I found a bottle of sherry and put my feet up. But late at night I went out to lock the front door and put up a chain, as recommended by the Sussex Police, I noticed an envelope that had got kicked under the mat, just the edge showing. With all the comings and more accurately goings, I had not seen it. I opened the letter.

It was from the Premium Bonds, bought years ago, a tidy sum.

And then the bomb blast hit, the tremors that had been building up all day erupted through the ground, through the floorboards and into my very being, I was free at last.

FOUR
H

I am a practical woman and knew I had to sort things out, but at the back of my mind many ideas were beginning to form. First I needed to find the Will.

There's a saying that those who keep a tidy desk never experience the joy of finding something they thought irretrievably lost, so it took me hours of rooting through the sideboard drawers, the papers behind the kitchen cups, my bedside cupboard and then I remembered that I had left it on top of the wardrobe so old Harry would not have a chance to add a codicil, like they do in the Agatha Christie thrillers.

The following morning I started making some more calls.

I texted Harry's relations and a spoke with former friends with increasing incoherence and a lack of control which meant I could not keep up a pretence of grief for the departed husband.

I called Freddie, Harry's nephew. He was supposed to be in the city, a trader no less. Well, that's what he told us. He and Harry never got on, but then very few did get on with Harry. I kept in touch with him because Harry and me, we had no children, but Harry used to say he would look after the lad, leave him a little something. We didn't see Freddie too often, and when he did turn up it was never with the wife and then usually wanting a loan.

I did think that I should speak to him. The wife answered the phone and told me that at 7.15am she was just getting up and it was too early to speak and to call Freddie on his mobile. Didn't listen to me, I knew I was gabbling, she always made me feel nervous. I just couldn't find the right words.

It took me another hour to find his mobile number, hate them, cannot ever remember them. Freddie was just getting off the train in a rush,

'You alright H?' he said.

It was not really a question if you know what I mean. I said I just wanted to speak to him, but he replied he was in a rush,

'Give you a call at the weekend.'

'When?'

'Look, I don't know,.'

'Well,' I said, 'I might not be around.'

'Don't be daft H,' he said, 'where would you be going then?'

And that was it, not a question but a very telling silence. Perhaps he was in the Tube and lost a signal, but I am not so sure. Shame really, so I altered the list, and most precisely crossed them both, deleted, gone.

At 10.30 I had rung my sister in law, Gwen, Freddie's mother. Harry had never got on with her either, and she did not approve of me. She'd recently moved to a bungalow in a more prestigious part of Lopeham. I asked her if she got the text, she hadn't read it so I told her Harry had died.

'Really?' she said, 'what, what say? Look, can hardly hear, don't have time to chat, just packing, leaving soon.'

She never talks in sentences that woman, you would think she suffered from shortness of breath, but I have come to the conclusion she just doesn't like using the energy needed to engage in meaningful communication.

'Where are you going? Hospital?' I asked, wondering if it was yet another visit to a hospital. She is an expert in the art of imagined illnesses, there are a few so well versed in the symptoms of hypochondria that for a time baffle doctors.

No!' she trilled, 'a cruise.'

'That's nice,' I said trying to mask my insincerity, 'I would like a cruise too.'

A short silence, then in a rush, 'Oh I don't think it would be your thing, too noisy, foreign travel, you know and what about Bertie, you couldn't leave him. Sorry must go.'

So I considered how much nicer my old dog had been, what a companion. Hah! Hope the crew and all the passengers come down with E coli and are quarantined for weeks in some seedy hot tropical port. Though what would happen if I just turned up on the same at the last minute, oh her face then!

Yes, her name came off the list too.

Midday, the impact of the shocks was beginning to reduce. They say that about bombs don't they? First the flash, the realisation that the world was changing, lights, flying debris, then silence and sadness and then picking yourself up from the rubble and carrying on.

So, I thought, 'lets reconsider the list'. Looking through the phone book so many dead names, then Sally. I remember Sally as a babe, my best friend's daughter. Her Mum was the first to go. Gosh I do miss her still.

At 12.15 precisely I phone Sally.

'Oh Auntie, how lovely to hear from you. Tell me what are you up to?' For a moment you know I couldn't think of anything to say, I am never up to anything, well not in recent years. Then I blurted out, 'poor old Bertie had to be put down,' and without thinking, 'Harry too.'

'Cripes, what, you put Harry to sleep too?' and started laughing.

But she doesn't give up. 'It's a lovely day, can I pop over and see you? Mum really loved you, you know, and I should love to see you. You are the only one who knew her as a young girl. How about a spot of shopping?'

My heart soars, what unexpected joy.

That began the walking out of the bomb blast with that moment of peace, the reconstruction, looking, perhaps to a new start.

A month later I had cleared all the boxes in the spare bedroom. I contacted a local house painter and to his surprise gave him my keys and told him to decorate throughout as I would be going away. I rented packing cases from the storage depot, checked everything in and sent them off for a 12 month incarceration along with those who have downsized from large house but cannot bear to part with essential bric-a-brac and unread books. In 12 months I would decide what to do.

I had both Harry and Bertie cremated, retrieved the ashes and put them in plastic boxes on the mantelpiece over the sitting room fireplace. I lined them up neatly beside the others, retrieved from their hiding place. That little ceremony completed it was time for a chat to Stephen.

FIVE
H

I had first heard of Stephen when Harry thought he ought to sort out his finances in other words seeking a pathway through that treacherous swamp littered with the skeletons of those who could not distinguish between tax avoidance and tax evasion.

Harry had been informed through contacts in the local pub that Stephen was a retired bank manager from Tunbridge Wells. Not true, Stephen, first all was far too young, and he was made redundant when advanced computers were delivered through the Bank's HQ in the distant City of London. I am not saying that the algorithms of the computers did much to hasten the demise of the City of London, but you cannot ignore such a coincidence.

Can you imagine a bank employee these days who was known, trusted and respected by his bank's customers? I was told that Stephen had been in the same branch for a few years, giving kindly, safe and reliable advice to the many customers through the glass screen. When he left to live on the outskirts of Eastbourne, able to buy a little house there, a number of former customers, many bemused and bewildered by changes in banking staffing, that dreadful internet arrangements and worst of all the closure of the branch, persuaded him to become their private adviser.

I had met him twice with Harry but now it was time to look him up again. He was so kind and helpful sorting out Harry's pension, making sure he had thought about 'the little woman', I think that he meant advice about Harry's Will. I had sat silently through the discussions smiling from time to time, at first inwardly seething about being referred to in those terms and then slowly realising that is what I had become, not little in stature, but of little significance.

I phoned Stephen and it took him more than a few minutes to remember me. 'Let's meet up, I can come to Lopeham,' he began.

I stopped him immediately, I knew that once he set foot in the town, he would be recognised, possibly even followed and then everyone would wonder if I had been left a nest egg, come into funds as it were. Without mentioning my fears, he appeared to understand, so we arranged to meet in Lewes.

'There are loads of cafes, we could meet at the one just outside the station. If it's a nice day we can sit outside. Do bring any papers you want me to see.'

I always liked going into Lewes. From time to time I used to catch the train and wander around, just to have a change of scene. It is a very hilly town, so different from where I lived. The Lewes trick is to walk from the station to the bus depot then take a bus right up to the top end of town and wander downhill.

The café was busy, but quiet, so many were working on laptops. I am told the curse of working at home is that after a very short time the silence of the house, the awaiting domestic chores, the weeds growing in the garden are frustrating distractions. That is why people and women in particular like to go out to work and escape the drudgery and monotony of the house. I just wished I could have done the same. Cafes have been quick to cash in on this, providing space, coffee and social contacts. So, when Stephen and I met up, we did not attract curious glances, just another two holding an informal business meeting.

SIX
Enter Stephen

Stephen had not looked forward to this meeting. When widows insist in meeting well away from the abode they had shared with their deceased, questions around wills, codicils and tax avoidance of dubious legality which formed the foundation of any consultation. He was well aware of the former wives and partners of old Harry Griffiths, and on the death of each, money poured into funds held by that curmudgeon, from life insurances in the main and twice from the successful prosecution of a care home.

He recalled the last Mrs Griffiths, like the others, he paused for a moment shocked he could recall how many former wives there had been, but did remember a vulnerable young woman, much younger than Harry and that same mousey, drab appearance that seemed to grow as a parasite within the bodies of these women until they met early and unexpected deaths.

Stephen liked Lewes, he enjoyed the energy the small town exuded and in an attempt to blend in, had chosen to wear his new linen and rather colourful jacket. He arrived early to ensure he had a table with some space around it. Clever management of the cafe had designated the tables at the back with access to the veranda for those with the very young children whose minders were unconcerned at the noise or mess made. Two young women on the next table were talking about holidays, seemed they liked resorts although not the resorts like Bournemouth and Bognor Regis, but all-inclusive resorts in Turkey or the Seychelles where, they agreed, you meet very nice British people. It seemed daft to Stephen to go all that way and not meet the locals, where's the fun in that?

He did not recognise her immediately, only when she walked up to his table did he realise who she was, standing hesitantly before him.

'Stephen? It is you isn't it? Thank you for coming all this way,' and looking around, laughed, 'not the usual Lopeham scene is it?'

Stephen looked up, then looked again and to give himself time stood up and went to order a coffee for her. As he swiped his card at the counter he looked back wondering what had changed. She still wore a drab mushroom coloured sweater that drained any colour from her face. Her hair lay unkempt on her shoulders, but as the sun came through the cafe windows, actually gleamed like a spring primrose emerging from the winter grasses. And more than that, she sparkled with an energy he had never seen before in the Griffith wives.

As they sat over their drinks, Stephen began, while shuffling papers that emerged with lack of order from a shopping bag,

'You look well, after all you have been through. My sympathy again on the passing of Harry.'

She nodded as if it were of no import and added,

'And Bertie too,'

Bertie? A relation?'

'No my old dog died, must say I miss him more.'

He gave her a quick look, a smile just edged on her lips, her eyes looked mischievious, so not a grieving widow.

I understand,' he said, giving her look of quiet acknowledgement, not judgemental, more appraising. He turned to the papers again.

'You do understand that you are secure, Mrs…er, what would you like me to call you?'

'Call me H, everyone does.'

He coughed and shuffled, 'an unusual name, but it does distinguish you for all others.'

She laughed and agreed, then more seriously turned to the papers lying on the table.

At the back of the cafe one observant young woman said to her friends,

'Will you look at those two. Must be a first date, sitting so near to each other not touching.'

'Those were the days,' sighed her companion trying to get a toddler to sit down while breastfeeding a baby. 'Bet it's an internet date, they look sort of secretive, muttering to each other.'

'She looks as if she can take care of herself, but look at him all spruced up, bet that's a new jacket, hope he has cut off the label.' And then ironically added, 'he doesn't look like a mass murderer, so she will be safe.'

And her friend said, 'yes but will he?'

SEVEN
H

I looked at all the papers on the table, there were so many, it was daunting.

Stephen began,

'Harry's Will is very simple and you will have his pension, not a fortune but enough to, well, have some fun. In fact Harry told me that you are the best of all his wives, the one H couldn't drop.' that old joke but it was surprisingly touching. But then 'Fun,' what could he mean?

Stephen continued, 'there are no pockets in shrouds, that is what I tell my clients, don't wait for a rainy day, do something you have always wanted to do, explore the world for instance,' he hesitated noticing my shocked look, 'or perhaps do up the bungalow, new kitchen?' now I had a look of pure distain.

He struggled, for he was a kindly and helpful man, 'how about a cruise?'

I practically choked on my latte, which was disgusting anyway. The thought of going on a cruise, locked in with thousands of unknown people, who might get into fights, get food poisoning, face hurricanes and worse made me tremble.

'Let's change tack,' I suggested, pleased at my first attempt at a nautical joke.

Stephen looked at me, 'I can see you are not one for the normal cruise, not your scene is it? But think about having an adventure. There are many ships that only have twenty or thirty, passengers and go to some exciting and little known destinations.

I think it would be up your street. One of my clients spoke very warmly about a cruise on *The Syndicate*.' You know my dear H,' he said patting my hand in not quite an avuncular fashion, 'I think a break now would do you the power of good. I will look after everything here. Spend your winnings on a treat.'

It was a nice hand, I did not withdraw it, in fact I gave it a little squeeze. Looking closely at Stephen I could see that despite his haircut, his new jacket, he was much younger than he seemed, in fact about my age. I liked the idea of having fun. No one had ever thought of me having 'a good time' but somehow the thought had great appeal. To his surprise I looked at him, and held onto his hand. I could see he was looking at me with some surprise. Had he noticed the change in me?

Old habits die hard, I could not bring myself to say much other than attempting to state quite calmly that this was the best advice I had ever had, and would arrange something that very day. We exchanged contacts and how we could keep in touch from any part of the world and he assured me that all my finances would blossom under his care.

I sat in the sunshine for an hour, had another glass of wine and suddenly thought the world was looking good.

EIGHT
Stephen

Stephen sat in the train back to Eastbourne, oblivious of the sun shining on Firle Beacon, deaf to the surrounding chatter of other passengers, all in singular conversation with the unseen on their mobiles bemused by his encounter with H. He liked an ordered life, and he was aware that in that brief handholding few minutes, his life was about to change. He thought that Lewes with its little meandering ways, locally called twittens held ancient powers. Then, more pragmatically contrasted small shops and businesses that rarely stayed too long, because all passing trade is on foot, only attracting business from the physically fit; so different from Eastbourne.

While Stephen was travelling away, the twittens were aloud with the students from the college trudging up the hill, chatting, bored and tired until a very good looking young man was spotted putting a poster onto a display in the window.

CRUISES WITH A DIFFERENCE
Want an adventure?
Maiden trip
including mystery destination
The Syndicate

'Will you just look at that!' gasped Tara who had just turned sixteen on that very day and had a keen eye for local talent. A young man, who was stretching to put the final touches of the display in the new travel agents gave her a wink.

He was in his twenties, tall, lean and tanned. Although his hair was blondish with tight curls. He had the most extraordinary eyes, dark brown with an oriental lift. As he stretched up to fix another poster, the admiring crowd could see he had tattoos on his upper arm, a lovely pattern of whorls, gentle lines encompassing shells. He shirt slightly opened at the neck was the start of a head of a lizard.

Mobile phones were out and in no time whatsoever, other students had deviated off their normal routes home a small gathering formed. He, on the other hand, was both pleased and embarrassed and stumbled away from the display and back into the shop.

Attracted by the noise an elderly couple wandered down the twitten.

'Oh my god, would you just look at that.'

'What Dilys?'

The tired reply, from an elderly man whose strength was severely challenged by the hills and twists of the Lewes streets.

'Jim look, an ideal holiday, just what we need.'

Jim, wise in the ways of his wife, and being reasonably confident that she was more attracted by the virile young man in the window than the trip that was being advertised, took the path of discretion and they both entered the little shop to the envy of the girls gathered outside.

Jim looked around what was in reality a very small space, whitewashed walls, wooden floors, not the glamour of the agents on the High Street - carpeted, comfortable and coffee offered to loyal customers.

Jim had fancied himself as a man of the sea, experience drawn from living in coastal town of Seaford, occasional trip out to catch whiting or mackerel, and long observation of the yachts passing by.

To break the silence and, in his opinion, not to show over enthusiasm about the 'Cruise with a difference' Dilys made a sly comment on the magnificent tattoos, especially the head of the lizard that popped up unexpectedly as the young man sat down and produced some brochures. Wonder what else he had down there? the thought shocking even her.

'This is no ordinary lizard,' he said, 'this is the magnificent Komodo dragon.'

Then apparently trying to get this couple to focus on business he buttoned up his shirt, the Dragon receded leaving just a nose, its wavering tongue and one eye, looking at Jim with some intent. A file opened and the beginning.

'This trip is expensive, it starts in West Australia and so the airfare return to Perth is extra to the cost of the cruise. Will this be a problem?'

I can of course book the flight for you.'

The young man was unsure, difficult to tell with the elderly what money they had and what money they were prepared to spend.

'No problem,' a breathless intervention from Dilys who was catching the excitement of such a venture, and, perhaps more.

'Let me show you recent photographs of the yacht.'

Jim hesitated, he had been thinking of a cruise ship.

'This is one of the biggest yachts, it is owned by a Russian businessman who unfortunately is unable to make use of it now, and we have leased it.'

'Bet he is in prison on the run,' Jim uncharitably muttered, but then gasped, for the yacht, unlike the ones in Eastbourne Marina was in fact huge, almost a naval battleship.

It takes 20 passengers and 8 crew. The interior is luxurious and of course it has extremely powerful engines and navigational gear for ocean going trips. 'No swimming pool,' he laughed, 'but passengers can always take a dip in the beautiful clear ocean waters with dolphins.'

The young man realised he had their interest, 'There will be some extra charges for additional wines or any special culinary dishes you would want to order, is that a problem?'

NINE
H

I distinctly remember being extremely curious, how could you have a cruise when you don't know where you are going? I supposed all the passengers have to have extraordinary faith in the captain and the crew is competent in navigational skills. Was this what my doctor and vet and now Stephen, referred to? What a coincidence!

When I finished my third glass of wine, the intervening time between the first casual sip and the last more vigorous swig was put to good use. First, was the surprisingly warm feeling I had towards Stephen - a surprise for even before the death of Harry I thought my future was to disdain men, become a nun or a librarian perhaps; and then on the third that it was the day to do something, to take that first step and it was fortuitous that the second step led me into the twitten, occupied by a number of young people looking in a shop window. As I approached, an elderly man pushed his way out of the shop muttering, but I noticed the woman give a cheery wave to someone in side.

Then I simultaneously took in the poster in the window and the young man within, who I joined, entranced or rather hypnotised by his glorious tattoos and there and then signed up. When I said no expense to be spared if he would please book Business Class for the return flight and that I could pay now before I changed my mind, I could see his hands shaking. He was so kind and so beguiling, I had no problem telling him about my recent good fortune, in unexpected wealth and the arrival of long wanted freedom.

I liked the thought that I would be taking off at the end of the month. It would not be not long enough to get in a panic and think about cancelling the venture, but enough time to pack. I left the little office and wandered down the High Street in a bit of a daze, I had never done anything so quickly, but after all I didn't have anyone to look after now.

What do people wear on cruises? I wondered, I looked in shop windows, all those sleeveless dresses and shorts! Huh I'd surely catch a chill.

The next day I rang Sally.

'Sally,' I said, 'I have some news, I have booked a cruise.'

And Sally said she was so pleased for me and asked me where I was going, a river cruise or perhaps the West Indies for a week.

'Heavens no,' I laughed, 'I could run into Gwen if I did that.'

I told her I had booked a mystery tour of the Pacific Islands. Sally was shocked into silence, 'We start in Australia and then onto an unknown mystery destination.'

I heard a gasp 'Wow' and then,

'That's just great, good for you, you deserve some fun.'

It suddenly hit me that this is not what everyone would be saying.

I told Peter and Angela next door and a predictable response 'Who would have thought?'

Angela looked at me strangely, 'Well,' she muttered in a thin-lipped way, 'Now Harry and Bertie are gone, you have your freedom.'

Did I see a jealous glint in her eye, and a rather resentful glance at her husband waddling down the garden path in an identical though a larger size sweat shirt to her own.

I told the nice girl at the corner shop and she said, 'Well I be blowed,' and even Arthur our long-term post person, we cannot call him a post man, was so kind and advised me about not leaving post collecting on the hall mat, but said to me, 'I hope you will manage.' What did he mean? Mind you I had a bit of drama. It was one thing finding my list, now changed by the way, but I had the same old ding-dong trying to find my passport.

So the day arrived for me to leave. I had no one to advise me, and I certainly was not going to speak to Gwen. I had bought a wheelie case, and for the cruise, a new nightie, a skirt, cotton trousers and three t-shirts. Then initially with some reluctance at the expense, three new bras and knickers, suitable for all occasions. I put in my old summer dress, lots of wear left in that. I got fancy plimsolls for walking around. I put in a paperback and a pack of playing cards. Oh yes some sun cream and a new toothbrush.

The plane took off at 10 pm. I still cannot see what's in all this flying nonsense.

At first it seemed fine, a glass of wine some very acceptable food. But looking at those in the economy section I realised that for those passengers it was no different from being on the village bus, and almost as uncomfortable.

PART TWO

In which the first death occurs unnoticed and unmourned. The once in a lifetime adventure begins for some, but none predicted how it would end.

ONE

No one really noticed the first death.

Six hours into the flight and everyone was sleeping. The plane somewhere over Iraq the oxygen supply had been reduced not only to encourage slumber but to limit the demands for alcohol and beverages.

In the galley a small group stood drinking and chatting, a bored member of the cabin crew and a young man with a tattoo of a komodo dragon. Eventually a signal was answered reluctantly by the steward, 'God, I thought they were all out for the count,' he muttered while adjusting his face to the 'ever friendly ever helpful nothing is too much to ask for', member of the crew.

A passenger was slumped in a seat, a woman sitting next to him was shaking the unconscious body, though, in the experience of the steward, that particular soul had long departed. A forced wail started then stopped, for strangely as she glanced at the steward she gave a wink, a quick grin, before the wailing started again.

The captain was summoned, a call went out for a doctor, but no stir from the slumbering passengers. Death was confirmed. The body was moved back through the cabin and put into a cupboard behind the galley. No further announcements; no emergency landing; no drama, just a quiet death at 40,000 feet.

From: hgriffiths
To   Sal123
Subject   Arrived
Dear Sally, Just arrived in Perth Just waiting to be picked up to go to the Syndicate. More soon, Much love Auntie H

From: hgriffiths
To: Sfinances
Subject   Safe arrival

Dear Stephen,
Just a quick email to say I have now arrived safely in Australia. I am looking forward to the cruise. The weather is very good here. Sincerely, H

TWO
H

We were picked up by a minibus after an exceedingly long time going though customs at Perth Airport.

With superb planning several long distance planes landed within minutes of each other, resulting in a long line of weary passengers waiting in a queues to get through customs.

The experience of negotiating Australian rules is a major culture shock for any British traveller. We are used to silent and empty tables at Heathrow, with the rare appearance of a uniformed officer and of course everyone choosing Nothing to Declare route.

Not in Perth, where everyone was checked. A form declaring we had no vegetable or animal matter had to be signed before we entered the final lap. A person in front of me had a carved stick, wooden of course, and it was with reluctance that it was passed.

A British couple were found to have not only some apples, but inexplicably three packets of prime British bacon. These were confiscated with due drama, senior officers called in, all cases re-opened and re-examined, and the couple taken away. No living thing animal or vegetable are let through it would seem exception of the disembarking passengers and they with some reluctance.

We waited a further hour, the couple who had been embroiled with customs emerged. 'Stupid old fool,' the woman hissed,
                        'Thought he could allow bacon through.'
Someone offered a sympathetic noise, but was met with,

'He had to pay a fine, that will cut his allowance on the cruise, we're not made of money, you know.'

'Lucky to get off that plane alive,' someone said wearily, 'Suspected the sea adventure would be hazardous, but a man died just near us, couldn't sleep for all the fuss.'

'I think they were going on the same trip as us', another offered.

We had to wait another half an hour, but there was no sign of the new widow, nor any communication to our driver, eventually we set off towards the harbour at Freemantle.

In the early morning light, my impression was that I had come a very long way to see a place that looks just like outer Croydon, endless stores and office buildings. It was only the houses, the majority bungalows that were different. We drove for nearly an hour, peering down long straight and silent suburban roads. And it was chilly, wintery and bleak.

We eventually came towards Freemantle, once a busy dock where thousands landed in the late nineteenth century hoping for a bright new life. Did they meet the convicts that had been there for a lifetime, who laboured with the harsh stones and rocks which built the city? did they meet the local aborigines driven out from their homeland and sent into the vast waste of the interior? I doubt it.

My companions took little notice of this history or gave it much thought. They were not planning to stay, but to launch themselves into the new challenge of the cruise.

Seeing a large cruise ship ablaze with lights, there were cries of excitement from the passengers in the minibus, now finding new energy as the prospect of boarding such a magnificent ship was in sight. But they are to be disappointed, as they continued on to a lonelier darker part of the quay, finally stopped by a smaller ship. Even in the dark, and to put it kindly, it had seen better days and that must have been the distant past.

It was just as in the brochure, but lacking the gloss and the tropical background. It was about 100 meters in length, lights shining from the cabins and the towering impressive satellite dishes reached out to the harbour lights. The more observant passengers could see the chipped paint and a bit of a bash on the upper deck, but wisely did not comment.

As we all tumbled out of the minibus, it became evident that we would have to carry our own luggage onboard. The commotion of cases was yanked roughly from the bus and thrown on the ground. It was clear that the driver was frustrated, angry or just plain tired at the long delays at the airport and the atmosphere was not in any way helped by the last to emerge from the bus, the couple who had not only drank the plane dry of champagne on the lengthy flight from the UK but tried illegal importation of meat goods. The man started yelling at the driver. The brief synopsis of that exchange revealed a curt but ominous sound, the driver's response to an order to get off his bus and help with the luggage, followed by a gesture which left no doubt that help was not forthcoming. It was left to the man to struggle with all the luggage up the gangplank, while a woman stepped ahead, with an impressive command of, 'Oh for god's sake Frank, do hurry up!' while looking around with the air of one who had done many cruises before.

Then a surprise. A taxi raced up and the recently widowed passenger from the plane scrambled out. To the sound of shouts and clanking chains, she just made it up the gangway and tripping, looked at me and laughed.

My first impressions were highly satisfactory: luxurious carpets, a Persian rug; coffee table with a vase of silk flowers most tastefully arranged; some paintings on the wall, strangely of snow covered houses in the deep forest, though more keen and critical eyes, noticed gaps where, perhaps, the former owner had removed some; and most important a wide bed, no bunks or hammocks of course. and finally, two deep and comfortable chairs to relax in which looked out to the window, though at that moment all that could be seen was the dismal dark harbour with its silent cranes, stacked cargo, gang ways awaiting incoming ships.

The bathroom with its marble walls had obviously been ordered to suit very macho tastes, I observed, the bath, enough to take a swim in, and a huge shower, enough to hold three adults, enough said. Were the taps gold? Impossible to tell. There were cupboards and a wardrobes, though which made me realise I did not have enough to fill even one. There was a notice in English and Russia not only about laundry, but that is was possible to buy additional clothing or jewellery when the boutique was open. This was the only indication of the nationality of the owner.

The noisy hum of the ship suddenly changed, great clanking sounds, vibrations, lights flickering was harbour wall was receding as the grey light of the winter revealed the granite stones, the grey seaweed and even the grey cardboard coffee cups floating on the surface the promised fun adventure and sunshine began, or at least what we, now the passengers thought.

First was the gentle lurching of the yacht leaving the harbour, the safety of the Swan River and to our small group, the impression was not that we had sailed with purpose towards a distant horizon, but had meandered wistfully away from land, the wake of the little ship wobbling in zigzags just as the sun started its journey from the land, racing up over the rooftops of Freemantle.

Were the seagulls shouting with delight or with warning cries? The Hopi Indians in central America believe that we are travelling backwards through time. We face our past experiences and see them receding, sometimes in a good light and sometimes not. But the future to come is behind us, they say, because that is why we cannot see what will befall us.

How like this trip.

From: Sal123
To: hgriffiths
Subject: Safe journey
    Hi my favourite auntie, OMG cannot believe you have gone so far. Have a lovely time. I'm keeping an eye on your place xxxxxxx Sally

---

From: sfinances
To: hgriffiths
Subject   Bon Voyage
Good morning, Delighted to get your email. Weather here is very mixed. Have a lovely holiday, Regards, Stephen

---

THREE
H

On the first morning, we are all told to muster in the lounge. We gathered in silence, reluctant to begin conversations. Those early moments had all the charm of a dentist's waiting room. The early camaraderie of the meeting at Perth Airport, the limited exchanges on the minibus had evaporated as we gradually gathered together.

Rarely understood by those unaccustomed to the English that the class divisions are as acute as ever. Hierarchy may not just be expressed through the condition of clothing, for a battered and torn tweed jacket may be worn with pride by the aristocracy; jewellery as an indication of wealth and thus indicating the owner is superior to others in the United States for example, does not necessarily give the same guarantee among the English, (though that is not to say it does not give rise to envy), too much shows lack of sophistication, little and preferably old, does not. And then there is voice, accent, and one reason why the Scots and Irish are loved by the English for they are seen as classless, while the English, with the impeccable daily demonstration of the royal family, seek to develop, to reflect such cultured accents...or for those with true confidence abandon the whole exercise and almost resort to a rough imitation of the working man.

As we sat down we all scrutinised our companions and knew we were being examined: clothes, new, bought specially for this trip and still uncomfortable, or old, survivors of other cruises; hair, cut colour; hands, nails, rings; accessories, but still silence, that final giveaway of voice to be guarded.

The decision facing those experienced in cruises, in package holidays, is that committing to a friendship, to establishing regular companions for drinks or a seat at meals too early, could be a disaster and to find oneself landed with the biggest bore for the duration of the holiday.

Until one voice, a woman standing at the back.

'Morning everyone, my name is Dilys.'

People turned, people looked, a curt nod from a few, a raised eyebrow from others. Undeterred she continued.

'So I paid for this trip and old Jim is in the coroner's office, nothing I can do for a week or two while they do an autopsy. No fuss I said, don't want to take his body back to the UK, so cremation in Australia, sometime. They weren't going to arrest me, and I realised I could make it to the ship.'

There were gasps, some shaking of heads as the passengers heard this announcement, but I just laughed and said, to give her some support,

'Good for you, I waited just a bit too long.' Now this could be a friend I thought. And then a second brief thought, 'I know her, I've seen her before,' but then the thought disappeared as quickly as the morning mists that linger on the fields in spring.

The Captain entered. All the passengers were curious to see the man who would have our lives in his hands for the coming weeks.

A quick glance, a silver haired, tanned man, with a face lined with years of facing the seas, but a second and longer look revealed more and disturbing features. First, his eyes were not the keen sharp eyes that I had seen on local yachtsmen sailing around Eastbourne ever watchful for the hazards at sea, no, these were rheumy eyes, crafty eyes. He was not tall, about average height but he was so thin, not slim and fit. His uniform hung on him, perhaps he had inherited it from the former Russian crew. And his hands were stained, I doubt if it was from oil, more from the Russian cigarettes the smell permeating his breath and his uniform; cruel strong hands, enough to strangle a victim in the dark; and finally as he moved forward a reptilian movement, one limb at a time, a leg, then a shoulder movement, another leg, slowly purposefully, watchful.

But how strange it was that impressions are so very different. 'He looks like an old sea dog,' I heard one passenger say to another, 'we'll be safe in his hands.'

I doubted this. To me he looked like a pirate, not a gallant swinging from the mainsail, no this man looked like a thug, and again doubts about this trip began to rumble in the very depths of my being.

The Captain was immediately joined by my friend from the Lewes Travel Agency. They stood before us. My friend introduced himself as Bruce our expedition leader and with the captain looking on in glum silence. Bruce explained that this voyage on *The Syndicate* was an adventure into the unknown. The Captain stood up somewhat reluctantly I thought. He looked around, he was sizing the women up, for his gaze swept over the men and me, but rested on Dilys and some others for a few seconds before coming to a full stop at the woman who had arrived so late on board yesterday.

He began to speak. I couldn't put an accent on him, he was, I supposed, a child of the seas constantly travelling. First he put a chart on the screen to show in detail where we currently were. As far as I could see, we were very far from any land and heading further into the deep ocean. At the top and bottom of the chart were coloured lines, these, we were told were shipping lanes which we were to avoid. 'How lovely' I had thought, to be so far away from anyone on this over populated and hectic planet. I mentioned this to Dilys, and her response was surprising,

'What would happen if we had an accident, ran into something?'

'Not likely, out here? Look out the window, just the wide ocean.'

'Yes bloody nothing, its weird, not even a seagull, didn't think it would be like this,' then a pause, 'we could run into a whale, or sink in a storm.'

The Captain ignored this observation and assured us that the weather ahead was calm and that we should enjoy the trip, that we may be followed by shoals of fish, though too far out for dolphins. He said we would take a circular route to our mystery island and would be passing remote atolls and uninhabited islands.

He finished with an upward gesture, easily misinterpreted, but saying that the ship had two powerful Zodiacs. They would bring us to shore at remote islands and were powerful and safe lifeboats. With the ending of reassurance he left the bar.

Bruce stood up. He introduced the crew, Paul, James and Rahmin but did not explain what their actual role was.

He told us that they were not only to find a mystery island but to find ourselves. This elected a coarse remark from a man at the back of, 'have no problem…'

Bruce glared and continued.

'We may be holding daily yoga sessions and times of meditation. We want you all to respect the peace and power of the ocean.'

'Oh goodie,' a voice from one of the women passengers, 'I have always wanted to do yoga and do you hum, you know during the meditation?'

There was a collective groan from the room.

'We might consider that approach at a later date,' a tactful reply. Then a sudden change, Bruce changed his stance, his shoulders back, his head up, his voice assertive.

'You will have read in the conditions that there will be no internet or use of mobiles on this trip. We are approaching the point where all iPads, all phones must be handed in. You have one hour to make final communications. I assure you each device will have its own box and you can see where it is placed in a safe in the Captain's office. You can watch the safe being locked if you wish.'

I was astonished that I had apparently agreed to hand in my new mobile phone when I signed up for the trip. I didn't recall this condition, perhaps in the very small print. Bruce went to say that too many trips were ruined by passengers constantly on their phones making unnecessary calls, or more seriously revealing our destinations. He said we were allowed an hour to make last calls and explain the situation, then all phones would be handed to the captain and kept securely.

To: Sal123/
From: hgriffiths
Subject: News
We are going to hand in all our mobiles etc to the captain so we can experience peace and calm on the cruise. As you know that won't make too much difference to me, though some of the passengers seem very worried. All well, with love H

To: hgriffiths
From: Sal123
Subject: Re news
Wow that is awesome! I expect you'll be doing yoga too. Have a wonderful time. XXXX

To: sfinances
From: hgriffiths
Subject   news

45

Dear Stephen, Just a quick note to say we are now handing in our mobiles so that we can enjoy true peace and calm on this stage of the cruise. The weather is hot and sunny. Sincerely H

To: hgriffiths
From: finances
Subject: RE news
How kind of you to contact. I am jealous, you must be on a wonderful trip. Do contact when you return. Lovely day here in Eastbourne Kind regards, Stephen

---

By 1pm all the phones and iPads were handed in. By 2pm many of the passengers were displaying manic withdrawal symptoms. With no phone to hold to an ear, without anything in hand, some were forced to actually enter into conversation of some length with first a partner then with those nearby, while others, unused to such enforced social contact, paced the yacht with blind intensity.

FOUR
H

And so the endless 'bing-bong' that signals food began. I was hungry and breakfast was good, lovely hot food, lots of strong tea, I took my time because it was the first time in years I hadn't had to cook my own breakfast. But when I finished and came up on deck, I noted with sadness, no birds nor whales nor dolphins gambolling before us. Strangely I missed the plane trails a constant sight for the residents of Lopeham under the flight paths into Gatwick, Heathrow, Southampton and seeing those more exotic trails as planes which, I was told, fly daily from Schipol made their way to Brazil. From the deck the seemingly empty ocean surrounded our little world.

The couple who had incurred the extra expense of a more spacious cabin thought they could pop into the Bridge and check our routes, our speed and the seamanship of the crew. But the door remained firmly locked against intruders. When I tried even to look through the glass panels, I was waved away. Was it security or secrecy? Nonetheless as the days went by I got very adept at nautical language, and knew my stern from my aft, which is an unusual, but no doubt, useful form of vocabulary for sea travel.

We were now 13 passengers due to an unfilled place, an unlucky number it is said.

My first impression was that all the passengers appeared to be so very similar. There were male and female couples and four of us travelling alone. We were all from the south of England. Of the couples, the men were older than their female partners, not frail but, what used to be termed 'spry'. I viewed them with a semi-professional eye, my experience at the retirement home coming to fruition and reminding me what Harry might have been if we had done this cruise some years ago

On reflection the couples mirrored my own experience of marriage and partnership, the men did look elderly but their female partners just did not, late middle-aged is the current term I have learnt. While the men wore shirts and blazers and obviously newly bought deck shoes, their partners had bright dresses, hair styles of an amazing array, and such manicured fingers and toes that they glistened among the mass of rings and bracelets even in the middle

47

of the day. Of these couples, one was the most mismatched.

He was elderly, with ophidian movement he slithered across the room barely using his limbs, his eyes darting everywhere, his tongue constantly licking his lips. She was tall, much younger about my own age, a trace of a foreign accent and a wardrobe to meet everyday, every occasion with something different.

A few women formed small groups, but I was never invited. Nor was Audrey the young woman so desperate for the yoga sessions.

Two were experienced passengers of cruises, as they informed anyone within earshot, both had much in common, sturdy reliable women, pillars of their community, their social status therein won on their husbands' ranking in the golf club, on the trout fishing lakes or even the cricket team. A title spat at first, along the lines of:

'We retired to Bognor Regis a few years ago, charming little town.'

'Oh Rita , Bognor, oh really?'

That wonderful use of 'Oh really' which covers everything from pure distain to mild curiosity.

'We moved to the coast, Hove, actually.' A plus mark to Melanie.

I watched from my corner as a strange dance, a ritual began. First it was the hair, one would touch her hair and the others would gradually join in, touching smoothing and stroking oh so delicately. Another would start with her face, again touching, and the others peering laughing touching stroking all with intent, quiet conversations, exchanged glances, were they sympathetic, approving or even hidden behind hands, disapproving. There was even stroking of breasts with appraising yet nonsexual looks, and then as the group formed a closer huddle one stood and the stroking continued on her backside. Slowly while reading a magazine I realised the reason for this curious dance such as may have been seen in a harem, was Botox, or plastic surgery. My god I thought how much of the women are real? Will they transform during the cruise, like aliens on a spaceship revealing the underlying horror?

Through all this I looked on with my straggly hair, my unpainted nails but realising that to question with some jealousy, 'why couldn't I ever get to look even a little glamorous for once?' would not elect any helpful response.

It was soon discovered that standing on the deck area at the back of the yacht was a thrilling experience, watching the wind blowing the waves and dolphins dancing alongside. But my companions did not join me even though I called into the bar area, and this was just what many had paid all this money to see. I assumed the fact that hair would be disturbed kept them locked behind the large windows in the stultifying and artificial atmosphere of the bar. I paced the decks, looking even more wind blown than on the onset of our voyage, but I noticed I was acquiring a tan and that my hair was beginning to bleach in that mixture of sunshine and sea-salt.

The days had their own rhythm. We got on first names with the waiters, James and Paul, though when I say first names, we were informed that those were their names, but they never used ours.

Self restricted to the bar and 'leisure areas' an informal sex separation was established. After breakfast the men settled down to serious conversation about their former professions and work. Frank was always first to settle down, I wonder if he was trying to escape his wife. Joe was a keen golfer about the same age as his comfortable plump wife Melanie. Sometimes they were joined by Nigel and Robin both single it seemed.

Strange how these 'bachelor' groups form into an animal kingdom. I had seen on BBC programmes about animals in Africa. Old lions, old elephants group together on the fringes of the herds, eventually content to let the younger males take over, fed up with the endless battles to preserve their mating rights, and perhaps just having time to chat about things that older males like to talk about, the monologues led by Call-me-Joe and David-please-not-Dave. And listening to this group of older human males, it was just incredible that in this little ship how many had single handedly won a battle; led a company; been a major player in the stock market; saved lives; rebuilt London. Not one was a lowly worker, not one had ever encountered failure. Talk was also of the men's clubs they now joined, and the class system emerged as they talked of rugby and admitted to following, on the news only the fortunes of Brighton and Hove Albion. Not for them the football clubs of the north, nor London of course.

Of all the men I thought Vince the most interesting. He rarely sat in the bar, preferring his cabin on the top deck. He was one of those men that looked middle aged when they reached their twentieth birthday, they remain unchanged for the next fifty years. I noticed he liked corners, back to the wall, his eyes continually scanning the room. I tried talking to him once, but he was absorbed in a book on the reptiles of the Polynesian Islands and Southern Oceans, He was polite and distant, so I gave up. He was a man with a problem I was sure, and perhaps a cruise was a way to either solve those issues or hide away for a time.

I watched I learned. There was something sinister about them that small clique of women. It took me a day to realise that they were watching the men with the intensity of a snake about to strike. Nonetheless when Dilys and I passed by, they would look up with a smile, friendly but with unspoken questions in their eyes.

One morning one did look up at me and said, which I thought most unfortunate

'I heard your husband passed before you left for this trip, how convenient.'

To which I replied, 'And yes my dog too,' as I was still grieving for my poor old Bertie.

WE'How touching,' she replied, before returning to her book. That was my first conversation with Jen.

When we first left Freemantle, there was a certain discipline in the dining room. Dinner was formal and waiter service. We were all allocated tables. Those with accommodation on the upper decks sat near windows which opened up onto the sun deck and the stern of the ship. Nearly every evening an officer joined one of the tables for dinner. Dilys and I sat near the back just by the door to the kitchen or galley. The English class system is artificially preserved, now based on money and bling rather than association to the monarch if only through a chance relationship with a minor royal.

As the passengers sat down for dinner they would wait anxiously for an officer to join them. At first it was only the captain, still in the uniform that seemed too big for him, though gleaming white, and one other male officer, all very smart, almost too smart, too suave. The tables without the gift of such a visit tried not to look on, tried not to overhear the conversation, although, I could one woman tried to wink and flirt, even from a distance, though ignored by the captain.

On the third evening the woman officer attended. We had not been introduced to her on that first night. She wore a very sexy interpretation of navy uniform, the skirt was not so much well fitting but tight, very tight in my opinion, and rather short unsuitable for a seagoing vessel should a storm hit. She was very glamorous, long hair curling around her shoulders, a husky voice with an East European accent. Was she a member of the crew when the Russian owner was aboard? The male passengers were torn between lust and an unspoken concern that a woman was possibly driving their ship.

I had seen her around the yacht, aloof walking with a sense of purpose, to the bridge, to the galley, sometimes talking to the waiters, but not actually doing anything. Unlike the other crew, she began to join the passengers for an after dinner drink. There was something inherently untrustworthy about her as she repeatedly and cleverly returned the conversation encouraging the passengers to discuss their wealth and how they invested their money. And idiots that they were, they revealed far too much.

FIVE
H

That night we encountered the first storm. The yacht had excellent stabilisers, so during the first days of our voyage, in the surprising calm sea, we had motored along just like crossing a pond as the saying goes. But that night we were really tossed around. I was grateful to the Russian for his wide and comfortable bed, no single bunk for the wealthy, then I considered he might be in prison and on a hard bunk and he thinking of the luxury he once knew.

By morning the storm had either blown itself out, or we had sailed to the other side, as dawn saw us staggering out onto the open deck behind the bridge, drawing in deep breaths, grateful to be alive. No one wanted to admit to being scared or seasick, and few approached the breakfast buffet with the enthusiasm of other mornings.

Dilys came up to me.

'The change has started,' she whispered, 'can't you feel it?'

I did not feel anything myself, but having experienced that day of the bomb blast back in Lopeham, back into my fast disappearing former life, I could not deny her moment.

'I could feel it when I realised we would be so far from land.' She continued thoughtfully, 'and I don't trust the crew. There's only five of them, taking turns one bridge driving this bloody yacht the next thing in the galley doing the cooking. I even saw one of the waiters with a hammer and tools fixing a broken catch. When Jim and I went on a cruise to South America every member of the staff had their roles, their place.'

I protested, 'but this is an adventure, this is something new for all of us. We are different from those on the more traditional cruises, we are going have fun and experiences to last us a life time.'

Why I was quoting a section of the brochure promoting this trip I do not know but I thought in a comforting mantra. And strangely, because she also seemed comforted by this, I told her about Gwen and just how ghastly it would be if she had turned up on *The Syndicate,* this too was odd because I never ever talked about my past.

We sat looking at the gradually calming sea, the sun reaching up into a cloudless sky and laughed about cruises and holidays. Dilys had been on many cruises, up and down major rivers, islands and resorts around the world. She told me about the uniformity of life on all cruises, the sense of dread when she and her Jim encountered people they had met on other cruises and the inability to escape from them, trapped for weeks with some boring couple.

Until Dilys turned to me, 'your husband, Harry was it, died before you left. Hmm…left you a little nest egg, did he?'

I had to close my eyes, the sense first of vertigo, the crushing pain as I raced back through time landing with a crash in my bedroom in the Children's Home with Chardonnay Lucas leaning over me and with quiet menace, 'see you had a visitor today, did she leave you anything? Sweets? Dope? Know your Mum's a junkie. Or perhaps a little money for your nest egg?' And then being dragged off her unconscious body, which lay on the floor, blood seeping from a head wound.

I opened my eyes, looked at Dilys and saw her flinch. I thought that I must not lose this clumsy attempt at friendship, there had been so few chances in my life. So I took a deep breath and smiled,

'He wasn't well off, a bit put aside for a rainy day. Looking back on it, its strange to think that the vet and the doctor all recommended this trip.'

Although I pretended to look at the sea, I saw from the corner of my eyes, Dilys giving me a questioning look, perhaps she was re-evaluating her approach to become friends.

'Lucky you, at least you know where you are, me, well Dr Parvin warned me a trip might not be so good when I told her about *The Syndicate*, but then thought I needed a bit of a break, But I am not so sure now that I knew what my Jim was up to with our money.'

I was shocked, had we both been patients of the same doctor whose prescription was to take a break? I did not pursue this nor did I comment on the fact that it put us here in mid-ocean and it was possible that only the captain knew where we were.

But she went on, 'did you know the girls?' she waved her hand to the covered seating area behind us and where all morning seasick casualties who had gradually emerged seeking refreshments or alcohol or both, 'are jealous of us, more of you of course.'

I turned to face her, 'jealous of me? Don't be daft! What them, with their hairdos, their manicured hands, facelifts and god-know-what-else-lifts?'

She lent forward, 'look and listen, your old man is dead, right, and you've got your freedom and a bit of cash. Me? Well my fella is dead and gone, though I really don't know what awaits me when we get back. Men of this age...' and again a gesture to the cabin, 'are likely to take off with some floosie and leave you high and dry.'

She sat back, message delivered, and then with a slightly misty eyed look at the far horizon added, 'so, at long last I know where he is now, shouldn't be able to do much damage.'

SIX

The next death happened on the third day as the yacht braved the deep and lonely ocean now far from the shipping lanes and less obviously far from the overhead aerial traffic routes. It was one of the men from the top tables. The passengers were looking forward to a stop on a small island to replenish stocks.

Just like the death on the plane, a quiet crash as a chair toppled over a few gathered for the morning buffet breakfast interrupting Dilys who was saying how much she was looking forward to getting on land. Then there was the sound of knives and forks falling on the floor.

'Good God!'

And

'Oh dear,'

and the very English

'Don't stare dear.'

Dilys looked up,

'Well…what do you expect?'

With a casual glance at the body now on the floor she announced, 'it's David, Rita's other. This is *The Syndicate* after all.'

What an odd thing to say.

There was the now familiar procedure somehow observed on the plane, a junior waiter checking pulse, a senior though non-medical officer declaring death and some perfunctory wailing by the widow.

'Oh David,' Rita cried, 'you weren't supposed to go today.'

Through copious tears, she gave a quick glance at Dilys who later confided

'Yep, he died of death, end of, like my Jim.'

While Jim could not have a burial from the air, and was the passengers assumed, in a fridge in a mortuary in Perth, the captain made it very clear that David would be buried at sea.

I could see through an open door the Captain looking onto where the hasty preparations for a makeshift coffin were underway. Bruce, Rahmin and Adnan were making a box, rather fragile, but then it was not made to last long in the sea.

I overheard Bruce saying, 'this is all wrong, he shouldn't have died this week, I thought he was one of the fittest ones,' and then on seeing the furious face of the captain fled further down into the bowels of the ship.

What with the tropical heat and the lack of space in the ship's fridges, a burial at sea was hastily organised for that very evening. The ship was slowed almost to a standstill, which meant it lurched around in the gathering swell. There were a few words hastily read out by the captain, and a passenger.

'I am Nigel,' he began in the belief introductions were important, continuing, that although he did not know David well, having only met him on the cruise, he was a jolly decent chap and had been honoured to be his bridge partner. The widow dabbed her eyes and the very rough coffin, was lowered into the seas, and to the obvious relief of the crew, sank beneath the waves.

There was an invitation for a drink in memory of the deceased, most quickly went to the bar failing to observe David's coffin, or more accurately wooden crate bob up in the churning waters, and it seemed for a time it was trying to follow the ship, before sinking once again to the depths as a jolly party was getting under way.

SEVEN
H

Landfall at last, although there was not much land in this huge ocean. We stopped, or more accurately, anchored a little way off the harbour for a day. Tied up were yachts like our own but strangely silent, no crew no passengers. Just as Dilys and I were leaning on the rail looking at the activity in the harbour. Bruce and Frank joined us, Frank, he of the smuggled bacon and the dominant wife.

'It's a tax dodge,' said Bruce looking sadly at these magnificent craft. 'The fat cats buy them and leave them and write off all sorts of costs to dodge paying a tax bill they could easily afford.'

'I knew people like that in the golf clubs around Uckfield,' Frank offered.

Dilys looked at the houses, 'an island like this could be somewhere they could get to and escape if the authorities are after them.'

I could see she was thinking if she could invest in the local economy.

'Or the mafia,' Frank surmised, 'you wouldn't want to have them after you.'

I wondered if he had experienced an encounter with the dark side of financial dealings, but on reflection thought it more likely to be his wife. She definitely had a mercenary view of life from what I could observe with her gold bracelets, her designer silk scarves, her extravagant sunglasses, though her husband was at best dowdy in an old blazer, the most outrageous item of clothing. Definitely an odd couple. On the other hand, there was more to Frank than I had originally thought.

As we were approaching, I could see that the island was one enormous pyramid soaring unexpectedly from the ocean floor. The harbour provided a safe haven in the endless ocean. Behind it the town climbed up the steep side of the mountain.

Houses were strewn randomly, a mixture of dwellings, some definitely more sophisticated that I had anticipated. We could see magnificent villas, some with tiled roofs, walls a blaze of colour from the Bougainvillea flowers of oranges red and yellow. Shaded verandas overlooked the ocean.

Bruce pointed at one, 'that is definitely a legacy of French colonisation, that guy knew what he was doing.'

'What was that?' I asked.

'He traded in everything, rare animal species, even rarer plants, vanilla of course, art from those washed up escapees from Paris and of course slaves as a side line.' I was shocked, not the slave trade.

Bruce looked thoughtful, started to move away, muttering, 'still goes on in a small way, so look out!'

And left us to help with the mooring. Further out front of the harbour wall tied up to the buoys were about a hundred little craft. They didn't look like they had been recently to sea, on deck were crates of beer lashed down, baskets heaving with fruit from all myriad of lines and ropes. People were moving about, mostly long haired scruffy young people. I heard of couples taking off to sail around the world in these little vessels, and was awe-struck that they could survive the storms we had encountered.

I would have loved to meet up with these alien creatures. Was their escape to an adventure as exciting as it had once seemed? Did the couples manage to live harmoniously for weeks on end? Did they ever get fed up with a diet of fish? That question was immediately answered as we took the Calypso to the harbour, a huge sign:

Pizza Parlour, only one around for 500 square miles.

And we could see, from our yacht that it was packed out!

We were given strict instructions on our visit to dry land. It turned out to be more or less a dash to a market before being herded back onboard and a quick take off in the early evening. We were given strong advice not to make conversation and not to show any identification. 'The police are very corrupt the Captain had advised and they will want bribes.' But I was not so sure, and considered that this stop over was not totally legal in the first place.

The crew went back and forth on the craft stocking up on fresh vegetables and fruit and crates of beer, even three clearly marked: Tesco: Highland Spring Water.

We, the passengers, wandered towards the market, just a small covered area with women selling small piles of fruit and vegetables. It was busy but peaceful. We were looked at, or more accurately watched, as we walked around stepping over discarded vegetable leaves, avoiding sleeping dogs, smiling at the kittens playing in the sunshine. All around us pervasive and strange smells from the dried fish, the odd chicken in a bamboo cage and the fruit. But it took some time to find the strongest aroma, sweet and lovely, it was vanilla. I would have liked to buy some, but it would not last in my cabin and the thought of trying to get it back through Australian customs was daunting.

I noticed Vince picking up some dried fish leaves and plants, but not buying to the disgust of the market seller, but inspecting muttering and replacing them. As I watched, another passenger, Nigel walked by.

'That's Vince all over,' he remarked with a sad smile, 'he's only interested in plants and animals, a right amateur biologist, watches all the David Attenborough TV programmes on a constant loop.'

So Nigel was interested in Vince but this was obviously not reciprocated.

Further on there were stalls of cooking pots, brushes and then the only bit of fashion items, collections of cotton skirts which were very bright so I bought two. But there was nothing in the way of beauty products, a bit of old laundry soap seemed to be the main item until I spotted some small bottles of perhaps shampoo but the labels were in Russian. Dilys bought a necklace of shells from one of the hippy characters. The young vendor said she had come out from Australia with a boyfriend but they had split up and she was stuck on the island. As we were leaving, I saw Bruce approach her and lead her off behind the buildings.

Dilys was still looking through another table of stuff so I slipped always to follow the couple. Was it for a bit of quick sex, a rough and tumble among the market crates? I thought she might be a vulnerable young woman, trying to get some cash, I knew of that situation, so I walked around, just to make sure she was safe, or at least that is what I told myself. They were standing very close, heads together, but it was not sex, no they were on a mobile phone in some intense conversation. A mobile! I started to walk towards them.

'Can I borrow that?' I asked somewhat naively, for their reaction was first shock then anger,

'Clear off,' snarled the young woman, 'bloody spy before I smack you one!'

Bruce held her back, 'she's one of the passengers' he hissed, 'leave her alone,' then to me, 'Jay has a problem with her phone I was just trying to get a better signal. No need to tell anyone OK?'

Unconvinced I walked back to Dilys. Perhaps Bruce had been out to the island a number of times and would know the young people who washed up around the islands. Dilys had not noted my absence and I decided to say nothing.

Then shouting, I looked down to the quay saw the captain with the two Zodiacs, it was time to return. I let the island with some foreboding. I could not leave a message, contact Sally or Stephen to tell them of this little adventure. As we sailed away I saw the young woman scrape her foot in the dirt road as if eliminating all trace of our quick visit.

EIGHT

Back on board *The Syndicate* left the island at some speed, rocking the large yachts moored by the harbour wall, which caused one head to appear and curse.

It was the consensus of many that this angry seaman who appeared to have bought his attire from a catalogue designed for wealthy 'matelots' that he was probably a drug baron on the run and hiding in the harbour.

As Dilys, Robin and Frank were looking back at the island when they were surprisingly joined by Frank's wife, who after all these days had remained in the bar or leisure area.

'Hi, don't know your names, but I'm Rosa, we're on a kind on honeymoon aren't we darling?'

She grasped Frank's arm not a gesture of love but of possession. Frank gave that kind of cough men give when not wanting to answer a question, but smiled benignly.

Rosa pointed at the large craft now bobbing about wildly in the wake of our engines.

'Look at those Frank,' and he did,

'The Captain told me some are for sale, and wouldn't it just be lovely to have our own and be able to do our own cruises. The Captain said he could find a crew.'

'I bet he did,' thought Robin who was not the first to notice she always talked a bit too much about what the captain says and does. Frank did not answer his wife, but hesitantly suggested

'Come along dear time for a drink before dinner.' And so she left the group without ever asking what their names were.

The little cruise ship had a limited entertainment schedule for the after-dinner hour. This consisted of a bridge night, a games night and then *'Entertainment by a member of the crew.'* The crew had little talent, one tried a couple of sea shanties, but was drowned out by several passengers, who put new and amusing lyrics to the well known tunes.

The female officer, did a dance that was met with stunned silence from the gents, reigniting their firm beliefs that women should not be spending time driving ships but doing much more feminine work, wearing very little and in doing so keeping the chaps happy.

There was a talk scheduled.

KOMODO DRAGONS.

To the surprise of many who had booked up their trip at various pop-up and short lived travel agents along the Sussex coast, they recognised their very own travel agent, now washed and scrubbed, but still looking very nervous. Even more surprising he had acquired a nomenclature, 'Expedition Leader,' and even a name, 'call me Bruce,' like many of the crew no family name just a badge.

Bruce had insisted that everyone attended his talk because, he said in this region the dragons are found on many of the islands and may be on our Mystery Island.

Vince surprisingly pushed to the front so he was immediately in front of Bruce disturbing the pattern of chairs obviously put out for couples.

The young woman, she who had wanted yoga sessions, went to sit beside him. 'Hi,' she said, 'I'm Audrey.' 'I'm Vince,' he replied, and that was the end of their conversation.

Bruce began his talk, but it developed into a verbal pas de deux with Vince. The aim was to describe the Komodo Dragons who live on the islands we were passing.

Bruce: The dragons can grow to over 10 feet long and weigh 150lbs,

Vince: And more, one is in a zoo in Australia that is the heaviest recorded;

Bruce: They have a varied carnivore diet, they eat rats, and can gorge on large animals, deer and possibly people. Their razor like teeth and the venom cause uncontrollable bleeding and in the animals, infection in the wound. They follow their prey until it dies.

Vince: They are cannibals too and will eat the young of other dragons.

Bruce: True, so the young will climb trees to escape the mature adults who are too heavy to follow. They can dash a short distance, but a fit person could out run them.

Vince: (with a nervous laugh), Well that's us doomed, not one of us could do that!

Vince looks around for support but is met with stony looks.

Bruce: (hastily intervening) Please don't worry where we are going, the local villagers have an agreement with the dragons, attacks are very rare, and they live in harmony

Vince: But this does not include tourists, so at all times we should stay with a guide. Bruce tell everyone about their reproductive cycle.

But at this point Bruce and his anxious passengers had had enough. Bruce left quickly and Vince sunk back to his silent corner. Audrey looked at him with admiration.

The plan was to arrive at the mystery destination the following morning.

The presentation, the thought of large predators unable to distinguish between man, woman or any large mammal, had upset the more elderly passengers, and as they retired to the comfort of their cabins, reviewed silently or with a sympathetic partner, whether this trip was to be more adventurous then anticipated in the safe streets and twittens of Sussex.

The cries during the night, far from bliss or ecstasy overheard by the night watch, indicated the nightmares that wandered through the yacht as it approached the destination.

The sea swell had built up during the night. The dawn was not met by a gradual calming of the waves as happened a few days ago. Enormous rollers ran under, over, and beside the yacht with sinister intent. But *The Syndicate* was a wise and a crafty warrior of the high seas, the occasional bumps and chipped paint evidence of past battles.

The passengers had two options. One, to cower within their cabin trying to lock into a bed to avoid being flung about. The second, to go out and face the demons.

Did the seas have demons as the much feared djinns of the deserts?

NINE
H

I seriously gave the moment some considered thought. I could die alone, trapped in a cabin of fading luxury or get up and face the elements. It was after all what I had signed up for.

So I put on some warm clothes, for I was sure the winds, the drenching of the sea spray would be chilly. I lurched along the silent corridor, past cabin doors firmly locked. On the upper deck I saw Rahmin looking terrified. I tried reassurance. Me! What was I thinking, I had never been at sea in a storm, but find myself saying:

'Are we nearly there yet?'

'We are we are,' he pointed, 'look, the volcano!'

Holding onto everything I could I made my way to the open deck area, managed to open the door and felt the full force of the magnificent storm. I heard a scream from behind me, it was a Rahmin,'

'He'll never make it, he's mad,'

And that was the last thing I heard for some time.

PART THREE

Where the charms and dangers of human, vegetable and reptilian origin, are discovered; where strange accidents occur and where the passengers learn more about Komodo dragons than they ever thought possible, and where they are led to face a monster of demonic proportions.

ONE

Three years before our story begins, on an island, not our Mystery Island, but a large and fruitful island full of good things for Komodo dragons to eat, and to find entertaining ways of passing the days while lying in wait for their next victim to come down a path, the dragons were uneasy.

The first to sense forthcoming changes were two young females. They had been playing with some abandoned car tyres, ripping them apart with the joy that only a young dragon can experience, when whoosh a tsunami of a wave just lifted all 18 kilos and perhaps more of these young females and slung them into the air like plastic bags and then into the receding seas, where one week later, and a journey of some distance, hungry and really furious two female dragons managed to swim ashore.

Komodo dragons do not need a male mate to produce fertile eggs, something female zoologists, observing these captive reptiles, had, on occasion, envied. The two females realised that they had actually been washed up on a pretty good place, and immediately began to dig nests, produce eggs and generally cause havoc to unsuspecting wildlife and the occasional domestic pig. When the eggs hatched they were all male, so it was fortuitous that the two females were not closely related.

The human inhabitants did not notice them at first, partly as the dragons only ate once a fortnight and generally kept themselves to themselves, but as the youngsters hatched, rumours began to spread. On the whole they were tolerated, by the islanders, on one hand because an encounter with a Komodo takes great skill to remain alive by the time of departure. Hunters did not die immediately from their bites, but sometime later. On the other hand the Komodo's population did not expand unduly, partly down to their cannibalistic habit where the young of another was easier prey that chasing the odd creature that was washed up on the beach.

At this time, however, the Komodos all became very quiet sensing that change was in the air. Some retreated into dark burrows, no longer watching to ambush any stray animal but to remain hidden, undetected. Two took to the seas, voluntarily to leave the island, only to return, thinner but wiser some weeks later.

For the first time in living memory a ship approached intentionally, not a shipwreck, not a yacht in distress, not lost mariners, but a yacht in full sail and confidence. Against all tradition, those on the dunes suddenly rose up, a cry and shout and sudden movement. It broke tradition, it broke the sense of normality, it offended the elders, but it surely excited the young kids as everyone turned and to their astonishment, saw a large yacht in full sail, gently approach through the reef in the place thought only to be known the most experienced fishermen (and who had suffered painful rites on sensitive parts of their bodies to obtain this knowledge) and gently land on the beach.

To the gasps of the villagers now bewitched and unable to move, a young man shouted, leapt overboard and ran up the beach. It was a lost son, one taken with good intention to be educated in Australia, a sacrifice a family had made so that the island might learn about the world outside.

There was rejoicing feasting stories to tell, dances to be danced, all while the Komodos hunkered in their burrows deeply suspicious of this most unusual behaviour. Until the young man realised two things first that all the island inhabitants were gathered and even he, with the arrogance and confidence of youth, could not believe it had been planned for his arrival. Secondly, something very big was happening for a palaver to be called.

He asked what happened and roughly translated this is what he heard:

'It's a curse that has befallen us.'

'The dolphins are dying, we are doomed.'

'We are sick from the stench.'

and more seriously,

'Our volcano, our mother is angry.'

And then they were shown the plastic. They were told of previous plans of sacrifice where upon the old women and young women looked militant, the sacrifice of pigs (there was coincidental grunting from the pens). But the young men said the world had to know, this was a disaster caused by others. And so for days they planned what action could be taken and a month later sailed off determined to take action that would involve the media throughout the world.

TWO
H

At first I didn't open my eyes. Was I in a bath and if so why was I lying face down? I could feel my bottom and my feet gently rising up and down. My hands were warm, for once no aches and pains, lovely, like they were in a warm pair of gloves, though come to think of it slightly scratchy. I coughed, painful, something in my mouth, salty water.

I opened my eyes and found a small crab looking at me. I moved and he or she retreated leaving a pattern of footprints on sand. In the silence, I could hear the movements of this small but malevolent crustacean. I raised my head. Now I was transfixed by a circle of malefic seagulls, unsure whether to start picking at my bones. I raised an arm to wave them off, with accompanying words once heard coming from my old Nan when the postman surprised her in the kitchen and she was just in her old nightie. Water ran down my arm making pools in the sand, which the crab and the gulls and myself considered with some bemusement. Where was I and how the hell did I get on a beach? Well at least its not Bognor I thought. So, I was not happy but I was not unhappy either.

Then I remembered being on deck, the surprising cold, the fierce sting of the seawater. I remembered we were due to land on our mystery island.

I got to my feet very slowly and began to move away from the unforgiving ocean. I felt so heavy, the water cascading out of my clothes. I found I was wearing my old dress, the one with long sleeves, a jumper, my very long knickers and my new plimsolls.

I could not remember why I had put on so many clothes, something about cold?

As I continued to spit out water, to the amusement of the birdlife, their numbers began unexpectedly increasing, I recalled the one and only life-saving class I attended, only because I fancied the lifeguard when I was thirteen, and but lacking that essential prerequisite of being a competent swimmer. We had to jump in the pool, fully clothed, whereupon I sank then bobbed up.

'See,' he said gravely, 'air can get trapped in clothes and it keeps you both warm and bouyant and certainly you,' he said pointing at me, 'your school knicks will do the job.' Children in care homes at that time had mainly serviceable but unfashionable clothes let alone underwear. Everyone laughed, I was mortified.

I heard a sound, I stopped, still dripping, observing the crabs and the birds were departing. I turned, and there, striding across the sands, a man, silent, confident, a hunter for sure and for a moment all I could think of was my long and very wet dress, and that he was wearing very little at all.

We looked at each other in mutual curiosity. Beyond magazine photos perused at the occasional visits to the dentist I had never in my life seen anything like this man. Up close he was not too tall, but his body was very muscular. He had black hair long and curly, and a beard all tight curls but still bristly looking, though both well kept. He was covered in tattoos. Not the ones I remembered old men in Eastbourne sporting, badges of army, regimental designs, or one with 'Mum' or a surpassing number of odd female names. No, these tattoos were black against his brown skin, ornate geometric designs. And then, and then I saw with horror, that on this chest he had the same tattoo as Bruce, a dragon with its lizard head pointing to his neck, its body encircling his chest.

A long bag hung from his shoulder, and just a leather skirt thing hung down over his private parts, but my attention focused on a very long bow and some very dangerous looking arrows.

Silence for a while, then he made the universal gesture to follow him, a nod of the head and a small gesture with his hand, so I followed him up the beach, there was nothing else I could do. I looked around. The storm had died down but with some reluctance because huge waves rolled in from a grey and dismal horizon, crashing against some wall or reef exploding white fumes soaring into sky.

There was no one else washed up as far as I could see, so with some trepidation and much curiosity, I started a whole new adventure.

I picked my way up the beach, littered with dried coral and some skeletons of fish, crabs and birds. The sun was blisteringly hot and it was obvious that I was not keeping up. At the top of the beach were palm trees, but behind them thick dense woods, bushes, creepers with just a path wandering through. I thought when we reached the trees that it would be cooler, but the heat just seemed more intense.

What struck me was the silence. Did the birds recognise the shape of the hunter moving stealthily along, did my clumsy walk, still hampered by my clothes, scare the monkeys and other wildlife? Then with sickening realisation I was certain that here could lie snakes of monstrous size, and oh my god, a Komodo dragon. I tried to speed up, to get as close as possible to my guide on the grounds that if there were a snake on the path he would step on it first. But he kept the same social distance, moving faster or slower as I made my clumsy but tiring efforts to get closer.

I don't have a good sense of time, but it seemed to me that we had been walking for ages. My hunter did not move fast but with steady determination, looking back at me, but not offering any word nor any help when I tripped over or stumbled. Occasionally he would look up as a scampering noise indicated the rapid departure of what I assumed had been his target, but he made no effort to raise his fearsome bow, but just sighed deeply and carried on, in what I recognised now as a very stoical manner.

Emerging from dense tropical forest, I saw the first signs of the village. It looked lovely. There were about twenty round houses, several larger ones were on stilts, children were playing around, a few animals were grazing nearby and at least one dog was sleeping in the shade. It was quiet, peaceful for about five minutes. For a moment I had a shock, it was so clean and tidy, no rubbish, no plastic bags, cans of lager, sweet wrappings that frequently litter, village greens at home, but then wondered if these people actually did not have those essential trappings of twentieth century leisure.

Two seconds later, pandemonium, the dogs noticed me and started barking and howling, the chickens took to the grass roofs, wild birds screamed from tree tops, pigs, yes pigs raced around in a meaningless way, perhaps they thought this was preparation for their immanent slaughter. Children shouted for parents, parents, well mostly women, came running out of their huts and quite suddenly this peaceful idyll became noisy and threatening. My hunter did not turn into my saviour, for though he had never touched me through our long walk, now he grabbed my arm and led me along as he might some prey he had brought to feed his family.

This thought began like a little piece of Japanese knotweed on the patio and within nano seconds had developed into a mysterious weed, up rooting the paving stones, invading the very foundations of my being. The thought was:

THESE PEOPLE COULD BE CANNIBALS

The men were tall, strong and like my saviour covered in tattoos some more ornate than others. But what I noticed was there was no uniformity of skin colour, hair colour, no uniformity or height or, to come to think, of it width, this was a very mixed bunch of people.

To prove my point the villagers formed a circle around me, pressing closer, silently until one elderly woman left forward pinched my arm and looking back at the other smiled. It seemed that relief and tension spread among the people, some chat, which I thought they were all agreeing about something.

The circle began to break up and three women approached me, holding up their left hands, three fingers erect and one and the thumb pinched together. This seemed reassuringly friendly so I just held up a hand too, which made them laugh and they indicated I should follow them to a nearby hut. I had to bend down to get through the doorway and entered into a dark but surprisingly cool place. I just collapsed down onto a mat all energy drained. I was offered a drink, never quite found out what it was but I was beyond caring.

A young woman came into the hut with a baggy sundress and indicated I should get out of my heavy and still very damp clothes. More women crowded into the hut, waiting with the same anticipation perhaps of me at a strip club, though I was certain it was a more professional.

I hesitated as children peered in through the open doorway, come crawling in for a front row viewing. A glance around, and I divided the women into two groups, young and definitely old. The young group wore an assortment of clothes, loose t-shirts, shorts one or two in the same type of baggy sundress that had been given to me. They had tight curly hair, and like the children, had blonde streaks. They looked fit and well fed, when they smiled they had gleaming white teeth in very good condition. In contrast the older women definitely looked old. Not only was their hair less groomed, scraggier somehow, their faces were deeply lined and one had a sort of paint on her cheeks. They wore sarongs, casually but securely, tied. Nonetheless they also looked well fed, almost plump in fact. I had to stop thinking about their food source.

There was no chance of getting away with a discrete change of clothes. Although I turned my back on most of the crowd, children

71

had crept into the furthest corners. As I started to take off my outer layers, a cry or sigh went up from the surrounding spectators. I began to feel I was the parcel given to the children's party of pass the parcel. I got down to my undies, but it was firmly indicated these should go, but I was handed the dress. I saw my clothes, my lovely but still damp plimsolls, disappear out the door and handed over to the men I presumed from the noise of chatter.

Once I had got on the roomy sundress, I had to admit it was cooler than my tight clothes, and a nice feeling of breezes through my underwear-free body, I haven't felt like that in years.

I was led outside and everyone sat in a circle around me. Some of the children had decided there was not much fun to be had and wandered off. There was an expectant silence and shuffling and from time to time someone would lean forward and touch my arm, gently poke me in the back, feel or sometimes tug my hair, and once someone peered into my mouth and while I felt this was unthreatening it was disturbing. It took me several minutes to see my hunter was not among the group nor were several other of the men that had originally met us when we entered the village.

We continued like this for some time, it was worse than getting to a funeral early and sitting in an unfamiliar crematorium looking at unfamiliar people with a sinking feeling you might be at the wrong funeral, while at the same time, giving that weak almost smile at those who appear to be looking at you with some curiosity while searching for a face you recognise.

Until, as we all searched for some form of communication, one particularly aged woman said, 'syndicate,' and all the others suddenly clapped and cheered. One old woman took care of me, cackling 'thynidatt,' over and over again while rubbing my head, friendly but decidedly odd.

She turned and said, *'u alright ten?'*

I couldn't believe my ears, just like greetings at home as blokes passing each other use the stroke greeting. It goes like this:

'You alright then?'

'Yeh, yourself?'

'Good.'

Enough recognition and so they pass on.

Then she said, *'nem bilong me Susie'* Lots of gestures and pointing at chest, then a poke at me. Right I had it, I smiled and told her my name, then put a finger to my lips. She nodded, *'new bling u'*, she said, '*woman.*' And that suited me just fine.

On the second day it struck me how similar life in this little village was to Lopeham, for the women that is. The women's housework was to sweep up fallen leaves, pack the kids with grandma (I assume it was their grandmas), and picking up containers prepared to head off to work. I followed them going out of the village because I was nervous about being left alone with the men. The women carried baskets on their heads, and one or two plastic jerrycans. I offered to help but was met with a kindly refusal. Just as well, for the path through the forest was uneven and I was still so nervous about snakes, spiders and Komodo dragons. When monkeys howled, I leapt sideways, when parrots screamed I leapt backwards, in fact I was a walking traffic hazard to my fellow workers.

We were climbing steadily upwards and the steamy heat intensified. We stopped for a while, the women looked at the scratches and bruises caused by my nervous tripping, falling, clutching at branches and began to apply leaves and salves. I now had a chance to look at them closely.

Although fit and able to move steadily up this mountain, the older women were definitely more wrinkled, lined faces were not ugly for there was a sense of wisdom and laughter in those lines. The young girls had amazing teeth. Strong and glistening when they chewed a piece of grass, but among the older women gums glistened in the sunshine for many of them had so few teeth. What had happened? I wondered.

I saw that very few women had the extensive tattoos of the men. One older woman had horizontal lines on her leg, and perhaps given the respect of the others must have been a marking of rank. As we walked nearly everyone plucked strands of leaves, stalks of flowers that were pushed through bushy hair, fixed onto the dresses and shirts they wore. One young girl approached me and tried to push a frond through my hair, but tangled and grubby as it was, it just fell out to the laughter of the others. Friendly I assumed, but intensely curious as more touching of my hair and rubbing my arms began again, just like last night.

It was only when we reached a high point and I looked back at the sea, did I realise how lucky I had been to arrive on this island relatively unscathed. The huge rollers were beginning to reduce, but

73

the spray and the early morning mist meant I could only see the beach below.

Silence shattered, the women leapt up, fingers pointing and a chanting starting, was I right? Were they really, clapping laughing dancing and singing, 'Syndi, syndi syndicate!' I then as I followed their fingers pointing to a reef a section I could not see on my ascent.

Oh ye gods of the oceans the depths below there was the hulk of a ship, no my yacht, rising and sinking beneath the waves. Like a great whale trapped on the rocks.

THREE
H

From where I was standing, transfixed, I could only watch as two large canoes approached the wreck of my ship. I felt a sudden passion for this brave vessel. It still carried my dream of escape, of adventure and a new life.

I had not spotted any canoes on my brief stay on the beach two days ago. Even I could see that it was dangerous manoeuvring, the canoes riding in and out of the surf until a cheer we even could hear. I could not see what was happening until about an hour later seeing their return journey, one canoe lower in the water than the other.

Pots, baskets and jerrycans were thrown to one side as all the women raced back down the path to the village with me following noticeably faster than my upward climb, I reached them just in time to meet the canoes on the beach.

Boys and young men launched themselves into the sea and helped pull the canoes up and out of the water. Boxes, cartons, plastic wrapped trays of tins were slung on the beach to cries of delight, then slowly, very slowly two heads emerged above the rim of the boat, looked at the assembled cheering crowd and ducked down again.

Two women were lifted out, one started shouting. I was shocked, it was Audrey, she who had planned to do Yoga and meditate, now dishevelled, screaming hysterically with remarkable lack of calmness. No spiritual karma to be seen. The villagers stepped back as my noisy former shipmate lashed out and mistakenly, I am sure, knocked a little child flying.

There was a moment's silence, everyone looked at the child who picked himself out of the sand, dazed but very quiet before the perpetrator was grabbed by the women and marched up the beach towards the woods. Laughter from the children, shouting from the villagers and screams receded gradually to be overtaken by the sound of the now gentle waves breaking on the beach and the sea birds crying above us.

I was left alone with the second woman, my silent associate, from *The Syndicate,* not yet a friend, just someone who had experienced a shared event, although I still could not recall the collision with the reef. I felt duty bound to offer guidance.

'You'll be OK, just keep calm, I don't think we are in any immediate danger.' Silly words, it made me feel like a Girl Guide instruction booklet published in the 1950s, especially when accompanied by an inept and clumsy pat of the arm.

For the first time I looked at her really close up. In the ship she had been aloof and come to think of it mainly silent. She was tall, well taller than her anguine partner. I could not fail to have noticed her on the cruise. She had the most extensive collection of 'trouz, that lovely Gaelic name for things in pairs. She wore breeches, chinos, cute dungarees, slacks and even bloomers.

Over which she had a bright multicoloured selection of blouses, bodices, slip overs, tank tops, cardigans and sweaters. By midday each day on our cruise she had exhausted my fashion vocabulary. But now, in contrast, she had just those very little shorts and a vest, of a masculine cut I thought.

She turned to scrutinise me, and it would appear that I had failed to pass some test, to stimulate any curiosity. But the movement interested me. She did not turn her head but moved her whole body, perhaps she had hurt her neck I wondered. She looked dazed, had she concussion?

I spoke again, I told her my name.

'Hey, remember we were on *The Syndicate* together, yeh? Are you OK?'

Her whole body turned to face me while she regarded me in silence. Only her eyes moved. I was not sure if I detected a slight choking sound. I moved a little nearer, perhaps she was hard of hearing and no doubt in shock. No movement in her face, blank uncomprehending. Her beautiful unlined features, no shock no anger, no joy at arriving safely to shore.

I think she said 'Jen,' but was not so sure for it was then I thought it might be the curse of Botox. She turned her full gaze on me, and then began a rapid blinking, most unsettling. I felt her shudder, then I noticed two different coloured eyes.

'I have my bag don't I?' she asked, but the bag was securely tied onto her waist. With difficulty she raised her hand to her eyes and was in some distress.

'Have you lost your contact lens?' I asked, 'can you see?' She groped my hand, 'Don't worry,' I really sounded more and more like that ghost of a girl guide, 'I'll take care of you.'

But my generous offer was met with a wail. It was when I was disentangling myself from her clutch that the most disturbing event occurred since I was washed up. Her hand, still grasping my arm, fell off. She stood back, minus hand while I looked on with horror and the appendage that was beginning to cut off the blood supply to my shoulder.

She came forward, I cringed, but she clipped on the hand, unbuckled it from me and again made a choking sound, was it laughter. I have read mass murderers can be very jolly just before their tenth killing.

Quite suddenly she lifted her arm, ripped her hair from her head and slung it across the beach. A wig, no wonder she could sport so many hairstyles. Strands of hair, somewhat disturbingly became entangled into the ocean. Not quite shaven headed, one handed, she threw back her head and laughed.

'Arthur went to the cabin to get some things,' she began.

'Who, who went to the cabin?' I asked horrified I had a sinking feeling, along with Arthur.

'Hah him! he's gone. Good riddance,' she spat

'Why?...' I did not finish my question

A venomous glance, 'I made him get some things, just in case.' She was calmer now.

What things Arthur went to get, I never found out for, as I looked at her, I was reminded again of the handbook on the dangers of the Komodo dragon.

We sat on the beach my strange companion and I, looking at the horizon in silence.

Eventually, 'the yacht is still there, perhaps we could go out and find your...things?'

I was hesitant in drawing too obvious a point. No response at first, but then a nod and she stood up

'Tomorrow,' she hissed, and with a nod of her head, began to follow the footprints in the sand towards the woods.

'Be careful', I warned, 'the komodo dragons hunt as the night draws in.'

She turned, 'Bah! she sneered, 'don't you remember that we are the same washed up creatures as those first dragons, pathetic, doomed!'

While this might be a true observation I thought it needlessly over dramatic, for any Komodo that arrived here must have swum some considerable distance and would be immensely strong and possibly the most intelligent of survivors.

We clambered though the trees, no moonlight to show us the way. For the first time I experienced that dread of the dark where roots and branches that were hardly noticed in daytime, take on a hostile presence, slapping you in the face, tripping you up and seemingly full of bustling little creatures that disturb the leaves as you pass by.

By the time we got to the village only a few women were sitting around the dying embers of the central fire.

The group that had been gathering nuts and berries from the hillside were there, and waved a friendly greeting. Jen was greeted with some curiosity, not the intense scrutiny that I had encountered. To my surprise, she sat down quietly and looking around seemed to be strangely at peace.

FOUR

Stephen woke up with a smile. It was unusual for him to remember dreams, but, as he lay in bed he listened to the build up of cars, buses and HGV's passing the top of the road, the planes going into Gatwick every few minutes, comforting sounds, loved sounds, telling him the world was alive and ready to go. His dream had been of that lovely lady from Lopeham.

Stephen divided females into three vague categories:

Category one: *Girls*

Girls ranged from two years old to an indeterminate stage in their twenties, unless they were middle-aged partners of golfing friends, who brought "the girls" drinks at the club.

Category two: *Women,*

Women were generally reserved for those he did not like.

Category three: *Ladies*

Ladies were special, once a lover, more frequently female friends or favoured clients.

This lady was different he thought with a smile, a dutiful wife, kind, caring and importantly a dog lover. She did not ask for anything and was both surprised and delighted at her good fortune. He lay back in his bed and thought she must be lying in a hammock on some South Sea island sipping cocktails.

And the more he thought the more he realised that she had a strange undiscovered beauty, a lovely laugh, and in his dream, a stunning body. It dawned on him with a slight feeling of apprehension that he had not had any text or communication for some time. Later in the day he would send a text, nothing formal, just a 'hope you are having a good time.'

These thoughts lowered his spirits. He looked wearily out at the grey skies, which, without any dramatic line of a horizon, lurched into the churning grey sea. He wondered if he had been precipitous in taking advantage of the redundancy package from the bank, like rushing over a cliff to a new future. He missed that chatter of the staff, even though in his final years at work had become shrill and nervous as their numbers reduced, other branches closed and fraud and scams on his favourite customers increased.

The move to Eastbourne was driven by a need to get away from having to pass his beloved bank, now closed and a restaurant chain in its place. He had visited it once with a client to find the gents in the basement where the strong room had been, his office part of the kitchen. He could have wept.

Eastbourne offered pleasant flats and apartments, a theatre, and a regular trains to London. Despite its reputation for being a convenient place for the elderly to retire, the town had a university campus, language schools and employment, so the there were many people of Stephen's age group always around. However, the theatre was fair at best and the trains unreliable. Getting to London was easy and his former clients were ever faithful. Though he could never, not ever, no not once, state either in speech or in writing, that he enjoyed seeing the women released from the care of crotchety old partners and start a new life often with money they never thought they had.

Another contribution to his depression was a letter posted in Australia originally to his old branch, and forwarded on to him. Normally the bank was reticent about posting on mail, but this envelope was adorned with strict instructions, **Personal and confidential URGENT please forward if necessary** on the back and the front.

He opened it with some foreboding to find it was one of his former clients.

Stephen,

Jim died unexpectedly on the plane, on our way to Australia. It was natural causes and his body is still with the coroner's office in Perth. I decided not to abandon my holiday plans so I am boarding The Syndicate this morning. It's a mystery tour, so it could be quite an exciting venture.

Can you look out our finance papers? I think you have a copy of Jim's will. Everything should be straightforward.

Contact you on my return,
Dilys Jones

Stephen sighed. He remembered that couple only too well. He was not too sure that Dilys' confidence in her late husband's financial matters were straightforward. He recalled a difficult meeting with Jim to discuss his gambling debts and Jim's ill advised plan to cash in his pension.

Nonetheless, it was a surprise to learn that Dilys was on the same cruise as his client from Lopeham. As the morning progressed the sun began to climb and stare weakly down on the Promenade, he became anxious. His texts to that Lovely Lady, Harry's widow had not been answered. The last he heard from her was a rather nervous phone conversation telling him she had booked up on a cruise and taken off at very short notice and then a text to say she was on the cruise. She promised to keep in touch, but as he looked at the calendar on his computer realised it was some time since he had any communication, no responses to his emails, no postcards, nothing.

FIVE
H

Over the next few days more survivors stumbled in, alone or accompanied by a villager. Most were in a state of shock. The survivors had suffered prolonged ordeals, which made me consider that my immediate and sudden arrival on the island though painful was less traumatic.

We all sat on the sand, as they told tragic stories.

One group of five had actually managed to get into the small Solos, which were not more than an inflated rubber tub. There were four passengers, Rita, Melanie and her husband Joe and Adnan. The yacht had hit the reef so suddenly and keeled over on one side just above the water line so their liferaft could be launched into the turbulent waves. They were swept out to sea away from the island and eventually collided into some rocks that soared up from the ocean bed, thin remnants of volcano plugs, now a sanctuary for birds. They sheltered in the lea of this outcrop until the storm abated. As the hot and humid days continued they knew they had to find water in rain pools and to see if there was land nearby.

It seemed that everyone was adamant that at least one stayed with the liferaft, so Joe left to climb the rocks.

Joe was a confident sixty something and I did recall his endless stories of keeping fit, going to the gym and haunting the rural lanes of Sussex with his cycle club.

There was a yell and Melanie said she could see Joe, then a scream and she saw Joe fall into the sea. At first he bobbed up and waved, they'd thought he was OK, but to her horror she saw a shark attack.

Melanie wept, 'it was so sad, he fought the shark for a short while, but lost the battle. There was nothing we could do.'

Rita put her arm around Melanie, describing how they had all looked on in horror as the final traces of Joe, his blood and the shark disappeared. It did not cross anyone's minds to dive in and attempt a rescue, it was all too final, yet another piece of evidence of the sinister aspect of the ocean, so far removed from this idyllic pictures in the brochure of *The Syndicate*.

Total silence had fallen on the little group until Dilys asked the obvious question,

'And then?'

'We could see a canoe coming this way, we started shouting and yelling and pointing down here so they could land near us. A rescue party perhaps. And then we had second thoughts, we had heard of tales,' Rita stopped and looked pointedly around, 'you know,' she whispered dramatically, 'cannibals!'

In the telling of the tale, I could see we were all visibly upset, but the women were, how can I express, stoical in the face of such tragedy. But then we English keep our emotions very hidden.

Our brave waiters had hung onto the wing of an aircraft that had unexpectedly floated to the surface in the churning seas. As they came towards the beach it was as if they were hanging onto a table.

A canoe was sent out to help them, where they pushed their makeshift life craft back into the seas to continue its eternal journey on the ocean currents. It was a shame, in my opinion that they did not take better notice of the markings and serial numbers. The young men were exhausted and sunburnt but told us they had survived, once landing on a coral reef that had some fresh water pools.

However, there was no sign of the Captain, the female officer, Bruce nor Rahmin.

Strangely I noticed that there were more female survivors among the passengers. Frank said he couldn't find his wife, the glamorous Rosa, when the shipped crashed into the reef. He assumed she was missing probably drowned in the dark and the chaos. Poor woman.

It crossed my mind that when we were on *The Syndicate* the majority of the passengers appeared to be established couples. 'Singletons', that hideous item of the travel agency manual assumes to be both diplomatic and tactful. When we registered for the cruise there was that lone character Vince, the yoga loving Audrey and a very nice chap called Robin. However, now many had lost their partners at some time during the voyage. It was highly reasonable as it turned out, that some of the male companions who were elderly and in many cases considerably older than their female partners did not make it. Secondly, I thought very privately that these men would not be missed, they had continually hung around the bar, their conversation loud and boring, their competitive bullying to get the most attention of staff and their slobbering over the female officer was nauseating. But what really struck me was that there was no sign no evidence of the captain, the officers of *The Syndicate* nor of Bruce, all experienced mariners we had been told. Where were they?

In the following days we all fell into a routine. The villagers were extremely welcoming. They were generous with their food, dressed the burns, put leaves on cuts and bruises and appeared every concerned about our welfare.

From a store some clothing was given to us. Susie produced well-worn shorts, t-shirts, one startling dress of patchwork materials of every kinds and lengths of cloths. 'Get on bloody quick,' she instructed as we picked through the pile. Audrey chose cloth to make a sarong, though initially lacked the skill to stop it continually unwinding. Jen picked through, occasionally sniffing at the t-shirts.

'Odd,' she commented, 'this one definitely smells of some perfume.'

Frank raised an objection, 'I cannot wear this,' he wailed holding up a worn but serviceable t-shirt, 'I only like shirts with collars, long trousers too.' In other circumstances we all would have been more understanding, perhaps even showing a modicum of sympathy, but most us of realised that whatever protection we were going to get was in that precious pile. So Frank was given first looks of distain, which had not raise one bit of comprehension, then more communicative suggestions along the lines of getting a life, and finally 'Oh for God's sake do shut up.'

Melanie was a little more understanding.

'I always noticed that Frank was so careful with his clothes on the cruise. Lovely ironed shirts twice a day at least, always wore socks too,' she mused. 'Pathetic,' spat Jen, 'who do you think did all that laundry, not him, vain little prick.'

'Leave them to it,' I suggested taking Jen away. 'I noticed you smelling that t-shirt and it's odd they have a ready store of clothes. Perhaps there have been others, before us here.'

'Then where are they now?' Jen said, adding quietly, 'there is more going on here than meets the eye.'

Once the clothing had been selected, the remains were bundled up. Susie gestured that returning to get more was not negotiable and that the hut was completely out of bounds. Punishment for trying to get in was communicated by violent gestures, extraordinary facial expressions, but it was the lying on the ground and groaning, that convinced us of the message… Keep out! In the following days, Susie was concerned that we should not get too sunburnt. She and the other women put coconut and oils on us. At first the men had mixed reactions, one or two thought it was a bit of a lark to be massaged by the women, but there is massage and massage. The type given to all of us is what athletes get, asexual, tough, occasionally intrusive. Hair was examined, ears peered into and from time to time mouths examined as if we were a collection of little kids.

'They're keeping us healthy, that's what all of this is about.' observed Jen, who that day had to be held by two burly women so she could be oiled thoroughly.

Two days later, this proved to be true. Frank, who insisted on walking barefoot had cut his foot on some coral. It quickly became sore and red, hard to describe, he suddenly collapsed in a faint.

We all stood around trying to remember any first aid. Did we sit him up, put his head between his knees, put him in the recovery position, pound his chest? Melanie offered to give him the kiss of life although it was plain he was breathing fairly easily.

Susie rushed over, calling the other women that were around. We pointed at Frank's foot, which by now was very red and sore, in fact so was his ankle. Frank was lifted up and we were directed not to our usual hut but to the long one at the back of the village.

Inside Frank was lain down on mats. I looked around the hut. It was beautiful. The roof was held up by enormous wooden poles and was thickly thatched over stretching to the supporting walls, giving shade. Apertures in the walls let in pools of sunlight and breezes from the sea.

Susie pushed everyone out, except for Jen and me. Jen gave Frank's leg a cold professional examination. 'Nasty,' she said, 'seen this in the war, might lose his leg.' Frank whimpered.

'Jen a bit of diplomacy please' I whispered then to Frank,

'You'll be OK, try to relax,' this produced even more groans than Jen's predictions had elicited.

Susie returned with a syringe, razor and a mush of green something. She expertly jabbed Frank's leg, causing him to suddenly relax, even produce a goofy grin, set to with the razor cutting the wound and more besides, then slapping the poultice on and finally bandaging it. Both Jen and I are suddenly respectful of this woman's skill.

'Him OK now, sleep and rest sometime,' she ordered. Jen walked forward and gave her a little hug.

'You were a nurse?' she asked,

'Yeh one small time, Port Morsby,' replied Susie, 'long long time ago.'

SEVEN
H

Each morning following my arrival on the island, I was for the first time in my life, woken by the cockerels shouting abuse at each other threatening to claw each other to death, no dawn chorus but a fearful racket.

I chose to join a small party of women to climb the hill and forage for fruits. I found that I could climb with some ease now and was even trusted to hold baskets. Their pace was slow and methodical, and while I thought at first it would be better to look upwards for any dangling fruit, the women kept their eyes strictly downwards and frequently glancing to the side of the path. Once or twice they would stop, a rustling sound, once a scream of a creature being caught, then an ominous silence. A hand gesture to me indicated snake, bird, cat and then another gesture started but ceased with a shudder. What was out there? I resolved to stick as closely as I could to the group.

I was trusted to hold baskets while the others looked for fruit. It appeared to be plentiful, there were hairy round berries that had a delicious white centre, bananas of different shape and sizes. There was quiet chat among the women, one or two pointing out a fruit and telling me the name. I learnt more about instructions like 'Stop' and 'Quiet' which were instantly obeyed. I learnt 'Pick up the basket' and Move along' and 'Catch' as a fruit was thrown over to me. And on these expeditions the beautiful sweet scent to the vanilla that grew from wild vines permeated the air and calmed my anxious soul.

Each day we visited a different part of the forest and gradually I got familiar with the winding paths. On the whole it was a lovely restful way of passing the day. For the first time I began to feel useful, doing something I actually rather liked, not hard when compared to the last few tedious years in Lopeham, traipsing down to the shops on a cold and damp day, or waiting in for deliveries, carers, but rarely friends.

One day I saw one small troupe of monkeys eating fruit just a few metres above the path. They immediately scattered as the women threw sticks to chase them off the fruit. The sticks were not thrown with much force, though their accuracy was fairly good. Just a message between the two groups. The monkeys retreated not too far, knowing we would eventually move off and they could return.

I went to the tree and thought I could climb up easily to the first branch and collect the fruit myself. I did not see many birds, we must be off any migration route, so those which had landed were the same 'blow ins' like myself. There was a little bird there, rather pretty, it started to hop towards me, 'how tame,' I thought, 'perhaps no one bothers to hunt it and there are so few around.' Suddenly a yell and I was dragged back landing with a thump on the ground. As I clambered to my feet they were again chucking sticks at the bird with intense accuracy and a great deal of force. The eldest woman began a dance, at first I almost giggled, so like charades when I was still a kid. She moved forward to another, hopping like a bird, she was stroked, she smiled, and then her companion writhed, twitched and suddenly lay still. This was repeated again and again until all my new friends were lying on the ground. Then as one stood up, looked at the bird and then at me. The warning was clear, the bird was dangerous. 'Were the feathers poisonous? Oh my god there was no one I could ask. For all its beauty our island had malign features.

While I was up on the hill with moments just to stop and think, I began to draw up a taxonomy of survivors a much reduced number since our full ship's compliment on leaving Fremantle. It started by taking on what could only be described as traditional gender specific activities.

There were three categories, though movement between these became more fluid, less marked as the days went by:

Category A consisted of those that at first tried to follow their lifestyle they had aspired to on the ship. The women started by sitting on the beach, finding small corals to attempt a manicure, flowers to weave, unsuccessfully into their hair. Rita and Melanie often went to sit by the village women, looking at the weaving. I uncharitably thought how like it was to the awful hobby classes in Lopeham, a way of spending an hour perhaps less tedious than an hour at home.

The men spent hours, lounging back, looking at the sea and continued to talk about their past business successes while others nodded, not listening, but instead dreaming of their own histories. Except when Frank was speaking, and then interest and guffaws, chortles and some comments such as 'You old goat,' and 'well fancy that.' Except here was one disquiet, a sense of unease at the number of their companions that had met unexpected deaths.

Darting among this lumbering, slumbering group who began daily to look more like sea lions on a beach, ran the waiters from *The Syndicate,* James and Paul, still being so professionally charming, delivering freshly cut coconuts, offering nuts and fruit as if this was a charming and eco-friendly resort of the most exclusive sort.

Category B were those that tried to keep busy. From time to time Frank and Nigel fashioned hooks and with rescued pieces of rope or twine, attempted fishing from the rocks at the end of the beach. Vince, followed at first by Nigel was active in catching fish. I was told that after looking them, holding them carefully in his hands, he would release them back into the sea as long as they appeared unhurt. Those that had got bashed, he kept, but when they were about to be cooked, he dissected them, silently and with intent curiosity.

On the other hand, Dilys led a group to the beach every afternoon where they sat in a circle drawing on the sand. I thought at first it was some kind of art class, until I was invited to join in.

Dilys wanted some advice she said because and I quote, 'You had it all sown up before the cruise even started.' I noted the admiration in the group's eyes as I approached. Puzzled I sat down and looking at the inscription on the sand realised it was arithmetical calculations.

Dilys began, 'this is what I get from Jim, about 10k in the bank, the house, the car, his shares, his pension, and we are trying to work out the tax.' Others joined in pointing to their calculations, all the recent widows, but those still with surviving partners looking on with enormous interest, like vultures waiting for the lions to finish feasting. When I informed them that I really didn't know but all my finances in the care of a lovely guy in Eastbourne, I heard to say,

'What a hussy, and her old man barely cold in the grave,' but Dilys said,

'You don't mean Stephen do you?' and then more thoughtfully,

'you know my Jim, went to see him just before we left. The old bugger.'

She gasped with growing horror,

'Don't tell me he tried to change his will, sell his shares, cash in his pension?'

With a scream she ran up and down the edges of the incoming tide as the waves and ripples deleted her carefully worked out financial plans, destroying her hopes and dreams for a new future.

Category C were those that really tried to help the villagers provide food for their unexpected guests. Surprisingly Jen with occasional help from Robin turned out to be keen gardeners , went out with the women to forage, gradually becoming knowledgeable about what to pick and what to leave well alone. Adnan and James were popular among the younger men, I supposed they had sea going skills and they often went out on the canoes coming back proudly with strange but nonetheless tasty fish.

It was only Audrey, she of the snake eyes from the ship, she who had to be dragged from the canoe, who remained in a hut nearly all day, only venturing out if she were accompanied by at least three of her former ship mates. The villagers appeared concerned, and though they tried to tempt her out with food or songs or playful gestures, she would howl and cry, or rage and spit. Any time there was a goat or pig roasting on the open fire she would get even more hysterical, I wondered if she had been a militant vegan. I am not sure what they believe in or what their diet really is, but I heard stories of them attacking mink farms. I never met any, so I am not sure if this is true, but I know lots of vegans in Lewes and Brighton because all the cafés have vegan 'options' on their food list and even the supermarkets have a special set of shelves. Each day Audrey would emerge and scream mindlessly, the only distinct words were "Where are they all?'

Were these early and tragic signs of dementia? I know it can strike at any age. If I approached she would scream out, 'Get away, you are in their power!' I did begin to wonder if Saga Tours had a system to deal with this type of crisis, and made a note to self that I should find out when I returned to Lopeham. But then I thought of all the elderly and lonely people there and reminded myself that by neighbours and fellow former carers would have more insight, more practical experience. To be honest she suffered a similar fate with our group. From initial sympathy and gradually weakening attempts to help, we all became bored and left her to it. Sad really but then we were focussing on our own survival.

Nonetheless it was Jen who stood out. What a metamorphosis! I once saw a horror film where someone turned into a spider and we all know of witches who disguise themselves as beautiful queens. Jen's hair, once shaved beneath the countless wigs began to grow. In the recent days, Jen had turned from the most glamorous arm candy, to a self-assured and proud leader, a warrior in waiting, one handed and glorious in a new found life.

It took us some days to realise how clean and tidy the village appeared. There was understandably no litter, a blight on the towns lanes and even woods in Sussex, so much so it went unnoticed until it was not there and those were rare days. There was no waste from food. Any meat was eaten down to the bones and then these boiled to nothing, only husks of vegetables were left and those put on compost. There was absolutely no waste.

The village had gardens, with simple stockades to keep goats, pigs and small children out. There were larger and stronger stockades where animals ready for slaughter or with young were kept in at night. We were a group of assorted women, none of us in our first flush of youth and many in the menopausal stage of middle age. We soon found that a mixture of yams seemed to keep the symptoms at bay and in fact some of us seemed to blossom with this herbal mixture.

Jen turned into a keen and skilled gardener, with the simplest of axes and implements she could cut and dig. She had built up a real friendship with the older women, who stayed in and near the village with the dual role of keeping an eye on the garden and looking after the little children. I wondered if it was her one hand and use of the prosthetic that bonded Jen to the matriarchs and leaders of the community. Nonetheless I was absolutely certain that her ability to take her hand on and off, to bash passing spiders with deadly accuracy and to cause respect from anyone getting in her way, especially the young men for whom she had a strange attraction, sealed her status as top woman of our group.

Children of the village were fearless. The very youngest sat near us working, or sleeping in simple hammocks which Jen would absently minded push from time to time. Ambulant toddlers played nearby arranging sticks and stones, piling up soil becoming covered in mud and dust. Jen would sometimes wander over, sing a song, or just give one a cuddle. The older ones were the most adventurous, obviously fascinated by the stranger and her hand. They would touch, feel and pull at it, essentially curious, making

Jen laugh as she would pretend to touch them.

She noticed me standing and looking at her.

'So,' she began defensively, aggressively, 'what's with you, always looking and staring?'

I weighed my words carefully and nonetheless kept a safe distance.

'Jen, you're great, of all the people who would have thought? I mean, you look so happy and I don't know, kind of alive, if you get my meaning.'

'Oh yeah, well I like this life. I have a role at last, never really liked kids but these ones are fine. Lots of the women have lost their teeth, so losing a hand is no big deal anymore, seems I really fit in.'

She looked for a second happy and content but in a spasm, she choked, gasped and turned to me.

'I left my so-called family when I was fourteen, never got a chance to return.'

Her eyes glazed over, she started to draw patterns in the soil. And then in a trance-like state she told me that she had no memories of her mother, and was first in the care of her grandmother, she gave a wry smile. Then she wept as she recalled the nightmare when neighbours killed her grandmother.

'Bloody wars, bloody men,' then she screamed, 'I was sold, sold sold!'

I was shocked, I had never met anyone who spoke with such sorrow. I was not sure what to do. I recall Woman's Hour advising just listening when someone needs counselling, not hard for me as no one really listened to me. I waited, tried to look as if this was not such an unusual occurrence, when she slowly raised her head and looked right at me. Quietly she said, 'thank all the gods and all the demons for *The Syndicate*, right? Surprised you came on the trip as you had it all sorted.'

A village woman looked up when she heard the word *Syndicate*, and once again the women stopped their gardening, their child minding and danced around in a circle, joined by Jen, singing over and over again 'Syndi, sindi syndicate'.

As I took Jen's hand to join the dance, I said quietly, half to myself, the unspoken truth,

'You may have been sold, but I was bought.'

EIGHT

In Lopeham, at that same moment, Wendy was struggling down to the shops, head low against the chilly wind catching the last of the overnight rain. Passing the bungalow, she paused and for a few moments thought about that couple that had lived there, the old man dying and his widow just taking off. While she was suspicious of at the behaviour of the newly bereaved widow, departing so quickly, Wendy, as Neighbourhood Watch self-appointed person, remembered the couple as exemplary neighbours who kept themselves to themselves, no trouble, never any disputes over hedges, pets, parking or god forbid visiting relations, silent and in the main unseen, just the ticket.

The post van drew up and curious to see if there was mail to be delivered to the silent house, she waited, pretending, most unconvincingly that she was looking at a passing malevolent seagull.

'Morning, Bill,' she said, proud after all these years that she should not only be on speaking terms with a postman but also know his name.

'Morning,' replied Arthur, for Bill was not his name nor had ever been, but he knew these people. How they loved three letter names for postmen, dustmen, plumbers and builders, but not doctors or estate agents. However, he was wise enough never to contradict these people now he was instructed to refer to them as clients.

'How are you this morning?' she enquired without displaying a curiosity, as to his well-being, but as a precursor to a far more interesting question.

'Mustn't grumble,' the stock reply of someone who does not want to stop and chat.

And now the question…

'Number 17 still away? I haven't seen her for some time.'

'Can't say,' replied Arthur, though he knew as all post people do, that one occupant was dead and other was on a cruise.

With determination, head down, envelopes guarded in his large and capable hands, he walked on, down the soulless avenue, past the house where Peter and Angela looked out, past all the faces along the Avenue, peering through windows and curtains of variable cleanliness, all hoping he would stop at their door.

93

An hour later Wendy was returning from the shops, when, ever vigilant she observed a hire car passing up and down the avenue. The driver looked bored and had a glazed look in his eyes, but in the back a florid woman, with unnatural tanned skin, earrings, bangles and wrapped in a large scarf was leaning forward giving directions to the driver. Wendy paused wondering if these were the upmarket thieves that Sussex police continually and rather depressingly warned the many local residents' groups to be on the look-out for. She did not think he looked the violent kind, though she was not too sure about the woman.

The car passed by again and she could see the woman tapping the driver's shoulders and his wince of annoyance. A car window descended, a voice emerged from the car,

'Excuse me, but are you local!'

Wendy wondered how this could be said without any suggestion that it was grammatically a question. But the day was stretching ahead of her and this encounter would be food for the next meeting of the Lopeham Resident Group.

'Do you know if the occupiers of number 17 are around?'

Wendy was now cautious, this fitted the bill of the police warnings. Her righteousness gave her courage.

'And who are you when you're at home?' she enquired not displeased at this firm handling of the criminal classes.

The driver gave a conspiratorial wink at Wendy as his passenger curtly replied,

'I am Gwen. My sister in law was widowed some months ago. I have been away on a cruise,' she patted her hair and examined the tan on her arms, just to make the point that cold bleak winters in Lopeham could not be suffered for the whole winter. She continued,

'I did hear, but it might only be a rumour, that she came into some money and I did wonder....'

She gave a pause, an alteration of tone, to continue with

'I just hope she is safe...'

But that sounded extremely unconvincing so Gwen tailed off uncertain how to finish the sentence. But there was no need, Wendy caught the point exactly and pointed looks, a minute nod of the head, and an even more minute lifting of eyebrows communicated Gwen.

'I can make enquiries,' mumbled Wendy her mind already on

how she could find the information. But, as the window was about to close her car window, she leant forward,

'So why are you interested?' she had a feeling there was more than a general concern for her neighbour.

'Oh well, you see,' began Gwen, 'I am a relation, though by marriage you know,' a nervous laugh, 'and I haven't heard from her for some months now, I just thought I would check on her.'

The car window was wound up with some force, another tap on the shoulder of the long-suffering driver and they were off.

'So nothing to do with sudden riches then,' thought Wendy and continued home thinking for the first time that Lopeham was not such a quiet and respectable place after all.

NINE
H

As I wandered back to the village thankful that Jen did not follow me, a group of the men returning from the beach, stopped, fell silent and waited for me to lead the way. I was not sure that this was due to any courtesy but I had the distinct impression they wanted to see where I was going. It was the first time I realised we were all being watched. I thought about the previous days; thought we were just following the villagers, to collect fruit, to go fishing or when the evening came some might just come and sit near our fire. Then I remembered Robin and Frank who had wandered along some of the cliff paths, or Vince who often went into the woods while all the time some of the young lads would follow, offering to show a way, point to birds in the most friendly fashion. If they thought I was trying to escape, they should, I'm my opinion, have their heads examined! I was happy on dry land. What did I have to go back to? Would I face the sea in some flimsy canoe? No chance.

Although a few minutes later I did think about Sally and Stephen too if I was truthful.

The sun began its spectacular collapse into the ocean. I was entranced each evening. The sun would attempt to slip surreptitiously towards the sea, but as it got to more than half way there was a great acceleration, crashing into the sea and sending up a final spasm of light, so unlike Lopeham where the sun just meandered downwards and with a sad and lonely gasp disappeared from view leaving behind the evening twilight, as if undecided whether to remerge or not.

I went to the hut I shared with Dilys and Rita, but sat outside, hidden, looking as the men stood huddled, whispering and anxious. It struck me that there were far fewer male passengers than female survivors, in fact there were even fewer village men all told than when I arrived washed up on the beach. I looked at the survivors with renewed interest.

Nigel had travelled alone, I recall he said his wife did not like the thought of an eco tour, and wanted to go to Lanzarotte with her sister, Frank's wife was missing and presumed drowned in the disaster, and now Robin and Vincent, appeared to be close friends travelling together.

It wasn't just that some of the older men had not made it to the village, but there were also young village men missing. Perhaps mad Audrey was right, where were the men, and where for example was my finder?

The next day as dawn was coming through the trees, I heard a commotion from the beach. The men from *The Syndicate* were grouped in the centre of the village, listening watching and strangely still. I left my hut and approached them. For the first time the circle widened so I could join them.

There was that curious shuffling, looking at feet, coughing, that people do when they are nervous, want to speak but search for the right words.

'Don't think we have ever had a chance to chat, seen you around.'

Nigel began hesitantly,

'Seen you talking to the girls of course, what survivors, 'he continued with a nervous laugh, 'and working with the village women, yes, splendid, splendid.'

Nigel's mammoth effort at communication screeched to a halt. I waited expectantly.

'Yes the girls,' began Robin, 'tough lot of women especially these days.'

More shuffling of feet and glances around, coughing, shaking of heads restarted for at least a few minutes.

Then comments such as Jim, nice bloke knew him at the golf club, then David, didn't see that coming and Joe what an end, and so it continued listing their fallen shipmates.

Nigel suddenly sprang into action and with a gesture from him all the man fell silent.

'Actually, that's not what we would like to talk to you about. You speak to the villagers, have you noticed anything odd? They all seem to be waiting for something.'

I did not comment that I had noticed we were continually watched.

Nigel continued.

'When we were rescued, I found a mobile which had been dropped on the deck of *The Syndicate*. Course it got wet and one of the young fellows from the village said he would take it and dry it out. Now he and the phone are gone.'

Nigel continued, "don't want to worry the girls, but we have searched all around, even up the mountains in case they were trying

97

to see if one of them were using it, trying to get a signal, but just no sign of it, men or phones.'

I thought of the Komodo dragons, but if they had attacked the party they surely would have spat out a phone.

The early commotion had now moved towards the village, shouts and a particular yell that was recognised.

'Good god they have Frank!'

No one dared move, but all looked as through the trees a group of boys and women had a struggling Frank in their grasps. They marched up to us and with disgust threw him on the ground, making wavy motions with their hands. And then they returned to their work, the boys to kick a ball around.

'What's going on old chap?' enquired Robin, who if old fashioned in his outlook was kindly, plus he was the only one to help Frank to his feet.

In a quavering voice Frank began, 'I got up really early before dawn, and I crept down to the beach. The sea was really calm and I thought I could swim out to the wreck, there are still parts above water jammed on the reef. Another storm and it could be totally lost.'

The others looked at him with a mixture of respect, disbelief and admiration.

'Got a pool at home,' he said recognising the looks, his voice gathering strength, 'got to keep fit, the second missus is quite demanding,' he said increasing the looks of admiration, 'do at least 50 lengths every day.' Some now increased looks of disbelief as they glanced surreptitiously at the portly girth standing before them.

'So what did you find?' asked Robin.

'That's the thing, that's what I want to say if I get a chance, I couldn't even get in the water.'

'What do you mean?' asked Nigel, who was among the sceptics.

'Bloody villagers came screaming down the beach, yelling and waving hands and as I tried to get through the waves, they actually leapt in and dragged me back. I thought I was going to be killed, started all this wavy business you saw it.'

I could see the men were really upset, perhaps they had been thinking of trying to get out to the wreck too, but did not have the physical prowess or stamina to make the swim. Over their shoulders, I could see the boys now stopping their game and looking at us and starting again these hand movements. As we all turned the pantomime became clearer, one waved his arm twisting and turning, then grabbing a pal standing close by, where upon the pal fell to the ground writhing and flailing around, followed by groans and an instant death. What a performance, just like Lopeham Am Drams on a good rendering of Macbeth. He stood up to applause from his friends. But this was no death by stabbing, this was poison, these were sea snakes.

'Sea snakes,' I gasped, 'they were protecting you from sea snakes. They are so venomous, you would have died. You need to thank these guys, they have saved your life.'

Frank looked as if he were going to faint, Robin sat down heavily on the sand, Nigel gasped and bent double with a howl,

'How will we ever get off this island, we are trapped?'

And I wondered if we would ever become fully adjusted, come to love our captors all fall into the Stockholm Syndrome.

TEN
H

It was as if those cries and groans from men who thought they were abandoned, who would never return to the life they knew, to the societies where they had acquired status, stirred the elements.

Deep in the woods the Komodo dragons moved languidly, silently, away from the beaches towards the high volcano. In the stark north, canoes returned without fish and were hauled far up the beach and anchored more securely than ever with vines.

The woods fell silent as the birds too began to seek shelter. The villagers began to collect anything left outside, shooing the chickens into a small hut and the pigs and goats driven into the shelters. A hot breeze came in with pernicious intent, while the sky darkened.

That night fierce winds lashed the coast. In the village, sheltered by the woods and a distance from the coast, the houses and huts shook and rocked and swayed, but did not break, the thatched roofs remained strong. The surrounding palm trees almost bent down to the ground, springing back if there was any lull between the gusts.

Worst of all was a howling, a screeching, a shaking of the ground. Of course we survivors did not believe in demons, devils, malign spirits, that entire pantheon of angry gods, but on the other hand each found themselves becoming somewhat open to suggestion. As the storm intensified, we gathered in the largest hut, there was a comfort that they might all die together. A feeling reinforced when at first three dogs, then a shabby old cat were joined by two piglets, a small sow and a goat. No one had the strength or courage to resist their entry or even query how they had been left outside, and so through that storm the group formed a strong bond not only with each other but with the livestock of the village.

Dawn crashed in silence, which was almost as scary as the rampage of the winds and chaos of the night. How could such a storm just stop and not peter out in a polite and somewhat regretful way as happens in Sussex? We helped the villagers haul back any articles that had got blown into the trees, relocated the animals and swept up any leaves that had come into the centre and all learned that fallen leaves can hide snakes, spiders and worse.

The new-found domesticity was interrupted by boys running out of the woods and all the adults clustered around in a circle. It was obvious deep discussion was being held. Could this be more disaster?

ELEVEN
H

One of the women, an elder of the village, broke away and came towards us with a smile. She hugged Frank, to his astonishment and taking hands and saying 'Syndicate' over and over again, she pulled him towards the path to the beach. We all followed in silent apprehension deaf to the receding cries of Audrey, like a banshee in days long gone. She remained in her hut peering through the door.

'They are taking him to sacrifice him, they will kill him, they will kill you,' But to be honest by then I could not care less as we followed in a haphazard formation without curiousity but with a unified determination not to be left behind in the village.

As we emerged through the trees, we stopped in shock. There, on the horizon soared the hulk of *The Syndicate*, sinister, menacing. We thought it sunk well beneath the waves on the seaward side of the reef, but the storm must have lifted the brave ship up again into the light, but not a natural light, not the bright tropical light we had become accustomed to. This light was grey, silent clouds hung overhead, and again the unnatural silence. Even the seas were in a discordant harmony, the waves diminishing before our eyes, and in some areas the sea was unnaturally flat, torpid, as if reluctant to reach the beach.

This in contrast to the activity of the village. Canoes were tugged down to the beach, some large enough for fifteen or more. Shouts and waves and we realised everyone was going out to the wreck.

I started more or less at a trot, but was overtaken by Jen.

'Got to get my own clothes,' she yelled as she passed me.

'Got to find our phones,' shouted a very energetic Frank and so, like a parody of the 100 metre sprint we all raced to the canoes. We were all helped in, except Robin and Nigel who were firmly told by some highly explicit sign language, to push two of the canoes out. Then they scrambled aboard, with little dignity but with a great sense of achievement.

I had never seen the large canoes before. They were a simple but classic design. Each had an outrigger, which made them very stable, though in the lagoon and especially on that day the sea was far from rough. Each of the larger canoes had six paddlers, men and women, while the passengers huddled in the centre. Smaller canoes followed, there were shouts and laughter and a race began. It was exhilarating and the first bit of really good fun. But when I looked back to the beach I suddenly realised that the reef seemed to be a mile or more from the shore and our little island began to look fragile but so beautiful in the darkening skies.

As we got nearer the hulk, the shouts quietened to a silence but *The Syndicate* sensing our approach began to screech and roar, sway and lurch in the seas beyond. Were these the songs of the ship, the dirges of the dead crew, the killer sharks and dolphins that circled the outer reaches of the reef? Our lovely ship was impaled on rocks, the prow jutting proudly to the skies, higher than we had calculated from the beach.

The paddlers slowly, cautiously manoeuvred the canoes alongside the reef, finding places where rocks and stone had become embedded into the razor sharp corals giving a smoother surface to hold. There was total silence, we overawed by the hulk looming above us, the villagers warily looking out for sharks.

The young boys were the first to leap on the reef, and secure the vine ropes from the canoes onto shards of the reef. Then one slung a rope with a hook high and after a few throws it was lodged on the railings. The boy clambered up with the same skill I had seen the boys climb the palm trees.

We waited below, our necks craning to see what was happening, the paddlers still keeping the canoes at a near but safe distance from the rocks. Suddenly a yell and a rope ladder came hurtling down.

Frank and Nigel suddenly stood up in their canoes, and even tried to jump onto the rocks. The paddlers hissed their disapproval, and were instructed to sit down and wait. Frank became angry,

'I need my phone you idiots,' but got a shove in the back and a fist put in his face, so he shut up.

Surprisingly our former waiter Paul clambered up the rope ladder and a very short time later, two more ladders were slung down. Now there was a real scramble. Frank with amazing energy leapt onto the reef and started up one of the ladders, slowly and much more cautiously followed by Nigel, then Jen. I think I was one of the last to attempt the ascent. I had no faith that I could make the climb and I hate heights, but, but I was not going to be left in the canoe on watch duty for marauding fish with large teeth and even larger appetites.

It took me about many painful minutes to complete the climb and then try to stand on the sloping deck. I was pushed aside by the villagers who were acting as a team. Stuff was being brought up from the lower decks; blankets, ropes, boxes of first aid materials, axes that were part of the fire escape equipment, tins of food, wooden chairs, in other words almost everything that was moveable. At one point there was an ear-piercing scream, it was Jen. She emerged ashen but triumphant. She had found her cabin just above the water line, happily located some skirts and matching tops no less, but sadly the remains of her husband, partly eaten she casually observed, by a shark that was swimming along the corridor below.

I was tying the tins into blankets and securing them with ropes to lower to the canoes when Frank and Nigel came to find me. Frank was shaking and Nigel looked as though his blood pressure had reached dangerous levels. They almost collapsed onto the railings by me.

'What's the matter?' I asked. It seemed a daft question in the midst of this apparently chaotic salvage operation.

'They've gone, they're not there,' he put his head in his hands, he scraped his fingers through his hair, he rocked and swayed.

'What's gone?'

'The phones! The phones you idiot! We got into the bridge, and, god all mighty, the safe was open and the safe was bare. What are we going to do, we are lost!'

'And the money, but chin up, old boy,' ventured Nigel, then abruptly stopped as he realised that any chin heading upwards would be his as Frank barely restrained himself from decking him one.

'Don't you realise, you old fool, that someone had opened that safe and taken everything out and where the hell are they now!'

A thought that had been at the back of my mind for several days now blearily made its way forward.

'Did you see any bodies around?'

Nigel let out a sob.

'I saw some bones, in a shoe, I think it was the purser, I cannot be sure.'

We moved with care over the deck and peered through the vitreous glass into the bar area. There floating in some suspiciously dark water were literally bits and pieces, shoes, a cap, bottles, even a large jar of olives. I assumed the sharks and their lesser pals had been in while this part of the ship had been under water. So no obvious human remains.

I thought for a while.

'Jen says she found the remains of her husband, I was lucky I suppose, I was thrown overboard when the ship crashed into the rocks.'

Robin said with sardonic humour, 'that was some crash! We were all thrown off our feet. Thought at first I had had too much of that cheap rum old James kept pressing on us. Then the yells and shouting and directions to get on deck in the dark, it was a nightmare.'

'But did you see the captain, or the officers, or Bruce or the rest of the crew?' I almost yelled. 'Where are they? They are not on the island, there are no bodies on the bridge.'

Nigel turned towards us, his reflection caught in the glass, his eyes glazed, like a zombie, he took a step forward, staggered, righted himself then screamed, 'Where are the Zodiacs?'

As with one movement, like spectres of the living dead, we raised our heads upward to the space behind the bridge. They had gone, all three of them.

The strong Zodiac boats with engines, and on which we would have explored the islands, the creeks the coral reefs, the inlets where we were to learn snorkelling.

Gone.

The boats we had been assured were strong, the engines capable of going through the wildest waves, the outer skin impervious to the sharp coral, the teeth of predators.

Gone.

The three spaces where the boats had been secured were now gaping, arms of one beam slightly swaying in the wind.

'Could they have been wrenched away from the holdings?' I ventured though I knew the answer.

'Of course not,' a reply in unison, 'the bastards, they've taken the boats, they've escaped.' Frank wailed.

But why, I wondered, did they head out to sea, with our phones, while we struggled to the shore? Before I could begin to articulate these thoughts there were shouts, yells, whistles and looking over the side I saw preparations to depart.

I looked back, *The Syndicate* had offered me so much hope for the future and I now realised I was fond of the brave little ship, over two thirds still below water. It seemed she clung onto the reef just to give us some last gifts.

The return journey was very slow. It was like those channel relay crossings for non-exceptional swimmers. Some of us were not so much encouraged but actually thrown overboard to swim alongside the laden canoes. We swam for as long as we could, occasionally getting a tow from a canoe, and when truly exhausted got hoisted in and some other unfortunate jettisoned out. The villagers were singing and laughing, but we, the passengers, were silent, remembering the bodies, the silent sharks themselves trapped in the hull. When we reached the beach everyone came to help unload. We watched the joy of blankets being hauled up, some clothes finding new owners, food and tins being examined and the ropes, the axes, the tools beginning to be fought over.

The vitality of the villagers was catching. Jan paraded around in a bright dress and flowing scarves, smiling extensively waving her prosthetic hand. Paul and James had found a guitar undamaged and were trying to strum out some kind of rhythm, I could not call it a tune, others banged coconuts, their gentle vibrations carrying across the waves.

As the evening fires were lit, we all had different stories to tell, the horrors and the joys. Tins of beer and a bottle of wine were opened. It was our first party. We all recognised we were the survivors, we had a safe haven and for some the discovery of tins of baked beans and rice pudding offered more comfort than could have been imagined.

Nonetheless, Frank, Nigel and myself had now formed an unlikely trio as we were the only ones who had noticed the missing boats, the absent captain, some of the crew, and more seriously the loss of our phones, laptops, iPads and all means of communication. This was information we hesitated to pass on to our now rejoicing comrades.

TWELVE
H

The storm returned.

I had wondered why there had been such a frantic salvage effort, I suppose I thought we could return to *The Syndicate* for a more extensive search but those hopes were dashed. Throughout the day and the following night, the intensity of the wind that blew us back into our huts, the lashing rains, horizontal, were terrifying. It was not only Audrey that was paralysed by a primeval fear of the spirits and demons of this alien island, this unknown culture had unleashed. We heard the groans, the screams and the final screech and knew our ship was being pulled from the reef and sinking forever lost in the endless fathoms of the sea below.

In the aftermath of the storm, we were gathered together with all the villagers. "Syndi sunk Syndi gone," said one woman with gestures, looking sad. We nodded in agreement and congratulated her on acquiring one more word in English.

Typically English and perhaps of the last generation that had attended school before Britain joined the European Union, the majority of the passengers were very slow to attempt to learn the language of the villagers. The English in particular have a belief that learning any foreign language proficiently will turn them into barbaric natives, as it is their belief that only by speaking English can the sanity and the most sophisticated culture of the world be saved.

From time to time, someone would say he or she heard a Spanish word, but that was in the context of finding a bottle of wine in the stores. Nigel swore he heard one man say '*skruvmesjel*' when searching among the tools and then picking up a screwdriver. 'How did he know that word, its Swedish?' Gradually we heard the odd word in French, Italian and even an impressive curse in Gaelic, according to Audrey, her first sign of a return to sanity and contribution to any conversation, as she recalled the same word when her grandmother dropped a saucepan on her foot.

On this morning there was little need for linguistic analysis. Susie, reinforcing her position as the village leader said "*u pickum up, yu glong we.*" And without a doubt we were on the move.

First everything that was moveable was gathered up.

Some stores were taken back to the beach and loaded in the largest of the canoes, those with the outriggers and the strongest of all the paddlers set off. I was apprehensive when the canoes left. First they were loaded with precious provisions, and second it meant the departure of more of the young men. I noticed the canoes were not loaded down, in fact there was quite a bit of space. The canoes rode high in the water as they took off through the gap in the reef and around the rocks at the end of the bay, out of sight in the still turbulent seas.

During the morning, we loaded up all the baskets of all the produce and stores, chickens were loaded into bamboo baskets. When finished, large bags were taken from the huts. We did become apprehensive, when an assortment of shoes and sandals was thrown on the ground. All the men, women and children came forward, picking out a variety of footwear, which disturbingly had a large number of non-matching flip flops. We were pushed forward to choose. We were surprised for we had become used to being barefoot, our feet generally hardening as we walked the paths and even the rough sands of the beach. But there was no arguing. Susie threw two towards me. Like a bad day shopping in Eastbourne we all had sandals, trainers, flip flops of every colour, some leather and every 'ethnic' some plastic and a few well- worn rubber boots.

Audrey had a moment of panic, when she could not find a matching pair.

"Why only one shoe?' she wailed as she rummaged through eventually giving up hope of finding a pair. But curiosity and a fear of being left behind had got her out of her hut.

It was such an efficient operation, it must have been done many times before.

Frank observed the going will be rough.

'If we all have to have footwear, it must mean we are going to climb the volcano.'

The order *'glong'* roughly translated as 'get going' was issued. As we left the village I looked back fondly at this place that had given us such a haven and noticed the villagers looked back too, but anxiously at the gathering clouds on the distant horizon.

THIRTEEN

At first, both Sally and Stephen were pleased to get emails

To: sal123
From: hgriffiths
Subject: update
Hi, DW,Captain returned mob for 5 mins. Having a super time,
tomorrow we swim FOMO! Orb so b4n.
    H

To: hgriffiths
From: sal123
Subject: re update
Wow auntie are you getting the jargon! XX

To: sfinances
From: hgriffiths
Hi, DW,Captain returned mob for 5 mins. Having a super time,
tomorrow we swim FOMO! Orb so b4n.
    H

To: hgriffiths
From   sfinances
Subject: contact

Thank you for the contact. Regards Stephen.

Stephen could never remember a time in his life where it could
be said he enjoyed sport. Recalling the brutality of school rugby,
the tedium of cricket and the chill of school swimming pool, he
had avoided most physical activity except the stroll along the
Promenade in summer. Recent warnings from his doctor to adopt
a less relaxed life style were heard, and, after some consideration

Stephen had taken up golf, surprised there were so many in his age group. He suspected many were escaping the joys of being a father to very young children. His well-founded belief that as a late beginner to the sport, not too much would be expected, and, sure enough, he found he could amble around a golf course with ease and as a reward replace any lost calories in the club bar afterwards.

Despite this unremarkable start, he was pleased to find himself on a list to play in a friendly tournament for new members from three local clubs. He was driven with three companions to Lewes for a match. He was paired against Charles who he had known from his days in the bank, now retired locally, but doing some part-time work. Charles had been his mentor at work and in fact had before he retired had recommended Stephen to some customers.

'What's life like in Lewes?' Stephen asked, not really interested, but putting down his ball ready to take a swing.

'I like it,' replied Charles, 'always something going on, always little odd events. Last week the police had to smash into a travel agent's, a neighbour had reported very strange goings on, some talk of a drugs bust even a missing body.'

'Really,' replied Stephen, somewhat urbanely. Drugs bust were not unknown even in the sleepier parts of Eastbourne and he never believed in missing bodies, missing people yes, errant husbands fleeing crooks, yes he knew all about them.

'This one was queer, lots of rumours typical small town gossip.' continued Charles. Stephen now lifted his club, shuffled his feet in what he hoped was an imitation of the best golfers.

Yes', mused Charles, 'it centred around one of those pop up shops and a bloke recruiting suckers for a non-existent eco-cruise on a ship called *The Syndicate*.'

At which point Stephen's struck his ball with such unexpected force that it was caught in the high strong winds and carried over the cliff and onto a greenhouse below.

'What did I say?' thought Charles as he pondered yet another letter of complaint to the club secretary and endless meetings of the level of compensation to be paid to irate neighbours.

FOURTEEN
H

The trek was, by any description, arduous. We could look up and see the path, a tortuous track, steep in places, sinuous, convoluted, winding itself up the side of the volcano, with detours to avoid the smoke issuing from vents.

We left the sweet scents of the woods, the aromatic vanilla, the perfume of the fruit trees to the dry and toxic airs seeping down from the volcano.

The older village boys led the way, most carrying the heaviest of the boxes, bags and baskets. These they had tied with vines that looped across their head and forehead and rested on their backs. They had to stoop as they moved forward steadily rhythmically and with great care along the uneven paths. We followed in the middle of the great line. I noticed how much fitter we had all become during our stay in the village. Though we had all lost weight, well flab to be honest, we had actually toned up, we were, to our astonishment quite fit. We were all given differing loads, an estimation on what we could carry. Interestingly Audrey was given a long bamboo and the task of keeping the pigs in line.

This was not difficult, the intelligent pigs had no intention of remaining behind and in the main trotted along in an amiable way, stopping now and again to look with curiosity into the undergrowth. Jen and I kept an eye on our companions, who from time to time tried to reach a fruit, look at a flower. We were continually warning, 'That's poisonous, watch out there's a spider, didn't you see the snake?' until they all kept their hands solely clasped around their packages, their eyes fixed on the path, hardly daring to look around. The dogs scampered behind us, occasionally taking a short cut through the bushes and appearing ahead, and once coming back with some unfortunate bird that they scrapped over.

The path began to zig-zag up the lower reaches of the volcano. We were reaching the outer limits of our former explorations from the village. We were leaving the familiar vegetation, for spiny bushes, scrubby grasses and the whiff of sulphur.

Now we really appreciated the assortment of footwear. The rough path might have cut our fairly hardened feet, but now we could feel the torrid heat seep through the soles of the sandals.

Even Frank, who had been pig-headed about wearing a delightfully floral pair at the start of our trek, put them on his burning feet.

We could see the boys ahead climbing confidently, when there was a scream, boxes dropped, chaos as we bumped into each other.

The boys dropped their loads and ran straight down across the steep shale to find out what was happening, picking up sticks as they ran. Susi and the other village women who had been behind us pushed their way forward.

'*Wazup?*' demanded Susi and Robin transfixed, ashen pointed to a large rock on which sat the largest komodo dragon, its evil fetid stench reaching us as its tongue flickered around is mouth, it huge claws twitched on the rocks, and its eyes, its awful eyes stared right down us us. In its jaws the last remains of an old goat that had wandered off the path.

'*Ya bugger off*' yelled Susi, a remarkable appropriate use of English, understood by the dragon who stepped back into the undergrowth, leaving a stench behind. The boys laughed and dropped their sticks returning up the scree to their fallen bundles.

'*Komodo go me,go u*', she said to us, then pointing back, '*bad , bad comin, komodo comin me comin u. She be Matilda.*'

It was evident that the Komodo and Susi if not the others had some kind of understanding. Susi had looked unafraid at the dragon and it had returned her gaze with reptilian equanimity. From which exchange I guessed that another storm was coming, we were all going somewhere and it looked like the Komodo was coming too. So we set off again up the increasing steep paths, silent and afraid, uncertain again of what the future would hold. We were pressed, shouted at and occasionally thumped if we stopped too long.

The sun was beginning to set when we reached the crest of the path. Even though the winds tore at our clothes, ripped through our hair, chilled our sweating brows we all stopped and looked back. Where was the calm and tranquil bay? We were for a moment disorientated then began to realise with sadness that the bay was lost in storm clouds, the sea invisible beneath the low and blackening clouds and the trees bent to the ground in the angry winds. I hoped the men who had left in the canoes were safe. I was not brought up in Sussex without a deep respect for and fear of what the sea can do.

Once we dropped down the far side of the climb we faced the northern section of the island. The change was dramatic, though we were sheltered from the wind and the storm, the land ahead looked stony and inhospitable.

There was a shout from the leaders who had stopped on a level piece of ground, enough for everyone, including chickens and pigs to set down. A fire was lit and basic food prepared and shared out. We were thankful for the blankets salvaged from *The Syndicate* and with some nostalgia for its logo stamped on the material, wrapped ourselves up and slept soundly to the snores of people, the grunts of the pigs and the odd disturbing shuffling nearby of some unknown creatures.

I swear the cockerels that morning had not waited for the dark to leave nor for dawn to arrive before they started up the most god-awful racket. I cannot say everyone stirred in their sleep and gradually awoke, more it was an activity from deep sleep to be on your feet. The boys almost were in a competition to load up first. We were helped with our loads, Audrey who by now had formed an affection bond with the pigs, counted them carefully, found one absent youngster and had them lined up with a precision that would have won prizes in any agricultural show, then we started on our way, down the winding path. From time to time I could hear, '*Bugger off,*' at the back of the line. About an hour later, I looked up the zig-zag and saw the last woman, I am sure it was Susi, followed now by four Komodo dragons about 30 metres behind her but receiving a shout and a wave of a stick when they got any nearer.

By midday we were exhausted, but had managed to reach some shade. Strangely the boys made a little fire, very smokey and shortly afterwards, there were shouts and we could see some more young fellows climbing up the path. As they reached our group there was initial good humoured punching that is a recognisable and universal form of greeting among young men, then they approached Susi with a bow of respect and stood back with no shame and gaped at us, occasionally approaching and touching, curious but not hostile, asking the ubiquitous greeting, '*alrighthen.?*' while we stood still, nervous and unsure how to respond.

The final leg of the journey was easier in some ways. The new lads took up some of the heavier bags from Frank and Robin who were looking exhausted, we women they ignored. Not unsurprising I thought given the muscles of the women in the village group.

Audrey in her newfound role, would not tolerate any interference and attempt to take control of the pigs.

Melanie stumbled unused to the stony paths, making gestures which indicated 'I'm a really going to be sick,' as we passed by some volcanic steam erupting from the rocks nearby by.

'I'll tell you one thing for sure,' she hissed over her shoulder to me, 'this is the last time I ever taken an eco-holiday, Bloody David Attenborough, if it wasn't for him, Joe would never have thought about taking a cruise like this! Oh for the beaches of Bournemouth, oh for the Blackpool Promenade, the sweet smells from the kebab shops, the fish and chips!'

And well behind us were the Komodo dragons who had sheltered in a cave watching us thread our way down the path, ever vigilant always waiting for that one opportunity, silent malign.

FIFTEEN
H

It took us two days to reach our final destination. The path was easier than the climb over the volcanic fields, and we followed the path twisting along the coastline. The storms did not appear to cross over the high ground behind and for once the feared volcano had offered us safety in its shelter. In contrast however, was the sea. We had become used to the usual gentle waves of the lagoon and the clear waters where we could see most life leading a benign life in the shallow waters.

Along on this coast there were no reefs. Huge rollers swept in, dashing themselves to pieces against the ragged rocks below. At one point Nigel looked sadly down,

'Those rollers are one continuous wave that may have travelled thousands of miles across oceans, never ceasing, never impeded until they come to this ignominious ending.' Then almost imperceptibly muttered, 'perhaps it will be the same for us.'

While some of us kept our eyes firmly on the path, Jan stopped and revealed how differently we regard the world.

'This is magnificent,' she said, dropping her load and, stretching her arms out, she shook her head and her growing hair flowed out in the wind.

I thought for one ghastly second she was going to have one of those hippie moments, that she would declare herself in tune with the elements, higher beings and turn vegan, but not Jen.

'Wouldn't this make a wonderful tourist resort? I could get surfers, hang gliders, bring out bands, have nightclubs. What do you think?'

I did not reply, for it wasn't expected. Few people expect me to reply to their questions. Personally, I thought it was a daft idea, but Jen had taken the same manic expression she had when she was first thrown out of the canoe by her rescuers so many weeks before, and forbear to utter a word.

The path reached lower ground. I had hoped the going would be easier, but instead we trekked around the edges of mangroves. We would occasionally slip on mud, or the path suddenly sinking beneath those with the heavier loads. From the silence of the volcanic fields we could hear birds above us calling and screeching giving warning of our route. The chickens in their bamboo cages began a cacophony of noise. Looking up I am sure I saw one raptor, an eagle, a hawk or perhaps some kind of vulture. Whatever it was the chickens recognised those calls and did not like being in the open.

We could tell we were approaching a settlement. The silence that had fallen among us was broken. First we noticed the path went from something the average foraging animal would make, to a neat and fairly wide track. I even noticed the potholes were recently filled in and made a mental note to write to East Sussex County Council on my return to the effect if a village on a godforsaken island could repair paths then surely something could be done on my dangerous potholed route to the shops.

It was Robin who noticed the plantations.

'Look over there, all the bushes are in a straight line,' and sure enough the further we went the more precise the lines of trees, bushes, vegetables were, some divided into strips. Around were fences of thorn bushes, all trimmed unnervingly to the identical height and width. All in all, not dissimilar to the fences and pickets in the allotments at the back of my house. But after the gentle chaos of our first village this felt uncomfortably strict. And then we noticed our village companions had fallen silent, even the young lads now marched with military step, their backs straight, their shoulders back and even their loads were balanced exactly on heads or backs.

Susie stepped up beside me. She pointed back up the path we had taken, '*Hiya linda*,' she said with a sigh, then pointed forward, '*Hiya orreby*,' and with that all the survivors moved forward with a sense of foreboding, such that Audrey, sensing even her little herd of pigs were apprehensive, began a muted wail like a kitten in distress.

We entered the village in silence, abandoning our haphazard departure from Linda, to adopting a military formation. The dogs came to heel, the pigs and goats walked in pairs without any assistance from Audrey, the boys and their heavy loads in lines of four, and then us, then the women in pairs with the eldest bringing up the rear. Absolutely no sign of the dragons, just the winding path leading back to a happier place.

The houses in the village were uniform in design.

Smaller dwellings backing onto the plantations, built in close proximity. Houses facing the sea were larger, some with the thorn fences we had seen in the plantations marking off areas had palm trees, hammocks, seating.

'See they go in for zoned housing schemes,' muttered Jan beneath her breath, 'Looks like social housing back there and housing for the toff along here.' So like villages in Sussex I mused. However, the silence was disturbing, where were all the people, where were all the dogs chicken and pigs that had so happily meandered around Linda?

The road opened onto an area of open ground where a large number of people were gathered, all standing in silence as we approached. At the front were four very large men, tall, muscular, hard eyed. Two had thin bones through their noses, one through an ear lobe.

One guy had both sets of bones plus some pretty impressive feathers in his lush curly black hair. Perhaps more eye catching, tattooed on every part of their body that we could see and for sure we could see most as only a tiny loincloth covered their parts. In silence, they watched our approach.

The boys dropped their loads at the feet of these impressive men, and stood back. With huge dignity, Susie stepped through the lines of women, passed us, and stood before the men. There was a bit of a staring match, then the biggest guy said the ubiquitous words of greeting: *'u all ri ten?'* and the ritual reply *'ye good an u self'*

The four men now started to walk towards us, Susie following behind them. '*Syndi?*" one asked. We nodded in reply, but worried and concerned, how did he know about the shipwreck? They paused in front of Jen and me. I noticed that as they approached the village women kept their heads down and appeared to huddle together. But not Jen, she drew herself up to her full height, for she was a tall woman and looked straight back.

The guy with the feathers suddenly lent forward and grabbed Jen's arm. Sadly for him he did not realise that her prosthetic hand was concealed under a bundle of cloth she still held. *'U cum me?'* he said imperiously, and to us who began to step forward to protect Jen, shouted *'u bugger off,'* but the speech ended in a strangled scream.

Susie's eyes widened in surprised admiration, the women

behind put their hands to their mouths to stop laughter, as Jen, dropping her bundle, turned to face her aggressor. She grabbed his arm with her prosthetic hand, which she was obviously tightening. Sweat glistened on his face and he tried to hold on to her.

'Let me go, you big bully,' said Jan calmly as if to a child. She was released. She recovered her hand before he could see it. She pointed a finger at him.

'I am not your woman, OK.'

To which Susie offered an unnecessary translation to the astonished men. Recovering their dignity, they marched back to the head of our group, orders given and activity started. '*Nem Bosai, big man*' said Susie, and laughing we made our way into the village.

'You just watch out for that Bosai,' I whispered to Jen, 'think he fancies you.'

To my surprise, for I was expecting Jen to make some kind of sardonic reply, she looked after him, a thoughtful expression in her eyes, "Could be a bit of alright, a bit tasty if you get my drift.'

All our baggage was sorted and put in separate huts around this main square, the pigs and hens were found pens, the dogs sorted themselves out, interestingly not facing any challenge from the only two resident hounds. Fires were lit, food prepared, but all in silent efficiency.

As dark drew in Susie came forward, '*Here u night,*' and mimed sleep. She pointed to a long house. We followed, all of us, up some steps and at the top there was a basic shelter about 30 metres in length.

It was obvious, even to Audrey who was beginning to look dangerously wild-eyed, that we all had to share this space together. My fears began to emerge out of the dark nightmares of my subconscious, would I be bought again?

I did not sleep that night. Nightmares of the Children's Homes returned and something darker, unformed images lurked in the shadows of my mind. I slept with my back against the wall, away from the snoring men who as any elderly bachelor group, had established themselves at the furthest end of the long hut.

As dawn broke we were shocked to find this settlement was at the end of an inlet. High cliffs soared out to the open seas, the waves visible as they roared past the narrow opening. It gave our group time to undertake just a little boasting,

'How like the fiords of Norway,' commented Melanie.

'You think so?' Not a question from Rita who was not expecting a response before continuing, 'I thought so much like that wonderful trip we had to South Island in New Zealand, you know.'

I could see a battle of holiday experiences to the more exotic locations was about to begin, when Audrey ventured, 'probably you are all correct, but I bet we are among the few that have ever been here.'

Silence fell and it reminded us of how far we were from home and in such an unknown place.

On that first morning, I could only assume the sun had risen. Unlike the blazing and glorious explosion from the seas that we had seen daily on our arrival on the island, the sun here climbed slowly, blearily, hesitantly. Long black shadows seeped across the inlet, one side in darkness the other slowly emerging into the sun light. Sparse vegetation clung to the cliff edges. Where there had been rock fall, their roots lent over the edges of the rocks like the baleful talons of some long dead sea eagle.

There was an unnatural stillness in this cove, although we could hear the scream and roar of the enormous surf crashing against the distant cliffs. There were no soft calls of the forest birds here, though malevolent sea birds rode the thermals, screeching abuse at each other, to their nesting companions on the cliff face and no doubt us, bewildered and fearful, standing on this lonely beach.

Suddenly it came to me that the real difference was the smell, no sweet vanilla here, just salt and the smell of dead things emerging from the sea, cast on the lonely beach.

There was surprisingly little activity that morning. The elders sat outside the house talking quietly. The hens had been let loose to scratch around, and the pigs taken out of the stockades to wander around looking for scraps, but neither group wandered far from the huts. Even the normally active women just stood around. The children caught the mood. For once the endless football games were played with disinterest, stopping every now and again to peer out to sea.

They were all waiting for something, some event, someone.

SIXTEEN

Stephen woke up with a hangover. He was normally an abstemious man, mindful of health warnings, concerned that living alone had its perils. But the previous days had tested him beyond measure. About ten days after his golf match in Lewes, he had received a poorly worded email from Charles to inform him the golf club insurance had refused to compensate the owner of the greenhouse. Further the owner of the greenhouse had put in a claim that would have surely paid for a summerhouse of massive proportions. Stephen, well trained by the bank searched for an aerial shot of the garden of the claimant verifying his belief that only a basic structure could fit in the garden of the modest property, and replied as such to Charles. He added that given the propensity of golf balls to sail over the cliff at Lewes the club should invest in high fencing. To which there was an acrimonious retort from Charles about the sanctity of view by the population of the town to the heights of that particular Sussex Down and a sharp reminder that National Park had severe planning restrictions on fencing.

What annoyed him the most was that he could not find any more information on the police raid in Lewes. Telephone conversations with any member of the constabulary were impossible.

The switchboard was only interested in those reporting crimes. The local papers had not taken up any investigations into the departure of the tenants of the pop-up shop. A freelance journalist told him that the pop-up shop scene was just that with the down side of tenants popping down, going off with the swag and popping back up elsewhere.

He was also niggled by the fact that now he had heard from three different sources, that a cruise on *The Syndicate* was not the normal holiday venture that he had assumed. He was disquieted at the news of Jim's death. He had never trusted Dilys, there was something cold and calculating about her, so no wonder that Jim had squirrelled away substantial funds. Stephen could not recall, as his head was throbbing, where the money would end up in the event of his client's sudden or unexpected death but he felt sure there was a substantial bequest to the campaign to re-open the old railway line between Lewes and the town to Uckfield, closed with spectacular lack of foresight to transport needs some eighty years ago, so no windfall for the widow there. Did Jim think that his wife might hasten his expiration while on a cruise? Stephen chastised himself for watching too many Agatha Christie thrillers on the TV.

Nonetheless he had to admit that he was now truly concerned about his lovely lady from Lopeham. As the days passed she assumed a seraphic, virtuous, and unworldly demeanour in his mind. He had gone from the admiration of this brave creature venturing into the unknown with new found independence to thinking that enough was enough, that she needed someone to care for her and that someone was to be him. But that would mean action. Although he would not admit it, he had been disturbed by her last text, the modern and casual use of language seemed strange coming from the woman he thought he knew, but then she was meeting new people and having new experiences.

First he would check out what was happening with her house. There was suspicion that she may have returned and failed to contact him. He caught the train. For some unacknowledged instinct, he thought he would make himself more anonymous, less easy for some client to spot him. He found a large raincoat, not worn for some time, finding he must have lost weight in recent months.

A trilby, pulled down over his eyes, a scarf around his neck, the recognised disguise of any self-respecting private detective.

Stephen alighted the train, marvelling at the defunct use of the word. If he could alight on leaving why could he not just light when he got on for his return journey? Musing on the vagaries of English, he was rarely inept in his work but could he describe himself as ept? He did not notice the beginning of the rain.

Head down and still distracted he took several wrong turnings down the closes, the avenues and the roads. Unsure that he had in fact reached the right road, he asked a passing postman for directions. Arthur confirmed that in fact Stephen was on the right road, but watched him as he walked slowly down one side looking at the house numbers.

'That'll take some time,' mused Arthur, well aware that many occupants thought is too lower class to have numbers on their houses and instead invested in daft names such as, "Laurel Lodge, Little Spinney, Brook Cottage, without rhyme of reason, other to confuse deliverers and post people.

Arthur's were not the only watching eyes. In matching sweaters, Peter and Angela stood together by the living room window, watching Stephen's slow progression along the road.

'Funny day to take a stroll, in the rain and no dog.' Peter observed, knowing that almost no one would choose to walk on a cold rainy day unless driven by the needs of their beloved dogs.

'Don't much like the look of him, all wrapped up like that,' agreed Angela, but doing nothing, they stood observant drinking in unison their cups of herbal teas.

After walking up one side of the road and then the other, Stephen was fairly sure he had now found the right address. The front of the house looked neat and tidy as he approached the front door. He hesitated, his courage faltered. What if she had returned and opened the door? What if she were annoyed that he had come here unannounced, uninvited?

He stopped and listened. The house was totally silent. He peered through the letterbox, perhaps there would be mail on the floor if she were still away, but he could see none. He peered through the sitting room window and with his heart breaking, he saw a pile of letters neatly stacked on a side table, He turned and just leaving the property was stopped by a woman, who though also enveloped in raincoats had a well-built figure, muscular rather than obese, who challenged him,

'What are you up to then?'

She adeptly placed her shopping trolley pinioning him against the fence. No escape. Stephen was desperate,

'Just unexpectedly in the area,' he gasped, 'wanted to see if my dear cousin was in, take her to lunch you know?'

Wendy eyed him with deep suspicion, trying to recall her training on Neighbourhood Watch. This man was well dressed, she recognised a raincoat of distinction, probably old shooting gear, and educated, upper class accent, so no burglar in her opinion. She released him, moving her shopping trolley a few centimetres at most. But it was enough. Before she could say she was a member of the Local Watch and a local resident of some standing in the community, Stephen was away with a turn of speed that surprised them both.

That afternoon, Wendy phoned Gwen. She needed to check if

Gwen knew about this so-called cousin.

'Gwen I have some news,' she began while pouring a very large sherry for herself and settling down for a long conversation.

Gwen sighed. Wendy had taken to calling her frequently, suggesting meeting for lunch or coffee in Eastbourne. But Wendy's news of a man, perhaps a private eye, lurking around her sister in law's house really interested her. It was only from neighbours that Gwen had learnt that H had left for a cruise, confirming her suspicions that she must have some into a tidy sum. Not shared with her relatives she sniffed. Gwen was curious, and so she agreed to meet in that jolly little café by the Martello Tower in Eastbourne.

The following day at eleven o'clock precisely, the two women met. There was some perplexity on what hot drink to choose. It seemed to them both that the ever growing list of different coffees, different milks, teas and what was chai was not something either wanted to admit. Then there was some artificial hesitancy about choosing cakes,

'I really shouldn't, but they look so tempting.' With the result, it was some 30 minutes later they could begin to engage in meaningful conversation.

However, to their horror a voice behind them said without pausing for breath,

'Oh Wendy, can I join you? Its such a horrid day and I thought I really must get out and Peter is in a foul mood, so why not have a coffee and here you are'.

Wendy had no choice as Angela sat herself down, with just a nod to Gwen. Wendy continued,

'So glad I saw you. Peter and I saw this most peculiar man walking up and down our road,'

She turned to Gwen needlessly explaining,

'It's a very quiet and respectable road and though we keep ourselves to ourselves, we do keep a watch on who is passing by.'

'I bet you do,' thought Gwen and Wendy simultaneously.

'Looked like one of those very doubtful men, dirty raincoat, hat pulled down, thankful there were not children around, though seemed to be taking an interest in next door,' continued Angela, stirring her coffee and unaware of the glances between her companions. Wendy was sure she must have been seen talking this stranger, so she was deeply suspicious of Angela.

Heavy rain lashed against the café windows, causing the women to look out, glad they were not among the drenched passers-by.

'Good heavens, there he is,' exclaimed Angela, as Stephen, cold wet and totally depressed walked by.

'Yes you are right, well who would have thought, in Eastbourne a man like that!' said Wendy thoughtfully looking at the rain.

Gwen was silent. She drew herself up, she shook out her hair, she stretched her neck like a cobra about to strike. She was sure she knew him. Old Harry's financial adviser she was sure. So, what had he been doing snooping around the house in Lopeham? She would find out.

SEVENTEEN
H

On the third morning at Orrible, a well named village, everyone was called to the main square. Unlike the previous days, there was to be no volunteering for activities. We were all given orders. To us it appeared chaotic, because it was chaotic, we did not understand at first, but sign language and again the use of some peppered European words and phrases, made things clear.

Audrey, Vincent and Robin were picked out, and from instructions it looked like they were to be in charge of keeping an eye on the animals. Audrey was delighted and started off following the pigs around, chatting to them in a totally barmy but benign fashion. Vincent was told to stay put. I did not understand, until Susie went up to him and with gestures indicated that if the Komodos came into the village he was to drive them off. Vincent paled and had to sit down. He tried to explain that though he had an academic interest in the reptiles, getting physically close and even to enter into some kind of dialogue with them was unthinkable. Not one of the villagers appeared to understand so he was given a big stick and asked to repeat '*bugger off*' several times until Susie was confident he was up to the task.

Robin, Paul, James and Frank were led to the young lads, and with gestures to keep an eye on them they began wearily following them as they scampered towards the cliffs.

The rest of us were marched in silent formation back along the path to the plantations. The women were led to different sections with instructions to weed hoe or gather some of the crops, the men to repairing the stockades or to cutting down brush to extend the planting areas.

Jen and I were told to begin to dig a trench the length of the first stockade. I was to dig the heavy ground, she to plant seedlings in my wake.

'I saw you had problems sleeping last night,' began Jen, 'you were crying in your sleep.'

I kept my head down concentrating on digging. I fought panic, for this was dangerous territory for me, no one could know my terrors. If they surfaced I would drown. I did not trust myself with this spade, one swipe…

I replied in the speech of a long forgotten and troubled teenager. 'So what, we all have bad nights what with what we've been going through, and what about you, what's the story of your hand then?'

Jen did not pause in her planting, her prosthetic hand sweeping away the dirt while the other gently put the plants in, covering them almost tenderly.

She started in an absent-minded way and to my surprise said she had been born in London. What surprised me was that she said she went to school in Croydon, and that's where I was found. Funny to think we could have gone to the same school but for our dysfunctional families. What was odd was that when her parents split, her father came back one night and kidnapped the kids, her and her two brothers, shoved in a car just like that, on a ferry and wound up in a war zone. Another year later they told her that her dad had killed her mum that night.

I looked at Jen, she was working robotically, her eyes on the ground, never looking at me. We continued in silence for some time. She stood up and stretched, lifting her arms to the sky, then wrapping them around her like a child does on a cold day. But there was worse to come. Words flowed from Jen, perhaps she had never really spoken about those times.

'I was given to an elderly couple I was told they were my grandparents, but I never really believed that. The night before my father and the boys left, the younger one, Kevin, held me and cried, sobbed more like. He did not want to fight. He was actually dragged out of the door at dawn and that was the last I saw of them. Of course, I didn't know that at the time, I just waited for Kevin to come back.'

I was shocked, I had seen kids separated then they came into care, when a foster family could not take more than one child or even worse when adopters only wanted one and would reject the others.

'Oh Jen how did you cope,' I asked gently and of course that little girl cried for her brothers and was terrified when the bombs got closer and closer.

'That couple were grasping, cunning, evil I was their servant, got some schooling from a women's volunteer group though. There was one woman and she and I would talk secretly in English. All I can say was I survived.'

I noticed the other workers looking towards us. "We got to keep going. Get back to the trench Jen,' for a time we worked on silently, me trying to imagine the horrors Jen had encountered and no doubt Jen trying to forget.

'And then?' I asked, hesitantly.

'And then…' a moment of silence, 'you want to know, so here it is. It took them years to tell me Kevin had been killed within a week of leaving me. I could never find out exactly how, when or where, but I am sure he was killed by my father ashamed of a weeping son. I heard the old bastard lived longer than his eldest child.

Then when news came that he had eventually been blown up, I planned to escape. They were losing the war anyway, that ragtag and bobtail lot, failures and misfits from around the world. I was glad the foreign troops had come to our area. But, since there was no money coming in for me I was put up for sale at 14 years old.'

'And were you sold?' I asked quietly.

'Not so you would notice,' she replied enigmatically.

'I thought I would get away in all the chaos, so I took that old couple's gold horde. They had antique rings, bracelets, ugly but valuable. But being young and stupid I did not have a plan where to go once I left the village, so within days I was caught, taken to town. They cut my hand off. Me! A fourteen year old girl! It was roughly bandaged so I didn't bleed to death and then thrown out.'

'My god almighty, that's dreadful,' I looked at her in horror, but she gave a wry grin.

'Well I was saved you might say by a British medical orderly who found me lying in the road. He smuggled me into the camp and treated the wounds. He even got me flown to England as a war casualty, false papers, a home for heroes etc. So, I finished up with a great false hand.'

'But the payment, did he want paying, there is always a price?' I asked.

'Of course. He was not only older than me but needed cover for his drugs running business, developed from his years in the army, suppliers in every country I think. He treated me well, lovely house, beautiful exotic wife, but I was the go-between. See, I spoke the languages of most of the suppliers, so some advantage of being in the war zone with the kids coming from everywhere. And I could learn others languages easily, every cloud as they say.'

She paused again, 'you know I am beginning to understand what the villagers are saying, my goodness what a mix it is.'

I thought long and hard before I asked,

'And did you help to end his days when *The Syndicate* sank?'

'Best you do not dwell on that too much my friend,' and I silently agreed. There are times when ignorance it truly bliss.

EIGHTEEN
H

This regime of work continued for another four days. We all developed bonds with the villagers. Paul, Robin and Frank became extremely fit and had already formed teams for football, rugby, cricket finding not only the boys but all the people left in the village joined in. First teams were drawn up on gender, then age and finally ability. Paul who seemed to have some games training found some of the older women were fantastic out fielders in cricket.

But it was Nigel, who one night drew our attention to something we had seen daily, not really taken much notice of. There were no sick people among the villagers.

The next morning we undertook a surreptitious survey and compared results. Nigel and Robin, both schoolteachers at one time or another, said all the kids had great teeth and, except for a few cuts and bruises, we were very healthy. The babies too were bonny, looked after the energetic grannies because the mothers were in the plantation working. Nigel said the same was true of the men, although the leaders were large, they were not obese and the others were lean and fit. We pondered on this for a time. Was it diet? Everything we ate was very fresh for there were no fridges. Was it a diet strong in fish, with the odd bit of chicken or pork for special occasions? Was it that the island was free from diseases, such as measles and if so, were the islanders in danger of a virus that we might have brought in? Then Audrey began to panic and suggested there might be some culling of the sick and elderly so that they did not use up resources, but this was dismissed.

Then Jen offered, 'there are women in early pregnancy, and there are babies, but there are no new-borns and no women in late pregnancy, so where are they?'

On the fifth day in Orrible, the weather changed. We had become reluctantly used to the crashing waves on the cliffs at the entrance of our sheltered have To my astonishment the sea was now quiet, so quiet in fact that the silence woke us up early.

As we emerged from our long house, we noticed everyone climbing the cliffs and moving towards the headland. We followed up the precipitous path. It was the first time I had climbed up there.

Our walk to the end was terrifying, the headland was narrow, no more than 3 metres wide at most, with a sheer drop on both sides to the evil black rocks below. There was silence as everyone looked out to sea, now and again pointing at a movement in the waves. Nigel was sure there was a passing school of whales, Robin saw seals or sea lions exploring the rocks below for shelter. The warm breezes lulled us into a blissful rest, we sat on the rocks almost sunbathing, when there was a shout from the youngsters, pointing and then the most wonderful singing from everyone.

We leapt up and straining our eyes, we could see first some movement on the waves, then approaching canoes. The singing carried over the waves and then we heard a responding call, at which the villagers turned and sped back down the cliffs to the village, some of the young men dived into the sea to swim alongside the canoes as they came into the inlet, as we clambered cautiously down to the beach.

There were three canoes and to my surprise they contained not just the missing men from Linda, but also Adnan and two young women holding new born babies.

The canoes were unloaded. One had all the provisions salvaged from the *Syndicate*. There was tinned and packet food, dried milk, and catering packs of instant coffee, tea bags and cans of Australian beer.

In the scramble to help although help may not have been the correct word, I noticed how we, the passengers grabbed the things we most missed. It revealed much about our priorities.

Melanie dived in and grabbed packets of soap, Rita plucked industrial containers of hand crème from the depths of one canoe. It made me realise that these two women, who had formed a very close friendship, had so missed essential cosmetics, which had made them feel beautiful and young, though not always achieving that dream.

Crates of beer and bottles of spirits were carried away by singing islanders very much helped by Frank and Nigel. However, it was Jen who quietly, without any fuss or drama, picked up all the First Aid boxes and medical equipment still safely in their cartons.

As emptying the canoes was nearly completed, I found a page of a newspaper stuffed under a seat, damp but readable. It had last week's date on it.

So, the canoes had called in somewhere else during the storm, somewhere with communications and a clinic at the very least.

There was no working in the fields that day. There were preparations for a huge party. Much to Audrey's annoyance, one of her favourite pigs was killed for the feast. That will teach her to have favourites and give it titbits all the time so it grew fatter than the others. The two babies were passed around, inspected and given a quick cuddle by everyone. Susie had one young man beside her all evening, the proud father I assumed. In the light of the fire songs were sung and dancing was frantic and joyful. We joined in, Jen was amazing singing and dancing, Nigel sang a sea shanty, Dilys and Rita sang old Beatles numbers but in the dying chords of 'Hey Jude' I felt lonely and wondered how Stephen, that lovely man in Eastbourne was doing and if he ever thought of me.

The next day we were told to rest, though rest was only a comparative term. The supplies were first sorted out again and packed into the huts. I realised there was no one ownership of anything. Our attempts to hold onto items were met with firm resistance. Melanie and Rita were persuaded to hand back their creams lotions and potions, Nigel's bed was searched, successfully for the tins of beer and I reluctantly gave up a packet of instant coffee. Everything on the island was shared there was no fighting over possessions. Was this the secret to such a successful and healthy community?

That morning there was another example. It was decided to make a new waterproof shelter. The boys went out to cut down saplings and others shimmied up trees to cut the large fronds from the palm trees. The roof was thatched, the wall made of brush and woven rattan, beautiful and all created from sustainable materials. We could not do much except watch and learn from this highly co-operative and good-humoured work. Then we were called in to help sort out everything and load them into the shelter. Jen took charge and the islanders left it to her, recognising she could read the labels.

Vince had continued, unnoticed, his duties as Komodo watcher. He continually wandered over the trees and bushes, peering into the undergrowth, looking up trees. Occasionally I could hear him clapping and the odd shout of 'hello my girls.' In the afternoon, I followed him.

'What are you doing Vince?' I asked.

As he turned towards me I noticed he had changed over these last few days.

'Just checking my girls are OK, they were very hungry yesterday, but I think they snaffled that old cockerel,' he grinned. Then becoming serious, 'I just love this place. It is so beautiful, so quiet. Look at the birds up there, magnificent soaring on the thermals.'

I must say his words made me look again and what I had previously taken to be rather battered vultures, but he was right they did have a magnificence about them.

He took my hand and reluctantly I followed, he pointed out flowers, orchids for sure but I had no idea of the others. He pointed at the little birds just above his head.

'Watch out for that one,' I warned him, 'he's a poisonous bastard.'

Vincent laughed, 'I know the boys told me, but he means no harm.'

He could see me looking at him and without turning his head he said,

'Here I have been truly happy. I walk around these paths and see plants and wildlife I could never even begin to imagine.'

There was a rustling nearby. I nervously looked around. A snake slithered across the path, but in silence we could hear movement and Vince continued, unhurried,.

'Hey Matilda,' he ordered, 'you know better than to come here so bugger off.' The rustling sound diminished as a large creature departed. "

'That was Matilda, the largest of the Komodos, the queen in fact. I have named them all. Lovely intelligent creatures, understand every word.'

Our walk had taken us down to the little beach, so very different from that of Linda, no long sands, just a stony bit of land that met the sea.

'Good grief will you look at that!' Vince gasped in wonder.

Just above the water line, two young Komodo dragons were tossing, chasing, throwing a cardboard carton.

'My god, they're playing, look you have got to be a witness!'

Although I have learnt to tolerate the dragons, I was extremely frightened of them, with their cold and calculating stare, their hideous flicking of tongues.

'Why? What's this all about?'

Vince groaned, 'the one time I need a camera, a phone anything to record this and here I am just with you. No offence,' he quickly added, 'but it has been claimed that dragons, young dragons do play, but it has only been recorded once in a zoo and then the dragon was on his own. This is fun co-operative play.'

I looked again at these two creatures, and yes in a reptilian way perhaps they were having fun. We all learn in strange ways.

I later walked back alone reflecting on the change in this lonely man from Worthing and the change is his life releasing him from the prison of his life on the south coast in England to the wild freedom the island offered.

The evening was very quiet compared to our partying of the night before. But the silence had a secretive quality, we noticed the looks from the islanders had changed. We could hear, but except for a few words not understand what was going on. They were in quiet discussions with the returning rowers from the canoes. Only Adnan were included but not our former waiter Paul who was firmly pushed out. I could not swear to it but I was sure he said,

'I know about the plan,'

He got another shove and one very hostile look driving him back to us, wringing his hands and starting to moan. There was not hostility I was sure, but the looks of all the islanders, had changed from mild curiosity to something more challenging.

The morning found Audrey standing in the village square, her arms outstretched making weird noises. Every now and again she broke into, *It is the age of Aquarius,* and *My sweet Lord,* proving she was a wannabe child of the 70s. Two dogs sat near her one taking up the sound with a howl, the other whimpering from time to time. The goats kept a safe distance under the trees and even the pigs observed her from beneath distant bushes.

Susie joined me looking on from a distance.

Wasup?' she asked,

'*Duuno,'* I replied pleased with my competence in the island patois. I walked down to Audrey.

'What's up my friend?' I asked gently.

'I am communing with the Mother Earth, I am talking to the

moon,' she replied. 'there is change coming, the moon last night had strange colours and now look, look at the sun. It is rising over there.'

She began to hum again, tunelessly, monotonously. I felt despair creeping over me. I had seen dementia start in many of old Harry's friends in Lopeham I could not cope with it here, facing all those growing needs and losing the person I had become quite fond of. And yet I turned to look at the rising sun. Audrey was right, it seemed to be lighting our dark little haven earlier than usual. The light was shining through a cleft in the cliffs. It is the equinox!

From behind us there was singing, chanting more like. From the trees the men came out with drums of hollowed wood, dressed and painted in white, feathers in their hair. Behind them the women waving fronds, waving garlands of flowers. They came down to the beach and stood in line where the rays shone through the fissure in the cliffs. They raised their hands to the skies, then lowered them down to touch the ground, all in unison. The drumbeats grew louder, the chanting stronger occasionally broken by a shout from one of the older men or a high pitched wail from the grandmothers. But as the sun reached the top of the cliff and exploded once again into the open sky, silence fell. Everyone dropped to their knees, including Audrey, who had joined the women's group with ease. Silence. Then with one groan, one fearful and one sad sound. Everyone rose and slowly gradually walked away to the tap of one lone drum, into the trees beyond the beach.

Audrey rejoined us. 'Something is going to happen. They were all waiting for today.'

NINETEEN
H

It was sometime later that morning that the ceremonies ended, the men returned to the bushes then re-emerged, nonchalantly, minus feathers. Did they imagine we did not recognised them in their regalia? We thought it more diplomatic to explore that question later.

Time was difficult to judge in those weeks, but I think it was about an hour later, when the shoe bag was dragged out and shoes were dispersed, and thrown at us. Most of the villagers did not seem to bother.

'I don't think we are heading back to Linda,' observed Nigel. Sure enough, nearly everyone assembled facing towards the path over the cliffs. There was to be no question, no resistance, we were to be in this march. Despite her pleas, Audrey was not allowed to remain behind. Only the very elderly men women and the very young children waved us off. Even the dogs who followed for a very short time dropped back to the safety of the village. Not a good omen I thought.

In fact, compared to our trek from Linda, this was well organised we were in the middle of the column with strict instructions to keep in line. That was a superfluous order, for as we started the climb, the evil drop on one side onto the crashing waves and rocks beneath and the jagged face of the cliff to our side.

We were headed north. Once or twice the track led us inland, giving us some respite from the winds blowing in from the ocean. On the first inland sortie, we were all pleased to find a safer path. We were soon disillusioned, the path did not take a straight line, but wandered around rocks jutting out from sandy soil, over soggy march where we had to take off footwear to prevent it being sucked off our feet. We had to leap the gullies, some fairly deep, where the water ran off the high grounds towards the cliffs and over to the sea. Only one had a makeshift bridge of narrow planks. This required confidence and balance and some help from outstretched hands to help us over. We stumbled through patches of thorny scrub. In the calm air of the inland stretch. News of our invasion of this area went around the entire population of island insects that fresh blood was on its way.

Susie and the women gathered some berries to spread on our

135

exposed skin and we were handed frond of grass to swish the offending bugs off. Nonetheless they regathered, swooped landed with precision on unguarded skin and took off before the leaves settled painfully on the victim. Our procession began to resemble one of those processions in Spain during Lent where sinners flagellate themselves to atone their previous wrongs. Melanie, always prone to drama even began to hum hymns and moaning that we were all sinners for surviving the shipwreck. Until a combination of shouts to 'shut up', from some and a timely reminder from Jen to Melanie that she had not stayed behind to save Joe, resulted in a welcome but uneasy silence.

The sun was reaching noon, when a shout from the front indicated we had reached to wherever we were going. We were puzzled. We had arrived at a desolate headland. Here, the winds whipped in from the sea. It was Frank who noticed it.

'The wind direction has changed, this is a northerly, what is happening?'

The villagers approached the end of the spur and began to descend. We paused before joining them. Catching our breath from the long struggle across the plateau we looked out to sea. It was alive with blossoms or fish swimming and darting their way through the waves. Reluctantly we were prodded, and hanging onto the cliff face we too followed them, down around steep corners and then to a large flat rock only some twenty metres above the waves.

Then we could see the horror before us as we beheld disaster and the anger of the villagers as they turned towards us.

TWENTY

Stephen awoke to the sound of chanting from somewhere in the neighbourhood. His house was in a pleasant but mundane, conventional street. A street, well more an avenue, where neighbours did not really know each other. The sound was not unpleasant, and Stephen's view of the world was a tolerant one. Nonetheless intrigued he peered from his bedroom window into the adjoining little gardens. There was a couple in the garden next door, just a little younger than himself, singing and lighting what he hoped were joss sticks.

The scent wafted up to his bedroom window and with a sigh he recalled that the lovely lady from Lopeham must now be on beaches, perhaps with the scent of blossoms or exploring hidden temples with the heavy scent of joss sticks from praying local villagers humbly beseeching the gods for a better life.

He left the house a little earlier than usual and for the first time encountered the couple on the avenue. He stopped them with a very polite 'good morning' and 'How nice to meet you' and then, receiving a friendly response, asked the key question., hesitantly, not wishing to offend, 'I heard you this morning, lovely sound you know, but why were you singing?'

The young man smiled, 'it is the equinox, days now change, the sun departs to leave us for the long winter nights. We must send the sun on its long journey with peace and be here to welcome the light back in the spring.'

The young woman said, 'I am so pleased you heard us. I saw you looking from your window. This is a time of change, we are entering a new cycle. We must find our spirit, our inner peace.'

With a promise to meet up at some time, the couple set off down the avenue. Stephen looked at them in wonder. Their conventional attire, suits, briefcases, smart haircuts belied this gentle approach to life. Stephen was energised by the encounter and with great good humour, bought his newspaper and went into town for an expensive cup of coffee his favourite café.

He opened the paper. Usual news of untruths being hidden and untruths being revealed. Did the Prime Minister say during that awful turmoil that he would be 'rather found dead in a ditch' or 'he would rather dine in Shoreditch?' the jury was out among journalists.

With a sigh, he turned the pages then found a report about a wing of an aircraft turning up in a most unexpected location in the Coral Sea. Attached to one wing was the remains of a large wooden crate in which there was a skeleton and evidence of some clothing and a pair of stout leather shoes.

'How very odd,' he mused. There were many reports of aircraft missing over the vast Pacific Ocean. Didn't Amelia Earhart go missing, though there are myths she actually landed on an island but was never discovered. The wing of the aircraft must have been very large and how did it get entangled with a crate. I suppose the little fish could get in and eat the body but not the sharks.

Must have been a good carpenter for the crate to last so long and the best of English made shoes too.' The article continued:

Experts have flown from Java to the site where the aircraft wing has been washed up. One team are to verify whether the wing is part of a missing flight. Air traffic in Perth Western Australia, lost communication one hour after take off. One hundred and twenty passengers and ten crew are declared missing.

The second team is to take DNA samples from the body in the crate. Local sources have said that fragments of remaining hair would indicate the body is European. Foul play is suspected.

Stephen turned the pages casually and resumed his coffee. He really liked this place. It was nearly full but silent as those 'working-from-home' worked on an assortment of IT equipment. How odd, they have escaped the office but still want company. He could not think of anything worse than working in isolation 'at home', with washing, ironing or even young children begged for attention.

He resolved to go into town and get himself the latest model of a Notebook, something he too could work in the quiet social area of a café. Perhaps the young couple were correct, this is the time for change. With determination, he rose from his place, thought about leaving the newspaper for others to read, but decided against. With a jaunty step he left the café and headed for town already thinking of the new progammes, the sites he could load and the films he could watch. To give him credit he did have one very fleeting thought about loading games, but with the same speed dismissed the idea.

Two hours later Stephen had not only bought a sleek, shiny and compact Notebook but had it loaded with programmes suggested by a dauntingly enthusiastic salesperson, who with hypnotic speed of the fingers as they raced across the keyboard, showed Stephen the additional programmes he wanted As he was about to leave the shop another customer pointed at Stephen's newspaper,

'Hey man,' he said gently, 'you don't want to be reading that old stuff, get online, find out what is really happening. No censorship there, mate. You can find the real stories.'

Stephen who thought he was pretty up to date given the bank had provided good IT training, was shaken.

This could be the opening of a new world he thought walking home, opening the door, plugging in the Notebook and finding it was true, a whole new world was about to open up.

First he searched an article about the missing aircraft and to his astonishment no less than two hundred sites flashed up. He looked at reputable newspaper links, then was drawn to blogs and posts, some outlandish, but he thought great fun. He had not realised how many aircraft go missing, especially over oceans. In his working lifetime over 50 airplanes were declared missing, no one knowing what happened to the passengers. He sat back and considered the information. It would not seem a total surprise that the odd wing of an aircraft would float in from time to time on shores, but why would one appear to be towing a crate with a skeleton? Being a man proud of his prowess in logical thinking, he considered that the plane must have contained the crate with the deceased person.

Half an hour later he dismissed that idea. From his extensive work with the elderly who on occasion died on cruises and the body flown home for burial, he knew that bodies had to be in lead lined containers and secured in the plane's hold. The idea of cruises led him to think of burial at sea, and he was aware that on occasion that could be a far more casual dismissal of a corpse. No ornate coffins but something that should sink rapidly and then disperse the contents back into the food chain. On a small ship they would not carry ornate coffins, something very simple at the very most. He thought the process very basic and yet in such harmony with the elements. Whoever, thought it was dust to dust at the end of life given the human body is 80 percent water or thereabouts, he mused, so water to water is a far more appropriate ending.

The thoughts stayed with him as he went to bed, and followed him through the night as yet again he returned to the thoughts of his lovely lady. She was on a small cruise ship. And now the growing concern for her safety began to build.

From: sfinanceservices
To: hgriffiths
Subject: News
Please excuse me for contacting you, but I would like to know how your trip is going? I hope you are having time to enjoy the beaches and the sunshine. The weather here is very poor, raining daily I regret. Regards, Stephen

---

From: hgriffiths
To: sfinanceservices
Subject: Re News
Hi Stephen,   Yes everything ☺ BTW Cap retn phone 2day. NN2R H

Stephen had to call next door for his young neighbours to translate.

Stephen thought he might go out to Lopeham again. From 6 am to nearly midday he dithered. What would he do, say, if she had returned? What would he do if she had not? As the early mists retreated, his mood improved. By midday the sun shone and the bright autumn day gave promise of good things to come. Abandoning his old raincoat he wore his new navy parka and rust coloured slacks recently purchased, threw a scarf around his neck and took off to the station.

Instead of his former cautious approach to the house, Stephen now strode confidently along the avenue. His heart nearly stopped when he saw the front door open, then returned to nearly normal when he saw a young woman just about to leave. He turned in the gate.

'Excuse me,' he began rather officiously for he was unaccountably nervous.

'Is the property owner at home?' and then noticing a startled gaze, continued, 'I am a friend, well a sort of friend,' and she being a sympathetic person replied,

'No she's not here, still away on holiday. I am her sort-of niece, my mum was her best friend and I am looking after the house.'

Stephen was both relieved and strangely happy.

'You must be Sally. Could I talk to you, I am a little disquieted.'

Inwardly Sally thought this was a strange approach, such a formal use of language, but then looking at him in his obviously new clothes took pity. 'Is this aunty's fancy man? She thought with a suppressed giggle. But then thought he would suit H.

'Look come in the house, we can't talk here.' Sally had spotted the ever vigilant Peter and Angela, peering through their sitting room window, both in matching jumpers, coffee mugs in hand.

Sally reopened the front door and led Stephen into the kitchen diner at the back of the house. It was bright and clean, the garden was small mainly patio, but well kept. Sally noticed him looking around.

'It's lovely isn't it?'

Stephen agreed.

'You cannot imagine how dismal this house was when Harry was alive, old skinflint, wouldn't spend a penny on anything that was not for his benefit; plenty of the best whisky for him and nothing for her.'

'I know,' offered Stephen, 'the minute he was carried out feet first, she got to work, a new kitchen, new bathroom, carpets, the place redecorated and even the garden relaid. Seemed she'd come into some money of her own.'

He told Sally the advice he had given and for a while they comfortably chatted about their shared friend. Eventually, Stephen said,

'I am pleased about the cruise, but I am rather concerned. I tried to keep in contact, but it seems all the passengers had to hand in their mobiles.'

'Yes I thought that odd, but then it was an eco tour and those guys are into mindfulness and well-being. So I suppose being detached from the internet might be OK,' agreed Sally but her words heavy with doubt.

'I have had two texts from her in all this time. The second one was strange, not like her.'

And for proof, Stephen got out his phone, 'Look at this, I had to go next door to my neighbours to get a translation. What do you think, I expect you are into all this language?'

'Stephen I am worried,' said Sally, 'you don't think anything drastic has happened, after all we would have heard if it had sunk or something…. Surely?' but the doubt was there, stronger now, leading to full scale panic.

'Come on,' said Stephen, 'lets go back to Eastbourne and contact the police or the authorities and report the ship missing.'

'Or,' began Sally, 'say we have an important message for a passenger.'

So they both rushed out of the house and down the avenue with purpose ignoring the surprised looks of Peter and the fact that Angela was reaching for the phone.

TWENTY ONE
H

The monster had shown up with artful cunning, for that is the way of successful monsters. First fragments, small pieces of a skeleton had arrived and the villagers noticed the gay colours, even brought strands back from the beach to decorate their houses. Did the monster recognise that this island would provide the safe haven which had been offered to humans and animals in the past? That we cannot know. One balmy night, with the moon majestically gliding over the phosphorous lights in the sea, one bag made its way to shore. At 2am the very same night, the space station swiftly progressed across the silent island, lighting the way for other bags, other strands to follow the first intrepid voyagers. As the sun rose in the clean blue sky, they gathered, collectively forming the behemoth that was there to stay.

The bay heaved as it gorged on dead fish, trapping dolphins in its tentacles, a writhing mass of squirming plastic bags and cartons and strings and ropes and fishing lines and nets which choked the life out of all living matter. As with all monsters the villagers first noticed an unpleasant whiff that grew and exploded into a disease ridden obnubilation covering the whole surface of the bay killing all that lay beneath it.

We all looked down with horror.

The entire bay was thick with plastic. It was entangled on the rocks, it was strewn high on the cliffs. Entire plastic bags bobbed around, pushed landward by the prevailing wind from the north. Some appeared to be bundled in repugnant blocks, 6 metres square, the ends fraying, stretching out like the tentacles of some mythological beast from the very depths of the ocean. It was an obscene island floating in from the sea, crashing into the once pristine cliffs. Like the monster Caliban its progress moved with the silent rage of its condition.

The horrific mass stretched out the length of the inlet. More was coming in, but the currents must have secured this abominable, moving island into the bay.

We could only look, paralysed by shock. I didn't suppose there was any of us among the passengers who were not aware of the impact of plastic on the environment.

I was sure all of us would have tried to bring their own bags to the supermarkets and to be conscientious as possible about recycling. But at that time not one of us had followed up what actually happens in recycling, though aware of plastic being dumped at sea. After all, there were no instances as far as we knew, of rotting plastic islands washing up around Eastbourne.

Melanie broke out of her trance and tried to get back to the path up the cliff, retching as she went. Audrey tried to follow, wailing with more intent and strength of purpose than usual. Nigel and Jen stood stoically on the edge of the rocks looking down at the seething mass, alive, malignant, deadly.

Jen said, 'we can see stuff coming in from the headland, so why isn't it building up even higher?'

I was so stunned I couldn't think of a reply.

'Perhaps because everything is being shredded on the rocks,' suggested Robin hesitantly, 'I saw a TV programme about micro plastics in the ocean.'

More David Attenborough I thought, his wisdom follows us around like a benevolent deity.

It was Vince who stood the nearest looking down.

'It's moving, the mass is moving, it's on a whirlpool.'

We looked down again. He was right, the mass was moving in a deadly spiral, the centre some 80 metres from where we stood. I saw a football bobbing along, avoiding the centre, rising up then fall back into the mass.

Vince pointed, 'look a whole load of trainers,' and in among the mass several pairs of trainers swirled and, reaching the centre, gently disappeared.

Rita screamed, 'my god there is someone trapped!'

A hand bobbed up a lubricious gesture, two fingers in that well-known gesture of utter contempt. We searched for any sign of a body, then Robin said, 'rubber gloves, they're rubber bloody gloves!' and as if on cue the hand disappeared sucked into the seething maelstrom.

But there were bodies in the mass for the stench was unimaginable. Dead and dying fish and dolphins were trapped. Solitary birds dived in to peck at the corpses only themselves to become trapped.

Jen turned to Susie, in words and gestures asked, 'how long has this been here?' Susie pointed to the skies and counted 24, more gestures. Jen was puzzled.

'She means 24 moons,' yelled Audrey.

So this plastic has been coming in for two years at least.

Robin said, 'but where is it going, how big are the underground caves?'

And as if to answer the distant volcano gave a huge belch. We turned to see that even from our location, hot ash erupting from the volcano and dense black smoke that soared up to hit the white clouds. A murmur of rage came from the villagers. Bosai stepped forward looking more menacing than ever before.

'You clean up, You hostages.'

As the village group and our band of passengers made a return across the bleak plateau to Orrible. We moved slowly, more or less in silence, broken by Melanie being sick, once actually on the narrow pathway between rocks at which point she got a cuff across the ear from Susie. Audrey tried a humming sound but was told to shut up by Jen. We were shocked, miserable and to be honest, guilty.

Looking back I am not sure which had the most impact on me the plastic or the more immediate problem that we were now hostages. With hindsight, I could see that the care the villagers took to make sure we were well and cared for had stretched beyond normal hospitality. I would not have gone along with Audrey's suspicions that they were fattening us for some cannabalistic feast, but though we had been given tasks and encouraged to help not one of us had to do anything beyond their physical capabilities. So we were to be traded for something. But the question was to whom and for what.

I walked back alongside Jen. I could see her opening and closing her prosthetic hand. I could see a purpose in her stride.

'No bastard is going to capture me without a fight,' she hissed, the trauma of her childhood was re-emerging. I tried to reassure her. The villagers had been kind, other than the first encounter with Bosai, none of us had been physically attacked.

'Play along with them,' I advised, 'let's wait and see what's going to happen.'

Nonetheless, we were worried about the future. This was a definite change in how we had regarded the island. The idyll of a little paradise was slowly slipping away. All except Robin.

Unconcerned as to his possible fate as a hostage, Robin walked head down, not noticing the rocks over which he had stumbled just a few hours ago. He did not look at the plants nor the views that had captured him on the way to the cove. He ignored any remarks that passed his way. He was deep in thought, trying to remember what he had ever learnt, possibly through TV documentaries and the distant lessons in geography at school so many years ago.

He muttered, barely audible, 'the island must be on the 'Ring of Fire,' that circle of active volcanoes that stretched around the Pacific. That's where we've landed,' and later, 'right in the pathway of volcanic activity, islands springing up from nowhere, others being blasted to smithereens and collapsing under the waves. This must be a fairly recently formed island.'

He developed a monologue, in short he wondered if that was why *The Syndicate* had been shipwrecked. Perhaps the island did not appear on sea charts. He had read they were often not up to date. The island was very small and often obscured by cloud or emissions from the volcano so not observable from passing satellites unless they were doing a highly specific search, and what would trigger that? The island was off the usual shipping lanes, otherwise the plastic would have been spotted. It would seem the currents had collected all the plastic negligently dumped in the sea, from rivers, shores, and ships and directed it all into the bay where it was trapped.

He stop and then asked me 'but even then, why is there not a mountain of the stuff. The whirlpool is sucking the plastic down, but to where and what happens to it?'

TWENTY TWO
H

It was dark when we arrived back in the village. We all gathered together. Audrey continued to whimper. She wandered off in the gloom towards the pigpens where we could hear her gently singing to her favourites joined in by their gentle grunts.

Paul went outside and kicked a ball against a tree but for once was not joined by any of the village kids. I could see Adnan sitting close by one of the young women of the village deep in conversation.

In our communal hut, I knew none of us could sleep, though we were all exhausted from the long trek. We had taken up a strange relationship. I think we were all fairly damaged creatures that were washed up on this island. Unlike our television counterparts, we were not driven by sexual desires. Except for the lads from the crew, none of us were particularly young, and although I had at first thought Melanie at least would find comfort in the arms of one of the men, the idea must have palled over the intervening weeks. With the exception of Frank, the men muttered and passed the odd comments about 'the wife' and 'didn't get up to much in recent years,' which seemed to me that with sadness and some nostalgia their sex lives had diminished if not disappeared.

Our diet and work schedule did not help revive our libido. Everything was hard for us. Not only did we have the work routine, but we found that without the appliances we were used to, washing ourselves and our clothes in cold water, lighting and keeping fires going, helping preparing food was exhausting. We only stopped when we were unwell. But now what we had thought of generous nursing, applications of balms for cuts, herbal brews for fevers, were in fact that the village was focused on keeping us alive and well.

That night, in the dark, Frank began to speak. Unusual for him to speak without a question first being posed. He was normally a quiet, reticent man. He began, softly at first, 'I wonder what happened to Rosa. Do you remember her, such a live wire, such fun?'

It was not a question, no one answered in the dark, sensing Frank would continue anyway. While he sighed deeply I tried to remember her. She seemed a lot younger than Frank, beautiful I

147

think, always with long black hair, which she tossed around or moved with her hands constantly.

He continued, 'I met her on a cruise. The wife, my first wife to be accurate wanted to get away. I wasn't that keen to be stuck on a ship for weeks with god knows whom.'

He didn't sense the irony that while we were not stuck on a cruise liner we were stuck on an island that was rapidly losing its charm.

'I remember that year. I had taken early retirement. Found myself at a loose end. Funny, I had looked forward to giving up work, the ghastly commuting and always being passed over for some whippersnapper.'

'Too right mate,' a murmur of sympathy from Robin, 'been through that myself.' Frank did not seem to hear and went on,

'Things were tough at home, god, teenage girls! If they weren't arguing between themselves, they were arguing with me. And the wife, she always took their part. And they had changed, where had my sweet little bundles gone, how did they become such harridans?'

He was silent for a while. I could feel if not see Rita nodding, and a quiet mutter of 'they grow up, that's the problem.'

Frank started again,

'She thought that getting away would solve our problems. I agreed to the cruise, and that is when I met Rosa.'

Jen grunted, 'well at least you both survived that one,' which, though to the point, was rather cruel.

Then there was silence. An unusual silence. The external night was full of sound, the wind in the trees, animal cries, odd bird calls, a strangulated scream, another predator though at this time of night it was unlikely that the Komodos had felled another victim; and the usual silence from within our hut littered with people turning, sighing, getting up and popping outside. No this was true silence for we were all awaiting Frank's confession.

'I couldn't get Rosa out of my mind, she haunted me,' Frank began.

Jen grunted, 'see all the woman's fault again, give me strength!'

Frank was undeterred,

'I used to dream of us together, a bright new future, and I searched for her at the end of the cruise and found her living in London. She said she was unhappy. I just thought we would talk, have some fun, but things ran out of control. And one day I just walked out, left the wife, the girls. New life you know?'

The silence from us indicated we did not know. We waited.

'At first it was just that, fun, but then it became so tiring. Non stop, out in the evenings. Parties with some odd people. Went to a nightclub for the first time. She demanded attention you know bed-wise', he groaned. 'All the time.'

'Well why not?' muttered Dilys, but was told to shut up.

'It must have been about six years after I left the wife for Rosa. One Saturday, Rosa was out, and there was a knock at the door. When I opened it, opened it,' he repeated with a sob, 'there was the most beautiful young woman with a lovely little toddler in her arms.'

'Look William,' she said to this beautiful child, 'this is your bastard grandfather. Thought you would like to see him once and let me tell you, neither of you will ever see each other again.'

Frank wailed, 'then she turned, my lovely daughter, and walked away towards a car, I ran after her. Where do you live? I didn't know you had a child. Why didn't your mum tell me?'

She turned and snarled at me like a wild cat,

'she didn't tell you because she's dead. You never bothered to see her, find out about us.'

She put the child in the car, it seemed he looked at me with the same hostility as his mother.

'You know,' Frank sighed, 'when I was with my wife and the girls I never used to dream of them, but now every night they come to me. Sometimes I am in my garden shed in the old house and they are outside. Sometimes I try to get to them, but my legs won't move.'

Silence, then Jen spoke

'And do you now dream of Rosa?'

One word cut through the night. 'Never.'

TWENTY THREE
H

Frank's revelation had disturbed us all. We stumbled out into the dawn, the light unusually misty and sombre. We all had our own thoughts about cruelties we had inflicted on others or thoughtless actions that had caused hurt. We could not meet each other's eyes, fearful we would burst into some confession or, even worse, hear one from someone else. Only Audrey seemed impervious to the atmosphere chatting benignly and happily to the pigs, while Vince gave her a hand rebuilding one of the stockades.

We did not have the strict work routine that had been part of the first days at Orrible, so we sat around, shocked, wondering about our future which did not look too good. It must have been mid-morning when we noticed Robin was missing. I think it was Frank who casually noticed he was not around. We did not move just glanced around. Vince ever mindful of the dragons, walked over to the bushes, around the back of the huts, asked Audrey, who stopped a wobbly yoga poise to the obvious admiration of the pigs, to say she had not seen him.

'He'll be back for the midday meal,' said Paul, ever the vigilant waiter. 'Never known Robin to miss food.'

But midday came and food was eaten and midday went and still no Robin.

Susie noticed us first as she walked into the village with some children. Paul had gone out to the plantations, Frank had started up the path to the inlet and the rest of us peered into huts pens stockades. '*Wasup?*' she queried. We hesitated remembering that Frank had been treated roughly when he tried to swim to the wreck. Like small children we attempted to look as if nothing had happened of any concern. Audrey started that awful humming, Nigel stared at stones by his feet, I attempted to look interested in a passing bird. It was of no use, Susie was a true village woman, well used to counting children, pigs, dogs, chickens and the menfolk. Nothing escaped her roll call. Nanoseconds later she said 'Robin!' then dashed into her hut, and gave a yell. We could see the precious shoes and sandals strewn inside. Robin had got some shoes and that meant he was intending to go far.

Shouts, cries, bad attempts to use a battered conch shell eventually brought everyone to the centre of the village.

Bosai lined us up, a now rather pathetic group of pale faced older hostages. He marched back and forth, with very effective body language and gestures, which indicated we were in deep trouble. Dilys attempted to say we did not know where Robin had gone and got a shove and a nasty glare in return. Rita started to snivel, joined unexpectedly by Paul.

'I am only a waiter, I don't know these people,' he said disloyally, and then shut up receiving similar mutinous glares from us and a shove from Jen.

This attracted the attention of Bosai who I assume had not recovered from her rejection of his early advance. He stepped up right in front of her, stuck his face millimeteres from her and yelled 'Robin!' He waited, apparently pleased with himself at this show of force, but then shocked as Jen did not flinch more move back, but yelled, 'Dunno!'

The villagers looked on with interest. I could see Susie was concerned that such a challenge to Bosai might end badly, but then Jan said more quietly, 'Dunno' and took his hand. 'Lets go.' and with gestures, 'lets look.' Bosai suddenly smiled, stood back and started to give orders. Search parties were organised and each one of us assigned a group. It made sense, if they left us all in the village alone, we too might scarper.

One group was directed back to Linda. They had strict instructions to look for any remains from an attack by the komodo dragons. Vince wanted to go with that group was punched back. Another, thankfully not including me, was directed to go down onto the narrow beaches and along the shoreline rocks. Gestures indicated that he may have fallen from the cliffs, intentionally or accidentally we wondered. To his horror Paul was selected for that group but somewhat comforted that Jen would be at his side, with it seemed, Bosai at her side. She was undaunted by a scramble down by the churning seas. In fact, she made some comment about checking out the bays and inlets for a possible holiday centre.

Vince and I were given shoes, not a good start. I knew somehow it would fall to us. We were to retrace our way back to the plastic hellhole. Worse, our accompanying villagers were making bundles of food, rolling up the bamboo mats. It looked like we would be out overnight.

As we started the steep climb out of the village, we could hear the other parties calling out Robin's name. Responses came from the birds and the occasional bark of a dog. I could hardly bring myself to look down from the narrow paths that hugged the cliff edge. The wind seemed stronger than on our first trip, would Robin have fallen and if so would we actually ever see him before the waves dragged his body out to sea?

We crossed the barren plateaus slowly. We spread out to see if Robin had fallen into the crevasses and mires that crossed the bleak terrain.

After three hours the sun began its dramatic descent, now unnoticed, except that the mats were laid out in the shelter of some rocks. A small fire lit, food distributed and as we lay down, chilled miserable and scared, I saw one young man awake. He looked at me and smiled, waved a stick and said, 'Dragon, snake, spider', so he was our night guard. Through the night, the guard was changed, the fire kept up, and only once did I hear the shout of '*Buggeroff*' and a stone thrown.

Morning and we continued. We did not shout. The bleak winds blowing over the plateau would have carried our voices away. But to be honest the stench from inlet, the plastic, the rotting corpses was enough to stop us breathing deeply. We put whatever cloth we had over our mouths and noses. This time we knew what to expect and I think that made the horror even worse.

We searched around the headland and moved further on from the point we had returned on our first trip. Vents from the volcano spewed sulphurous fumes. For the first time, I noticed pools of boiling water, but around the pools insect life was teeming. I spotted one very small lizard approaching a pool perhaps to catch and feed on this extraordinary life. Overhead a bird I had never seen in any other part of the island hovered, perhaps our lizard hunter was itself in danger. Vince was entranced. He burbled with excitement. After several verbal explosions from him like,

'Look! Wow! OMG! (and, I tell the truth) gosh!' was told to keep quiet and listen.

We must have been searching for several hours, when suddenly I caught sight of a body lying on the rocks on the edge of a chasm. It was Robin. Steam or smoke billowed up around the rocks, he must be overcome, poisoned by their toxic fumes. I shouted at to the others and pointed. My heart sank. Was this the first death among our group who had hung on so tenaciously to life through all the drama of the shipwreck, the loss of friends and partners?

PART FOUR

In the unlikely setting of the sedate town of Eastbourne the true danger of going on a cruise is realised, and among the cacophony of explosions and fireworks, a plan is devised to launch a rescue mission; the survivors slowly adjust to life on the island and despite no further unexpected deaths, all feel homesick; in Lopeham deep suspicions lie and Stephen meets some very unusual people.

ONE

Stephen and Sally returned from Lopeham and went straight to the Eastbourne police station. The initial interest of the local police waned to minus zero when they had to admit the ship had not disappeared within the coastal reaches of Eastbourne, or the Channel or even the far flung European waters, but somewhere, as the police receptionist said, 'oh somewhere out east then?' The officer advised the dejected pair just to Google missing ships.

They met up later in Stephen's now favourite café, he with his new Notebook. The first article they opened on missing ships had the discouraging sentence:

Every year more than two dozen large ships sink or go missing taking their crew with them.
Last year over three thousand 3,112 containers fell overboard at a cost of $50,000 per box. Most were lost in the Pacific Ocean.

Sally gasped in horror but a horror based on local knowledge. Accidents were caused by collision, overcrowding or catching fire. Anyone living on the south coast knew of the local small trawlers that were practically mown down by the huge commercial trawlers who ploughed the seabed and all life therein and thereon, often with no obvious personnel on the bridge or lookout.

'Surely SOS messages would have been sent,' she said. 'There must be some record. When are they due back to Australia? Perhaps they are not over due.' She added without much conviction.

Stephen was now worried. He had after all tried to trace the stories of the missing airplane and no distress messages were sent or picked up, and only indefinite rumours of plane wings appearing lent credence that a plane had crashed in the ocean and not been hijacked to a remote destination in Central Asia.

They trawled through lists of reported missing ships, but *The Syndicate* did not appear. They searched for travel agents that booked places on eco cruises, but disturbingly could not find any reference to the cruise. Sally was sure information had been deleted, finding a single reference left on the web from over 18 months ago.

Stephen, provoked by sleepless nights and nagging worries,

informed Sally quite formally that he would get to work on the missing vessel and they would meet again.

Mid October and the annual primeval stirrings in rural Sussex began to emerge. In fields throughout the county, towers of wooden crates and anything inflammable began to reach for the skies, every evening lorries, trailers even family cars unloaded anything inflammable.

In the houses the last of the costumes were sewn, mended, expanded to meet middle-aged paunches, or cut down for young children.

In sheds and barns, in deadly secrecy, the finishing touches to the effigies, politicians, parking meters, local demons (once it was a village shopkeeper) and of course Pope Alexander VI the all-time baddie. And in even more secrecy in sites only known to the inner brethren, stockpiles of fireworks were kept.

These were the preparations for bonfire. Barcombe, Crowborough, Mayfield, Little Horsted, Wivelsfield Green, Rotherfield, Rye, Uckfield, all towns and villages of such gentle names that belied the intensity of feelings expressed in the fires. Torchlit parades, and by torches that means posts of burning cloth bound with tar, were carried through the dark lanes to the sites.

The village events started at the end of October and continued through to the second week of November. Each evening was all finished off with fireworks, flares screaming up to the night sky, bangers rattling windows, people walking back to the pub and then perhaps too much beer downed

In the early days the skills of firework making were developed locally. It was said that this art form originated and developed in Tudor times. First Henry VIII was forced to employ an Italian demolition expert to blow up Lewes Priory during the Reformation, then his daughter Elizabeth entrenched the tradition to resolve a problem.

Huge amounts of gunpowder had been sent to Lewes in the event of the predicted fight on the Sussex coast against the Armada. The gunpowder was stored, it is said, where the grim Lewes Prison stands today. When the threat of the Armada had diminished, wise councillors thought Lewes too rebellious a town to hold such an arsenal and safe transport back to London could not be guaranteed. Orders went out for the gunpowder to be taken just a short distance to the top of Mount Harry and blown up for the entertainment of the local people. And the local people, thinking of the old Saxon Fire festivals agreed this was such a good idea, that, in one form or another, the good townspeople continued to blow up things.

Stephen was well used to the cacophony of bangs, the night sky filled with strange lights over the autumn nights. He sat alone in his flat listening, looking out the window at the flashes illuminating the darkness and thinking. His campaign to start a new life had faltered. He mastered the new computer system, had installed apps, found more news sites and once wandered into the unsavoury world of internet chat. But still he was uneasy and more to the point was lonely. Unusually for him, a man of habit and self-discipline he could not sleep. His mind was racing in time with the passing days and though just in his thirties, he could feel his life draining from him, the future was dark, cold and empty.

There was a moment of light. Charles, his former golf partner had invited him to Lewes for November 5th. Charles was a decent chap and somewhat ashamed at his outburst at Stephen, mollified by the claim for damages against the golf club for the spectacular shot of Stephen's, onto the greenhouse below the cliff had not been successful.

Charles' invitation was quite specific.

'Come at midday and do stay the night, all hell on public transport and the town will be closed to traffic. We can have a pub lunch then wander in to see the procession. We can watch the fireworks from our house.'

Stephen took the train, arriving at 12 o'clock. It was the first time he had been in the town for November 5th. He was astonished, in fact disquieted, to pass so many boarded up shop windows, to hear the occasional small banger being let off and to experience a general air of excitement. Schools were closing early to allow for the infamous school run before the traffic was stopped. Children and young people were gathering in the doorways, plans being made for meeting later on.

Charles offered a short walk to a country pub, and walking in the fresh autumn afternoon, Stephen found himself unburdening his worries about *The Syndicate*. There's something about speaking on topics not normally approached, while walking looking around and rarely at a companion's face. Outwardly Charles appeared sympathetic, years of working in minor posts in the diplomatic service, but inwardly was derisive.

'How could cautious Stephen get enmeshed in this conspiracy, god he'll be on about the Twin Towers,' thought Charles with an inward groan.

'Let me think on it,' he promised.

Stephen was exhausted from watching the parade of thousands, dressed bizarrely as Tudors, Native Americans, and Zulus, all in random order and intermingled with bands of varying musicality, bugles, drums, glockenspiels banging out 'Sussex by the Sea'. Enormous effigies were dragged through the streets, a close resemblance to several politicians national and international who incurred the displeasure of many. Their fate to be blown up with great glee later in the night. The procession from the Cliffe of the Vikings, with their burning torches, hundreds of people or more, sinister in dress and marching with precision took a different route as was their custom. They began in the old Saxon part of the town and entered what had been the Norman part. Old traditions linger long. Bangers and firecrackers let off, people choking the streets and all with laughter and great good humour.

Crowds began to disperse to the bonfire sites, youths slugged alcohol from an assortment of containers, young girls, giggling in safe groups, parents sitting at home worried while others lost their virginity, boys, girls usually, although a surprised and willing more adult member of the community may have found themselves joyfully finding love among the bushes, in the shadows of the fires. All combined to leave Stephen at more of a loss, observing such primitive excitement with such little aggression. 'How do they do it?' he wondered.

Later and back at Charles' house there was no let up. The friends could see the bonfires were lit at various high points, plus on by the river and the fireworks began. The night sizzled with bright lights, the Downs rebounded the enormous explosions. Stephen, with a comforting and large whiskey in hand, observed,

'If there were an invasion tonight, the Red Army making a surprise start to a war no one in this town would take any notice or even remark that the American strategy of Fear and Awe would have any impact.'

Charles, well used to the traditions of the 5th muttered agreement, and just as one spectacular rocket reached for the heavens, said to Stephen

'Been thinking old chap, know a fellow, he's unshipping insurance, might be able to trace what has happened to your ship.'

But unspoken Charles considered that he might contact a former colleague who had moved to Cheltenham and was rumoured to have contacts at the very least with security, government not commercial as he had pointed out to his sceptical wife. After all a missing ship might have terrorist connections, been carrying arms, or drugs. Yes, a quiet word, no need to worry Stephen further.

TWO
H

We raced across the sharp rocks. I could not speak, could not shout, a combination of dread and reluctance to breathe in the noxious fumes. Our two village lads got there first and in a new approach to First Aid techniques gave the body a sharp kick. A hand lifted, a head turned, it was a very cross Robin then being pulled to his feet.

I caught up with the others unsure whether to hug the escapee or add to the punches now given by Vince.

'What were you doing? There's no need to end your life, it's a sin, we'll get rescued' a list spilled out from Vince, his counselling skills contrasted poorly to that used by the Samaritans as they gently talk people back from the cliff edge at Beachy Head.

'What the hell?' choked Robin, now, we thought safe in the hold of the strong young lads. 'Let me go, what are you doing?' as he was dragged away from the chasm, 'I was just trying to find out how the volcano works.'

'Are you completely mad?' shouted Vince, 'volcanos explode up from the centre of the earth, they spew hot rocks, they burn people alive, they cool down, new island, end of!'

It was, I recollected with some admiration, an excellent summary of major geological phenomenon on the birth and death of volcanos. Sadly, this exchange was terminated. A strong vine was tied around the still protesting Robin by the lads and to be honest I was too shattered to intervene.

We started the run back to Orrible and I do mean run. First it was more downhill than the climb up, but the perilous path along the cliff side was done faster. I was continually prodded in the back by the rear guard, ensuring that neither Vince nor myself tried to head back. As we approached the final headland, they shouted and yelled, so by the time we got to the village nearly everyone and had assembled to watch us stumble in as the dark night fell. There were only a few fires, nearly everyone had been to the search. Children pushed themselves forward, watching I think to see what punishment would be meted out.

It was the hostile silence that was the most threatening. Robin was taken to a separate hut, still tied, and a guard placed outside. We were given a very sparse meal and again went to our hut, silent except for Vince who kept muttering that Robin had completely lost it, until told by Dilys in an unusual alliance with Robin, that it was so unlike him, he must have had a reason and asked, several times, to repeat what he had said when we found him.

The next morning the whole village assembled, silent, watchful. Somehow we had broken a contract we never knew we had been signed up to.

Bosia led the procession of elders. Was he the Great Panjandrum, a simple guy pretending to be the great leader, or just a highly competent and wise village chief? A man followed him closely, wearing just a simple sarong. The other elders entered from the largest hut, all in full regalia. Drumbeats sounded and drummers followed the procession.

Susie walked behind, for once head bowed, avoiding our eyes. Two lads brought out a carved stool. The runes were not good.

Without a word of command the villagers formed a semi-circle. With some shuffling and rearranging it was men and boys on one side, women and girls on the other, and, like village football games the children just pushed to the front and sat on the dusty ground, wide eyed.

Bosai stood and with gestures that needed no translation indicated that we, the passengers, had always been safe, always fed. This was met with nods, and quiet sounds of 'yeah'. Bosai sat on the carved stool. Robin was brought forward. To my astonishment he threw himself on the ground.

We waited for cries of contrition, we waited for please, for mercy, we waited for wails, for fear of a forthcoming punishment, none came. To our astonishment, Robin began digging frantically in the ground while at the same time grabbing stones pebbles and putting them in a heap.

'Well he's lost it,' observed Dilys, 'gone bonkers like my husband did,' a strange comment which we had no time to explore.

In many cultures there is a tendency to accommodate those experiencing lunatic behaviour and about four minutes into Robin's dramatic display, that look of 'has anyone brought the tranquillisers?' appeared to cross the faces of the chiefs.

Robin turned to us and shouted, 'the volcano, Pyrolysis, plastic, it's the answer!' and he yelled and danced around in a continuing manic fashion.

'Bet Susie's got some cream for that,' observed Rita, 'My David used to have piles, ruined our lives.'

Audrey watching began to shiver, 'he's possessed. I always

knew that part of the island was evil. He's been taken by the spirits, I must touch his karma I must call back his guardians.' and so began her maddening humming, standing with a little more expertise on one leg until simultaneously she toppled over as we all shouted to shut up.

However, Vince, Frank and Jen looked on more thoughtfully.

As the day progressed, I began to consider words, which in modern life, in my experience, that we have lost, words that went with a slow and ponderous past.

As the elders talked, conscious of the watching village, they were obviously courteous, deferential to the chief, but nonetheless firm. Proceedings were formal, the emperor advised by his wily mandarins. The word *Palaver* came to mind, now attached to meaningless but lengthy discussion. My one visit to a local town council meeting back home somehow came to mind.

Robin, by this time was silent though kept scratching at the ground growing more alone as we weighed up the future. On occasion one of the search party was called forward to give an account of what they had seen the day before. It was now obvious that the man in the sarong, who we had never noticed before, whispered to Bosai. Must be the political adviser, the Dominic Cummings of our small nation island. Even we could see that the tolerant friends from Linda were attempting to ameliorate any punishment being considered. Then with great dignity, as the sun reached noon and no shade was easily obtained, the elders left and we were all herded into one hut.

The shocked silence of siesta time was broken as we all turned on Robin.

'What the hell are you playing at!'
'Have you gone completely mad?'
'We will all be killed now!'

'And eaten,' that contribution from Audrey was met with shouts of…'Oh for (and here you can insert many words) sake, shut up!'

For the first time in many months we were all conscious of the intense heat of midday that dragged into the afternoon, only relieved when the sun made its spectacular descent into the sea. We sat and we sweated. We were still and we were silent. Nothing moved outside, no children playing, no hens clucking about, no birdsong.

Gradually we turned to Robin who appeared to be coming out of some kind of trance. Not that he had been a swivelled eyed loon, of sixteenth century drama, medically speaking, but it had been a near thing.

He lifted his head, sat up straighter and spoke.

'Consider the plastic.'

We groaned but he raised his hands, 'stop think you idiots, think about what you saw.'

The horror returned before all our eyes, the endless mass of plastic, the stench of the trapped dolphins, birds and fish.

'So the currents are dragging in tons of plastic every day, so why isn't the island covered with it?'

Now we were curious.

'Dunno,' offered Rita, never quite the intellectual, 'once a teacher always a teacher, so I expect you'll tell us.'

Robin glared at her took a deep breath and continued, 'You saw the whirlpool, the plastic being dragged down,'

'And the nets and the all the poor dead creatures,' ventured Audrey, 'I might write a poem about it,' her comments met with a tired and resigned, 'Shut up!' from some of us.

Robin continued, 'so that is why there is no mountain of the stuff, that is why its not covering the island? But the whirlpool must have been there for years, so where is it going?'

Now we were interested.

'Its being dragged down, down, down, down.'

He was getting manic.

'Into the volcano?' asked Rita,

'Good question, no but I think it definitely being drawn into fissures in the rocks and being heated to great temperatures.'

A question from Frank, 'and then?'

'That's what I was trying to find when I was grabbed. There is something seeping out in that cove on the far side, to me it looks like oil.'

'So?' again a surly question from Rita.

'So my good woman,' a bad start to answering a fair question, 'it is known that plastic burnt to a high temperature will reduce back to the oil from whence it came. The force of all this debris through the passages around the hot volcano are similar to an industrial incinerator, something that would cost millions to build.'

I thought of the ugly incinerator along the coast from Eastbourne. Jen looked thoughtful.

'And the oil returns to the seabed, is that bad? And what about the fumes, surely they are toxic?'

'Probably,' an off hand remark, 'but then given the actual stench from the sulphur and the heat from the lava, who is going to go near that area?'

'So it could have commercial value?' the ever entrepreneurial Jen again. 'We could get ships to dump plastic near that current.'

'I don't think so,' replied Robin, but considered the possibility. 'We would need aerial photographs to seen how much plastic is in that island stream that is already coming in, but it might be worth thinking about, a natural way of dealing with the stuff.'

'But we should be banning it outright,' muttered Vince and got a sympathetic hug from Audrey, with a 'too right' from Vince.

'We could alert the world to this phenomenon, it might be the best solution, returning plastics from whence it came.'

I could hear the fervour in Robin's voice and then from Jen 'and make some money.'

'We've got to get out, get away, we have to find a solution.'

More fervour, then the silence returned when Frank ventured, 'How?'

'I have been thinking, why no rescue.' I was hesitant to share my own nightmare,

'Surely this island is known, marked on maps, seen from satellites?' Robin, said, now regaining his confidence and authority, I supposed from years of being a schoolteacher.

'There's several reasons. The easy one is we are off the usual shipping lanes, the second that with many of the Pacific small islands, it is presumed this one is uninhabited, third, the constant smoke from the volcano obscures sightings from planes or perhaps satellites, but finally I think we must be inside the area where there was significant testing of atom bombs and so is thought to have high level of radiation,' he continued, noticing our shocked expressions,

'But the latter is wrong I am sure, the people are far too healthy, but I did notices some strange crystal like rocks that might be formed by the nuclear blast off the coast in Western Australia in the 1950s'.

There was silence, the evening had begun and still the village was in lockdown. We were again shocked, unable to speak for there was nothing to say at that point.

Susie came by, normally our good friend our counselor, adviser, would not even smile, taciturn, eyes cast down, she left some food to eat alone.

The evening ritual was more hasty than usual. A young lad came around with embers, hot charcoal and then threw leaves on them to smoulder in the centre of the hut. He too left without a word or a smile. Rita complained, as always about the smoke, and Robin as usual reminded her that the smoke deterred the mosquitoes and other flying creatures of the night.

'Remember,' he said, 'Malaria and dengue fever was rife in Sussex once people built chimneys in the houses. Nothing like a smoky fire.'

We coughed and agreed. But the smoke, the charcoal stirred memories.

A flash of lightning lit the skies and in the distant that sharp clap of thunder particular to the tropics.

Rita gasped, 'Look a falling star,' and as we gazed toward the dark night sky more and more falling stars appeared, mixed with the distant flash of lightning, the sharp crashes of thunder rolling around us.

'Just think,' she was nearly crying, 'it must be Bonfire in Lewes. Oh god to think of those chilly nights, the leaves, the smell of the fires, the fireworks.'

Silence then,

'Always hated it,' that was Frank,

'Always rained, cold wet miserable waiting for the fireworks to go off, then when they did I had just got to bed. The cat was so frightened each year she shat all over the house.'

We looked at the falling stars and thought of fireworks, young people shouting and if on cue a scream punctured our night, though I recalled the foxes riding the dustbins Lopeham and their screams were one of joy.

'Never liked Sussex, only went there to get a job on this cruise,' ventured Paul, 'in Wales they have proper rain there. Had a scholarship to Cardiff University, cold and wet, not like these hot downpours. I will go back to LLangollen, perhaps.' We all muttered abstractedly the old joke, that's difficult to say and more difficult to spell."

I looked out and thought about home, the time before I was in care. I was a 'swallow,' one of the children of Irish immigrants who sent the children home to Ireland for the summer holidays, back to the intense love of my grandparents, good food, freedom from the London suburbs. I thought about the mountains and the gentle mist that clothed them in the early mornings, the cattle in the fields, the old castle, standing defiant. How strange that I could not recall rain, nor cold nor discord. It is a picture of a home, of people that are no longer there, though the same sweet mountain airs and the castle's sturdy stones keep me linked to that dream.

Jen stood up, breaks us all from our reverie.

'What's up with you guys?" she was angry, 'what's all this about home, bonfires, explosions? Have you never experienced war, gunfire, bombs, torture? I have, I have,' she was nearly crying.

'Calm down Jen,' an unwise interruption from Rita,

Jen yelled, 'do you really know what is going on all over the world, the petty wars, the misery, no one to trust, seeing things I shall never forget. Listen my friends and look around you. We have been thrown into the most beautiful place, with kind and generous people. We are safe. Let me tell you this will be my home, I will never leave it. So go back to your wet cold days in November, your anxious days wondering if someone will care for you in your old age. Take what is offered to you and remember this. When you return home will it be the same as when you left?'

THREE

Stephen looked around his living room, neat compact, ordered, much like himself he mused. He had a bottle of wine, some fruit juice in case Sally had to drive, some snacks in bowls especially bought this very afternoon and, for the first time in months, he actually had guests. A call from Sally the day before, breathless, and excited telling him that she had found a contact and wanted to have a meeting. Not a café, Stephen thought and so had invited them to him place where unobserved, they could review their progress on the search for H.

Gwen had taken to calling him every week with spurious excuses a grand circumlocution through weather, the state of the nation before coming to the key question,
'Have you heard from H?'
It took him several weeks before he hit on the proper response,
'No, but honestly Gwen I don't expect to. Surely you have, after all you are family, you must have been in touch since your brother died, to keep an eye on H, make sure she was ok?'
A question left artfully hanging in the air. Her silence marked her treachery. Over the months he had observed her covertness, avarice, even rapacity in hoping to get her hands on the bungalow in Lopeham and selling the plot for development. She was, he decided, a woman with a talent to make more enemies than friends.
She, on the other hand was silent as her deepest suspicions were fed by Stephen's evasions. He did not know that she knew of his visits to the bungalow. He did not know, that informed by the vigilant Peter and Angela, that all of Sally's visits were logged, plus his visit at the end of summer. Peter and Angela were also certain they had seen him having coffee with Sally in Eastbourne.
They both ended the call with a curt, 'must go, have another call coming,' from Stephen which Gwen did not believe for one moment.
At half past six Sally arrived with a young man about her age. They swung in with energy, enthusiasm and confidence, which shook Stephen, polite introductions and then from Sally,
'Gary works in Newhaven in the port, he knows about shipping. He's real cool with yachts too. Used to crew in the West Indies for real fat cats.'

Stephen, with remarkable self-discipline, outlined his progress in tracing *The Syndicate*. His Lewes pal Charles had been true to his word and had fixed up a meeting with his contact who had access to all of Lloyds' shipping registers. There was no registration of a cruise ship of that name. They looked at lists of ship travelling under flags of convenience, not an appropriate term he thought, as finding some listings arduous, confusing and among the opaque lines.

'Nice wine,' said Gary already holding out for a second glass. Stephen repressed prudish opinions, for Sally was sparkled eyed. He looked at them sadly recalling Somerset Maugham observing that there was an understandable distinction to be under forty but to be under twenty-five, as these two evidently were, was absurd.

'Yes,' continued Gary, 'I checked, do you know that on average twenty-four ships sink or go missing taking all their crew with them every year? But one of the reasons why ships go missing is that they turn off their AIS Responder.'

'A what?' though Stephen had a despairing feeling he already knew.

'It's the tracking device on ships, so on the internet you can see every ship in the world that is on the high seas. Captains have been known to turn them off in areas where there are pirates, because the pirates can see what ship is approaching them, or even if the ship is smuggling. So it is possible they have put into port somewhere perhaps for repairs, or have been captured.'

'But at least if they have been taken hostage they will be alive,' Stephen added.

'Going on cruises can be dangerous,' said Sally.

Stephen looked at her in astonishment as she stared at her note pad, and continued,

'Loads of people die on cruises, I read somewhere nearly 200 died last year. Of course many are elderly, have heart attacks, fall over board, mainly men I think.'

Stephen suddenly recalled Dilys, the grasping wife of old Jim, both were registered on *The Syndicate* he recalled, and wondered if Jim was still alive.

Suddenly a knock on the door, Stephen was not expecting anyone, but to his delight it was his next door neighbours, the kindly young couple.

'Hey didn't know you have visitors, we've come to celebrate, hope you don't mind,' for they were carrying two bottles of champagne. We're Ollie and Kate from next door and we've just bought a house, well, borrowed a fortune to get a house, so we've come to tell you.'

Stephen was pleased, the young people all were so friendly, drinks were poured and toasts drunk and within twenty minutes they were all talking about tracing the ship. Sally started talking about the strange emails and was showing them around again. Grasping their enthusiasm, their energy, a thought crossed his mind. Why shouldn't he take off, go and find H, rescue her perhaps. Ever cautious though he did not keep his counsel, and to distract himself from blurting out something that needed further thought, further planning and depth of courage he was not sure he had, and asked, 'where is your new house?'

'Oh its not new,' Ollie laughed, 'a bit of a wreck in Lopeham, a bit of a do-upper as they say, but quite near the station, has a garden, overgrown so a bit of a challenge.'

And as if he had suddenly become a fortuneteller, Stephen knew it was next door to H's home, and next door but one to Angela and Peter.

The next morning there was definitely change in the air. At half past ten, as was their custom, Peter and Angela looked out of their front window, again with matching mugs and sweaters, but with some concern as the 'For Sale' sign for next-door-but-one, not only came down but was joyfully pitched under the hedge by a very young couple. Peter and Angela, looked on, their coffee getting colder, as doors and windows were opened, paint pots, brushes and ladders taken out of a car and into the house. To their horror they could hear Radio 2 being played.

'Mark my words, this is the beginning of the end,' said Peter.

Angela saw Gwen driving by almost knocking Arthur over as he crossed the road. She saw Gwen's eyes open first in horror then in relief when she realised it was not H's bungalow which was to be the centre of imminent redecoration. She eventually stopped the car, and, as Albert observed, did not so much as try to park the vehicle but to abandon it some distance from the pavement.

Gwen for once did not hurry straight to Peter and Angela's house, but made a detour, attempting to look casually at the new arrivals. She went to H's house and rang the bell knowing there would be no one in. Nonetheless she was astounded when these new occupants approached her cheerfully over the joint hedge and informed her that the owner was still away but that they were going to keep an eye on the place.

'How very kind of you,' Gwen ventured, through clenched teeth.

Angela waved at Gwen to call in, and over a cup of warn coffee and a soggy biscuit or two, questions were posed such as

What is happening?

Who are they?

Where have they come from?

Do they know H?

And eventually

What has ever happened to H?

But, as each of them had their own concerns, not to be shared, they manifested that perfect mannerism of the English, by giving nods, some sighs, oblique references to the weather, 'It's turning out to be quite nice today,' a prime example of anti communicative interaction, but for those critical enquiries, answers there came none.

FOUR
H

Someone was crashing into our hut. We were woken up by Paul.

'Wake up, they are getting ready to move. The boys tell me that someone is on their way, it might be a rescue.'

It was like an electric shock. We all sat up, stood or even jumped up depending on our fitness.

How d'you know? What's happened? Where are we going? Who told you?'

All shouted at Paul simultaneously, as a Greek chorus but without the tune.

'The boys told me.'

'How do you know that?' asked Frank.

'Because I have learned their language while you all have been sitting around like mini members of the colonial service, too post-imperialist to learn a language for fear of going native. For heavens sake I learnt Welsh when I was in Cardiff'

Silence fell, we were astonished, learning Welsh! Also for we all knew he was right. We had only striven to learn essential words, for food and water, for comfort and to obey orders. Minimal strategy.

'For god's sake stop being so woke,' exploded Melanie, this from quiet Melanie, we all turned around and just stared at her.

'You just don't notice do you, running around with the boys, going out to the plantations, what we've been doing?'

We shook our heads, was this a minor rebellious cabal, only two members so far?

'We've been sitting with the women learning how to make those beautiful strong baskets,' Rita added, 'and they've shown us how to make ointments against the flies,' then giggled and looked archly at Robin, 'And other essential potions for the older woman,'

Robin blushed

Vince tried to protest, 'I have learned the names of the birds and flowers.'

'I tried to sing their songs,' muttered Audrey and we all recalled how the villagers had protested until she was dissuaded to go down that path of musical education. Ever practical Jen said, 'they've got some communications we don't know about, let's get out and find out what's happening.'

Walking out of our hut, I could see the daylight was different. In addition to the constant smoking of the volcano, the steam from the vents that were visible from all angles of the village, I could see dark clouds approaching, from a direction where I had never seen clouds with dark or fluffy white before. Now more than a strong breeze was beginning to whip up white horses on the water in the inlet, carrying sand and grit from the shale and sand, just enough to get into eyes, just enough to be irritating. The tops of the palm trees that lined the track to the fields began to bend, and I saw that many of the boys were out securing the fences and stockades. A chill of fear ran through me, a storm was on its way, and before it was carried the old and familiar signs of hurricanes, rain storms but far worse and more ominous was carried the stench for the plastic heap which belched and heaved from its trap in the north.

Activity was building up rapidly. Bundles of canes were in a pile, raffia baskets were taken from the huts full of fruits, yams, leaves and hens, those protesting at first then settling down. The shoes and flip-flops were thrown on the ground for anyone to choose two pieces of footwear, seldom a pair. The animals were herded out of the pens and stood around expectantly, the dogs remained under the bushes scratching and yawning, waiting, they had been through this migration many times in their short life span. We were not addressed in any formal way, but Susie organised us, indicating what we were to carry. And all this was carried out quietly and efficiently as befitted this highly structured but cold village community. There were some formal farewells between the villagers and in the main, I had the distinct feeling that there were pleased the Linda party was leaving.

With the exception of Bosai, who had spent some time looking at Jen. He approached her and made a little speech. Paul, who was nearby said, 'Jen he's telling you that he fancies you something chronic and if you ever return you can be his number one woman.'

Jen turned to Paul, 'tell him I'll be back, I have plans for this place and if all goes well, I may choose him to be my number one guy, but no guarantees, OK.'

Bosai laughed and looked smug, but as Jen turned to go, Mancy, the baby that had come on the canoe, new born all those months ago, the little bundle she had often and almost secretly cuddled, wailed and reached out for her. Touching his chubby fingers gently, giving a hug to his mum, returned to normal.

Just as the sun came through the morning clouds we set off. This time we all had bundles to carry, even Audrey who claimed she should be free to guide the pigs and goats. There was no need for this task, it was obvious to them, even before we realised, that we were heading back to Linda. Audrey was piled high with the bamboo and raffia chicken baskets and as she almost skipped along the path, sang, tunelessly of course, while the hens clucked in unison, a pretty sight as the further we travelled the more covered in feathers she became.

Robin walked at the back, more slowly than others. Although he too was weighed down by heavy packages all wrapped in canvases he would from time to time, stoop to pick up rocks, pocketed them before being urged onwards. Rita and Dilys walked confidently alongside Jen, silent for once, but there was an eagerness in their step. Susie led the march, striding out, pointing to the overhead birds shouting out, 'Welcome home,' the other women occasionally stopping, singing and picking leaves. Vince and Paul and some of his football team were at the very back of this procession. Vince was dismayed that well aimed stones thrown by the boys, drove the Komodo Dragons back from following too closely, or from peering over at us from the high rocks. Shouts of

'*Ya bugger off!* Ignoring pleas from Vince to leave them alone.

Looking at our group stepping out, smiling and laughing with the villagers, surprising themselves at how much of the local language they had picked up, I realised it was a journey homeward. We all looking forward to the peaceful haven where we had been rescued and so well looked after in those first days and weeks.

I wondered if we would find any attempts of anyone coming to rescue us. I think we all were heading back to where we were washed up with that unspoken thought. If any rescue party had come to the beach at Lindi while we were on the other side of the island they would not have found any trace of us. On the other hand, the weather on the Lindi side had been rough, monsoons bringing typhoons and lesser storms. But now the season had change perhaps a search party would set out. I was uneasy.

We did not really know or have evidence that anyone had escaped alive and reported us missing. Perhaps they had died. We could count those who had been lost in the storm and soon after, but there were some unaccounted for. Who would know we were still alive? If the captain and some of the crew had actually managed to escape in the life craft then why was there no rescue. The more I thought about it the more despairing I became, for it struck me that the whole expedition of *The Syndicate* was not just unconventional in the sense of an adventurous eco holiday, the sort of event some of us may have but on the ubiquitous bucket list, no there was something more.

It was a shock, thoughts repressed during our travels and struggles that, despite the length of time we had been away, so very few of us had left behind anyone who would miss us much. Some like Jen or Vince had fled partners or a former life, others like Rita had literally lost her husband under the waves and had no children to search for her. Only Frank had spoken about children, but they did not have any wish to contact him. I thought about home. Would my ghastly sister in law report me missing? Doubtful. Perhaps my lovely Sally, but she was young and though not thoughtless, would be tied up with her life. I did wonder about Stephen, but really I hardly knew him and I suppose he would regard me just as a client. For once I was genuinely homesick and wondered what I was missing back in Lopeham.

FIVE

In the late afternoon, Stephen, Sally and Gary met. On Stephen's laptop, they traced at shipping routes across the Pacific, they looked at areas where the Komodo dragons thrived, they looked at islands in with restricted access where there were military installations and or secret prisons, and they looked uninhabited islands.

Gary had trawled for notification of missing ships. While there was no official record that *The Syndicate* was 'lost', they did find some interesting postings. Some were identical emails from passengers to that received by Stephen and allegedly from H. In all the time that had lapsed there were only two enquiries about the missing ship, one from Stephen, of course, but the other from someone in Singapore asking about her son, Paul, who was a member of the crew.

It was, by chance the very same week, when Charles' friend, who did after all have very close links with security, received a response from the real spook, a young lad recently recruited with the 'new look' of security forces, that is with a background from a local comprehensive and not a degree but a higher certificate in IT.

Despite living in the age of media, internet and mass communication, the thing this young man craved was anonymity. He was clever, he was talented and he was bored, but to his delight he was nameless at his workstation, he was merely a code, even on occasion a letter, a chance to abandon his name Tyche, donated by a mother with a misunderstanding of Greek mythology or a mistake in spelling.

The request for a possible missing ship appeared to be ludicrous, until he looked more closely to where it possibly could have been lost. The Pacific was a very thesaurus of terminology.

There were islands, islets, atolls, large rocks and recently merged volcanoes. Some were connected in long lines by peninsulas, cays, reefs and bars, and one or two were isolated either forgotten or undiscovered. It was, he initially thought, a geological paradise for a pirate, a drug runner, an arms smuggler, or wanted person, until he scanned the flora and fauna of the islands to find the large number of venomous snakes, spiders, even birds and that before he read of the horrific Komodo dragons that roamed all lands, unchallenged, supreme.

He also looked closely at Stephen's emails that Charles passed to him. There were two facts that enlivened Tyche's dismally tedious day. First the area, normally patrolled by American security services was the scene of several missing planes, a number of recorded sinking ships. Second, a thrill he rarely expressed for 'it was not done' in office parlance, was the access he had to emails, chat on the internet and a myriad of secrets by the famous infamous. Most surprisingly, the communications of unknown and unrecognised people in whose thoughts might yet blossom paths to revolution and the overthrow of any government.

The latter he acknowledged was purely fantasy but it gave him a sense of power, a way of passing tedious days, a method of watching the friends and family of those second rate ex-public school boys who still stalked the corridors of power.

All of which appealed to his knowledge of chatter on the internet was that strange alteration of email exchanges from the passengers on the ship to friends and family in the UK. While these looked to assure of the success of the holiday, he noticed the abrupt and strange use of language from the most staid to that which he was sure his mother would never master.

Two days later, tedious tasks complete, Tyche decided to hack into the space satellites that constantly monitor the earth surface. He was highly skilled and even more highly devious, for he had found backdoors, trapdoors and the occasionally carelessly left opened front door of American, Russian, Chinese, Indian, Israeli Iranian, Korean (North and South he observed with pride), and quite easily, a few privately operated programs that operated satellites.

To give himself a reference point, he observed the south coast of England, the shipping lanes crammed with tankers, trawlers and even the smallest of any floatable craft loaded escaping 175 migrants heading towards Dover. He looked at the traffic fumes emitted by 20 miles of stationary traffic on the M25, the numerous aircraft trails of planes arriving and departing Heathrow, Gatwick, Stanstead and Luton, marvelling at he skill that was keeping those places apart.

He tracked back to the coast, noticing for the first time the plume of smoke coming from the incinerator in Newhaven. He was shocked. When walking along the River Ouse he had seen the smoke issuing white against the blue sky, benignly it would seem. But from space, that same plume was dark, black, a better indicator of the toxic plastics the incinerator was designed to burn.

During the early afternoon of the first day of his search, his section leader suddenly came to his desk and leaning over him said,

'What are you onto then?'

But did not wait for an answer.

'Good work, checking out the beaches, never be too sure who or what is turning up these days. Good initiative, keep at it Tyson.'

Tyche, well used to people not remembering his name just nodded. He had realised he was not expected to respond to any comments made by the section leader, or any other colleague come to think of it. They all worked in silence, most with headsets on to block any noise other than that of their choosing. Any eye contact, always accidental, was met with a frisson of horror before gazes returned to their own individual screens.

Tyche was now confident he could scan the region where *The Syndicate* had last been reported. And so, while terrorists communicated on obscure networks, financial skulduggery was afoot and plans for political mayhem were nearing completion, he worked steadily, obsessively searching, and in less than 24 non stop hours, had located an island that did not appear on any charts and was far off shipping and airplane lanes. He also found unusual mobile traffic, quite sophisticated coming from another island some 200 miles distant. Indeed there was significant activity emanating from a coastal settlement. Worth checking, he thought with great satisfaction.

SIX
H

Our walk back to Lindi was in stark contrast to the departure. Even I began to look forward to reaching the bay with some enthusiasm. For the first time I could look around and not have to watch every step, not gasp for breath at each climb or descent as we traversed the island, circled the tors and gullies. The beauty of the island was revealed as the morning mist rose. As we climbed that inland path up to the highlands that ran like a spine of a dinosaur through the centre of the island, we could look back at Orrible and marvel at its neatness and order. Now we did not have to endure their controlled and humourless lives, we could see from up here, the amazing agriculture those villagers had established. The stockades, the small fields where any local indigenous growth had been brutally discouraged, now seem to have such purpose in keeping that large community fed.

Even the now distant and still smoking volcano had majestic beauty. As we would pass through some grim and rocky outcrop, we would see beneath small areas of lush green vegetation in the tucked into the chasm and canyons far below, small. Among the rocks, even the dry sections on the paths crossing the higher sections of our trek, plants resembling cactus were in bloom, the flowers in bright contrast to the grey rocks.

At one point, Robin called Vince to look at one rock. We gathered around, for Robin's shouts and enthusiasm was catching. All is could see was some other green spongy growth.

'So you realise what this is?' We could not think of an answer that did not include the words, disagreeable green spongy stuff, and so remained silent. It was evident that Robin, like so many disastrous teachers, was posing an unanswerable questions to the victims trapped in their classrooms.

'This a moss or perhaps lichen,' he said.

We all nodded with varying attempts to humour him.

'So?' queried Jen.

This is the start of all plant growth on the island,' said Vince, stroking the spongy green stuff as if it was the hair of a maiden.

'Before long, seeds of other plants will grow on this and gradually all the island will be covered in plants and trees and that will bring birds and give food to those animals that were washed up on the beaches like us.'

Now Jen was interested. Looking around she said, slowly, thoughtfully, 'how long would it take? I mean for the trees to grow up here away from the coast? I could build pathways up through the trees, build hideaway glam camping sites where tourists could see the birds the plants, the animals pacing through the undergrowth.'

There was a suppressed laugh from Vince. Robin growled, 'Its not funny Jen, always the joker in the pack, I might have known such a comment from you.'

Jen turned, a hurt but angry look, tight mouthed, explosion about to build.

'No, Jen,' intervened the very quiet and kindly Vince, 'this process takes hundred of years, the point is that for these new islands that have only recently emerged at part of the volcanic activity on the sea bed this is an exciting discovery, it shows the whole island could be really viable in the future. But not in our lifetimes,' then he hastily added, 'well In this part, the coastal area is well colonised by plants.'

But Jen was still angry, 'well screw you guys,' and she picked up her pack and strode off. We all followed.

'Take it easy Robin,' I said to him once we had started our trek. 'Jen means well, and I think she is planning to stay, she has plans and ambition. And after all, unlike many of us, she has no one to care for her and she knows no one is looking for her.'

He turned to me, 'and you think she is the only one.'

So I was not the only one wondering about our future.

Looking back, it seemed that trek took about half the time of the outward journey. Then we had all been so frightened, unsure of why we had to move, and with no idea of what lay ahead. Each day we had been assaulted by new experiences, the people and their strange language where some words were instantly recognisable, though hidden among such strange words, sounds and even gestures. Now we were a group, our band of castaways, the survivors. We, who back in England may not have shared a second glance at in the street, who would for all the foot dance of the English class system would never had met socially, we now bonded. We hung together when faced with a culture that had seemed so threatening, even when we had been shown tolerance and acceptance. We did not seek to mingle with the villagers despite their interest and kindness. As proven in the history of the British Empire, this failure to learn a foreign language in case 'we all went native' and who knows then what would happen, resulted in us not mingling happily. Most of us had learnt the essentials of survival for example the vocabulary of food and water, the greetings, but not the nuanced questions such as, 'How's the day been for you?' And 'Who is your girl friend?' Only Vince,vAdnan and Paul, seemed to be fluent. Though I expected the most of the topics in which they were confident centred around football. Still no different from many blokes at home in Lopeham.

For the first time I realised that we were only a group out of necessity. We had splintered. The older men had yet again turned themselves into that band of old male animals, either confirmed bachelors or those who had lost their dominant place in the herd. They never seemed interested in the women, some like Frank viewing all female interest or approached with deep if not hostile suspicion.

Dilys, Rita and Melanie, slowly picked up their baskets I noticed that we women were all lean and surprisingly fit. We carried our baskets with ease, we walked confidently along the stony paths. We had all changed. The expensive tints and colours that had brightened our hair had long faded away. Susi had shown us all how to manage all our cosmetic needs, Our hair had grown longer only cut rarely, using coconut and plants oils, the women and come to think of it, shone in the sunlight.

It was Dilys who broke the harmony of that stage towards the descent to Lindi.

'Now we're heading back, I have got to thinking about Jim. I wonder if he's still in the morgue in Perth.'

And just as we were looking for words of comfort or condolence added,

'What worries me is what is happening to his Will. I mean he always said he had made arrangements for me should he go first. But if I am declared missing there are people who would like to get their hands on his money.'

I remembered the early days when Dilys seem to run classes on claiming of the estates of the recently deceased. I noticed Rita and Melanie also looked concerned.

Melanie wailed, 'it would not be funny if we got out of here and found the bequests from our dear departed had been grabbed by the in-laws, our houses sold from under us,'

Dilys continued, more quietly, 'or the bookies. Old Jim did have debts.'

'I know what you mean,' muttered Rita, always a quiet woman, always in the background. 'I could see what that bastard was up to.'

It was fortunate that path was rocky and the others were pacing away from us, nightfall in a few hours, other wise we would have stopped, gasped, sat around and had a long chat. But was not possible, we trudged on each of us processing the venom that had just been expressed by Rita. Silent Rita who seems to blend into any background, for goodness sake!

'I am sure you don't mean that,' I tried, only to be met with a hostile glance, a snort of derision.

'Why do you think we came on a cruise?' Melanie asked. We were silent with our own reasons in mind.

'Because I read that lots of people die on cruises. He could have caught Norovirus, been swept overboard, fallen down stairs, but that old bugger was watching me. He knew I knew, but he didn't know I knew until I gave him that pushback when he nearly made it to the rocks, yes back towards that shark. No one saw me doing it, but he saw the look in my eyes.'

Strewth, now we have a second homicidal maniac in our group.

'But I thought he was lovely,' ventured Dilys.

I did recall some mild flirting on board T*he Syndicate*.

'Think you were the only one,' snarled Melanie, 'always trying for a bit on the side. I used to put up with it, saved me the problem of the nightly groping, until she came along.'

'Who?' I asked.

'Her!' the answer spat out. 'She used to be a van driver. Always delivering things, always looking very smart, in her uniform. Bright trousers, bright shirt with a scarf, a veritable 1950s air hostess. All she missed was a dinky hat. Then it dawned on me that he was ordering an awful lot of stuff on line, then returning it. It was crazy. I thought he was going into dementia. Then a neighbour said how helpful the smart delivery driver had been, taking in the deliveries into the house, helping him unpack. Oh yeh! and staying for a cup tea as the old saying goes. I came home and found them at it, on my new rug in the lounge. So disgusting.'

'Blimey, what did you do then?' Rita stopped, put down her basket, 'you got to tell us.'

'Saw her keys on the table in the hall, so I took them, jumped in the van and drove it off. Wow! I could see her in the mirror yelling trying to pull up her trousers. Yep I drove off in her van, dumped it in a car park and left the keys in, even opened the back door. He was furious but what could he do? She managed to talk her way out of it with the boss. In fact and just my luck apparently nothing was stolen from the van. But I saw the look in his eyes and I could see he was after her again. So I booked the Cruise. Took me a few days to find a small old ship going off to remote islands. Thought I could polish him off unnoticed, then get back and start a new life.'

Dilys went over and gave Melanie a hug, then we all joined in. We all had our stories, hidden from public view in our struggle to keep alive. A shout interrupted the weak attempt at a group hug, and we picked up our baskets and started again along the rocky path. And turning a sharp corner we saw Audrey and Vince clamber down from rocks above.

'Just checking where the dragons are?' said Vince, while Audrey blushed and started to hum. We looked on with a pang of nostalgia, a small bit of envy is seeing the obvious joy of the young couple, and muttered almost in unison, 'yeh right.'

SEVEN

Stephen was experiencing a number of conflicting emotions. He had got up early pondering and caught the train to Lewes. He walked slowly from the station down the lovely Friars Walk, stopping to look at All Saints Church, the mother church, the oldest in the town, built it was said on a Celtic religious site with its proximity to the old Pinwell that must have given fresh clean water to the old settlement. Then beside it the Quaker Meeting House, set in tranquil gardens just away from the busy street. In the chaos that Stephen was experiencing in recent months the thought of finding a divine plan against which he should not struggle was appealing. Perhaps another day, he considered and walked on.

There were not many occasions he would walk down the Cliffe High Street. Lewes followed and maintained the town planning of the Normans, early arrivals for it was William the Conqueror's daughter who had come to live there, with the obligatory plans for an immense castle and a Priory. Most important of all she and her descendants built a wall, and inside that wall the Normans and their descendants, now mainly successful business people and senior academics from Sussex University, lived. Outside the wall was a swampy area, until the Fifteenth Century a marsh that had swallowed attacking armies, and was probably riddled with malaria and other nasty illnesses, but was where the Saxons had to hang out. Until the late Nineteenth Century there were actually two recognised boroughs on each side of the aptly named lazy (mainly) and muddy River Ouse.

He entered the Cliffe, now so vibrant. The weekly farmers' market was in force. Vegetables from nearby Barcombe, goat meat, goat cheese practically everything a goat could produce, lamb, chicken who had all been in the fields until recently, he was assured. There were cakes made by the enthusiastic supporters of the Women's Institute, a man selling wooden bowls, a woman selling knitting wools but best of all the stall selling the Lewes Pound, a currency only to be used within the town.

He continued over the bridge, stopping to look into Harvey's shop then continued on, past antique shops with strange and alluring windows. He noticed with a shock that one had a phone for sale so like the one he had in his parents house and then oh horrors an early mobile phone, a brick, both classed as genuine antiques. Where had the years gone!

A phone call from Charles the previous was as non-informative as anything Stephen had encountered in his long and distinguished professional career with customers of dubious integrity, and frequently with much to hide.

'Charles here.' The conversation had started unnecessarily for Stephen's phone had revealed the caller name and of course his voice was instantly recognised.

'Can't say too much but can you meet, Lewes, about ten tomorrow, something to run by you.'

Stephen had reacted guiltily, surely it was not about the outstanding complaint from the owner of the green house his golf ball had allegedly smashed all those weeks ago.

'Greenhouse? What are you talking about?' Came a terse response.

'No the other matter, I'll have someone with me.'

He gave directions to the cafe, and there the conversation ended, not on a request but an order. 'Don't be late.'

Stephen arrived a little earlier than had been arranged, sitting in an uncomfortable couch near the entrance. He watched the customers come in a very mixed crowd. Some young mothers with babies strapped to them which then took some inexpert unwinding and disentangling of the baby, who did not seem to mind. They sat in groups heads huddled together, some breastfeeding with benign confidence. Some men with noisy toddlers made a small group at the back. The toddlers running around unheeded while the young men chatted and continually looked at their mobiles. Perhaps it was to avoid much eye contact and to present a macho appearance during their child caring hours.

Lewes cafe owners had shrewdly recognised that, with the huge expense of commuting, 'working from home' was a serous option. As few could actually monitor the work hours which were actually done at home, young couples shared child rearing. So the cafes became a kind of playground for the fathers, an unexpected meeting place, tolerant of semi-supervised youngsters.

To Stephen's amusement, Charles of course made quite an

entrance. Before opening the door and coming into the cafe, Stephen could see him furtively look up and down the street in the manner of a bad 1950's thriller. He came in looked around the cafe, acknowledged Stephen and then went out, now waving his hand. From a nearby shop a young man crossed the street and together joined Stephen.

In many places the contrast between the three men might have have raised interested glances but not Lewes. Stephen in classic shirt, sweater and well-pressed trousers, Charles in a sharp and expensive business suit, matching tie and handkerchief in top pocket and a young man in tatty jeans, and oblivious to the weather a skimpy t-shirt, and well worn trainers with no socks. Hair, short at the front but a long and reasonable clean ponytail emerging from a cap. Stephen always thought himself non-judgemental, tolerant in fact to most fashions and religious edicts, but this, he thought must indicate some mental disturbance on this chilly day.

His views were compounded as they each ordered their coffees at the counter with a barista that had not attended charm school. Stephen thought himself well clued up in Eastbourne, but had not reckoned on the art of ordering in Lewes. It started well.

'A cappuccino,' ordered Charles.

'What coffee?' A gesture to the board behind indicated ten different brands, names of countries of origin and regions therein, even colours.

Charles did not hesitate, 'your best.'

'Me too,' added Stephen. He did not really want a cappuccino, but he did not have the mental strength to engage with the formidable list. Stephen then watched a new dance around the orders of the next customer

'Tea,' said the young man tersely. 'Chia, not dairy and the Indonesian green elephant.'

'Do you want, goat, oat, soya?'

'Oat, and a toast, gluten free.'

'Yes, which bread, do you have any allergy?'

'Yes, no nuts, oh must be local stone baked, and some jam, sugar free.'

'Of course, we'll take it to your table'

As they walked to a table at the back of the cafe away from the babies and toddlers, the young man observed.

'For a small town out in the sticks this is a real cool place.'

Charles replied stiffly,

'In Lewes we practically invented intolerance to anything edible or drinkable and the cafes have certainly cashed on this, and particularly here. Now let me introduce you to Stephen for it is he who has put us on the merry trip of discovery. Stephen, this is the excellent but enigmatic Tyche. We can't say too much, can we Tyche, but let's say he has been an absolute wonder in tracking down your lady, all very hush-hush.'

Tyche did not seem to be listening to this obsequious introduction so there were no handshakes but nods exchanged, Stephen tense, lent forward, and with a shock realised this 'young man' was only a few years younger than himself.

'So what's this all about?' he began,

Charles winked conspiratorially glancing around to see if anyone was trying to overhear their conversation.

'Tyche has ways and means you know, found something that might interest you. I told him about your search.'

They were silent for a moment the coffees, chai and toast were delivered. Stephen regarded the liquid in the chai with some curiosity, compared to what he always regarded as tea, this seemed to have to have the colour and texture of mud, and the bread looked tough, you would need good teeth to break into those crusts, he thought, so perhaps that's why the jam must be sugar free. But he was drawn back to reality as Tyche began to speak.

Stephen sat back in astonishment the breath knocked out of him, for once speechless.

'I found an island, right off the beaten track, its got an active volcano but it's possible, like 17 million to one that they might be shipwrecked there. But then we all buy lottery tickets with those odds.'

'And someone wins,' muttered Stephen.

'What I didn't like, are those emails you had from your pal.'

Charles interrupted,

'Tyche once gave evidence in a trial where the police had fitted someone up with a false statement. Poor bloke was heading for a long stretch when Tyche found the use of language totally alien to someone such as the victim and had indeed been written by an overworked copper trying to get a speedy conviction. Pity really as the bloke went on to murder someone a year later.'

185

Stephen was impatient, 'for goodness sake Charles! Tyche how did you find this?'

'Can't say, but it was fun looking. If your ship went down in the shipping lanes, some debris would be found and there has been none so far. They might have sunk near an island, but there have been no reports of people alive or dead being washed up. But the strange thing was that at the time of emails being sent that the captain had got all the mobiles locked up, the ship was lost on the GIS. Now that's not unusual in waters where there are pirates, but not where the last signals came from.'

Stephen nodded enthusiastically it confirmed his findings.

'Didn't like the language in the emails to you. Can't see your friend writing like that no matter what she might have taken a fancy to on her trip. Know what I mean, some oldies suddenly want to try out the drug scene, find out what they missed in their youth, and man, the choice is wide open these days.'

Stephen shuddered, surely not, but then did he really know H? After all they were not both oldies but he decided that Tyche referred to attitude not age. 'What do you think we should do now?' he asked.

'Get out there quick, I reckon someone is hiding something. I can trace the location where I think the emails came from, but somehow my money is on that island. Most of the time its covered by smoke coming from an active volcano, but there's a constant plume, reminded me of the Newhaven incinerator and I cannot work that out. There cannot be a full scale industrial incinerator operating there, but that's what the smoke looks like even though its mixed with the stuff coming from the volcano. They must be burning plastic, but there are no ships coming into the island, in fact there are not evidence any shipping. I suppose there might be the odd canoe. On the other hand, it does look there might be some human habitation. I thought I saw some small plantations but I am not sure. If the passengers are alive its a possibility they were washed up there.'

'Who could we get to check it out,' queried Stephen, 'is there a police force, navy, would they help?'

Tyche exchanged a look with Charles, indicating some despair, then with some pity turned to Stephen

'Two things man. There's a small chance this could be some secret base, Russian, American, Chinese, perhaps even us though we no longer have the capacity to maintain a base, nor keep it secret. It could be an old scientific station, hence the toxic fumes from an old incinerator.'

'You mean chemical weapons development?'

'Yeh possible, but an old one, abandoned, they are around.'

Charles grunted, 'surely not.'

'What about Gruinard off the Scottish coast?' snapped Stephen, 'the British government released Anthrax spores there as part of a chemical weapons experiment developed at Porton Down, and the place still remains toxic, unfit for human habitation.'

'That's what I thought,' agreed Tyche, 'but you know what there would be some track of activity or even buildings, and there is nothing to suggest it just a little tropical island a million miles from anywhere. So if you are up for it, the only way is to get out there yourself.'

An hour later Stephen had been faintly amused at Charles' attempt for cat and mouse manoeuvres in Lewes, which had distracted him from what Tyche had claimed. Charles had insisted they all left the cafe separately, slipping out the back though the car park and walking back along the river over the footbridge to his house near the castle. Very Norman of course.

Tyche said he would like another drink, for which Stephen was grateful as he knew the ordering process would take a few minutes and thus give him time to think while he considered the next move.

Of all the people in the world, the one you could have thought you could rely on not to cause mayhem, the bookies would have backed Dilys. Mercenary for sure, sad but not really definably bad, it was Dilys that was the catalyst to Stephen's next step.

That very morning, before he left for Lewes, he had received a call, which had concerned him. He recalled the conversation. He answered his office phone:

'Is that S. Financial Services?'

'Yes, who is calling?'

A hesitant reply, for Stephen never advertised and knew most of his client's voices well.

'You don't know me but the police have been next door and then called me.'

Stephen was polite but firm.

'I am not sure I can help, I do not deal with criminal matters.'

'No not me, my neighbours.'

'I regret all financial matters are confidential, I regret I cannot help.'

Stephen was about to cut the call when the voice said, 'its about Dilys and Jim Coppard. They don't know what to do about the body.'

Stephen gasped, his heart had a small spasm of shock.

He could hear the speaker take on a lung full of air and then spoke for some minutes without stopping. She began, 'I understand the Coroner's office in Auckland, New Zealand have contacted the Sussex police. Well it seems old Jim died out there some months ago on a plane they said, and his body has been in the city morgue and there is no sign of Dilys and she told me that she was seeing you just before they left on that cruise because she never trusted that old bastard, excuse me French, but he was and I knew she was worried about all his money going to the bookies and that you were a real gent and she felt so much safer since she spoke to you and I know they did not have many friends so I thought I'd call you.'

While the caller paused for breath, Stephen's immediate reaction was to employ hesitation phenomena, the phrases that are meaningless, but give the speaker time to think.

'Right, ok…so…well, thank you for calling me,' he began, 'that is most interesting…yes…well…ummm…'

And then with some concern, 'I am not sure what I can do. Did you give the police my name?'

The caller was impatient.

'Course not, it's private isn't it, the chat you had with Dilys?'

Stephen was not sure what line this might take, perhaps a threat, blackmail?

'All my dealings with all my clients are completely confidential.'

A rather prim and petulant tone had entered his voice.

'I know that,' his caller was better informed than he thought. 'If Dilys has taken off to the South Sea paradise and left him cold in New Zealand, well good luck to you girl, is what I think, but she ought to know that the police are sniffing around. Got it?'

And to Stephen's astonishment it was she, the nameless neighbour who cut the call.

So, on the departure of Charles from the cafe he felt his life turning to a new venture while he waited for Tyche to return with whatever liquid he chose, though thinking a glass of water might be more tasty.

When Tyche sat down, Stephen did not make eye content, but rearranged the pepper, the salt snd the paper napkins and said, 'I'll have to go and find them, but I don't know where to start.'

And to his astonishment, was slapped on the back by Tyche.

'Great man, I will give you every help I am dead bored but don't tell Charles.'

They exchanged covert communication details, and to please Charles who for all they knew might be lurking in a doorway to ensure they followed orders, did indeed leave separately.

Stephen called Sally and Gary and later that evening they met up. He did not at that point think it right to tell them about the morning's call, a dead and very cold body in the morgue in New Zealand, but did give them a synopsis of his meeting in Lewes.

Sally was really excited, 'I knew Aunt H was alive, I coming with you.'

Gary said, 'we need to get as close as we can to that island, and then I can get an ocean going yacht to that the final leg. I have done a fair bit of ocean sailing. Tyche will be valuable for communications. And I can look into chartering a yacht, perhaps from the near to the last email that was sent.'

There was a great sense of excitement and trepidation.

Sally said, 'I am in, not sure what I can do.'

Gary gave her a hug, 'tell you what I will give you a crash course in navigation. I know someone in Brighton marina with a fancy yacht and we'll take it out a few times.'

Stephen who had been silent, the thought of being on the sea for any time already turned his stomach.

'Give me the estimate of costs he began, unable to resist years of financial management from his days in the bank, 'I will see to that side, and I'll be able to fund the venture too.'

Then thinking that his days on the gloomy south coast would be even more barren should his team take off without him, and with thoughts he could stack up on seasickness pills, said, 'I'm coming too.'

EIGHT
H

There was no vestige of an organised route march back to
Linda. The village lads had been ordered to bring up the vanguard,
then darted ahead when Vince and Audrey had side stepped for
some investigations in the flora and fauna. The boys were taking
shortcuts leaping down the rocks while most of the line moved
sedately following the winding path. Robin and Frank were walking
quickly, once taking a small load from a young girl who was trying
to carry an assortment of baskets and help and young toddler. We
all were energised, even Dilys Rita and Melanie were striding out,
not their usual reluctant ambling, it was a kind of homecoming.

By early evening we reached the village. Each person gratefully
putting down their load. The boys had started a fire in the centre,
all the women were given tasks to inspect the houses carrying small
smoking branches to hunt out any snakes, large spiders, scorpions
and lizards. The smoke was extremely efficacious. I could not
count the unwanted wildlife, which left the huts, but one thing was
for sure, we could not stay long inside either. The smoke blistered
our eyes, the pungent aroma from the singeing leaves made out
eyes water and god only knows what damage it was doing to our
lungs.

I was surprised Frank offered to go around once more, just to
check that nothing had crept slithered or flown back in. It was only
later as I saw him trying to replicate the art of making the stick
smoulder. In a fit of nostalgia, he told me the experience of the
acrid smoke reminded him of the time he smoked 50 Senior
Service unzipped cigarettes a day, and many of those down the pub
where he met the other smokers over a pint or three.

The men made a tour of the village compound, checking for
the damage caused by the monsoon storms. The main huts were
almost perfect, though I noticed that some of the thatch looked as
if it had recently been replaced. Audrey, Vince and the children did
not need to coax the pigs and goats into the stockades, for they ran
in with the same sense of homecoming that we experienced.
Chickens practically flew from the confinement of their baskets,
pecking around that giving those little crows of delight that all
chickens, the cockerels too were picking up choice grains that had
fallen when the baskets were unloaded, offering them with chuck

of delight to their 'girls' before taking advantage of them. 'Just typical.' muttered Jen as she booted one over enthusiastic young cockerel away from a hen that was not receptive to his offerings. But the community activity was so reassuring, everyone helped, there were very few disputes over workload and one over possessions or food. That is how this little community flourished.

We were all busy for at least an hour, sorting and putting all the stuff away. Gradually one by one, we and our village friends sat down around the fire. I think there were only fifty or so of us that night. Susie and some of the women went to the store and came back with bottles of beer. I was not too surprised I knew there was a well-guarded stash that was brought out for special occasions, but it was a lovely gesture. We all felt as one, no longer strangers. Bundles of meat and vegetables were beginning to roast slowly in the embers of the fire, the light shining on our faces, the warm sand beneath our feet so comforting. The village girls sang a sweet song. We felt a huge sense of calm, tranquility even until Audrey said, 'someone has been here while we have been away. Not only are all the stockades repaired but there is a new one.'

We looked at the villagers, they were waiting for something because they had suddenly fallen silent. Then with a crash and leaping out of the trees and bushes, hurtled a group of men.

Audrey screamed and clung to Vince who conveniently was right next to her. Dilys screamed, but could not find anyone near enough to cling onto. Frank and Robin tried to show some bravado but could not even make it to the standing position. But it was Jen, the first on her feet and with a cry of joy said, 'look, look!'

But there was pandemonium, all the village was on their collective feet, there was running, there was chasing, there were screams, which we gradually realised were not of fear pain or torture but of sheer joy and pleasure. Nigel had eventually managed to stand up and was waving a stick ineffectually, perhaps to defend the honour of the passenger group. Among the running melee we could see one that looked different, European maybe. This person detached himself from the melee and stood with just one other man, looking at us.

'The bastard, the bastard its that bastard captain!' yelled Jen. We all stopped, literally open mouthed, yes there was the captain of *The Syndicate* being greeted and feted by the village and beside him stood the man I first encountered when I was washed up on the beach to many months ago.

The Captain stood on the beach, defiant but barely recognisable. He was no longer the debonair figure that stood on the deck of the *Syndicate* in his smart uniform, his careful coiffured hair. He was in rather battered shorts, was leaner, far more weather beaten. As the villages ran towards them, he stood proud on the beach, until the women in particular passed him by to give the men accompanying him full greetings.

It was Nigel who recovered first and marched up to him, I think might have even taken a swing at him if not stopped by Bosai, glaring with all the authority of community leader. Though held back Nigel yelled,

'What the hell is going on? Where have you been?'

Useless questions but enough to let the Captain know that Nigel was not feeling friendly towards him. The captain stood still, silent but watchful.

But it was Paul, quiet Paul who made the most chilling observation.

'Look,' he said to us, 'those village men are the ones who left just after we got washed up. Do you remember when all the canoes suddenly disappeared?'

While all around us there were sounds of rejoicing, we our little group of survivors and the captain stood still, a rock in the maelstrom of activity. More fires were lit, chickens despatched, preparations for a feast as the sun began to head down towards the horizon. For so many weeks we had felt ourselves so much part of this community, but the return of the men and the appearance of the silent captain forced us once again into the role of alien beings.

There followed a moment of reflection on both sides. One of those timeless moments, might have been a minute may have been an hour, though that is doubtful. I cut out all the shouting, the running, the laughter and could hear only my own voice in the deepest silence struggling to get words to emerge. Was it the impact of the shock? It was like drowning, I just could not breathe. I must have staggered for Jen was at my side, holding me, though I could feel her trembling too. Now it was our turn to watch. Suddenly, as a robot awakened, the captain, who had been so still, so silent, now moved through the groups of rejoicing villagers, as though searching. He spoke to one or two of the men who had been with him as they burst through the bushes. They were respectful but just shook their heads and returned to the party. He spoke apparently threateningly to some women, who turned their backs on him, glaring in open hostility. He returned to our group, now aggressive, mean and downright ugly. He shouted.

'What the hell has happened? Where is everyone?'

Dilys ventured, 'what do you mean?'

'You murderous old bitch, I knew about your plans! I didn't believe for one minute that your old man died unexpectedly on a flight. You couldn't wait to see him dead and buried, oh no not you! Died unexpectedly no way, bet you had it planned it all along. Think you've got all his money. Well we'll see. So cut the crap.'

As Dilys sank down onto the sand in a near faint, he turned his venom on Jen who unfortunately was standing nearest to him. He would have struck her, but for her raising her lethal prosthetic hand.

'Don't even think of that,' she murmured. 'what's up with you?'

He screamed at her and then us, 'so, where are the others? What the hell has happened here?'

PART FIVE

Where Stephen finds strength and even a commendable level of both bravery and recklessness and rescue is planned; but where the passengers encounter the worst of their fears; pirates are encountered and a slave rescued.

ONE

Stephen, Sally and Tyche began searches to charter ocean going vessels. Stephen resumed his daily visits to his favourite Eastbourne cafe, taking a childish delight in his surreptitious and probable illegal quest. However, on the second day, he made detour on his journey, thing he saw the ghastly Gwen heading for the station.

It was to avoid her, that Stephen had a Damascene moment, a flash of understanding of life outside his comfort zone. It made him reflect on how fortunate his life had been up to that very moment. Without any effort he had inherited funds from his grandparents to get on the property ladder at eighteen. He had wafted through university obtaining a moderate degree, he had fallen into a job in a bank and by the age of thirty could leave and set up a fairly lucrative business, all without effort, or trauma or a recognition that for others the dice had not fallen so well.

His new route took him past a church hall where a notice for the food bank stood by the open door. He had of course noticed the baskets by the checkout of all local supermarkets for donations of food, and the local people were generous, though the contents worthy but unexciting. Perhaps sweet biscuits and cake were not allowed, though excessive amounts of baked beans were. How come, he thought, that a wealthy place such as this glorious south coast town would have foodbanks?

There must be employment in the hotels, small and very large, though the tourist industry is fickle; there was an industrial estate, but he was not sure how much skilled work was offered; and finally he wondered how many employers of all the local employers paid more than the minimum rate ?

The majority of local businesses fell into that mid category called Small to Medium Enterprises, SMEs to the initiated but to the uninitiated it sounded like an unpleasant medical complaint. As most employed five or even fewer and were struggling in the post Brexit economy, even the boss had to struggle to get an income. It was well known that many of the catering supplying coffee and burgers, paid the minimum, though in their case there were vast profits to be had and sometimes with minimal tax payments.

A woman passed him, climbing the steps to the church.

Stephen stood back to let her pass and then noticed under the worn coat was the uniform of a local Care Home. She was lovely looking, he thought, a kind and gentle face, but so tired. He knew staff at Care Homes were far from being well paid, but nonetheless he was shocked. This foodbank was only a few streets from his usual routes he took through town and yet he had never been aware its existence. How many recipients of the foodbank were living in unregulated private rented accommodation, and though employed were trapped in an ever downward cycle?

Stephen's mood scarcely lifted as he entered the cafe. The pride and joy he had normally taking out his very expensive laptop was diminished. Did he really need this high-grade computer, with more buttons, features, apps and programs than he would ever learn to manage or even use?

It was of some comfort one of the staff brought over his usual latte (skimmed milk no sugar), with, 'morning Stephen, what's up with you today? Are you OK?'

Stephen looked up and mumbled a response, but he was strangely grateful for the interest, kindly meant. Disguising his interest he viewed the young member of staff with curiosity, was she managing on her wages, did she get the tips he occasionally left? He should check it out.

His mood switched from depression to incredulity as he began to search on Google for ways of chartering ocean-going yachts. He was bombarded with sites, and clicked on several at random. He could charter ocean going yachts of obscene luxury, with crews to prepare high cuisine foods, and presumably to drive the ship for a mere one million pounds sterling per week.

Stephen studied the brochures in a daze, photos of huge decks with couches, a dining area larger than his whole apartment, bedrooms with beds that defied the description king size. At least you could be seasick in comfort, though the thought of rolling around in such a huge bed as the yacht surfed the high rollers on the open ocean, made him feel queasy and here he was still in a cafe in Eastbourne.

He realised there are two worlds, those who gained millions even billions every year and who were hard put to spend a tenth of that annual income, and those that had almost nothing. It was like the sea itself he reflected. The large sharks had few predators other than themselves. They roamed the seas feeding on the little fish.

Perhaps, until the arrival of the sharks, the little ones edged in and out of the reefs, fed on delights on the sea bottom, until snap, lights out. At least they were eaten whole and not nibbled away slowly.

He continued to scroll down to more modest charters and to the blogs of lunatics that venture in small boats across the Indian Ocean, dodging pirates, aggressive whales, mountainous seas and distant havens. Perhaps they could hitch a ride with one of these more casual riders of the seas.

Stephen sat back to try to think out all the possibilities. In his experience he was aware that the extremely wealthy were vulnerable, they are their own worst enemies. They thrived on notoriety, on being different, despising those who paid their tax demands on time and without complaint. Like the sharks in the sea, they swam alone, trusted no one, took chances, short cuts with few to stop them. He could not recall one of his vastly wealthy customers, that he actually liked. There were some that rich, mainly the children of local landowners. Many were not very sharp, over reliant on inherited wealth and their position in the local society. But he thought they were doomed as the social orders of England underwent a silent revolution Money now ruled and there was little regard from whence it came, Russia, China, the exotic Khans, or the mundane successes of local bank robberies, money laundering.

'Are they the same as me, I am the same as them, though on a lower scale of expenditure?' He wondered then with resolution thought, 'things must change!'

But these musings made Stephen consider he could take a chance. He knew of a guy who 'allegedly' had connections with neighbours of repute, allegedly with connections to the Russian mafia. He had seen the usual tabloid stories of millionaires on the French Riviera or cruising in the West Indies and knew the owners never made the sea crossings. Could they act as crew and just deviate off course?

At the same time Tyche in his dark office console, had been cruising the marinas of Australia and New Zealand. Looking down on Freemantle, West Australia he could see hundreds of ocean going ketches and sloops, silent and still in the two marinas, more on the harbour side in dry dock, on gantries. He moved a mile or two to the Swan River, up to the city of Perth, and the same story. He covered in amazement the coastal towns and cities. He moved onward to New Zealand, Wellington, Auckland, and millions and millions of immobile sea-craft tethered to stanchions, like impatient wild horses, wanting to be free. 'Hey little boats,' he muttered to them from the great height of his satellite observation, 'Can I help?' But more in his line of craft, he searched for postings for lone skippers looking for crew, owners desperate for income to pay for their marine costs and perhaps not too fussy about possible charters.

Coincidentally, Sally was working along the same lines but looking at blogs. Searching online she found many accounts of ketches and sloops making long distance trips from Freemantle or Darwin. There were constant references to Ocean Passages for the World, the bible for long-distance cruising. From reading of the blogs it seemed the optimum time to leave and search the area, late autumn. In the northern half of the ocean the southeast trades should blow a steady 15-25 knots by July or August.

Extract:

10.135. Northern Australia to Singapore. From April to October, two routes are recommended, the usual route passing N of Timor, through Wbtar Strait and W~tar Passage into the Flores Sea, continuing W along the N side of all the islands and through Sapudi Strait to Selat Bangka or Selat Gelasa (10.35-10.42).

An alternative route passes either N or S of Timor and along the S side of all the islands, entering the Java Sea through Sunda Strait (10.33); thence as directed in 10.32.02.

From November to April take the Colombo route for that season, see 10.133.

She rang the others. 'What do you know about Freemantle? Find out and meet tomorrow.'

TWO
H

Our band of survivors grouped together, like a school of little fish fearful in the onslaught of the captain's rage, but defiant. Jen, the ever fearless warrior stepped forward, tall and magnificent in the growing firelight of the surrounding fires.

'And who the hell are you to take that attitude with us? Where have you been all these weeks? Yes you fled and left us, you bastard.'

The captain flinched.

'And who are you, you were never one of the passengers.' And then he looked and saw Jen's hand, the fist clenched ominously.

'Oh my god,' he whined, 'it cannot be you!'

For as I had noticed earlier this very same day we had all changed physically so much.

Adnan and James looked mutinous, but kept silent. Robin and Frank, shuffled their feet in the sand quietly muttering to each other. The noise from the surrounding fires grew, beers had been released from the stores, music and singing was beginning, the village was rejoicing on the return of their young men. It seemed the captain was a welcome visitor too. Darkness fell with practically the audible crash that is the tropical sunset and the night stars began to emerge.

'Let's leave this to the morning,' said Robin. 'Yes we have questions too.' And from the look in his eyes I knew he was thinking of his second wife and whether she was alive or dead.

In many respects the party that night reminded me of stories when a cocktail party, held in the British embassy of some South American capital, had been invaded by a local liberation group and the large gathering of ambassadors, first secretaries, and one, and only one, local politician had been held hostage. After three hours, they ran out of conversation, then were concerned not to divulge any of their state secrets as the sobering up process began, forcing a polite if frigid pall on any communication. They were trapped together for ten days, living on gradually decaying canapés, finishing the drinks, mainly alcoholic and carefully constructing increasing banal conversation. It was the modern version of hell.

We sat on the rush mats in silence, except thanking our generous villagers who came around with hunks of meat, grilled fish, baked yams and just one beer each.

We had not considered our lives in England for some weeks. Now we were forced to think about what had been going on in our absence. Having assumed the captain and the crew were dead, some were thinking whether their partners had survived. And if those partners had received a gentle push into the after life via sharks or the sea, who would know now?

After an hour, Frank got up and wandered up and down the beach, head down seemingly looking at his solitary footprints left in the sand. The full moon had now swung over the cliffs as he paced up and down.

'This is so sad,' said Audrey. 'I might go to him and sing him a song to quieten his spirit.' There was universal response from us to the effect that even if it did, and it would have been most likely to be ineffective, any song would have the opposite impact on us.

Audrey was distressed. We were now well used to her ways of solving problems, which often meant standing on one leg, hands stretched to the skies. In fact we were really impressed, as it was Audrey, the mad woman who had arrived screaming, terrified at all around her, that was the only passenger really at one with this island.

'Why don't you go to the beach, but keep a little distance from Frank?' suggested Melanie kindly, 'and do some yoga, I am sure it will help.'

The Captain overheard and sneered, 'so what's with you lot, gone native?'

We looked at him in shock, we had not so very long ago trusted him with our lives on the ship and had even been fooled into handing over our phones. We turned away and watched as Audrey got up to move towards the trees, Vince followed her, ever faithful, ever watchful. He called back to us, 'the girls are here, be careful,'

'What girls?' the captain gasped, and looked around expectantly, 'there have never been dancing girls here.'

'Idiot!' snapped Dilys, 'he means his girls, the dragons.'

'Hey Matilda,' we heard Vince almost croon, looking up to the branches that over hung the beach, 'get down from there, nothing for you just yet.' Then, with the authority learnt from our treks,

'Now bugger off before the boys see you and start chucking sticks at you.'

And unbelievably the branch shook and the grass swayed as a troop of dragons left dignified, hissing malignantly to search for prey in the deeper parts of the woods.

He looked back at us, 'they know something is up, they're not often out of their burrows at night, they are uneasy just like us.'

Dilys, still cross, muttered, 'Vince, his brains are addled, he thinks those lizards understand him, what nonsense. Those monster just smelt the cooking, that what they are after.'

Melanie looked up, 'well they are either waiting for the meat from the feast, or perhaps us, they are not too fussy, alive or dead, makes no odds to them.'

'You're all mad!' the captain leapt to his feet. 'I cannot take any more, we'll meeting the morning. Then you'll know why you are here. You are all fools, idiots and just face up to that fact.'

We watched him storm off, we watched the villagers rejoicing feasting singing and dancing, and felt more deserted, more lonely than at any time since our arrival.

THREE
H

The cockerels started their morning cacophony with unusual enthusiasm. The wind had changed from the usual on-shore to off-shore, bringing with it the tang of sulphur from the smoking volcano and surprisingly white plumes which must have some from the burning plastic on the far side of the island.

The villagers emerged slowly, one with what could only be assumed was a violent hangover, threw a coconut with some force at a lone cockerel with the unspoken order to 'Shut up and bugger off'.

We slowly gathered too. Even in this early part of the day, the heat was beginning to be oppressive. We had all become used to the tropical heat over the last few months. During the day we moved languidly with our tasks. We learnt that wearing some loose clothing. Most of the women wore sarongs, as did Vince, while the others kept to baggy shorts or like Frank what might once have been cut down tracksuit bottoms. This clothing was more cooling than exposing our skin to the sun, we learnt to use oils and balms from the coconuts and other plants to deal with any sunburn, scratches and insect bites. After painful weeks, we managed to go barefoot unless we were planning to cross the hot lava fields.

We gathered under the largest tree, one reserved for village parleys waiting for the captain. As the village life got under way, no one asked us to do our usual work but passed us by, silently, knowing we were to face some calamitous news. We too were silent, uneasy, each with their own thoughts about what the next phase would be. Nonetheless, Rita brought her basket weaving, which had become an obsession with her. Melanie, silent as usual, picked the earth from under her fingernails. She looked anxiously over at the plantations, asking Audrey if she was sure the gate to the goat compound was closed. Audrey also looked anxiously over the hens. 'Will we be long? The pigs need feeding.' She was ignored. Vince picked at the shells, silently turning them over, then chucking them away. Frank and Robin stood apart, anxious, watchful, suspicious. We heard a noise and as one we turned.

The captain emerged. After last night we no longer viewed him with the respect that sea captains rightly deserve, or in the case of cruise captains with fawning admiration of culpable passengers, occasionally not deserved. Before crossing the village compound, he looked back, gave an order, and emerging from a hut to follow him was my original rescuer, my hero who dragged me from the waves, as I was washed up on the beach. At first he followed the captain, eyes downcast, then as they both approached us, looked up, caught my eye and gave a gentle wave of his hand in recognition. Jen caught this movement.

'Do you know him?' she asked very quietly. I could not reply, I was shocked. I remembered a few men had disappeared when we first got to the island, some did return with the woman and her baby and provisions but my hero had not been among them.

'Sit down,' an imperious voice from the captain, and like very reluctant pupils coming into a school assembly we gradually sat down in a circle.

'So,' the captain began. Then I knew he was as nervous as us, for when people start an important sentence with *so* they are having to think very carefully about exactly what they say next.

He began again a little more forcefully,

'So you know *The Syndicate* hit the reef and sank.'

'We had noticed,' observed Frank, 'get on with it.'

My hero shuffled his feet, looked up and said in perfect English though with a distinct Australian accent, 'it was my idea. It's not about the money, exactly.'

At this the captain snarled, 'bloody snowflake,' he muttered.

'I met Bruce when I was at school in Australia,' he continued, 'he was on a gap year. Bruce would organise a trip, and chartered a ship, then we get the publicity, ransom money, good news all round.'

'Ransom money! Kidnapped! I don't believe it!' an unconvincing outcry from Melanie, though we had all suspected this for some time.

'Quiet!' the captain tried to re-establish his authority. 'The plan was to land you, then Ross, Bruce and I would sail to Darwin and start negotiations. But the ship wrecked made that plan impossible at first.'

'And you abandoned us, you bastard!' a pained shout from the usually silent Paul. 'I was one of your crew, you should have looked out for me.'

A snarl, 'you were only a waiter and who would miss you

pathetic fool!'

'Well I would miss him,' shot back Dilys, followed by similar 'me too.' from us all.

Paul looked around almost with tears in his eyes.

'Yeh, well my Mum will miss me and I have friends here now, so don't start on me!' He stuttered.

FOUR

It was Tyche who insisted they all met in Haywards Heath. This is a nondescript inland town, its sole purpose for existence was the railway station where three coastal routes met on the way to London. When the station was built the townsfolk took the wise decision of not living near the noxious smoke and the toxic ash of the early trains. In the post war years and the demise of the steam train, the station was bordered by supermarkets and an industrial estate, which surprisingly contained an expensive private hospital, while the housing stretched relentlessly in the opposite direction. However, the town stubbornly resisted to move any closer, leaving visitors a tedious uphill walk to parades of mundane shops. Advised by Tyche they all arrived separately and had to walk the quarter mile to the first of the anonymous cafes, mostly owned by chains. Hiding in plain sight, Tyche had advised.

The first to arrive was Stephen. Ever careful to follow instructions to take different routes and not to travel together, he had actually taken the coastal train to Brighton and then the train north, which eventually stopped at Haywards Heath. He made an attempt to look less instantly recognisable from afar, thinking that the awful Gwen might possibly venture this far. Instead of his immaculate pressed trousers, checked shirts and tailored overcoat, he was in disguise, chinos a polo neck jumper, even a newly acquired anorak. As he entered the cafe, he noted with some pleasure that the long list of Lewesian coffee options were not available. It was just coffee or tea. 'What a relief,' he sighed, thinking the places were long gone.

Next Tyche came down from London on the Thames Link direct from central London. He walked in confidently, jeans and t-shirt, only his trainers and a subtle waft of expensive aftershave indicating he was not an impoverished student and, his sense of purpose, that he was not one of the idle sons of the local bourgeoisie. He was followed by Sally. These days she had so much sparkle. Stephen noticed her hair was perhaps more blonde than when he first met her, and certainly all her clothes looked new. As she entered, she looked back and her face lit up as Gary entered. 'I came by bus, what a journey, none of them linked into each other.'

Tyche began, 'I have real news, I have been trawling blogs and emails from West Australia and there are many requests for crews to join long distance trips across the Indian Ocean, and Pacific.'

Sally interrupted, 'yes I was reading one written by two Irish people that left Darwin and sailed to south Africa in a tin can from the looks of it, even broke down at one point and just had to drift.'

Tyche continued, 'there are a surprising amount of these trips in all kinds of boats. But we need more than a tin can, so I have been looking and I think we have found something. There's a request for two crew for an adventure trip to look for Komodo dragons.'

'Strewth!' exclaimed Sally, her favourite expression borrowed from her mother, 'that's what Auntie H told me her trip was about. That was what *The Syndicate* was searching for. Is that a coincidence or what?'

Stephen looked down at his murky, gloomy liquid, sold as coffee, he remembered. 'It can't be, unless of course someone else is looking for missing friends, it could just be possible.' He stirred the liquid, 'but it 's worth looking into.'

'Done that,' said Tyche proudly, 'and booked two of you as crew.'

'Oh god not me,' Stephen nearly knocked his cup over, 'I can't go to sea, I get so sick,'

'What kind of vessel is it?' asked Gary, 'I am not going out in a tin can regardless of what others have done, and I am not risking Sally's life.'

Tyche was annoyed, 'don't be daft, would I do that? No this is a 38 foot Beneteau sloop. She is registered in the UK and looks beautiful. She has got sails so is not dependent on engines or fuel, can carry enough fresh water for 31days of sailing. The person who set up the posting is experienced and Gary you have good sailing knowledge and Sally too. Stephen, you should go out to Australia and ensure they have enough money for essentials, I will monitor you from my office. So how does that sound?'

'This is just totally brilliant, you are a star Tyche, can you reply to say we are on for it. It would be awful to lose this if others replied before us,' said Sally while reaching for Gary's hand under the table.

'Done it,' said Tyche, 'thought you would be up for it, and I took down all the other enquiries, so we are on.'

'Look the least I can do is get down to the travel agents and

206

book tickets for us three to go to Perth. I am happy to pay,' said Stephen in a rush of generosity fuelled by the thought that at long last he was on his way to rescue his lovely lady. He had a subconscious identity like a knight of old, for there had been talk of dragons, and while he did not have a white charger, Business Class on Quantas or Emirates from Gatwick would do nicely.

'Done it,' repeated Tyche, 'no problem Stephen my friend, I just got into your credit card, so its all booked and paid for, checked your passports are OK and so you are off the day after tomorrow.'

'But visas?' Stephen paused, 'done it?'

'Done it,' was the reply

Sally and Gary looked at each, laughed and muttered about leaving messages at work to explain their absence, but Stephen looked at Tyche seeing before him a guy who was great as a friend but who could be lethal as an enemy.

FIVE

Stephen, Sally and Gary started the most arduous part of their journey, which was to negotiate the departure to landside at Perth Airport. None of them were surprised that they had been upgraded to Business Class for the journey, techie's dark skills were gratefully accepted, but this location was well protected from his intervention.

They joined a long line of people slowly wending their way through the well-organised lines to customs. They were warned that absolutely no fruit, veg or meat, flowers, wood, insects, animals could be taken into Australia. All were subject to the same penalties as guns and drugs it seemed to Stephen, who spent the waiting minutes studying all the posters. Arriving at the head of the queue he was politely asked questions, then allowed to proceed. Though Gary and Sally's bags were opened and thoroughly searched.

Stephen waited for them so they could all exit together. When they walked through the final doors, they saw someone holding a card with their names, a relief certainly that the meeting arrangements were in hand.

A hesitant greeting all round, 'I am Bruce. Hi everyone,' and a reply of 'Hi,' then they dragged their bags out into blistering sunshine, momentarily blinded them, the heat coming as a blow. The car park was nearby, no long trail like Gatwick.

'Yeah, its a bit warm, here in Perth, but Freo is cooler. You are staying in an apartment block down by the harbour for a day while we get everything ready OK?'

While Sally and Gary sat in the back, of the minibus on their journey to Freemantle, their phones out and working, their heads down like penguins feeding their young, Stephen looked at the driver. He was a young man, late twenties or thirties. At first Stephen thought he was perhaps too casually dressed in a t-shirt, shorts and flip flops, until looking out of people walking through the city suburbs, realised this must be the national dress for young males. He was very tanned and had that stubble of beard that makes his generation. He had an English accent too, Stephen noticed. But it was his neck that caught Stephen's attention. The head of a lizard appeared to peer out from the top of Bruce's shirt.

There was something about that tattoo that Stephen struggled to remember. He was fairly sure he had never met the young man before, but nonetheless he was sure it was something of significance.

They drove for about 45 minutes, passed endless straight suburban roads of neat bungalows.

'Freemantle is where the yacht is moored. Its a little town about ten miles or so from Perth, the big city,' explained Bruce, his eyes firmly on the road. 'Same distance as Lewes is from Brighton then,' observed Stephen, and saw with surprise Bruce nod and then try unsuccessfully to disguise the movement that showed he was aware of that distance. 'I am sure there is more to him, I bet he is involved somehow in *The Syndicate*' thought Stephen, but did not say anything more, each man now silent with their thoughts.

They arrived in Freemantle, driving through the old port area, the harbour offices, the hotels and bars that had welcomed enormous numbers of immigrants arriving by ship in the Nineteenth Century. Bruce pointed to a round building on a hill.

'That was built in 1830 and is the oldest building in Western Australia can you believe. This place was the first stop for thousands of Italian migrants and you will hear Italian spoken everywhere, the Italian cooking and the coffee is great here, end of history lesson,' laughed Bruce now looking much more relaxed as the car drew up outside the apartment block.

After checking in, Bruce followed them into the apartment. 'I know its hot now,' said Bruce, 'but it will be cooler later when the doctor gets in.'

'What's this about the doctor?' asked Sally, 'we don't need a doctor.'

Bruce laughed, 'haven't been doing your homework girl, the Freo doctor is an onshore breeze that cools the afternoons and evenings here. Stops everyone going mad like they do in the rest of this country. So whenever we get going it needs to be on the morning tides. And by the way, walk over to the Shipwrecks Museum while you are here and you will get an idea of the rocks and reefs that have taken down hundreds of ships. Get some sleep and I will call in tomorrow morning to finalise out plans. We need to get away by Saturday.'

That evening they sat overlooking the silent marina. The metal ropes tapped without rhythm noisily against the masts, an occasional splash of a gull hitting the water were the only sounds. The air smelt different, perhaps from the Norfolk pines nearby, but more portably from the cooking on the Harbour eating places.

It was Sally who said, 'there must be hundreds of yachts, just moored here. Looks as if they are never taken out.'

'Just like every other marina in the world,' added Gary, 'what a complete waste of materials, but I suppose it keeps boat builders in a job. But he is as keen as us to get away. Let's hope he knows what he is doing.'

But that night none of them slept, but were awake realising the enormity of what they had taken on, the dangers along inhospitable an unknown coast line, the trust they had to have in the unknown Bruce.

Gary was terrified of sharks, and dreaded that if he should at any time fall overboard he would be in grave danger. He wondered how Bruce, who seemed to be an ordinary bloke, could afford the yacht and why he did not really question them about any direction, destination or even purpose for the voyage.

Sally thought about the heat. She tried to sleep without any air conditioning, but the breeze from the doctor was very light that evening and she sweated even though the door to her room opened onto a balcony. How would she cope own the open seas in the relentless tropical heat she wondered and further a she least experienced sailor, it would be down to her to do the cooking.

Stephen also lay sleepless for most of the night. 'What had he got his two friends into?' he thought. He was also worried that Tyche seemed to have control of his finances, how far could he be trusted, did Charles really know him? Thoughts sped relentlessly around like racing cars on an eternal circuit, going faster and faster and going nowhere.

The next morning, they blearily welcomed Bruce.

'We'll go straight to the Marina. At the moment the ketch is registered as Ivy Ellen, but that will get changed when we leave. She is fully provisioned, its taken me weeks to get ready. We can go out in an hour and just sail around so you get the feel of her, OK?' And turning to Stephen, 'why don't you come along too, we'll only be out an hour or two. Bring you gear so that in the morning we can just take off.'

And a short walk to the mooring and there she was, the most beautiful ocean going ketch imaginable. Even Gary with all his experience was impressed.

'It has sailed around much of the world,' Bruce said proudly. 'Just got here from Sydney, came out from Portsmouth last year.'

Stephen stepped cautiously onto the deck from the wharf. He promised himself he was only going to look around. All the deck seemed strewn with ropes and cunningly placed he was sure. Two steps down there was in a luxurious cabin area, seating for at least six, a large table in the centre, a galley down one side. And further in there were two cabins each with two bunk beds, even a shower and modern toilet. He was half tempted to suggest that he joined them, but quickly recalled how he loathed the sea and when he absolutely had to take a ferry, was usually violently seasick. Emerging on deck, he congratulated Bruce on his ship and added,

'I am tempted to come with you, but you may need space later on, er that is,' and here he noticed a glare from Gary, 'that you should have to pick up anyone on the way, perhaps...do you do such things?'

And to his surprise, Bruce agreed, 'just what I was thinking mate,' he said quietly.

During the morning, they checked and re-checked everything was working and that all the stores were onboard. Stephen was unprepared fort the heat, but Bruce was relentless in getting everything onboard and correctly stowed.

'Think this is hot,' he said to the group, 'inland up near Perth its at least another ten degrees above here, and in the centre of Australia even more.'

'God almighty,' groaned Stephen, 'thought it was only Saudi Arabia that had those sort of temperatures.'

'And that's without the bush fires, man when those get going the heat is dreadful and the fire service go out to try to put them out.'

They had all heard stories of the fires that had raged across thousands of hectares, and for once were silent, grateful they were near the sea. As the afternoon breeze began, Bruce suggested they all went out for an hour just to get used to the working of the yacht. A short sea trial was how he described it. Even Stephen was persuaded to join them, assured it would on the calmest of seas. To his own great surprise he accepted the offer.

The Freemantle heat, never as severe or cruel as elsewhere in Australia, was beginning to hit. Combined with jet lag, he thought he would not cope if left alone in a hot room waiting for them to return. And again unacknowledged, he had guilt the adventure which he had started might not turn out well.

Leaving the harbour, they could see a number of yachts of differing sizes, even a few motorboats out on the open sea.

'My god, there's a regatta tomorrow,' said Bruce excitedly, 'Perfect cover, We can start early morning and no one will notice we haven't returned.'

Nobody commented on the fact that Bruce wanted an unobserved departure as much as themselves.

They left the marina heading for the nearby islands. Loads of people to sailing about without any direction it seemed to Stephen. The largest of the islands was Rottnest. Bruce looked at it sadly telling them it had been a concentration camp run by the British where possibly hundreds of aborigine warriors had been incarcerated or killed, a crime only recently recognised by the government. It was difficult to believe, but it is said only one warrior escaped by swimming to the mainland.

'With all the development along the coastline its hard to imagine how hostile this coastline must have been back then,' said Sally.

'Not too much has changed,' Bruce said quietly. 'You can see the beaches and the nice houses, the ports and the ferry going to the island, but not too far from here the wild coast resumes, make a mistake and you are a long way from help, even if you make it to shore and that's before the sharks get you. Look there's one cruising about, just keeping an eye on us.'

Stephen withdrew his hands right inside the boat, his antipathy to the sea significantly increasing.

Bruce checked the radio, looked at the sky. The swell of the sea had increased, and although Stephen was pretty sure he had never actually screamed in his life, one began to emerge, but of an anguished cry of, 'let me off!' He was scared and he was feeling decidedly seasick. 'Relax mate,' said Bruce, 'we'll drop you off at Rottenest.' And so it was the Stephen was dropped overboard, not landed on a jetty, but forced to wade through shallow water up the beach in front of amused backpackers and to catch the ferry back to the mainland.

Later, in the warmth of a west Australian night, they gathered cooking a meal together. They were all quiet, the crew because they were exhausted from ensuring all the provisions were safely stored, the fresh fruit ready in strong bags to hang outside, that all the sails and ropes were in excellent working order. Stephen too was lost for words. He was ashamed of his panic on just a trip outside the harbour, but he saw what the ocean could deliver, even so near to shore.

That night he contacted Tyche. 'We have everything ready to go. Bruce seems to know what he is doing and they will set off tomorrow morning as the yachts go out for the regatta.'

'I know,' replied Tyche, 'tell them I will set the yacht's co-ordinates in two days time for the island. If all goes well they should be near in five days time. Don't worry I will follow them. In the meantime, you start contacting journalists with a scoop. As soon as we know more we'll start to splash the story.'

As dawn came up, the yacht slowly left the harbour in the wake of the huge tankers leaving the port of Freemantle into the shipping lanes, following the huge export of minerals, the sheep and cattle destined for slaughter in Asia and those empty returning to factories and plants to bring cars and just stuff back to Australia. Stephen watched them from the apartment, reluctant to draw attention by being on the jetty, waving a handkerchief either physically or metaphorically. He saw them silently hoist the sails, and turning across mouth of the Swan river, heading north and into the perilous seas of the Indian Ocean.

SIX

H

The only way for survival for the isolated communities of the tiny islands, lost in the enormity of the oceans, where humans live on the very brink of existence is to follow two important rules.

The first is to share everything. It was, to follow an over used expression a very steep learning curve for those who had been washed up, victims of shipwrecks, lost mariners, or pirates who were left on a desert island, to abandon the skills of cunning and acquisition and learn that work had to be co-operative, that food had to be shared in times of plenty and hardship.

The second was never to allow any dispute get to a level of violence. Raised voices were unacceptable, fights unknown and any threatening behaviour met with sharp disapproval for all in the community. The only exception was in the case of any child who let out the pigs, failed to feed the hens or who were ghastly to their siblings, which earned a slap or gentle cuff on the head.

So it was, that as the captain shouted and yelled, waved his arms in the air, the villagers began to leave their tasks and look anxiously towards us. The young men and boys gradually, silently moved to stand near Paul.

'*Stap isi,*' said one. '*No gut pain,*' said another.

'What are you saying? Who the hell are you to tell me what to do!' began the captain, then, observing that these young men were tall, immensely strong, and obviously protective to Paul, closed his mouth, while still trembling with rage.

'They are Paul's football team,' said Robin giving a diplomatic explanation for in any culture no one messes with a football team.

Ross laughed, 'at last, we can have a match against Orrible, perhaps against the other islands,' and I could see that he was imagining taking on Liverpool in the not too distant future.

'Hang on,' said Dilys, still smarting from the vicious words of the captain. 'What exactly do you mean, the other islands?'

'Shut up,' snarled the captain, but to whom he was addressing this advice was uncertain, was it Ross or Dilys? In the case of the latter his remarks failed to have any impact. She stepped right up and said with quiet determinism, 'what do you mean the other islands? Have you been nearby all this time? Could we have been bloody rescued weeks ago? Just what is going on?'

Susi now joined us. Her matriarchal presence certainly diffused the situation.

'Sit down, shut up,' she said with dignity, and that was just what we did.

'Ross,' she commanded, '*Now wasup, Tok tru*' then added to stress the meaning and in precise English, 'and no bullshit, yeah.'

'We did not mean you any harm,' Ross began, 'but we are desperate, we had to do something. It wasn't about money. Well, not at first. That would only be the final stage. *The Syndicate* was not supposed to crash. We planned to come in through the reef and then leave you safely here while we did the negotiations.'

'But it did crash and you left us.' said Frank thoughtfully,

'Not me, I stayed to see you were Ok didn't I? And I rescued you,' he said looking at me, 'you could have drowned if I hadn't dragged you onto the beach.'

'That's not the point,' continued Frank with quiet intensity. 'You, and the so-called captain, left in the only lifecrafts. We know some of the passengers drowned we saw their bodies in the wreckage. That's manslaughter! So who left with you, here and the rest of the crew?' Unspoken, 'and where is my wife?'

There was a silence, a hesitation in proceedings, during which the villagers gathered around. It was one of those moments when the sun paused in the sky, the space-time continuum gave a shudder, this pause seemed to measure the nano seconds, lengthening to a minute perhaps more, the silence deepened as we all looked at each other, suspicions growing.

Susi looked meaningfully at Ross, the kind of look that teachers give when expecting an answer and not tolerating any evasion. Ross looked intently at the sand. Rita put her arm around Melanie, who had begun to tremble. Robin had his hands on his waist, looking like he was measuring up for a fight. Frank had his head in his hands, a prisoner awaiting sentence. The men began to move closer. I noticed one or two had picked up large sticks and rocks. Sushi moved around obviously trying to calm the situation, but the restrained anger and frustration began to pour out from our group. Shouting began along the lines of :

Where are the crew?

Where are the lifeboats?

We haven't got any money!

Get me off this island!

But piercing into this cacophony came a primeval scream, a wail, a voice unrecognised. It was Paul, distraught, sobbing, stuttering. We were shocked into silence.

'What's up,' a gentle touch by Robin, though he was pushed away.

'Where's Rahmin? What have you done to him? He must have gone with you, I never found his body though I swam around the wreck for days! Is he alive?'

And then continued to sob, Paul's body wracked with grief

'Well,' I thought to myself, 'I didn't see that coming.'

Paul, defeated, did not want or expect an answer and went to sit on the sand at the back of our group. Two of the football team sat near him giving him some support I suppose though they may not have understood his act words.

Jen stood up and with the authority gained over the last few weeks said, 'just everyone shut the fuck up.'

And then turning to Ross and the captain said with some menace

'Now tell us, just how did you get here?'

On this Frank, who had remained restless pacing about, suddenly took off. It was a repeat performance of his bid to get out to the wreck all those weeks ago. And with history repeating itself, he was in a matter of yards brought down by the young warriors and he screamed and thrashed around.

'He's got a ship, he must have ship,' at least I think that is what he was saying as his face was somewhat buried in the sand.

When Frank was subdued, back in his place by us, Jen repeated her question this time with such intensity that the captain again flinched.

'Don't you start on me,' he was an animal realising he was trapped, snarling, defiant, but truly scared. 'And where's your husband poor old sod, I could see you are planning his demise on the cruise, did you pack your widow's weeds!' And this was met with such a slap from Jen he reeled backwards.

'Fuck you!' ahe yelled right inches face. 'Let's start at the end. So how did you get here and is this a rescue mission?'

Ross stood up, suddenly defiant and laughed, 'him?' he said derisively, 'he was just the muscle, stupid but cunning, a real latter day pirate.' And with that flicked sand in the face of the captain.

But this gesture drew hisses from the surrounding villagers, for this was not their way of parley. It was then I noticed that Paul, quiet Paul, had withdrawn from the pushing and shoving and had started on the path up the cliffs with two of the football team. I thought it best not to draw attention to their departure.

'So,' began Ross, 'two years ago, I knew we needed help here but could not work out what to do. Then I met Bruce in Australia when I was at college in Perth, and we thought of a plan. We'd charter a ship and do an ecovoyage, not to hold you as hostages but to raise the problem as a worldwide disaster.'

At this point there was a yell from Paul on the cliffs and then he came hurtling down that very same path that had so frightened us when we first arrived. He ran across the sands to us, well ahead of the following team. They too looked disturbed.

'No Ship!' he screamed, 'they got here in a bamboo outrigger, there's no ship, there's no rescue. Its on the beach around the rocks, you bastard,' and he launched himself unsuccessfully at the captain.

'Will you let me finish!' Ross ordered, and Paul surpassingly sat down, resentful, watchful.

'Yup, get on,' commanded Susie and after the usual shuffling around and sitting in the sand, Ross started.'

'Look we did get away in the zodiac to get help. We made it to the first of the islands. We did send messages back with the canoes. Bruce got a lift back to Australia from a dinghy. But we couldn't get another ship, we had no money.'

'And?' demanded Frank, 'so you got here in a little canoe and is that the way we have to leave? Because it's getting hot here in the sand and I have had enough of desert islands, so what's the plan?'

'The outriggers are great,' Ross began, 'islanders travelled all around these oceans, still do.'

Melanie stood up, 'look spare me the geography lesson and tell me one thing.'

And then both she and the captain asked the same question.

'Where are the others?'

SEVEN
H

Even in the parley centre of the village, the heat was intense. The group packed tighter to take advantage of the shade beneath the trees. A heavy silence descended as the pigs and goats took a siesta, as the hens made dust holes in the dry earth to snooze away the afternoon, the wild birds settled down knowing the predators of the night were still in the burrows, their holes and caves. The dragons. As ever languidly hunted among the trees and on the beaches. Even the scent of the bush, the vanilla plantation seemed to disappear in the unremitting onslaught of the midday sun.

Only Rita and Melanie sat on the sand already weaving baskets, somewhat reminiscent of that woman who sat by the guillotines knitting while heads of aristocrats were lopped off.

The captain, a survivor of several bar room brawls and worse, wisely chose defeat. With much suffering of feet, coughing and spitting, he began.

'Well we got to the island, eventually. You guys didn't notice we took a long way round, didn't want to be traced. I had turned the GPS off days before, and got your phones and stuff.' He stopped seemingly pleased with his cunning.

'Get on with it,' growled Frank, with menace.

'Right,' a pause for spectacular coughing, an attempt to spit checked by a glare from Susi.

'Well you all was picked 'cos we thought you would be loaded and when we checked your background there were not too many people who would miss you, at least for some weeks.'

'OOH!' wailed Audrey, 'that's so cruel,' but she got no further, Vince gave her a hug and she nestled in his arms reassured.

The captain began, 'right,' his favourite opening when in trouble, 'so we gets here but the weather turned leery and these seas truly bad. Ross here thought we'd get through the reef. And we didn't.'

'And we didn't' said Robin sadly, 'go on.'

'Well I, haven't been to sea for years without knowing we were in trouble. And that we were, weren't we?' Not a question but a statement of fact, continuing, 'so we gets the lifeboats damn quick. If you hadn't been all shocked and crying and shouting some of you could have come too.'

He looked at Frank, 'and your missus God she hopped onboard before all of us, get me out of here she says.'

Frank, fell back on the sand, his worst fears realised, his wife had survived.

The captain did not notice this and looking out to sea said thoughtfully, 'but we lost her at the first island.'

'You mean she died?' queried Frank, rather hopeful.

'Not her, she just took off dunno where she is now, she had a fight with the purser, lovely woman she was, but she didn't take prisoners, as they say, had a wicked way with a knife.'

Surprisingly he seemed somewhat misty-eyed.

'But I heard a rumour that they were planning to set up a bar together somewhere.'

'And the others?' Jen asked.

'Bruce took off in a rig when we got to the second island, The sad thing was I had to sell Rahmin when we ran out of money and had to depart bloody quick from PNG. So he could be around.'

Paul sprang up, 'You ruthless bastard, you sold him as a slave!'

The captain backed off, 'not a slave...exactly...just labour.' And then seeing the lethal look in Paul's eyes and the contempt and shock in those of the group, suddenly turned in a counter attack. He stood ready to run, then lifting his fist, yelled.

'Where's that chubby blonde, always fancied her, where's that neurotic bitch always complaining about her allergies? So what my friends happened to you, because there are a damn sight fewer of you that I would have thought.'

And quietly we heard Melanie say, 'Rita forget the baskets let's see if we could do a casket.

EIGHT

Out of sight of land, realisation of the enormity of the great ocean before them was both a frightening and an exhilarating experience. Watching the sun sink in the west and the clear night skies with all the stars, the mysterious constellations reinforced their feeling of being such insignificant creatures in the cosmos. On that first night, the winds were benign, and the sea without the huge swells that can be a hazard to small craft. The sails rattled, holding the ketch to a steady speed as Bruce asked them all to come down to the cabin.

Bruce was worried. Searching for diplomatic words, though the tension in his body, the sweat on his forehead was obvious. He began,

'I had something to tell you. Not sure where to being, I am sorry but I was not totally truthful. But now something strange is going on and I am not sure what it is.'

He looked stressed almost in a panic,

'This yacht is out of control.'

Gary nodded, 'yeah. I can guess. The route is changed on your autopilot. So let me tell you what is going on.'

'You don't understand,' Bruce's voice was rising, bordering on hysteria. 'I was going to tell you this evening, I was going to change the plans. We're not heading for the Andaman islands but heading north east into the islands out from Papua New Guinea.'

Gary began, 'cool its ok, we changed the course. I suppose we've taken over your yacht, not pirates but we need to get to an island where we think our mates are.'

Sally sat beside Bruce and when she had a chance to speak, 'listen, Bruce,' her voice disembodied, strange, almost ethereal, 'we are on a mission, we got find my dearest friend. I am sure she is still alive, but she was on an eco-trip and the ship has completely disappeared.'

There was an explosion, Bruce leapt up. 'What are you saying? Who are you?'

He looked out to sea, hanging on the rigging as the yacht cut through the evening swell. He questioned now quietly and in some despair, 'just who are you? I haven't got any money, far from it,' he gave a weary laugh. 'Just my bloody luck, in all the people who could have come I am out here with two nutters.'

Sally tried again, with less effort admittedly, to be a voice of reason.

'Look, we just want to use your yacht for a few weeks. We are looking for a ship, *The Syndicate* and we think we know where she is. If we are right, we think she may have run aground near an island north east from here. We've picked up very some strange messages, but there is definitely something going on.'

As Sally turned to look directly at Bruce, she was alarmed. He began to laugh manically, he screamed, he suddenly took off swinging around the yacht (without any safety harness), he clapped his hands, he tore his hair, then going down the galley arrived back loaded with wine and beer bottles.

'My friends,' he began, 'what the fuck is going on I do not know, but I am going to get truly hammered.' He opened a bottle and drank, no glass, made a spliff and sat back.

'Well, bugger me, who would have thought?' he laughed. 'Its where I am heading, no probs.'

He lit the spliff and inhaled.

'Gary my mate, you are on first watch and Sally my lovely on second.'

In the next hour under a glorious night sky and on a benign sea, they caught up onto amazing coincidence that had brought their two missions together, they all silently wondered that the work of the 'fickle finger of fate' was decidedly spooky.

Sally and Gary watched all night together. Uneasy and unsure now that Bruce had dissolved into a quiet slumber. They sat in silence together, watching the automatic pilot, making small adjustments to the wheel as if some ghostly pirate was still at the helm. Above them Orion's Belt looked down, upside down from its position above Eastbourne, but a comforting landmark in the galaxies above them.

Sally began, 'I know Tyche is clever, but I read once that life plays cruel and perplexing practical jokes on mankind by making us face so many contradictory elements together and leaving us to deal the callousness of the universe.'

'Wow,' Gary looked at her fondly, 'now that's a real philosophical observation! But you're right.'

Sally cuddled up closer to Gary, 'what I wonder, who, or what is playing tricks on us? At least we were kind of prepared, but for Bruce, can you just imagine the shock?'

Gary agreed. 'But what has been his involvement and what has he been doing all these past months? Sally my love, just get some sleep, you may have to take the next watch and we're going to have to be careful. We are still on the shipping lanes and god only knows how effective the lookout is from some of these old cargo ships.'

After a short time, Gary assured by the gentle snores from below, charged up his mobile and called Tyche.

'Hi man,' the laconic voice came out of Gary's phone, like a genie speaking quietly from the bottle. 'Been watching you. What a turn up with that Bruce guy. But bit of a surprise.'

But Gary now used to the satanic skills of Tyche was unconvinced.

'Oh yeah?' he answered, 'so how did you pick him?'

'Hours of searching, mate,' came the enigmatic reply. 'Leave it to you to find out more about him, think serendipity my friend,' and with that silence as Tyche cut all communication.

The Ivy Ellen sailed quietly and with dignity through the ocean. Her sails caught the winds without difficulty, she leaned only as far as required, she was a vessel that avoided drama. Sally and Gary met every day with amazement. First they had to navigate well away from the sinister cargo ships, stacked so high with thousands of boxes, not crates or containers, they were told but boxes which only came in two sizes to fit all international shipping. Once they saw the vessel loaded with live sheep and cattle heading to North Australia to pick up buffalo before heading east to the meat markets of Asia and the Middle East.

On the third day they were well away from the main shipping lanes. Sally, whose previous sailing experience had been along the busy highways of the English Channel had been apprehensive that they would be fighting treacherous seas, desolate outlook devoid of life. Not so. During the morning they were followed by a school of dolphins. As they leapt over the waves, Sally noticed they were looking at her, fearless and curious to know what this vessel so silent, without any engines, was doing in their patch of the ocean.

Fish swam beneath and once they glimpsed a small group of whales on their annual migration south. As they moved further into the ocean, they saw fewer sailing vessels, like themselves off on round the world ventures, but from time to time spotted fishing trawlers trailing long lines of nets.

Gary began to respect Bruce. Discipline was friendly but firm, hours on watch were kept, all had turns cooking, alcohol was restricted, safety harnesses had to be worn at all times, sun cream was an essential. However, when it came to social chatting, Bruce was almost taciturn, untrusting, but nonetheless driven to ensure they reached their destination. Gary was sure there were unspoken secrets, something that had severely affected Bruce more than the rescue mission.

It was later on that fateful third day when their venture took another turn. Towards the evening, they spotted a fishing boat. Bruce looked at it long and hard though powerful binoculars.

'Alter course,' he commanded, 'I want to keep well away. They've got excellent radio communications, look at those antennae and that satellite dish. I don't want us to be recognised.'

Gary added, 'looks like they've got powerful engines there too. Do you think they are smugglers, perhaps pirates?'

'Possibly,' replied Bruce, 'they may not bother us, though this yacht is valuable. We need to keep an eye on them. Still its unusual they are alone, normally they are in pairs. Keep a good watch tonight.'

As the evening drew in and the relentless sun eventually sank Sally was on watch. She loved this time marvelling at the stars. Bruce had shown her a map of the skies made from tiny front of bamboo interlaced with different shells. At first it looked like an extremely poor piece of primary school artwork, a table mat perhaps which would never see a table but would be treasured by a young mother as a sign of her child's genius only weeks later to fall to bits.

It was a shock to learn this was a most sophisticated map. Each piece of bamboo on the mat showed the major points of the compass, some shells indicated islands, other stars and weaving through them were threads of different colours. These represented the major ocean currents, but Bruce added that most early Polynesian sailors would dip the hands in the water searching for warmth and cold. Sally marvelled at the knowledge so nearly destroyed by the European explorers so confined in their inherent superiority, but their weakness in relying on untested naval instruments. She had read about the many wrecks off the west coast of Australia, the lives lost.

Although the side of the yacht rose some feet above the waves, she leaned farther to trail her hands in the water. She wondered if she could feel the difference in the water temperature, would it be cold indicating the Antarctic currents had reached so far north, or would the water be warm even in night cool winds.

In horror and with a scream she snatched her hand out. Something evil had wrapped itself around her hand, around her arm, heavy, a sticking toxic grey mass. She was paralysed with fear, she had read of the Kraken, huge squid-like creatures that legends and myths described as strong enough to pull down a ship with their enormous tentacles, sinking even the largest of the ships She had seen enough of David Attenborough's explorations of the sea depths to be almost phobic about what lived far beneath them. Her panic grew, she could not find a light and in the end her yells woke up the two sleeping men.

Gary had never seen Sally in such a state normally self assured, almost too analytical.

'What's up?' More screams from Sally.

Bruce shone a torch, 'Jesus, what's that?'

More screams from Sally, and as she waved her arms, frantically trying to shake off what had caught on her, slime and gross fronds like dead tentacles slithered down her arm onto the deck. Carcasses of dead fish, remnants of rope encircled with seaweed and molluscs, and other rotting vegetation gathered in a pool at her feet, then a bag, then a plastic water bottle, the label still distinct, dropped from this heaving mass onto the deck.

'Oh god almighty, its plastic,' groaned Bruce, 'just look at it, vile stuff.'

'Get this off me!' yelled Sally uninterested in the scientific analysis of what ever had caught her. 'Its not plastic it alive!'

She was right, a bruised and battered fish slithered, half dead onto the deck. In the moonlight, her hands were a ghastly hue of green, her t-shirt and shorts now covered in a grey mass of slime. Gary bent down to retrieve a struggling fish, not throwing it back but putting it aside for supper later on.

Looking at his distraught love, Gary did not want to hug her, reassure her for the stench was awful, and chose instead to go below to make a cup of tea. It was Bruce who silently got the hose out, washed Sally and the deck down with equal but thorough force. He did not say very much except orders to get below, and get changed, but not to chuck anything overboard which she had made a weak attempt to do.

That night none of them could sleep, Sally was still in shock, kept referring to the legends of the Kraken, Gary took over the watch quietly and efficiently checking course, checking sails, though it was hardly needed on this balmy night. Bruce lay on his bunk, the calmest and planning their next move but not anticipating what the next day would bring.

The sun was just coming over the horizon. Again for deep ocean all was going well, no heavy swell, no unanticipated squalls. The autopilot was set. Bruce said he wanted a formal meeting and they gathered together in unusual solemnity.

'Last night, Sally you discovered why we are on this venture. This ocean is full of rotting plastic, it sweeps along the top of waves in rafts, even like small islands. In storms it gets sucked down, trapped in reefs or rocks, floating like lethal bombs in the undersea currents and much of it is washed up, trapped in a bay on a nearby island. Every day more heaving mass has been washed in and then trapped. The islanders are in despair. That's where we planned to take *The Syndicate*.'

'You are mad, completely out of your mind,' Sally was choking, still in shock from the night's experiences.

Bruce hesitated, coughed looked unsettled.

'Go on,' said Gary wearily, for he knew what was coming up.

Bruce gave him a long hard look, then continued,

'We are approaching that island, we should be there within the next 36 hours all being well. You can see for yourselves the impact of plastic when we get there, not many people know about the island, standing alone and right off the shipping lanes,' Gary said, looking down, his head in his hands. 'We know all that, get on with it!'

'Our plan was to get a mini cruise together with passengers that had money but no close relatives that would miss them too quickly.'

Sally looked at him in horror, 'that ship had my friend on it,

225

don't tell me she's dead, been killed, is that what this is about?'

'Cool it,' replied Bruce tersely, 'our plan was to keep the ship at our island, then hold the passengers to ransom, to attract world wide publicity to the cause of the islanders, to get them help and to do something about all this plastic. But it all started to go wrong, even from the outset I never trusted that captain. First he took everyone's mobiles, laptops and all the passengers were without communication. He started sending rubbish emails in their names to anyone on their address list, at random and using language they would never use, thinking he was so clever, idiot!'

'We know,' said Sally more gently this time, 'that made us suspicious.'

'And then there was the shipwreck,' muttered Bruce, not noticing that at these words, Sally had stood up, belligerent, but before she could speak, she fell forward.

'What the fuck!'

Bruce leapt up, the yacht had crashed into something just under the waterline, it was like hitting a log on a country road. The yacht rose and groaned, its sails trying to pull it free.

'Get the sails down,' and looking over the side, 'oh my god, its fishing lines, miles long. Where the hell is the trawler, out here fishing illegally and no light on the lines. Get the axe we have to cut ourselves free.'

Bruce got the scuba gear from the deck locker as Gary returned with the axe.

'I'll go and try to disentangle the lines from the propeller, I am sure that's where we're caught, but both of you look out for sharks, they follow these nets for easy prey, though they often get trapped in the line too.'

Bruce slipped overboard, a line tied to him just in case he had to be pulled in quickly. They could see Bruce hacking at the lines and seeming to have some success, but as he surfaced, Sally shouted,

'There's a trawler out there and it's heading this way.'

Gary, with his experience of trawlermen on the south coast, knew that these guys would be far from pleased, and in fact if they took out guns and shot them all dead who would know? But they could not move despite Bruce's frantic efforts. The trawler was closing in.

Bruce clambered aboard, 'we should be free now,' he gasped,

exhausted, then, 'what the hell is going on there?'

Then they heard, 'Stop, help, wait for me,' and to their astonishment, a man dived into the sea and swam with Olympic speed towards them.

'Is he going to attack?' Sally was worried, then realised he must be desperate to dive in along the fishing lines and possibly in the pathway of sharks, when Bruce exploded.

'Oh my god, its Rahmin!'

NINE
H

The captain repeated his question. And one by one, the group muttered about what had happened to the partner they had originally boarded with all those weeks ago. I kept silent, after all I had lost my husband, not mislaid, not left behind, but genuinely lost him, in fact could hardly remember him now. But we all had a problem for we were recalling a life we had not only long forgotten, but actually had few plans to return to. The comments such as: he just slipped away, under the waves; he was asleep, I couldn't wake him;, he fell on a perch no I mean a ledge. It all sounded so trite but was actually accurate.

'So they're dead eh?' snarled the captain, then putting on a pseudo posh voice, 'Oh must like every cruise where there are sometimes a high number of deaths, among the men,' then back to his obnoxious leering voice, 'Do you dare to criticize me?' And then more thoughtfully and looking directly at Dilys and me, 'and my jolly widows, will you benefit from the wills, are you looking forward to a handy payment when you get home?'

Dilys was ashen, and I remembered her classes on tax relief or avoidance on the beach when we first got washed up. She may have looked pale, but she wasn't going down with a fight.

'My Jim died on the plane coming out here.'

'No doubt helped in his way, did you drop a little something into his gin and tonic on the way. I remember you were the one that definitely did not want to stay behind and look after his corpse, trying to avoid the enquiry eh?'

Then he turned and with dramatic effect said, 'don't you idiots realise my joke the name of our little cruise ship!'

And on that enigmatic remark, he turned a marched away, trying to find the hut where Ross' family lived.

We all got up too, silent. Melanie, the normally quiet Melanie turned with passion.

'Was I really once a chubby blonde?'

We did not respond.

She continued, 'but, you know what, that captain is dead right. I couldn't believe, that shark, what a champion, him and his and all his mates munched that old bastard to bits in no time. Just hope they didn't get indigestion.'

We looked at her surprised, she had normally seemed the quiet grieving widow just slowly getting on with life on the island. It suddenly struck me that she was one of the most changed of all our group, or perhaps like many, she was not at all changed, that the person we thought we knew was just a facade, a pretence. She stood, upright, slim from all the hard work, bronzed. Like all of us, her hair had grown and now a streaked alone and natural grey, which gleamed from the constant oils in this tropical heat, Her hair was tied back, always with a flower or frond. She wore her brightly coloured sarong with confidence, no nervous hitching up, no constant retying, which we all did on arrival, like the newly arrived at the swimming pool Spanish holiday resort.

Rita looked astonished at Melanie's words, then said, 'well said, girl,' and then walked away.

Frank looked after her, 'never really knew what happened to her guy, supposed to have slipped off some rocks.'

'Best not to ask,' said Jen firmly, while glancing at me, which I thought uncalled for as my Harry had died in his chair in Lopeham while I was at the shops.

It was that evening that Ross and Susie came to sit with us. At first they were quiet, but we had long recognised that this behaviour was a precursor to a serious statement of some kind. Like all the people in the world who are facing west, to the sunset, we sat on the beach. We were like our ancestors partly pleased to see the baking sun gradually sink down and pleased to welcome the cool of the evening. Were we apprehensive that this giver of life, this radiant source of energy, might decide to go away, never to reemerge in the morning mists. And like the people of the world we sat in silence, in respect to this eternal and wonderful spectacle of the sun's descent, of the changing colours of the sky and the shy emerging first stars of the night.

Ross began, 'Susie and I want to tell you about what we had planned. It's all gone wrong, I was stupid to think it would work but we had to do something. Everyone on the island agreed, well almost everyone.'

Robin snorted, 'Hah! You had a plan, well I cannot see much evidence of that, the whole thing has been a disaster from beginning to end.'

I could see Susie was taken aback by this, she may not be very fluent in English but she could understand far more than she could express.

'Enough, Robin,' I said, 'just listen, and take into account we are alive and well.'

'So,' another attempt at a start from Ross, 'before you came we stocked up on essential medical equipment, drugs, first aid and god knows what to keep you soft Europeans alive.'

'We're not Europeans,' interjected Robin, all pretences of diplomacy abandoned, 'we have the vote and I support Brexit, and England.'

For the first time in so many months of hardship I actually thought I was going to hit him, but everyone else chorused the usual 'just shut up', now with added colourful expletives.

'Then we got all the people who might need help away so the you would think we were totally isolated,' continued Ross.

'Oh my god,' said Jen, 'the baby, that's why the canoe came back with his mother, and all those provisions.'

Ross put his head in his hands, 'yes,' he said sadly 'and that was when we found out the captain had doubled crossed us. We thought he would get help, but all he did was sell everything to pirates.'

'Including Rahmin!' Paul spat.

'Including Rahmin,' Ross repeated, 'I don't know whether he is alive or dead, and the same for Bruce.'

'Paul you knew about the plan didn't you?' Robin asked.

Paul was defensive, 'no I bloody didn't, well I was fairly sure something was unusual about the trip, all the secret conversations, whispered exchanges, and then taking our mobiles. I suppose I should have known, got off at some point and left you to your fate. None of knew did we?'

James and Adnan agreed.

'Forget all that,' Jen was in command again, 'just tell us, if everything had worked out what was your plan, if not to take all our money!'

'You haven't worked it out?' Ross looked at us with some derision. 'The plastic, man the plastic! You saw the bay a heaving stinking rotten mess, a catastrophe. We hardly saw plastic until it arrived here about two years ago, the stream is relentless. We tried, we really tried to get attention, but who would listen to us? We are just little islanders on a remote island, no money, nothing but what the sea can give us.'

He was practically weeping. 'Even at college the Australians weren't interested, of course it would be different if the plastic found its way to the glorious and famous Bondi Beach!'

Vince said, 'but it does, Ross, it does. I go down to the beach in Eastbourne with friends and we pick up bags and bags of plastic off the beaches.'

'I help my village pick up on the verges,' said Rita sadly, 'and every week the same amount is dumped there, out of car windows, thrown off lorries, nobody cares.'

Ross looked surprised, and then continued.

'The plan was to hold you hostage and get publicity about the scourge of plastic and to release you when help came. We didn't want money, that was only to fund something to clear up the mess, to draw international attention. We chose you because first you had signed up to a ecotour off the beaten track, so would be adventurous, and you were all fairly rich, well very rich by our standards.'

'And,' continued Jen, 'none of us had people that would immediately report us missing.'

For a moment silence fell. We considered Jen's words. That view of ourselves had been cruelly pointed out by the captain, but then gradually like a cold sea mist gradually fading away in the morning sunshine in Eastbourne, we felt immensely uplifted. It occurred to all of us how much we had become part of the island, how kindly we had been treated. We were exceedingly pleased, for we were to be the solution, key figures in the Huge Fightback.

TEN

It said something for the seamanship and experience of the crew that no one said much, but got the sails up, even started the engine and were well away before the first shots rang out from the trawler. Rahmin lay on the deck, resembling, thought Sally, the jelly fish that had slithered off her only last night. They made fantastic speed, for the wind was picking up and within an hour felt safe enough to retrim the sails, slow down, take the strain off the brave yacht. Bruce again set the autopilot and called everyone down below.

First it was evident that Bruce was really shocked. He gave Rahmin a real man hug, 'oh man what happened to you?'

This was not the Rahmin that Bruce had crewed with on *The Syndicate*. What he saw before him was an emaciated young man, ribs sticking out, his hair, which had been very attentively styled so many weeks ago, was now dirty and long, just tied back with some string. His body was covered with bruises and cuts. His hands were the worst, even one of his nails was missing. As he tried to reply, Bruce could see he had even lost teeth.

Sally could not speak, she looked at him in horror. If this is what had happened to one of the crew, how would her beloved friend survive? Her Auntie H had never been abroad, as far as Sally knew, she had lived very quietly in a south coast small town just looking after an elderly husband. Why, Sally asked herself, did she encourage this madcap trip to a remote island at her time of life? But it was going to get worse.

As Rahmin began to recover from his escape, his dash for freedom and the growing realisation of what a risk he had taken, swimming so near the lines and perhaps even nearer to the sharks, he began to tell them of the Captain's duplicity.

'After the shipwreck, we all went to the life craft as we had practised, ready to help the passengers. But the captain and the purser released the boats. I was only on one by accident because I was there. In fact I rescued one passenger who was so quick, she leapt from the ship into the sea but I got her in. I could see the ship was stuck on the reef by the island so I knew once it was calmer the islanders would go out and rescue the passengers because they knew were expected that day.'

'So it was well-planned,' thought Gary, with some relief.

There was silence for a while then Rahmin continued, 'then I realised what a crook the captain was. He was trying to find a way of raising the ransom for the passengers. He has no interest, and that is putting it mildly in raising awareness about the catastrophe on the island, the mountain of incoming plastic.'

'Too bloody true mate,' agreed Bruce.

'But the project was more difficult that he thought. He was scared of being accused of kidnap and piracy. No one, the thought, was interested in a bunch of ageing British pensioners who could not look after themselves at best and not be of any value to the trawlers.'

He stood up and paced around obviously distressed, then described with some irony that they too had problems with the plastic that caught in their nets.

He said sadly, 'they did not make much money, some of the fish were inedible and the sharks were on us all the time. But I could not believe it when I saw the yacht and then I saw Bruce! Oh man! I thought you had died in the wreck!'

Rahmin was tearful again and they all gave him a clumsy group hug.

'Oh how very touching!'

The sardonic tones of Tyche boomed around the cabin. Rahmin leapt back in horror, and had it not been for the thought of sharks lingering beneath the ketch he would have disembarked without delay.

'What's that, who's that, what's happening?' Questions exploded from Rahmin like a hail of bullets, no pause for any answers.

It was unusual for the generally suave, laconic Tyche to sound concerned as he commanded.

'Listen, I think they may be onto me. You are only twelve hours away from the island if the forecast is right and sea conditions remain the same, Stephen is ready. He has contacted the media and press, so its all go now. Watch for the headlines:

'BRAVE RESCUE OF HOSTAGES'
'SECRET MISSION UNCOVERS ENVIRONMENT CATASTROPHE ON DESERT ISLAND.

I will have the satellite positioned for photos of your landing. You have the communications gear, so set it up immediately you land. Gotta go.'

There was silence, except for the rushing wind through the sails, they all looked at each other apprehensive realising the end of their adventure was approaching. Bruce again took the lead.

'We'll have a hectic day tomorrow, better to get something to eat.'

Like zombies they moved around, Sally started frying a fish she had inadvertently caught in the morning. Gary opened his favourite baked beans, Bruce took out the previous cargo of fresh fruit. Rahmin looked around still dazed.

'I cannot believe you came for me, I thought I was going to die on that trawler. And now I am here with you and a feast made in heaven.'

And after this sumptuous feast, though Sally could think of better menus, Bruce and Gary made arrangements for the night watch. While Sally and Rahmin slept the sleep of the dead, emotionally exhausted, still shocked.

Gary took the first watch, looking at the stars above, in awe of the insignificance of the Earth in the great cosmos and seeing the phosphorous glisten on the waves, disturbed by fish surfacing perhaps fleeing unseen predators, that they were lost in the vast ocean, sailing above a world, travelling over a complete universe beneath the waves beautiful, alien and dangerous.

As the first light of dawn lit the eastern horizon, Bruce came up on deck with two cups of tea.

'This is the best time of day', he said quietly. 'I love this part of the world. I lived on the islands when I was a young child. My father was an artist, a wannabe Gauguin. Some hope,' he added with a sigh. 'He was never a commercial success but had his dreams. I went back to England with my mother. I met a guy from the island when I was on a trip to Australia, he had been sent to school there, and we always kept in touch.'

'We have been planning this for over a year, raising money from friends and some groups.'

Gary hesitated, never very confident with words, he sought for a diplomatic response, and failing said, 'what the fuck do you really think you were up to? Didn't you realise that people like Sally, who dearly loves H, is distraught? She still thinks she might be dead, or injured or like Rahmin kept as some kind of slave?'

'Shit I know, I know,' Bruce replied, first looking at his feet, face hidden in a cup of tea, unable to face Gary. Then looking up at the horizon said, 'God almighty just look!'

Gary asked, 'is there a ship of fire, what is that?'

'Its the volcano, we're here!' And with more shouting down to the two sleeping below, got everyone on deck.

The winds took them. With fair speed they approached the island. They could see first the top of the volcano, then the surrounding hills, the trees cascading down one side, the high cliffs and then the surf crashing off the reefs. Bruce kept his eyes on the depth finder while Rahmin stood on the highest point forward, holding onto the mast. Then he gave a great cry, of fear, of despair.

Gary and Sally went to join him, excited to be at last at the end of their venture.

'Look look,' Rahmin continued to scream, 'see, its the Captain's outrigger, the one he stole, he's here!'

ELEVEN

And in the past three days there had been activity in England.

First, Tyche was interviewed with that strange, but quietly threatening manner in which government servants are interviewed, following the detection of possible misdemeanours. It is a process, requiring training and experience, for first skilled interrogators must determine whether the activity would benefit, first their own careers and secondly that of Her Majesty's government. Tyche was the new sort of recruit whose behaviour did not follow established patterns, but which may in the long run have its advantages.

He had been seen tracking a yacht, and shown interest in a remote island. At first there was concern that this might involve a detour to the islands in the Pacific where terrorist or more accurately political prisoners were incarcerated by a number of different nations unwilling to offer them trials or prisons in within their own nation. That did not happen, and yet Tyche had been vigilant in his tracking as were his minders observing him.

However, when Tyche entered the interview room there was, in his total confidence, a jauntiness to his demeanour which caused some slight consternation among those who normally interviewed more nervous suspects.

The usual introductions, which were intended to be polite, discerning and yet disturbing, failed completely. The chair offered to Tyche was not taken. Instead he did not so much march up to the polished mahogany table, so beloved by senior civil servants, as approach it with determination.

The interviewers flinched, the newly appointed chairman started to try to remember where the panic button was, installed some years previously following a distressing incident with the head of counter terrorism, who on hearing the Minister thought there would be no further threat, and therefore no further need for employment of someone of that grade, had attempted to murder the whole panel. A surprise when some of the panel, thought the diminutive, attractive female Chair would have been more diplomatic.

'Its great to see you guys,' began Tyche, 'because I have something to tell you.'

The Chair hesitated, was this to be a confession, but she

thought it unlikely. Tyche continued 'We have found the British hostages and we are just about to negotiate their release. It's all going to be all over the media in one hour, I just want to be sure the rescue party have safely landed.'

He then paced the room, 'this is going to be so big man, and will the PM be made up that this department has been working on it all these weeks!'

The panel, ever opportunistic, exchanged glances, comforted that they all looked equally puzzled, perplexed even. Not one had the smug look indicating they prior information.

Tyche turned to the occupant at the end of the table, 'you remember Boss, don't you when that info came in about plastic in the Pacific, something about one of the navy ships running into an island or a raft just made with tons of the stuff. Got caught around some of the underwater detection gear I was told.'

The Boss shifted uncomfortably in his chair as the rest of the panel moved to look at him, not just by turning their heads but their whole body. He made a small inadequate gesture, not yet wishing to commit to any side of this discussion.

The Chair realising his colleague was in some discomfort said in an icy voice, 'do carry on,' and, with a nod to the panel, 'most interesting don't you think?'

Tyche, who never grasped the derision contained in irony, told the history of the events; that the group was not some highly organised pressure group, but formed by just one young woman and a bloke from Eastbourne trying to find out what happened to a friend.

The panel were about to relax, after all the island and the rescue was well away from sensitive political areas, that the PM, who was in dire need of some positive publicity could claim success for the rescue mission, when Tyche dropped the bombshell,

'Of course it all went tits up when *The Syndicate,* with the hostages, was wrecked on the reef.'

'Language young man.' It was the first verbal contribution from the Head of HR to the meeting, feeling it was her right to insist on correct communication. Then realising she had been brought to the meeting as Head of Human Resources (Section only), only if a dismissal be considered, stood up abruptly, the sound of her chair breaking the silence, looking at her shocked colleagues,

'Are you telling me that people died on this foolhardy trip?'

And the Chair added, 'I hope there aren't any British casualties.'

And the Head of Section of Oceans and Small Islands queried, 'What about the plastic then?'

Tyche, who had been pacing the room, gesturing extravagantly to emphasise the personal achievement in following and advising the group, stood still, conveniently near the door.

'Yeah well,' he scratched his head thoughtfully, 'that's the thing, we don't really know. But the ketch is about to land, they've got communication, so if you don't mind I'll get back and check them out,' and with that he hurriedly left the room.

'Get after him!' the Chair yelled to no one in particular. Tyche's boss ran out leaving his papers behind, closely followed by others, though the Chair and the Head of HR remained behind.

'Interesting indeed,' observed the Chair absent-mindedly tapping her fingers on the table as if the action could give her energy to make a decision.

'Either he is brilliant or dangerous, needs watching,' said the Head of HR.

The Chair looked shocked and rose slowly to walk over to the window. Standing side by side they looked out at the cultivated lawns below so designed to offer no hiding place for any intruder.

'Might ask to see the Minister,' suggested the Chair addressing the glass before her.

'Good idea,' came the reply from the Head of HR, followed with, 'I understand young Tyche is well connected, if you get my meaning.' And with a nod left she room silently leaving the Chair rocking on her heels.

She suddenly moved, reptilian in her speed and intent. Going to her office and making arrangements for an immediate trip to London. It was no more than, 'Philippa, urgent meet at the club, will be of interest you,' then added obliquely, 'I do mean your interest.'

They met, but mindful of being overheard, left their mobiles, pagers, briefcases at the Club and took a stroll out around the busy streets of Victoria. The Chair outlined the amateur rescue mission, said there happened to be one of the newly commissioned frigates in the area. 'Had to drop-off some special cargo to the islands,' she muttered. The Minister nodded, somewhat surprised she had not been consulted and began to wonder under whose orders the frigate was now in Australia. Then considered that secret political prisoners may have been delivered to one of the island prison 'facilities,' and was grateful for that ignorance.

She began to consider the rescue mission.

'But why, and who is this renegade you have employed without it seems due supervision?'

The Chair had been a wily Civil Servant for many years, but still found herself annoyed, even angry at the petulant tones of the members of the Cabinet, their weak attempts to ape the language of the military, when all their experience of the army was in a dismal career in the CCF at school at best. Inwardly she shuddered, but nonetheless years of patience and endless cunning had armed her well.

'Minister,' she began the fight back ignoring the questions posed just a minute before, 'you will recall Charles,' but before she could continue, and a petulant interruption,

'Charles who, the royal Charles, a deceased Charles, be clear!'

With a sigh, the Chair replied, 'minister, the Charles who funded your campaign, the Charles who I believe is funding your positioning for the leadership, the Charles...' again she was interrupted.

First with a stupid question of 'how'd you know?' then wisely not waiting for an answer continued, 'so if we divert the frigate to pick up the hostages, send a message that the Navy are the brave sailors, that I acted promptly.' She glanced at the grubby Buckingham Palace now thronged with future voters, possible supporters and dreamed for a minute to two.

'Right,' she said decisively, 'send the gunboat, I'll get it though Cabinet, last item when they are all tired and bored," then laughed merrily at this arcane but still sinister command

TWELVE

In the days since Tyche's abortive personnel appraisal, the Minister, ever mindful that her involvement could be seen as marvellous, perceptive, insightful, action worthy of a much younger politician, was acting with unusual caution. She had attempted to talk to the Prime Minister alone, to get a go-ahead sanction in such a way that should it go wrong no blame would fall on his shoulders. The matter was raised in Cabinet. Not unexpectedly the Prime Minister successfully avoided any responsibility for the project, but as predicted it was nodded through for there would be no extra cost and some good publicity for the navy.

And so it was, the crew of the frigate who were enjoying a leisurely trip home, having been generously wined and dined by the Australian Navy and loaded with bottles of the fabulous Margaret River red wines, had to alter course out of Freemantle and be battle ready within a day.

As the Minister ordered her political adviser to construct a press release, stating the newly commissioned frigate was to make a call on a remote island to bring aid to offer help. It was, just in case, couched in the vaguest of language. The adviser pointed out that the hostages might not actually be there, might have been killed and so counselled that the crew had their arms at the ready in case of military landing under fire.

THIRTEEN
H

The following morning none of us could get into the usual rhythm of our work. Robin wandered up the path towards the plateau, Jen strode along the beach occasionally looking back, was she trying to see where her hotel would be best sited. Adnan was helping a young woman rebuild part of a stockade, but nonetheless he too was watchful.

I wandered along the path into the woods, looking for the vanilla plants that hung from the trees. The vanilla perfumed the air and I was sure plants hid well away from the path, but I did not venture in. I could hear the constant shuffling and from time to time the noxious odour of Mildred and her daughters and very closely related male dragons nearby. It struck me that I too had come to terms with these creatures who like me had been washed up on an island so far from home, so alien in many ways, but where we had all thrived, well, until recent times.

Suddenly there was yelling and shouting and a great to do. For the first time we heard again the less than successful attempts to blow conch shells, there was banging of the few metal pots and pans and then, as I ran back to the village, I could see preparations for a huge fire on the beach. Every child was running with branches, the men were piling a huge mound. Then more noise, Robin yelling from the high path, then seemingly swept aside as the whole village of Orrible came over the pass running as fast down towards us.

I never thought it an attractive community, their self-discipline, their martial approach to life was alien to me, but now I stared in amazement. The young men led the charge, their normally patched but clean shorts torn and dirty, followed by the older men and women surprisingly fast either barefoot or in the ubiquitous flip flops and up along the path slower but still moving at a pace, mother and the very young children, all arriving within half an hour of the leaders. Robin was the last to descent having been pushed to the side of the path by the oncoming hoard. Jen ran up from the beach and stopped gazing at Bosai, who had just screeched to a stop from his rapid descent down the path from the plateau. He, manfully and with great dignity, tried to catch his breath, not to gasp for air, to ignore the gash on his leg, which he may have cut stumbling across the rocks and disentangled some leaves that had caught in his hair. He drew himself up, looked around, looked only at Jen and said, 'they are coming.'

We all had our backs to the sea, having watched this invasion coming down the inland paths, and as one, we turned and saw a yacht coming over the horizon heading for the reef. There was a gasp from us and from the villagers of Linde. The children ran up and down excited, calling and waving. Some of the men pulled the canoes that were tied far up the beach and brought them down to the water line.

At first the ketch seemed to be travelling so slowly, but as it approached the reef it seemed to speed up. Was this just the perception of distance, or did the onshore winds pick up?'

'Will they know where the gap of the reef is?'

'Who are they?

'Is this a rescue mission?'

These questions where posed quietly, no one expecting a reply. I looked at the men by the canoes, they were waiting to launch a rescue mission, I was sure the roar of the surf crashing against the sharp rocks of the reef had increased. We all watched, rigid, fearful of a crash.

Nearer and nearer we couldn't breathe. I could see one of the crew, a young man, gesturing and calling back instructions, a girl on the back holding the fenders that protect the sides of the yacht when it is docking. The yacht zoomed through the gap of the reef.

There was a collective cheer as all the air we had been holding in our lungs just exploded. I found myself jumping up and down, hands waved, everyone laughed, the kids dived into the water to greet the slowing vessel. Frank gave the first coherent statement, 'man that was one bit of skilled seamanship.'

Even those of us who had limited experience of yachting were stunned with the confident approach and then the calm entry to the lagoon, the disciplined dropping of the anchor. We watched again in silence until I gave a strange sound.

'My god, what's wrong?' Jen caught me as I was about to collapse on the beach. Shock had paralysed me. I tried to wave a hand, I tried to find words failed, tried again with the momentous statement, 'well, bloody hell, that's Sally.'

I first stood rigid then ran from Jen's supporting arms, straight into the sea, yelling 'Sally, Sally!' I fell, I lost my footing I half swam I half paddled, I choked, for yelling while under water is not a great thing to do, but I arrived at the side of the yacht while the stunned face of Sally looked over the side. I clambered up the diving ladder.

'God almighty,' she was nearly crying 'is that really you?'

The disembarkation of the yacht was the most joyous event. Bruce was greeted, first with dignity by the village chiefs, maternal hugs froth elder women and those of a more flirtatious manner by the girls. Paul and Rahmin hugged each other in silent rapture, tactfully left to it by everyone.

Sally and I were entwined, my arm around her as I introduced her to my passengers, and the villagers. But it was only Gary, left for a moment who looked totally stunned, unprepared for such a welcome. He later said that as they approached the island he was not sure if we were alive, and perhaps they too were sailing into great danger and not this rapturous community.

The sun started its downward descent, fires were lit, a pig was roasted, pots of roots and vegetables put ready for the final cooking. The drums were about to start, when from one of the huts came a roar and out staggered the Captain. We had forgotten about him. Bosai looked with magnificent distain at the dishevelled figure.

The captain lurched around.

'What's all this about?' he yelled at Jen. She turned her face away in disgust as his foul breath hit her. 'And who the fuck are you to look at me like that?'

An unwise question to Bosai, who did not hit him but pushed him firmly sending him reeling back and into Rahmin and seeing the hatred in Rahman's eyes, began to appear to rapidly sober up.

'Oh fuck, Rahmin,' he whimpered, 'how did you get here?' And then without waiting for a reply ran to the edge of the beach and into the woods.

'Leave him Rahmin,' said Paul and Vince added, 'he won't get far not at this time of night. Matilda and sisters are on the prowl and hungry.' It was one of those hot nights, which I recall with such clarity. The full moon shone down with such benevolence during its slow progression from the west reaching into the eastern horizon to await the dawn. In the north the volcano occasionally

243

belched out white fumes, from time a red tongue of fire shot up then subsided quietly, without fuss. It was a spectacular sight in the night sky and I realised I would miss it if and when I returned to Lopeham.

It was the best party ever. We sang, we ate, we drank beers released from the carefully guarded stores, I even drank wine donated by Bruce, a wonder after so many months, practically non alcohol months. It was by order, that this night we would party and tomorrow the serious talk and parley would begin.

PART SIX

Where the neighbours in Lopeham are thrown into disarray; the crew of a frigate Prince Hamlet has to deviate from their passage home and are led to the horrors in the inlet, and where in London, politicians and civil servants seek advantage.

ONE

Life in Lopeham had continued through the English winter oblivious to the dramas challenges and once in a lifetime experiences of a one time resident. The weather from October onwards had turned predictably cold, but not cold enough for frost or snow. The grey clouds hung in the sky most days, regardless if rain was to drench the roads and gardens or not. Spring was late. Few people ventured out, so As Peter and Angela drank their morning coffee there was little to distinguish one day from another.
Until.

Through the morning rain they saw Wendy almost running or more accurate coming down the road in a fast trot. Peter observed dryly,

'Must be a spate of burglaries for our Neighbourhood Watch representative to move at that pace.'

Angela looked out sipping her cooling coffee thinking that they should change the brand from this insipid mixture, she added with more hope than enthusiasm,

'Perhaps there has been a murder.'

Peter looked at her severely, 'we don't have murders here, this is a very quiet neighbourhood, that's the sort of thing that goes on in London.'

Angela was about to comment that the neighbourhood was changing with all these young people buying the bungalows and doing them up, when they saw Wendy crossing the road, waving a paper at them. She was very nearly flattened by a car screeching into the avenue, almost on two wheels. The door flew open and Gwen, who had put on considerable weight since they last saw her, poured out of the car, and reached their gate at the same time as Wendy.

'Good grief there're coming in,' an anguished cry from Angela, moving at the approximate speed of light, scooped up all the old newspapers, straightened the cushion on the chair, took out last night's wine glasses and flung them into the kitchen slamming the door.

Peter went to the front door, waited for them to ring the bell or more accurately the Westminster chimes and during those minutes before opening the door he carefully smoothed his hair over his bald patch and just checked his flies were done up.

Any invitation to come in was redundant as both women pushed passed. Angela skillfully blocked any attempt to go into the lounge kitchen/dining room that overlooked the back garden.

Gwen started.

'You can never guess what's happened.'

'No suppose I can't,' a weary response from Peter who hated surprises and pub quizzes.

Wendy waved a copy of the local press:

DRAMATIC RESCUE OF HOSTAGES
FRIGATE DIVERTED

'So what is the problem?'

Gwen had no patience. In forceful language she outlined the content of the carefully considered press release that had omitted any location of the Frigate and only mentioning that some of the hostages may be British part of an ecotour, held on an island in the Pacific.

'It's H,' she practically yelled, 'I knew there was something wrong. Going on a crazy venture like that, what did she expect? I wouldn't be surprised if that shifty guy from Eastbourne wasn't involved. Looked it up just now, she cannot claim on her travel insurance, if ever she took out any cover, which knowing her I expect not,'

She paused for breath and taking in a lungful continued.

'I can see the house being sold to pay her ransom. This is a disaster!'

Even the normally obtuse Peter picked up that Gwen's concern focused on the house and not her sister-in-law.

Wendy sat down firmly that is to say she forced all the others that had been standing between the hallway and the sitting room to do the same.

'I'll put the kettle on,' said Angela wearily, hoping there were enough clean mugs.

'Want a hand?' offered Gwen, anxious to see how much of a garden they had at the back of the house.

'No,' snapped Angela, then more gently, but not without a degree of spite, 'you just sit down, you look as if you could do with a rest. Now wait till I get back before you decide anything.'

She went into the kitchen, found matching mugs, located a

tray, sorted out the best of the biscuits, the ones less shattered than the others, combed her hair, found a better pair of slippers and returned. But of course the discussion was well underway.

Wendy, from years of militant though largely ineffective watching the neighbourhood was in the middle of a diatribe against the youngsters who had recently moved into the avenue.

'And you tell me, what's happened to the couple who moved in next door? Was she a friend of H's, or was it her mother, and where is she now?'

'Who H? I thought you said she was one of the hostages?'

'No H's friend, didn't that girl then start hanging around H when Harry died?'

They all considered the mendacious nature of people especially the young.

'Came into money did she, your neighbour with that odd name? Some never have enough.'

This from Gwen, which caused a wry smile from Angela. Not seeing it, Gwen continued without any hint of recognising any element of hypocrisy

'We could contact the papers, say we are sure one of the hostages at least came from here, tell them H disappeared without a trace, say that young girl and her boyfriend have been acting strangely and now they are gone too.'

'Oh yes,' said Wendy, hoping gather would be enough time for her to get her hair done before the press descended, 'And don't,' she added 'forget to mention that weird bloke from Eastbourne.'

TWO

The Minister's Chief Political Adviser received a phone call from Downing Street. There was just a terse message to the effect that whomsoever leaked the story to the press would be toast and without essential bodily parts.

And even as that message was being received and regretfully understood, the British frigate *Prince Hamlet* was making good speed. The name had been chosen, partly to avoid using the names of any current royalty that are or might be involved in scandals and in recognition of the Danish shipyards and the designer and for some of the funding for high grade furnishings of the Captain's quarters, offered as a goodwill gesture from the Danish government. The British Navy felt the ship's name was a reciprocal gesture that was essentially cost free.

Captain Bligh stood on the bridge enjoying the excitement of a break from the dismal routine of making semi-diplomatic visits to, as he put it, 'the ex colonies'. Although he was comparatively young for such a command, (his father was an admiral, his uncle had influence throughout Whitehall), he had been surprised at the opulence of West Australia, the lifestyle and not a kangaroo in sight. Nonetheless he was aware that the crew silently resented his leadership, and now they were sailing in the Pacific, he had been teased about his name and questioned if the intention of this detour was to call into his distant relatives.

Lieutenant Johnson joined him.

'Spoken to the men, landing party ready, should drop anchor just after sun up, might catch them still sleeping.'

'Good. Landing boats ready? Medics got all their stuff?'

Sergeant Hayes came on the bridge. Bligh viewed him with some suspicion for he was on attachment from the Marines.

He saluted smartly, always sticking to correct often over formal behaviour around the captain. "All ready and in place,' he started addressing the captain but looking at Johnson. Then,

'Bloody hell Fletch look at that!'

As they raised their binoculars, the captain said to Johnson quietly.

'What did he call you?'

Johnson was too wily to answer, perhaps not realising there

that a character called or nicknamed Fletcher would follow Captain Bligh from the torture of his days at public school to his deathbed. Instead he said, 'is that a conflagration, is the place on fire, are they killing the hostages?'

Hayes said with authority, 'no its the volcano, info in from satellites, volcano often active, dense smoke is frequent.'

The captain thought, 'why doesn't anyone tell me anything?'

They kept to course, gradually seeing the island appear to rise from the sea as they approached. They could now see the volcano in the centre of the island, they could see the smoke although it struck Johnson that there still could be fires. Then, to their amazement, they could see a large number of people on the beach. Nearer and nearer they got. The crew was on maximum alert for an armed landing. And then the captain said,

'God almighty, what is that stench?'

THREE
H

As the early mists rose from the calm ocean, we could see a huge ship on the horizon and fast approaching. Robin, Frank and Jen ran up the cliff path to get a better view, Melanie started waving a scarf.

'Do you think they'll see us, I would kill myself if they just sailed by,' she cried.

'That doesn't look like a cruise ship,' observed Dilys.

We were silent, sick with apprehension, until Vince muttered, so as not to further upset Melanie.

'Can't you see, that's a warship, we are about to be invaded.'

At this point Bruce jumped off the ketch and waded ashore.

'Just got a message from Tyche, that's a British frigate come to rescue you,' he said solemnly.

There was a ragged cheer from some, but not all of us. The villagers now were gathering around us, not with any overt aggression, but as they say in management booklets, with firm assertion.

'Let's get one thing clear,' this from Ross, 'you are not going anywhere until the matter of the plastic is dealt with.'

We stopped shocked to be reminded once again we were hostages. Bruce looked out to sea and confirmed it was a British navy frigate, was to be putting down anchor.

We watched. It took about an hour, it was a kind of stand off. We looked at each other, they from more powerful binoculars, but we had the advantage of experienced eyes that could read the seas around the island with ease.

'Sharks are curious,' observed Ross, 'perhaps they have chucked out food or something, because those old white sharks are circling the ship and you don't often see that.'

In the unusual silence of the island, we could hear new sounds, then see landing craft being lowered. It was at this point that three things happened simultaneously: Bosai and Ross tried to push us back towards the huts with orders to get in and keep quiet; Jen, Frank and Robin came running down the cliff, shouting, waving and laughing; and then a new set of yelling. We turned, and from the far beach we could see the Captain with torn shorts, cuts on his torso in a canoe frantically making out to sea and desperate to get the attention of the Frigate.

'He'll never make it' observed Rita with cold detachment, but his desperation gave him strength, plus a fortuitous sudden calming of the surf. We could hear him screaming as he was making his way towards the Frigate.

All efforts to get us to the huts now stopped, while we watched the Captain.

'Never thought he had that strength,' observed Robin.

'Must have had a bad night out there in the woods with my dragons on the prowl,' added Vince.

'Encouraged him to leave did they?' laughed Audrey, her past fears sublimely forgotten.

FOUR

The crew of the *Prince Hamlet* lined up to watch the approach of the canoe. Captain Bligh raised his glasses.

'Doesn't look like the usual Pacific Islander,' he said, but without conviction for he had never met anyone from any of the thousands of islands.

'Bloody hell!' remarked Johnson, 'it's Robinson Crusoe,'

'Don't like the look of those sharks following him' observed Hayes, wondering if he had enough time to open a book and take bets on the likelihood of the guy getting to them intact, before the sharks struck.

'He's safe enough in the canoe,' offered Bligh, ignorant to the fact that sharks will frequently attack canoes and small boats. At this point they could hear the muffled shouts and screams coming across the water.

'What language is he using? Do you think it could be a terrorist attack?'

Johnson paused searching for a tactful way or replying.

'That's Scouse, Speke variety,' said Hayes in a voice that would not countenance any further discussion.

'Prepare to take the man on board. Stand down the landing party until we have interrogated that man.' And with a sense of purpose long overdue, Bligh left the Bridge eager to get what information he could.

As the sun rose higher, there was no more than languid activity on the *Prince Hamlet,* and even less movement on the island.

We were not pushed into the huts, for after watching the Captain being lifted onboard just as the canoe was snapped from beneath him, there was nothing to see.

Audrey returned to looking after the pigs and checking the hens. Adnan and his girlfriend wandered off to the beach, Rita, Melanie and Dilys took up their raffia in the shade of a tree. James and Rahmin sat in deep conversation. Vince wandered up the forest path looking out for the dragons and occasionally giving them a call. Robin and Paul kicked a ball around without enthusiasm and Frank just sat on the beach, his head in his hands looking downcast, I could hear him muttering,

'But what if she is still alive?'

The villagers all went about the normal morning routine, though did not go far from the village centre. The women did not get their baskets ready for a long hike up the mountain trail, but did some weeding in a nearby compound, the men did not organise any sea fishing but sat around the canoes talking.

Nonetheless all of us kept an eye on the frigate. At first we could only guess what was happening out there, what lies the Captain was telling, whether the crew would believe him or not. Bruce was still on the ketch and he gave a shout that caught everyone's attention.

'I've been talking to Tyche, and as you thought that bloody captain is spinning a load of lies. He's trying to convince them that you are all in extremely danger, about to be eaten no less. He's offering to act as mediator...'

Bruce was interrupted, 'I expect he is offering to undertake this brave task for a considerable financial reward,' this from Robin.

I was curious, 'how so you know that, how do you know what's being said? That's a navy frigate.'

Sally intervened and took my arm saying with the gentle words,
'Best not to ask.'

SIX

As the heat of the day took command of the island, the ship, the canoes and all the surface activity of the ocean, in London frantic conferences were held by Ministers and their advisers, by senior civil servants in several ministries in Whitehall, by editors alerting their overseas contacts hacks. Maps were found, few able to locate the island. Calls made to commission planes and pilots with bravado that could island hop along the way to get the story first.

Captain Bligh, to his annoyance, was ordered to take direction from Royal Marine Hayes for landing at first light. The crew who had spent a useful afternoon in the cool of the frigate's efficient air conditioning, had established a book of bets which numbered:

Number of hostages alive at landing

Number of hostages still alive after landing

Whether Bligh would be captured and killed by islanders

And finally,

Who owned the luxurious ketch anchored inside the reef.

Whether it was a fortunate misunderstanding or ignorance of island life that the mission departed the frigate silently just a good hour before sun up the following day. Some of the crew were chuckling, for loud laughter would be a serious breach of protocols (Invasion tactics Manual 2009) because the Captain's screams of 'Beware the dragons,' had followed them across the water.

'Pull yourself together man,' Johnson had commanded, 'do you think we believe in myths and legends, 'there be dragons' what nonsense!

But as the captain of the shipwrecked *Syndicate*, started rocking with shock and horror as he recalled his last night on the island being pursued in quiet determination by Mildred her sisters and sons, he failed to reply, just uttering choking gasps. Serious threats and the use of force got the captain into a landing craft. Bligh made a note to contact London to arrange for some advice on mental health.

SEVEN

H

The cockerels began their pre-dawn racket, normally it would only last a few minutes before they collectively realised dawn was yet an hour off and returned to sleep. It was normally a time of quiet before the heat of the day dropped in. But for most of us it was a signal to get up, start the fires for making a hot water, so of course we heard the landing vessels on their way. I went around all the huts making sure everyone was awake and so we gathered on the beach, a welcoming party I hoped.

The first landing craft had successfully negotiated the gap in the reef to the accompanying cheers from those on the beach. But the crew, misinterpreting our cheers of welcome for those of hostile intention immediately signalled to the second landing craft to find an alternative location.

To the horror of Vince, he saw them approaching the area much favoured by the dragons, and along with some of the village young men and Audrey, took off to warn them not to land. It was later he said he thought he could hear our crazy captain screaming 'not that way, turn!' and then silence.

The first landing craft approached our beach. Bosai stood at the water edge a true descendent of brave Pacific island explorers, ship wrecked mariners and the odd pirate. Tall and proud he wore full chief regalia and with face painting that would have been much admired by Australian cricketers. Then with growing horror, we saw him carrying old musket, which he began to wave in friendly greeting.

A shot rang out, followed by stunned silence. We could hear Bruce screaming from the ketch, but the landing craft was careering in the helmsman either ignoring Bruce or oblivious to his cries. Bosai stood proud, then he staggered and then he fell, blood pouring from his shoulder. Jen screamed, Susie and the women gathered around, men rushed forward, picked up Bosia and ran to the hut with Susie and the women following.

I ran down to the beach screaming weeping swearing, words I hadn't used since they took me into the Children's Home. It was evident this was not the reception the crew had anticipated.

We, the 'hostages,' attacked them with bare fists. As they jumped onto the beach, they were pummelled, knocked to the ground while the young village men stood back just waiting their chance to pile in.

Eventually it was Jen, who had been identified as a leader, stopped this brawl. Years of experience from skirmishes in the Balkans had given her sufficient skills and menace to be listened to. And, of course, the dreadful error was eventually recognised by the landing crew and some kind of peace descended, not a sure peace of course, but an acknowledged stand off.

It nearly flared up again. Johnson was about to pick up Bosai's old musket.

'Good grief will you look at this,' he began, 'must be two hundred years old.'

There was a collective snarl as a group of young men began to approach him.

'Put it down! Back away! Now!' a shout from Jen and years of obeying orders worked, as Johnson did just that.

Even I joined in 'you idiot, that gun is a sign of chiefdom, been handed down since the first shipwreck landed here.'

'Tell them I apologise, and tell them it is a very fine musket,' said Johnson with much dignity, which we did but so the stand off continued.

We all gathered outside the hut. Silence. We waited. The smell of the vanilla seeped down from the trees in the woods above the beach, the waves lapped on the shore, the pigs snuffled around contently while the chickens kept their endless and optimistic search from grubs among the shade of the bushes. I knew we were all thinking the same thing. We had at many times during our long stay on the island, dreamed of rescue, but we did not anticipate this. Gary and Sally sat near me and I could hear them muttering that no shooting or aggression was needed, that Tyche had specifically told the Minister that the island was peaceful. Jen overheard them and turned,

'These are men of war, guns and killing is what they are trained for. Do not be lulled into thinking that just because this was to be a peace mission that the training does not overcome all other reactions. This I have seen so many times,' and with that she spat on the sand.

Johnson said in defence of his men, 'I have sent for our ship's medic to come here. I'd rather keep the craft in the lagoon. Contact the second craft, why has there been radio silence? it's not necessary.'

Robin looked up and said with something of an evil glint inches eye, 'not surprised, that's where the dragons hang out. Didn't that wreck of a captain not want you when he fled in a canoe?'

Johnson was about to make a caustic response, even offer Where be dragons? Then hastily reconsidered that option and instead, 'What dragons?'

'Komodos, whole families of them, but I think Vince and the lads have gone to ask them to back off.'

'What here? Isn't this too far from…'

He was interrupted as Robin continued, 'yes like the rest of us, washed up on a storm, shipwrecked, but all mostly girls, the blokes fight amongst themselves.

'Yes paradise,' offered Jen, 'for some.'

The sun came up with relentless precision and again we waited. Johnson eventually gave permission for the landing craft to leave the lagoon and head back to the Frigate for supplies and a confidential update for London. Best to get his side of the story in first he thought.

I looked at the disappearing small boat and thought of all the peaceful months on the island. There had been a few accidents and occasional quarrels but no needless violence, no murders, no thefts. Life was hard and I suspected extremely short compared to the affluence of the South Coast of England where, to die in one's eighties was viewed with distaste, 'Why so young' people said at the funeral.

And then there was another noise, another landing craft coming around the headland. Its path lacked the precision of the approach of the dawn raid, and in fact its speed was variable.

'What the hell is going on?' shouted Jackson to no one in particular. And on the radio, 'Vessel 2, vessel 2 come in.'

No reply.

I could see Rahmin and one of the village lads hanging onto ropes at the stern, pointing to the gaps on the reef, and to my horror, not quite yet shared by Jackson, there was Vince driving! Shouts and yells could not be decoded, but it was obvious they were coming in, and there was a problem.

EIGHT

In England, Bligh's communications were met with varied responses from:
1. the verbal
'Good show, brilliant landing, showed the kidnappers we mean business'
2. draft headlines for broadsheets
Hostages live and rescued by British Navy operation
3. internet blogs
Imperialism raises its ugly head, villager fights for life.

In Lewes, Charles, with rare formality addressed his wife.
'We may have a journalist knocking on the door soon, best not to say anything.'
His wife looked at her normally staid husband, for a moment considering whether he'd had an affair or defrauded the golf club of the funds, until guessing at her puzzled face, said, 'no I helped old Stephen out about a problem, introduced him to Tyche, but let's wait and see, talk about it later, perhaps.'

Stephen contacted Tyche, 'When will they be home?'
Tyche replied to Bligh's communications so encoded no one in the department had understood the response, translated it stated:

New orders. Set up expedition to disaster site with immediate action. Cyclone alert approximate landing in 5 days.

NINE

Bligh had returned to the Frigate looking forward to having a cool shower, a tot of something comforting and possibly medicinal, there was the akvavit thoughtfully left by the Danish ship design team in the freezer in his cabin. The trip back to the frigate was through choppier waters than on his outward journey. He had felt the queeziness of sea sickness about to attack. The motion of the small landing craft as it bounced through the surf and then lurching onto the rollers of the ocean was far greater than anything he had recently experienced on the much larger frigate.

The comms officer greeted him as he clambered on board.

'Sir, message from London urgent.' Urgency was not what Bligh wanted.

'Message fully decoded?'

He was hopeful that it was work in progress, perhaps time for a quick sip. The comms officer replied that everything was complete and awaiting orders. Bligh wearily took a paper, went to the ship's office opened the connection and there it was in essence: 'get back, take as many crew as possible equipped for overland trek'.

He called a meeting and again was surprised that all the officers were ready to move. So much for top secret briefings from London, unless there was some form of telepathy in action.

He asked why so many of the officers and their teams were at a state ready to disembark, when a junior, taking for pity of the pompous Bligh said, 'got a text from my girl at home, it's headline news on the Mail, we are commissioned to find the reason for the kidnapping.'

To the relief of the crew and Bligh himself, it was agreed that Bligh and a skeleton crew would remain on the frigate and keep her on anchor just off the island. Any approaching cyclone would hit the further side of the island and so they should be sheltered. The landing crew took full provisions, especially medical supplies, food packs and naturally the odd bottle was slipped in. Bligh watched them leave, genuinely torn between wanting adventure, realising he was not the adventurous type, did not have many skills at rough living since his days in the Scouts, while at the same time wondering what was on the menu for dinner.

TEN
H

The sun signalled the ending of the day in a slow descent into the sea as the landing craft returned from the Frigate. It was a very different scene to that of their chaotic first arrival. Fires were being lit, and preparations for the evening cooking were underway. Bosai sat on a chair outside the hut, tall dignified and heavily bandaged around his upper arm. A ship's medic sat near him talking to Susi and Ross. Bosai's musket lay across his lap, his sign of authority re-established.

Little further away sat the crew of the second landing craft. Many of them had dressings and bandages, ripped shirts. They sat in a circle talking over and over about their landing that morning. First, where the coral ran up to the beach, it tore at their shoes when they jumped overboard. They had wanted a quiet approach, to circle around and approach the village from inland through the woods in a surprise attack. They had planned that the bedraggled and now semi coherent captain of the shipwreck might lead them, or at least show a path through the dense mangrove that bordered this beach, but he kept jabbering 'dragons! dragons!'

It was only when the last of their party looked back to make sure the landing craft was well away from the water's edge, that he noticed a large, curious but essentially malign lizard making its way towards them.

It was later agreed that they would not mention in any verbal or written reports of the panic that swept over them all. The crew scattered each trying to make the shortest route back to the craft, while the original first dragon was joined by others in an eerily well organised hunting party. The unspoken agreement among the fit and proud crew was that the bedraggled captain had struggled free from his captors and made it first back to the landing craft and was endeavouring to start the engine and abandon them to their fate.

We all looked up when the new landing crew arrived. Diplomatically Johnston approached Bosai immediately offering two boxes and cases marked with a large red cross and a bottle of malt whiskey, making a speech of apology for the misunderstanding on their first landing. Bosai nodded but made no move to pick up any of the offerings.

Johnson and some of his men came to join us. We introduced ourselves, knowing hard questions would soon follow. I decided to take the lead on avoidance tactics. I had a great advantage, firstly my husband had died long before I joined *The Syndicate* for a Once-In-A-Lifetime-Experience, an adventure written in my bucket list, and stressed that it was my friends in England who had initiated the search.

It was evident from his distracted expression that Johnson was attempting to formulate a question to resolve doubts that had been circulating around his brain like a lost sheep in the Cumbrian mountain mists, when Bruce reminded him that the expedition should be ready for an early start the next day. Taking this as a sign to end a delving into our personal lives, we got up and started to gather our stuff for the long trek. There was some grumbling from some, Rita and Melanie said they might not be fit to make the journey yet again, though to be honest, they were fitter that day than ever in their previous life. Dilys gave a show of reluctance more in solidarity with her friends than honest intent, for she had thought an expedition with handsome naval officers could lead two some adventure.

We went to the hut to look through what remained of the footwear.

Robin voiced what we were all thinking, that in the weeks we had been on the island our feet were definitely not pretty but they were toughened.

Frank said, with typical bravado, "not so sure I want sandals," but was reminded by Jen of the hot rocks around the side of the volcano.

'She's been spitting a fair bit of fire recently, seen rocks thrown to the skies and she is definitely upset about something.'

Frank, who feared all women, was not only dismayed that the volcano was a female and therefore unpredictable in his book, but could turn on him, fry him on the spot, just like his second wife.

Gary and Sally were nervous. I had to remind myself that though they were young and enthusiastic they were very new to the conditions on the island. They were still overwhelmed by the tropical heat once they left the breezes coming in from the sea, the sets of the fruits hanging from the trees and of course the ever sleepy and sweet scent of the vanilla vines. They had yet to met Mildred and her relations, but had now heard so many stories of the attack of dragons, their lethal saliva that infected and eventually killed all creatures they bit.

Sally wondered if she would be fit enough to make the trip, but I laughed saying that if I had survived the first forced march, it should be no problem for her. Bruce was very quiet, I knew he was torn between leaving the ketch with a cyclone coming and of course ensuring the naval team got all the information first hand of the great plastic disaster.

At first cockerel crow, we were up and ready to start before the heat of the day struck. Susi and Jen were to remain behind to look after Bosia, still weak from his wounds. Two navy ratings were also delegated to stay, to keep guard on the two landing craft and the ketch, which Bruce reluctantly was going to leave. The plan was to make the bay in one day. It was a daunting plan given on our first trek there we had two days of hard walking.

Rita and Melanie stood back as some of their baskets were chosen and packed. I shared their sense of pride. Of all of us who had been washed up, they were the most conventional if somewhat tedious characters. They had really bonded and at first I assumed they had little to do with the village women. That was until I saw them basket making. The first attempts were wonky, fell to bits and the fronds cut their hands.

But they had persisted, and though less glamorous than fishing, or farming on the vegetable strips, had made a substantial contribution to the village.

We all carried provisions, as before, some were able to take heavier loads than others. Selection was gender free as to the surprise of the crew and Bruce Sally and Gary, many of the village women, Dilys and I were given heavier loads than Frank and Robin. We took food, some blankets and material if we had to stay near the bay overnight. Bruce had cameras and his mobile. The crew carried some scientific sounding equipment and more sophisticated communications.

Climbing up the steep path once again, we all experienced very mixed emotions. It started with Dilys, always vocal when it came to complaining. What she said was: 'I hope this is the last bloody time I have to make this trek. It's ridiculous, they could have gone on their own, why do we have to be here?'

And on and on, though the path became steep, the stones more prominent forcing us to weave our way through, even her

263

voice began to fade in place of a weary puffing, and gasping for air.

At first I was irritated then astonished to realise that I was sad, that this was the beginning of the end of our time on the island. For so many weeks, looking forward to returning home had been an unquestioned target for most of us, but did I want to go home? I shuddered when I thought of all those dismal years in Lopeham, the long grey winters. Sally was walking beside me.

'What's up H?' she said so kindly, 'not like you to cry.'

Was I crying? I never, never cry. I stopped for a moment, put down my basket and looked around.

'You know I have had some very happy days here. For once no one knew about my background. I am safe here, there's no one here from the Children's Home, free from that man. Have a sense of purpose here, I have achieved things I never knew possible. I love this place.'

Sally collapsed onto the ground, her head in her hands. What had I said? Was the climb already too much for her? I put down my basket and sat beside her. She was shaking, laughter, tears, both. I put my arms around her. She looked at me blankly, then she looked around, and muttered, 'dear god give me strength!'

During this time we had blocked the path so the following people had to walk around us, not saying anything but concentrating on getting up the mountain.

Eventually Vince and the lads arrived, the vanguard of our expedition.

'Get moving,' he commanded, enforced with, 'Mildred is following us.'

'Mildred?' asked Sally, 'I don't remember meeting anyone called Mildred last night.'

'Just as well you didn't,' Vince added helpfully, 'she's the oldest of all the dragons and often follows us, but keep away from her, she is dangerous.'

Sally was on her feet immediately, pulled me up and said with a smile to take the edge off her words, 'you have no idea what trouble you have caused. If it wasn't for Stephen you would be here forever, no choice. Now stop being stupid and show me where we are going.'

Four hours later we had reached the place where before they had compared all night. We, the hostages, got some teasing from all the villagers, a lot of smiling and arm waving.

'What's up?' asked Gary.

Ross said, 'I am told that the first time they took this lot up here,' and he pointed randomly at all us, 'it took them all day and they had to camp here. Now look at them, moving up these paths like a true islander.'

We were all pleased, we had passed some test very well. Nonetheless we knew the hardest part was to come. We were not to descend to the village of Orrible, but to continue to the inlet onto the side of the volcano. We were given very little time to drink form the water containers and have a snack of cold vegetables. Then Ross picked up his pack.

'Come on, if we can keep this pace up, we should get near by nightfall.'

Once again we hit the hard thorny path leading to the inlet. We got bruised from stumbling over the gullies, scratched from the thorn bushes, the only vegetation along the route, and yet again feasted upon by every insect on the island. These seemed impervious to the oils and lotions we had brought with us, and to the sprays used by all but one of the crew.

He had apparently picked up the wrong cannister, and was now spraying himself with some revolting aftershave, but it did the trick and we noticed the insects hovering around him, uncertain whether to land.

By evening, we found a dismal shelter from the wind and settled as best we could. Vince and the lads reported they had not seen Mildred for some time and it was possible that not even she would venture into this waste land there was no evidence of living creatures. The rocks were warm beneath our feet and the malodorous sulphur blew around in the wind.

The crew was uneasy, even Hayes was muttering about the god forsaken place and the Comms officer was worried that communication with the Frigate was unreliable.

'There's something interfering with the system,' he said.

One of the crew did think it might be because their captain sounded drunk, but did not venture this opinion to anyone but the guy sitting next to him. The others were worried and offered comments about possible sabotage by China, Russian, possible terrorist groups that could cause such interrupted and incoherent messages from the Frigate.

Bruce said, 'don't worry, it's just the volcano, she doesn't like visitors,' and this was accepted as an entirely plausible explanation.

As we lay down for what we anticipated would be a far from restful night, Robin wandered back along the path looking at rocks, while Vince and Audrey, of course, offered to keep watch.

'I can sense if Mildred does decide to see if we have left any scraps,'

I thought it uncharitable to add for concern that the crew was having enough of a bad time, that those scraps might be their legs.

We set off just before dawn to the final leg to the inlet. The crew led the way with Ross and the young village men. Even though they had received a briefing from us, they could not know what they were going to meet.

The path was, I remain convinced to this day, strewn with more hot rocks which tumbled down from the vents on the side of the volcano. There was no gush of deadly plasma, these rocks were just warning signs. Every now and again the ground shook as we slithered across the moraine. And the further we went the more the sulphurous smoke descended on us, making us wrench.

Even Hayes began to look worried.

'Should we turn back?'

Not a question more said in hope that someone would take it up. He was firmly pushed by Ross with the order to keep going. As we approached the inlet, the crew began to gag, even to panic.

'Where are you taking us, what's going on, what's up there?' but all pleas, questions demands, orders are ignored all they received was a sharp dig in the back and menacing looks from us all.

The inlet heaved with plastic, rotting fish, screaming birds trapped in the ropes and fronds.

A nightmare.

But the sea was still, though mourning the loss of life in the abomination that crept in from the outer ocean. Hayes walked forward to the very edge, staring downward. Robin caught his arm and pulled him back.

'Be careful,' he said, 'if you gaze long enough into an abyss, the abyss will gaze back into you, someone once said.'

'Nietzsche,' I said to Melanie.

266

'Bless you,' she replied still concentrating on the crew.

I sighed taking comfort that Robin was better informed than others.

One member of the crew screamed. Caught in the swirling mass was a transparent mass and inside, the dead grinning face of a small shark. Leaping up as if to escape were the plastic gloves that we had seen on our first visit, still yellow, as if all the cleaners in the world had become entrapped. Shopping bags from around the world, tarpaulins plastic cups and bottles swirled. Another gave a piece of plastic that had been blown up near his feet a vicious kick. From the sodden mess a child's voice rang out, 'Happy birthday Happy birthday to you.' He leapt away nearly going over to join the demonic voice.

'What the fuck is that!'

Robin said, 'the tiny batteries in singing birthday cards cannot be recycled. Lucky I suppose it is at sea because the sparks from the batteries have caused massive fires in recycling centres.' Unimpressed with this tiny arsonist, the crew stamped on the battery till the child's voice was heard no more.

Recovering from their initial shock the crew began to ask questions and would have stayed longer despite the stench. But Hayes and Ross looking at the distant horizon commanded us to leave. Robin said, "They are worried about the cyclone, that it why the sea is so eerily flat, reckon we have only 24 hours at best.'

And so we returned to Linda, the village always a lovely sight sheltering behind the reef.

The crew had asked endless questions on the way down, none of them had seen a plastic island floating in the Pacific, but one thing was evident, they were on the side of our kidnappers and the attempt to bring this disaster to the very world that had created it.

Dilys and Rita moved swiftly along the paths in deep and conspiratorial conversation. I overheard bits,

'I will go onto Frigate, the chaps can pack into the ketch' from the ever resourceful Dilys.

'Perhaps I'll have to share a bunk with Hayes,' giggled Rita.

I could only admire their optimism, but it got me thinking about how we will organise our departure.

Hayes and Robin were also in deep conversation. Robin, rather breathlessly trying to give a summary of his findings about where the plastic was going, whether it was being burnt in the vents and fissures of the volcano.

'If this has been collecting for years, I cannot understand why the island is not completely buried by the stuff by now.'

Hayes looked thoughtful, but said very little, except to give a sudden yell as he saw Mildred on the path waiting for our return. A well aimed stick, a shout from Vince and she slowly and with dignity crept up the rocks looking down us, her tongue out testing the wind, our smells and location before slinking back under the bushes.

ELEVEN
H

We arrived back late at night exhausted. The village had lit torches on the last part of our route. I was so thankful I am not sure I would have made it otherwise. We were all sore, cuts, bruises, burns from the hot rocks and of course the shock of what we had seen. Even the crew refused to give a briefing to the waiting Johnson despite orders from the Captain, who we could hear shouting from the Frigate, all modern communications unnecessary. Johnson wearily turned off radio communication with 'Just let them rest, we'll contact at dawn.'

But I could hear tapping on the laptops and Johnson speaking quietly and knew they were planning something. I spoke to Jen and between us we kept watch.

Was it the thought of spending a few weeks at sea with Dilys and Rita, I do not know, but just before the cockerel started his early morning call, the crew were up, silently gathering everything together and about to creep to the shoreline. Jen as always well prepared, started banging pots, yelling, I screamed and roused everyone.

Bosai stormed out of his hut.

'Where the hell do you think you are going?' Was his communicative intent, though not expressed in English, and suddenly the crew was surrounded by very angry villagers and hostages. A parley was enforced, and an agreement of who would go where and with whom. It turned out to be an interesting exercise.

In the Children's Home, when I first arrived, we had often played the game where there is a missionary with one boat who had to cross a river with a tiger, a goat and a bag of corn. The boat cannot hold them all, and as we know, left alone the tiger will eat the goat and the goat the corn. It is an exercise in understanding suspicion and distrust. Our version, in the Home was not to cross the river, but who could be with the little ones to protect them at all times, who would stand watch, who could snatch hours of safe sleep and who would deflect the deadly predators that stalked the corridors, snatching the unaware.

The crew offered to go to the Frigate and promised to return with a second craft. This was met by jeers. 'Got to be joking. Why would we trust you?' and so on for at least ten minutes. I knew how the missionary must have felt, what better than to leave the tiger behind and escape to a new life.

I stood forward, 'I am an expert on this,' my voice was authoritative, I was looked at in surprise. 'My first question is to the passengers. Does everyone want to leave the island?'

As I anticipated, Vince and Audrey shyly put up their hands.

'We want to stay,' began Audrey, 'Vince sees a future the study of the exclusively female Komodo dragons,' this brought a smile to the villagers who had for sometime admired his persistence observing the dragons and even being accepted, as far it is possible to be accepted by the grand matriarch, Mildred.

Audrey continued, 'and I want to continue with my meditation and my music,' there was a collective quiet groan from the villagers, but no objection.

Then Jen stood up, 'no no no, not Jen,' I screamed inside, 'not Jen my strong companion, who had seen me through those early dark days.'

She looked at me, sadly. 'You know I cannot go back just yet, too many questions about my past, perhaps the police might be waiting for me, never really had a legal passport. And I have plans for the island, I think I can help, with Bosai here beside me.'

'Yes' I thought, 'they will make a good team.'

Ross put up his hand. I could see Susie was nervous, she stepped nearer to him.

'I want to stay, I have been away too along and this is my home. I have talked to Bruce and I will keep information going about what is happening with the plastic.'

Susie then went right up to him and gave him such a hug, it brought tears to my eyes, so that it is like to be a mother. I was envious.

There was a pause then Robin put up his hand.

'I have a question, will you be coming back? Definitely? For sure?' There were energetic nods from Bruce and less enthusiastic but confirming nod from Hayes.

270

'Well, I would like to study the actions of the volcano. I can set up a proper monitoring programme. I want to verify it the plastic is being burnt and I want to know if there are emissions from that process. Like it might be harming the island inhabitants.' He turned to Vince and Audrey who looked unenthusiastic then added.

'There might be an impact on our dragons.'

Vince said, 'Go for it, we'll help.'

Robin added. 'Leave me enough equipment and the cameras and I can send regular reports. Somehow we have to stop the plastic drift and clear up the abomination in the inlet.'

Ross turned to him, 'that's brilliant,' and then a quiet, 'thank you' and I realised Ross was fearful that he would lose us all.

Adnan, put up his free hand, the other clasped around his girlfriend and just quietly said, 'Staying.'

Dilys put up her hand. "If I return in the Frigate home and near Australia, I won't risk getting arrested in Freemantle.' She had just remembered her husband presumably still in the morgue.

She added very quietly, "then at least they'll have to extradite me from the UK.'

Said Rita, with surprising energy, 'I'll go in the Frigate too more room for my things. Can I bring my baskets with me?'

Melanie said with a mischievous grin, 'can I go in the Frigate, take a turn on the bridge,' she said with a sly smile and a wink at Hayes.

Frank stood. He coughed, he looked at his feet, then quietly said as if the words did not want to leave his mouth and soar into the skies, 'I will go back, but I have many things to think about. Can I go on the ketch? Would appreciate a chance to learn a little about sailing.' And that was agreed. I could see he was so fearful of finding out what happened to his escaped wife. 'I have no need to rush home,' he added sadly.

Now the minute had come, not the week, not the day but the very moment. We were all suddenly fearful of what was to come.

'Frank, are you sure you don't want to come on the Frigate with us?' asked Dilys, then added, 'I don't know what's waiting for me either.' And we all knew she was thinking of her husband so cold and so long in the morgue in Freemantle and perhaps a lot less money in the bank in Eastbourne than she was hoping for.

'Before you leave,' ventured Rita turning to Dilys,

'tell us now, how did your husband die on that plane?' An unwise question. Dilys snapped back, "and wouldn't you like to know with yours travelling the oceans inside that shark!"

'Leave it," Jen intervened, 'we all have things that are best left unsaid. This I know from my days on the war. Only H here,' she said putting an arm around my shoulder, 'joined us alone a respectable widow from Sussex and one who never makes judgements.'

I was very touched by Jen's faith in me and the others nodded in agreement smiling at me I thought, 'well let them go on thinking just that.' Though at that moment a shudder shook my body, my head rang, I could feel even my teeth chatter, spasms ranged throughout, more than electric shocks and I could hear the evil last words of that devil, 'look out gel, killed better women than you'll ever be.' Nobody noticed. I remained the one whose partner died in suburban dignity without a stain on his character.

Only I knew of the dark secrets, the horrors that were best forgotten. I forced myself to concentrate on the activity, the melee around me.

At the insistence of the villagers, Hayes and the comms officer had to remain on the island while the crew took Rahmin, Paul, and Melanie to the Frigate. There was almost an extra run to bring all the baskets so proudly woven by Rita and her gang, one a very good coffin, 'just in case,' muttered Rita with a meaningful look towards the captain of *The Syndicate*. Some baskets were filled with vanilla roots, some with the fruits we had grown like to so much.

With to-ing and fro-ing that would have done the missionary and his charges proud, ensuring that at no time did the craft only hold crew, eventually we were all aboard our vessels and ready to leave.

I was the last to go, appropriate really as I had been the first one washed up on that very same sandy beach. I had no control over my departure. Jen, the normally tough Jen, had thrown her arms around me and said with such a tender voice, one I had not heard before, 'go safely my dearest friend, my rock, my guide, my saviour. Dearest H now it is time to find your name,' she put her hands onto my face, 'now is time for change.' I could see tears in her eyes, but why?

Then Vince and Audrey stood by me. 'I was going to give you an egg to take back, but I cannot see a Komodo surviving in Eastbourne, so here is a garland of flowers,' and Audrey said, 'please take up yoga when you get back it will give you peace.'

What were they thinking of? But on the other hand a Komodo might do very well in the sunny climes of Eastbourne, slinking about the discarded rubbish, killing rats, cats and other unfortunates that were in her path.

And then my personal cyclone hit. Not the one forecast to hit the island in a few days, but my very own. Not a bombshell but an invisible, cataclysmic whirlwind, that lifted me up, crashed me down, not in Kansas like the famous Dorothy. What was this feeling? I was sad, I had tears in my eyes as I looked back to the island, to those waving us farewell and part of me wanted to stay with them.

Up to that day I had never felt sad, and I cannot remember crying as I was crying now.

I did not cry when I was dumped in the Children's Home by my addict mother, not for my good but so she could run her dealing without interference from me; I did not cry in the Children's Home, even when they gave me that little box of ashes and I certainly did not cry when they found my social worker dead in my room, though they gave me his ashes, saying, 'he was always so fond of you.' Too right. And I did not cry when Harry died, serial killer, though I do miss to this day my old dog.

So perhaps I was changing.

PART SEVEN

Homeward bound for some, and others decide to remain. The politicians are pleased with the outcome. Only H suffers as she confronts the demons from her childhood and reveals a darker side she has carefully hidden.

ONE
H

We raced back towards Freemantle. The unexpected cyclone had changed the weather pattern and the normal wind directions. I distinctly recall my first communication with Tyche. It happened when Bruce was seeking the latest and most accurate information on weather, sneaky fishing vessels, local cargo ships, other navy ships seeking us, oil tankers and the latest football scores. I joined Bruce, Gary and Sally marvelling in their use of language, the speed at which they resolved issues, and then, from Tyche no less, 'oh wowsie, wowsie don't tell me that's the famous H sitting next to you Bruce, she, the lost maiden that is the subject of the search? Isn't she lovely? No wonder old Stephen has lost his heart to her.'

I can truthfully say I was not impressed by this young man's familiarity nor the contact of his observations. 'Bugger off,' I snarled, but Sally laughed, 'you have no idea what's waiting for you. But it is true, without Stephen we would not be here, so prepare yourself to be nice.'

I went to my bunk to lie down, but in fact I was rather pleased. Thoughts ran through my head, first was around this guy, Stephen, standing on the jetty in Australia, what was it he really wanted, for life had taught me there was always a price. Then if I had changed, would he like the new me?

And in the dark recess of my mind, was the fear that if he did like me and if it ever came to anything, would he be safe from me, and mindful that absurd women often go from one abuser to another, would I be safe from him? And just what was I going to do with those boxes sitting in the store depot full of old photographs, bangles, necklaces and scarves?

Bruce was in command at the wheel, Gary and Sally stood on the deck with shouts of delight and surprise as they saw in the distance the high tower on Cantonement Hill at that stands above Fremantle once an old prison for the colonisers. It chilled my soul thinking of those sad blokes locked up looking over the sea and perhaps longing for home thousands of miles away. But my mood changed, for it seemed all the small boats had come out to meet up. An airplane flew overhead with a trailer reading, WELL DONE.

After passing Rottnest Island we were followed by a flotilla of yachts, in fact the entirety of sailing craft. People waved flags, tins of beer, bottles of wine. I was assured that the approach to Fremantle could not have been more different to our secretive departure. Bruce kept the sails up almost to the entry to the marina. It made quite a sight, for the townspeople standing along the harbour wall, a ketch coming into harbour after such an adventure. We were directed to a Pontoon by the yacht club. As we drew up, we dropped anchor and tied up, a procedure that took a few minutes for we were not the most skilled crew and we were all shocked at the noise of the waiting crowd. Frank stood hesitant scanning the crowd. We knew he was still looking for his wife. Many blonde cheerful women waved but none had her killer look.

Although West Australians revel in informality of dress and speech, it was evident that the Aborigine elders, political dignitaries, youth leaders, TV cameramen and women were all clustered on the front of the club. And there, standing back, shyly smiling at me, yes just at me, was Stephen.

Timing is everything as we all eventually learn. Would we have received such a welcome if…

Let me start at the beginning of what happened.

We were the first to make landfall. The Frigate had to shelter from the cyclone as the winds unusually swerved off the normal season course that batter islands and ships in its path. Bruce had a suspicion that it might they may have encountered navigational problems, but then the demonic manipulations of Tyche can be over exaggerated.

So it was that when we stood on Australian soil we were pushed and pulled, shouted at, all meant to be welcoming, but scary. What took me a few minutes or maybe more, was that the newspapers and photos of ME standing by the inlet, looking into the abyss of the plastic maelstrom were handed to us. A new satellite had just come into service with the specific task of finding the plastic rafts in the ocean. While it could detect plastic in minute quantities, finding the enormous amount in the island and then being able to focus on us was mere child's play.

We were clapped and cheered. We were asked to say a few words. Bruce and I had agreed we would try to get the press to focus on the environmental disaster, not the criminal act of kidnap. And all the time, Stephen and I just looked at each other, he standing back and waiting to see what would happen.

TWO

At the same time, in London a nervous Head of Section and the Prime Minister's comms team were sitting in Downing Street preparing press releases while watching the news channels. There was disappointment that the Frigate had been unaccountably delayed and radio messages from the ship were on the incoherent side. That could be left to later. The main question was how to capitalise on the successful rescue.

The Minister for Overseas Trade joined them. He was in an emollient mood.

'Well done chaps, now who was it that recommended the young fellow, you know, techie?' The head of Section raised a tentative hand. 'Brilliant, could not have happened at a better time, wonderful publicity for the PM he is delighted, good all round British action.'

The Comms officer looked at her laptop in despair. How was she going to translate the language of the Minister gained from watching too many programmes of the re-run of D Day, VE Day and other newsreels of World War 2?

She tried, 'British Hostage rescued from plastic horror,' but then thought that some of the early photos showed much of it had originated from Britain; then British hostages praise brave islanders,' but that might show they were victims of the Stockholm syndrome a condition where hostages form a close bond with their captors.

She mused on this, for some of them had actually refused to leave the island. Then inspiration, she just caught a reporter asking about the Komodo dragons and was struck by the reply:

'Plastic kills dragons.'

Three words, the essence of every political campaign since Brexit.

She looked up. 'Minister can I ask that now the satellites have great pictures and that there are still British people on the island, what you plan to do?'

The Minister looked down the table, he turned to his political adviser, he raised his eyebrows in question to the Head of Section.

'I am sure the PM will request that the Minister of the Environment makes a statement in the commons soon and we could set up a Public Enquiry to report by the end of the year.'

The Comms Officer, a brave spirit and therefore her career in Whitehall predicted to be short, said assertively but with controlled hostility, thinking she would not share her brilliant three worded slogan on this particular minister, 'so nothing, no action, no recognition of Britain's responsibility in the production of plastic?'

The Minister was startled, not expecting to be questioned for so far down the conference table.

The Head of Section quickly intervened, 'for your information, you should realise that plastics are an off-shoot of our oil industry and with the drop in oil consumption where the production of plastic is a significant by-product. We cannot be seen to be cutting back more than these environmental lobbies call for.'

The Comms Officer sighed deeply and did not look up, further shortening her days of employment with each breath. But the wily political adviser stepped in, 'can I suggest, with your agreement of course Minister?'

'Suggest?'' thought the Comms Officer, this is an order, so she looked expectantly ready to attack her keyboard.

'Could I suggest the following. The Minister recognises the urgency which the information from the satellites are revealing daily, and has begun talks with the oil industry, the manufacturers of plastics and the waste industry.'

'Gosh,' the Minister chortled, 'now that will keep me busy.'

'You don't have to do it all today,' continued the advisor, 'and the press release should also state that the Minister congratulates our security section which were among the first to alert the world to the plastic build up on the island.'

'Very good,' intervened the Head of Section.

'Perhaps Minister a word in the right ear for a bravery award for that woman who seems to be the leader of the hostages? It would keep her fairly on board don't you think? And let's use it as a bridge to Environment, might pay off in the future?'

'Terrific,' the Minister stood up, 'time for lunch, will you join me?'

The invitation excluded the Comms Officer, the Minister's departure marked with, 'could you have a draft on my desk in an hour, need to get it on the 6 o'clock news.'

It was happenstance, it was a perfect example of serendipity that the most junior Comms Officer was the one who picked up early briefings of a sudden outbreak of illness among market traders in China and briefly considered informing her boss, but then knew it would be wiser to leave his lunch uninterrupted.

THREE

Five hours later Angela and Peter turned on the 6 o'clock news. Angela screamed, 'Look it's H!'

Peter muttered without conviction, 'are you sure?' The unnecessary question threatening the diminishing happiness and stability of his marriage.

The phone rang, it was Gwen, 'have you seen it? I knew she was up to something, never liked her, untrustworthy and I was always suspicious of Harry's death, now look at her.'

Even Angela was taken aback by the spite, but in general agreed.

'I'll call the local papers,' she started and then with another exclamation as the press conference in Fremantle was beamed into Sussex. 'Will you look at that, isn't that the creepy guy who lurked around here months ago?

FOUR

H

It took us nearly a month to leave Fremantle. I had become fond of this little town hanging off the edge of the huge continent. And I did not want to rush back to my old life in Lopeham.

Fremantle had the same bloody mindedness as Lewes, the same enthusiasms for safeguarding the environment and the local peoples. Whereas Lewes cheerfully blew up effigies of politicians and world leaders, Fremantle resolutely refused to celebrate Australia Day, calling it Invasion Day and holding a party for One Nation the day before.

Frank said he was staying on in the city for longer than us. He was assured he could get a six-month visa. I thought he might try to go to the islands, a search for someone he really did not want to find.

We returned the boat, came to a peaceful settlement with immigration and negotiated advances for our story in a number of different publications. However, the most important part for me, was Stephen. It was the first time in my life that a man had done something for me. He knew I did not like being touched, so we just walked and talked, up and down the beaches of Freemantle through the parks, in the numerous cafes.

He told me about his search for me.

'Why me?' I had laughed, and he said, 'I don't know but I have always loved you' and I thought, 'gosh never knew that.'

And then he said, 'you are so beautiful.'

Gradually I told him in a strictly edited version, about my childhood, a very short and rather brutal account. I told him I never knew my father, but mother had entertained a number of boyfriends, not really friends looking back on it, just other druggies like herself. But it took me a long time to tell him about my time in Care.

'Well I went into care because I was pregnant, and only twelve years old. I was terrified, could not remember how I got into that condition, was probably drugged and raped at home. The baby only lived a few hours, but I insisted I had his ashes.'

Stephen just looked sad and gently held my hand. I could not stop talking now.

'The social workers did try at first but I was difficult, DLS appeared again and again on my notes. I would have been alright, except one day a new manager said that keeping the baby's ashes was morbid and he was going to throw them away. I cannot remember how it happened but he fell and hit his head, but I do know I thought, quick as quick, that I could be facing charges, so I cried and sobbed, sad I didn't know what had happened, and asked to go the funeral and when I found he had no family asked for his ashes too.'

I told Stephen the whole story, that narrow escape and I knew I did even at thirteen, that I had not fooled all the staff but now I think they many have been aware this guy was an abuser.

They thought me so sweet, 'just fancy,' I heard one saying, 'I never knew she had a caring bone in her body,' too right. But I did not tell Stephen that just to remind myself of my lucky escape and also that I had got away with murder, or manslaughter so I kept his ashes.

I told Stephen how I had drifted into Adult Care, not as a client but a worker in an old folks home. I liked the work, undemanding, had my own room as I often did nights. I told him about meeting Harry, but omitted the part about Holly's swift departure following a visit.

I said to Stephen as we sat on the beach in the morning sun, I decided to marry Harry when he asked, even though he was a bit older than me, and he has a house in a nice address and I thought I would be safe and in return I would look after him. Stephen put his arm around me and gave me such a sweet kiss, a touch that was not a grope. Then he spoilt the moment when he said, 'my dearest love, you are so sweet, so caring and you deserve a good life. You are a kind and generous woman, and I can see how much all your friends love you.'

'How wrong you are,' I thought, 'you don't know the half of it,' and then trying to see what the future might bring, 'what the hell am I going to do with those boxes in the storage department.' And with that sent an email booking the storage unit for another twelve months.

FIVE

The frigate eventually made speed back to Portsmouth. They had dropped off Paul and Rahmin in Singapore. The onward journey was unimpeded by computer failure, problems with the navigation and the crew working in silent unison so that the day of disembarkation of the passengers would soon arrive.

Rita, Melanie and Dilys found Captain Bligh's store of Danish spirits and continued to sit wherever they could find a space while they perfected the weave and materials for a sturdy yet attractive biodegradable and environmental coffin. Their departure from the ship did cause some well-disciplined eyebrows of the welcome party to rise and they marched down carrying their masterpieces, happy that their financial future was assured.

In the weeks after leaving the island and while we were in Fremantle, I had news from the island. Vince was commissioned to write a paper on:
Viable and meaningful interaction between island communities and komodo dragons
Audrey too had been busy while we were journeying back to Sussex, posting while standing very balanced on the beach, on You Tube, Songs To Sing To Dragons. She achieved 2,000,000 hits in less than a week.

Robin had to be treated for lava burns by the team left by the Frigate. But of Jen little news, other than, 'life is good, Bosai and I are one team these days.'

Gary and Sally returned to England a week before Stephen and I took a slower journey home. The day we arrived, the Minister's initial meeting with the oil industry had fortuitously also scheduled, so we were met at Gatwick for an interview. The whole topic of evil plastic had once again hit the headlines and we, and of course and the navy team and the Minister were heroes.

While we were driven to my house in a luxurious car paid for by the newspaper, Peter and Angela were being interviewed by the local press outside our house. I was later told of what happened as they were standing anxiously hoping to be on the local news:
'What do you think of your brave neighbour?'
'Do you know there is a possibility of an award for her bravery,

have you any comment?'

'Will this be an honour for this town?'

Peter looked on as Angela replied, silent in stunned admiration for his wife's convincing change of opinion, 'oh yes,' she gushed, 'we've always been such good neighbours, and I so admire what she has done. Actually it was me that persuaded her to take a holiday after the death of her dear husband. She had been such a good and loving partner to him, quiet rather mousy woman. Of course here we keep ourselves to ourselves.'

The press group was perplexed.

"Call her mousey, call her quiet! This woman doesn't know anything. Cut her out from tonight's transmission.'

And in the background, kept out of shot by another skillful cameraman, Gwen and Wendy tried to push in and have a word.

SIX
H

Of course, of this I did not know, though later told in great detail by Arthur on his postal round. But as our car drew up and we got out, there were shouts of goodwill, flowers were lying on the doorstep and there was even a balloon saying Welcome Home. It was beautiful, I looked around at all the smiling faces, the children clapping and thought, 'its not so bad here really.'

Gary, Sally and Bruce had got champagne ready and we stood in my front room, all spruced and tidy, the sun pouring in and then I noticed my plastic boxes and gone.

I turned on Sally, 'Where are they? I almost choked.

'Darling auntie,' said Sally so gently, 'I have put them safe, upstairs in a drawer. They are now all at rest in peace. Now is the time to move on.'

Stephen my lovely Stephen said,

'Here's to the future and to your name that has been lost and now is yours. Farewell H and welcome Hope.'

And they raised their glasses and said, 'to Hope, to the future.'

EPILOGUE

At that point just as the glasses were raised, the Prime Minister announced that the pandemic had hit, that we were all to be locked in our houses.

I, who had so dreaded returning to the noise and pollution of the south coast, could open the windows to the spring songs of the birds, and smell the awakening blossom. No planes, just the clear gentle blue skies promising the coming summer, time to reflect, time to move on.

And as you, dear reader, might already guess I did move away from Lopeham to live with my beloved Stephen. I could see trouble was brewing when Angela and Peter started wearing different sweatshirts and more obviously the day Angela wore a pretty dress. The inquest not a few months later, gave an open verdict on Peter's unexpected demise and to be honest I did not like her remark about following in my footsteps.

I have rented the house to Arthur who told me he had been evicted from his rural cottage when he retired from his postal rounds, and could not afford the increased rent. A wicked ruse by the landlord facing short holiday lets. Hah not with the lockdown!

Gary and Sally did not wait for the pandemic to end. But got married, a small group of friends and family in attendance.

Bruce worked in colourful websites promoting a variety of Holidays of a Lifetime cruises.

Pandemics bring tragic news of so many deaths, but there are also winners, and so it was that Rita and Melanie moved into a substantial house in the better part of Hove and from weaving one or two caskets a week, turned it into a successful business employing skilled young people as the mortality rate increased.

Bligh left the navy and took a course on counselling distressed mariners and discovered a huge pool of wealthy clients.

Tyche continued to move unobserved through the dark passageways of the internet.

Charles achieved his life's ambition when he was elected President of the Lewes Golf Club, though it was a very long time before he could park his car in the most prestigious slot in the car park.

Gwen had left for a cruise the day before the announcement, of lockdown throughout the Caribbean, and the last I heard she was on some ship that was running out of the luxuries that she so yearned for, and had been staring, unable to disembark, at some outer harbour wall.

And on the island so far away, plans are made to deal with the plastic, but more and more sweeps in. The island survives, the sweet smell of vanilla permeates the air, while the komodo dragon walk languidly, powerfully across the beach, through the woods in the everlasting quest for prey.

***

THANKS are due to the staff of Newhaven Incinerator for opening my eyes to the issues of burning plastic; to the bloggers who posted accounts of the sea voyages out of Freemantle, especially the dangers of getting caught in long illegal fishing lines, but most of all to my student who told me of the story of a party of people taken hostage by his grandfather on a very remote island in Papua new Guinea.

Plastic and the Volcano

Burning plastic in the traditional manner creates extremely polluting byproducts, as evidenced by the black smoke produced by the cup. But this didn't thwart Levendis, who noted that plastic contains the same amount of energy per pound as premium fuel.

"We wanted to tackle the problem by preprocessing the plastics," said Chuanwei Zhuo, a doctoral candidate in Levendis' lab. Toward that end, the team developed a combustion system that adds a simple step to the burning process that allows for turning plastic into a fuel that burns just as cleanly as natural gas.

That simple step has a daunting name: pyrolytic gasification. Instead of directly setting the cup aflame with a match in the open air, the team's reactor heats the material to a whopping 800 degrees Celsius in a completely oxygen-free environment. This causes the plastic to become a gas, which is then mixed with air before it is burned as a clean fuel.

ROSALYN ST PIERRE was born in Tipperary Ireland and grew
up in Surrey. She graduated in politics from the University of
Liverpool. She has an MA from the Institute of Education,
University of London. Her career involved working in international
education and travelling extensively throughout Asia, the Indian
Ocean and the Pacific. She was a country councillor for 12 years
when the Newhaven incinerator, Energy from Waste, was being
built primarily to burn waste plastic. During this time she was also
a member of the panel responsible for children in the care of
the local authority. She now lives in Sussex with her husband and
dog Micha.

Printed in Great Britain
by Amazon

84977251R00171